Princess of Prophecy

Copyright © 2024
Alexander Thomas
www.AlexanderThomasAuthor.com

Cover by Marta Susic Obucina
Map by Adriano Bezerra

This is a work of fiction.
Any similarities to persons living or dead, or actual events, is purely coincidental.

Manuscript 5 May 2024.

For Mary, a fighter.

Table of Contents

Ominous Prologue	1
Chapter 1 - Princess	4
Chapter 2 - Prophecy	11
Chapter 3 - Knight	20
Chapter 4 - Barbarian	30
Chapter 5 - Dunswell	36
Chapter 6 - Plains	40
Chapter 7 - School	45
Chapter 8 - Council	54
Chapter 9 - Hills	63
Chapter 10 - River	74
Chapter 11 - Haffleton	82
Chapter 12 - Bluntworth	87
Chapter 13 - Tavern	95
Chapter 14 - Feast	101
Chapter 15 - Visitors	112
Chapter 16 - Badlands	117
Chapter 17 - Caverns	126
Chapter 18 - Lich	136
Chapter 19 - Healer	146
Chapter 20 - Archives	157
Chapter 21 - Teacup	163
Chapter 22 - Peril	171
Chapter 23 - Bandits	178
Chapter 24 - Defenders	185
Chapter 25 - Champion	193
Chapter 26 - Fisticuffs	200
Chapter 27 - Negotiations	210
Chapter 28 - Battle	217
Chapter 29 - Assault	223
Chapter 30 - Victory	230
Chapter 31 - Night	236
Chapter 32 - Moonflow	247
Chapter 33 - Dragon	254
Chapter 34 - Bishop	260
Chapter 35 - Farewells	268
Chapter 36 - Home	275
About the Author	283

Offerdell and the Lands Beyond

Excerpt from The Chroniclers Guide:

Two rules must ye follow when chronicling the fulfillment of a prophecy.

First, each chapter must lead with an insightful quote from an authoritative reference work, so the reader knows the Chronicler is learned and serious about their craft.

Second, the chronicle itself must begin with an...

Ominous Prologue

Harken ye to the provenance of the accursed Teapot, lest ye sip tea of a slightly uncomfortable temperature.
Or have your homeland ravaged by the undead.

— Considered Revelations, Book 94 "Origin Myths Worthy of Some Serious Harkening", Chapter 13, Verse 5

In the beginning days, the Elder Gods desired a universe to play with. Being far too lazy and arrogant to do this with their own hands, they created a race of titans to build it for them, complete with stars and nebulae and termites.

Elder Gods, of course, are oblivious to the well-being of anyone else, including titans. So there was a lot of back-and-forth over the exact placement of continents, the cycles of seasons, and other questions around titan pay and break time and the treatment of subcontractors. Thus was the first universe and the first labor union created at the same time.

And though the titans were nearly gods themselves, with supreme powers and generous contract terms, some were bitter and vengeful about excessive interference in their artistic judgment and uninspiring overtime pay. These titans knew better than to complain to all-powerful, unpredictable Elder Gods, and so they took out their frustrations on their creations, and played with the new mortal races just as the Elder Gods played with the titans.

A particularly cruel group of titans procured a cursed Teapot and Teacup, which served tea that remained a few degrees too hot no matter how long you waited for it to cool. They also enchanted the ceramics to bestow immortality and other powers on their owner. They placed the relics, along with some tea leaves and fresh water, in a large Castle of Terror, in the middle of the Badlands. The titans proclaimed the Teapot and Teacup—and even the Castle itself—free to anyone that could best them in combat.

Mortal champions from the four corners of the earth (for at the time, the world was still flat) rushed to the challenge, with predictable results. Great warriors were smote with fire, great armies were swallowed whole by the land, and great wizards were smote with fire again, since the titans had a ready supply of fire on hand.

After a while the Bishop of the nearby town of Bluntworth decided she'd seen enough senseless violence, and asked the titans to lay off. But they only laughed at her, and mocked her backcountry accent.

So she sent messages to the greatest wizard of the age, the legendary Omondi, and he challenged the titans for the cursed tea set, even though he was more of a coffee drinker himself. For three days and three nights they battled—with short breaks every few hours as per titan union rules—but ultimately Omondi was victorious, and the disgraced titans slunk away to another part of the universe, where they could torment different mortals with different relics on a different planet.

Omondi put the Teapot on the mantle, so he could keep a close eye on it. Then he sealed the other relics away in chests, and cast spells upon them such that no mortal hand could touch them.

He waved to the Bishop, and she waved back, and for a few days, the earth knew peace. But then, just as Omondi was getting ready for the most important day of his life, his own apprentice stabbed him. For the promise of immense power had corrupted the junior mage, even to the point where he would betray his own master. He leaped over the fallen Omondi and grasped the Teapot, and all of its great powers became his.

Some of the relic's capabilities, such as opening wormholes to other galaxies or changing the melting point of vanadium, were beyond his simple tastes. But he was thrilled with the prospect of life unending, and the ability to summon the dead to serve him.

The Bishop cursed the apprentice, swearing that if anyone dared to pour tea with him, the relics would fail. The apprentice scorned her, and attempted to smite her, but being both clumsy and not very bright, he overdid his smiting, and caused a large earthquake instead. Mountains trembled, trees swayed, and a large wave swept a confused sea serpent into a small lake in the northlands, where you can still see him today.

But the epicenter of the quake was the Castle of Terror itself, which promptly collapsed in a tumult of stone and expensive roofing tiles, the tallest tower toppling over and flattening the entire structure with a mighty roar. When the dust settled, not even a single brick remained above the earth.

The apprentice, of course, had the misfortune to be standing in the center of the calamity. Though crushed under the collapsed Castle of Terror, he clutched the Teapot, and so it regenerated him as a lich.

The apprentice didn't know what a lich was, and had to look it up in a tome that had survived the cataclysm. Hunched over the book in a dimly lit cavern far underground, he discovered that a lich is like a zombie but smarter, and carries all their faculties and powers from the old life into the new.

In this case, the apprentice was reanimated as an undead magician of rather middling capabilities. Despite being trapped in the ruins of the castle, he knew that time was on his side. He could stay there for centuries, using the Teapot to grow in power and malice until he was a horrible Lich King, ready to conquer the entire world.

And eventually someone gullible would come by and free him.

Chapter 1
Princess

If you are able to choose, I highly recommend the job of Princess.

— *Considered Revelations, Book 16 "Practical Occupations", Chapter 3, Verse 7*

Far from the dangerous parts of the world lay the quiet Kingdom of Offerdell. It was a pleasant land, warm and verdant in the summer, cold but cozy in the winter, with a robust farming ethic and a surprisingly efficient postal service.

North stood the Teeth of Janks, dark mountains of sheer cliffs and ice that kept the barbarians at bay. The great river Halstrop ran as an impenetrable barrier further west, protecting Offerdell from the roaming monsters and predatory merchants of the wild lands of Kell. East lurked the Forest of Madness, through which no army would dare to venture. South sprawled the Flower Hills, which you might think were safe, but were actually infested with trolls and their two-headed cousins, ettins, and at least one viciously aggressive skunk.

No, the Kingdom of Offerdell was quite insulated from the outside world, leaving its citizens to tend their gardens in peace. This was to everyone's liking, especially the king and queen, who had little to concern themselves with save the counting of taxes and the usual ruling family's problems of orderly succession.

Fortunately, being a very practical king and queen, they had produced two royal children, an eldest Prince to inherit the throne, and a younger Princess upon whom to shower their love and affection, and of course marry off once she was old enough, which was any day now. The thing about marriage is that it requires not just one, but *two* people to participate, a truth known to most of the citizens of Offerdell, and so there was continual speculation as to *who* exactly the Princess might marry.

Would it be the swarthy Sir Chad of the Southport Borderlands, burdened with neither worry nor wit? Or perhaps the passionate Prince Juan Ramirez, known for his smooth conversation and

CHAPTER ONE: PRINCESS   5

charming smile? There was even an outside bet that the spoiled son of King Girard was in the running, since the royal houses of both countries were close friends.

But by far the most eligible suitor, and the favorite, was the dashing Prince Mikhail. Younger citizens of Offerdell swooned at the mention of the tall, dark and handsome Prince, with sparkling blue eyes and sharp black outfit. The older citizens noted his great wealth, increasing land holdings, and smooth speaking style. And he cut an exceptionally empathetic figure, mourning the recent passing of his previous wife, coming unfortunately on the heels of the death of the wife before that, which followed the heartbreaking demise of his first wife, all due to hunting accidents. The Prince mourned them all, a deep melancholy that lasted for over a day, seemingly not placated by the entreaties by friends or the outsized dowries of his late spouses.

It was generally agreed that such a fine young man deserved a break from the recent tragedies of his life, and that Princess Maryan of Offerdell was the perfect match, since she was of marrying age and went hunting all the time with no fatal accidents yet.

"You see, dear," explained the queen one evening, "he's loved by everyone, and has a fantastic estate. It's a beautiful castle looking over a river. And the trees on his castle grounds are always decorated."

"Decorated with cages containing condemned prisoners?"

"That's the thing, dear, he's romantic and witty but also tough on crime."

Maryan sighed as she looked out the window. From here, high up in a slender tower of Offerdell's palace, she could look out and see the bright fields of the kingdom spread out before her. To the east a small thundercloud sped towards her, casting a shadow on the ground, a shadow which followed the road with unerring accuracy.

Maryan frowned. "Mom, did you invite Prince Mikhail to dinner tonight?"

"Oh, I'm so glad you approve!" The queen clapped her hands together. "Given that all of the kingdom will be celebrating the May Day Banquet tonight, your father and I thought this would be a perfect opportunity to get you love birds together. You know, in case he needed to ask you any important questions." The queen winked at her.

"Mom—"

"You know, dear, the palace is so dreadfully quiet these days. I miss the pitter-patter of little feet, don't you?"

"Mom—"

"Oh, my, is that the Prince already?"

They looked down at the shadowed carriage, moving swiftly towards them on the road, pulled by two mighty gray chargers. An escort of troops in bright red livery rode before and after.

"An impressive entrance, don't you think, dear? I just love his honor guard."

"They're Death Knights, Mom. They're undead, sworn to serve Prince Mikhail forever, and they suck the soul out of anyone they kill."

"They have sharp uniforms, though, don't they? So few young men these days take their appearance seriously. It's refreshing." Her mother stepped back from the window and smoothed her skirts. "Well, dear, I'm sure you'll want to get ready. You need to look your best tonight."

"Mom—"

"And wear some nice grandkids, all right, dear? Oh my, did I say grandkids? I don't know where that came from. I meant, wear some nice *bracelets*. They'll make your wrists look thinner."

"Bye, Mom."

"Of course, dear, see you at the banquet tonight."

Once the queen had left, Princess Maryan selected a black dress from her wardrobe, and a pair of chunky boots.

Her maid-in-waiting raised an eyebrow as she tied the belt in the back. "Isn't this what you wore to your uncle's funeral, Your Highness?"

"It's perfect." Maryan regarded her hair in the long mirror. Her brown curls perched up in a severe bun. "What would you say are my least attractive bracelets?"

"The bronze ones with wyverns, definitely, ma'am."

"Fetch those, will you?"

The maid-in-waiting rolled her eyes but dutifully trudged back into the deepest recesses of the closet.

A powerful knock shook the door. "Hello, can I come in?"

"Of course, Dad."

King Albert of Offerdell strode into the room, his quick gray eyes taking in the window, her dress, and the table in the corner. "I see you still play those silly games. Isn't it time you grew out of them?"

"It's not a silly game, Dad. It's the siege of Allendale. You gave me the book yourself." Maryan strode over, gesturing at the small figurines, carved knights and infantry of blue and red on a detailed map. "The defending infantry had lined up here, then the opposing line made a charge around the right flank—"

"Yes, yes." The King waved at the board, then turned his back to it, facing her squarely. "But it's time to move beyond tactics and consider *strategy*, Maryan."

"Such as?"

"Such as alliances, and the creation of those blessed family bonds which bring distant countries together in peace, a peace which provides superior strength." He stroked his trim beard, shot through with regal streaks of white. "Anyone can win a battle. But winning a war, now that's something special."

"I wasn't aware we were at war, Dad."

He laughed, a hearty belly laugh that shook the room, rich and long and utterly insincere, in the way of all kings. "Here, stand by me at the window. No, not that close. There, like that. Now, look out and tell me what you see."

"What do you want me to see? Sharks circling us?"

"That's my girl. The world is a dangerous place for a small kingdom. We must be ever vigilant, my dear."

"You always say that."

"Yes, well, *now* we put those words into action. It is time for you to think of how you might best contribute to the kingdom's safety and security."

"By marrying a vampire?"

"Please, my good Maryan, you should stop making jokes about Prince Mikhail's teeth! He's a good man, despite what his subjects say."

"Yes, Dad."

"Now, I'm sure you must be nervous. There's no need to be. Once you get to know him, once you settle into a routine at his mountain stronghold, once you see our combined armies out on maneuver, you'll realize what a wonderful choice you've made."

"Isn't Prince Mikhail just using us to get our iron mines? The same way he used Estoria to get their grain reserves? Or how he used West Archerfield—"

"Now, now, my dear, I wouldn't put too much stock in rumors. Especially when they are inconvenient for my larger plans."

"What if I choose *not* to marry Prince Mikhail?"

"That would be inconvenient too. By the way, I invited him to meet you before the banquet. He'll be waiting in the garden. I thought it might speed things along."

"Wonderful."

"See you at the banquet, dear." The king stopped in the doorway. "Remember, Maryan. This is your chance to contribute to the safety and security of Offerdell."

"Got it, Dad."

He nodded and left.

The maid-in-waiting returned from the depths of her closets with the two wyvern bracelets. "Here you are, ma'am."

Maryan studied the bracelets as the maid-in-waiting fumbled with the clasps. She'd been told that one wyvern was sitting on its haunches, about to leap forward in a terrible charge, while the other was coiled back, ready to unleash a mighty gout of flame. Yet whether by her ignorance of wyvern behavior or poor execution on the part of the jeweler, the animals most looked as if they'd eaten something which disagreed with them, and were each dealing with it in a different way.

"These are perfect. Thank you."

"You're welcome, ma'am."

Maryan walked down the stairway and through the eastern halls to reach the palace's central garden. Many servants bustled through the passageways, preparing for the evening banquet. One or two turned to greet her, but upon seeing the princess's furrowed brow and clenched hands, dropped their heads and waited silently for Maryan to pass.

Maryan bit her lip. Why did her parents meddle and arrange these meetings instead of letting Maryan meet people on her own? And what would she say to Prince Mikhail when they met?

CHAPTER ONE: PRINCESS

She passed under a graceful marble archway, entering a bright garden with many rose bushes contained within crisply trimmed hedges. Here and there, a statue loomed, making it difficult to spot others. Maryan wound along the paths until a shadow reared up and blocked her, and she stepped back.

Before her stood Prince Mikhail, resplendent in a long black jacket embroidered with silver filigree, white ruffled cuffs sticking out of his sleeves. His dark hair was slicked back, one lock falling over his pale forehead, while his blue eyes regarded her with twinkling menace.

"You are just as beautiful as I'd been told." The Prince bowed imperceptibly towards her.

Fear flashed through Maryan and her breath caught in her throat. She'd intended to look severe and funereal, but now it occurred to her that Mikhail might prefer that fashion. "Thank you, good Prince." Maryan hinted at a bow in response. "I didn't see you there."

"Most people don't." He proffered a box of light purple, tied with a darker purple ribbon. "Chocolates from Estoria."

"Thank you. How does one transport chocolates over so great a distance in the heat of the spring sun?"

"By avoiding it, of course." He waved in annoyance over his head. "The sun is a harsh irritant, an inhabitant of those less-civilized kingdoms of the south, and I have devoted my life to weakening its influence over the north."

"Some people like the sun."

"Yes, but some people like ketchup with breakfast. There's no accounting for taste. Please, grace me with your presence a moment longer."

They walked along the smooth stone walkway together.

Mikhail noted her bracelets. "Are your wyverns unwell?"

"They're fine."

"This is all happening so fast," said Mikhail as he crushed a gardenia on the path. "I'm already head over boots in love with you."

"Heels."

"Say again?"

"Head over heels."

"Yes, that too." Mikhail stopped and clasped her hand in his, holding it to his chest, his cold blue eyes peering deep into her soul, as if searching for something small that had fallen down a grating.

He was close and musky with a hint of vanilla, and Maryan exhaled sharply to expel the scent of him. "As you say, good Prince, this is happening very fast."

"We are but two ships, tossed on a mighty ocean of love." He sighed. "Alas, oceans can be dangerous, and this one requires that we unite in holy matrimony within the month."

"Indeed, good Prince, I am not aware of such an ocean."

"It's a big world, and there are many oceans, some of which are chiefly concerned with love and matrimonial deadlines falling ahead of the summer campaigning season." He gazed at her with wide, puppy-dog eyes, his canines protruding over his lower lip to complete the look. "Someday I will explain it to you. Perhaps while hunting."

"I think, good Prince, that I will not sail on such an ocean."

Mikhail tossed back his head and laughed, like sparkling showers of spring rain cascading down, forming rivulets of laugh water that washed topsoil all over a patio you'd just finished sweeping.

"Your laugh is both lyrical and annoying, good Prince."

He stopped laughing, but kept the wide smile that featured his teeth. "Accept my proposal before the next full moon, or I'll lay waste to your kingdom and take you and your iron mines anyway." He let go of her hands and turned to leave. "Do enjoy the chocolates. They're made with fresh lavender."

Chapter 2
Prophecy

Everyone loves a good prophecy.

— *Considered Revelations, Book 27 "Things People Love", Chapter 8, Verse 12*

Many countries celebrate May Day, coming as it does after the cold winter, when the sun has conclusively won its battle with the long nights, and peasants can raise their mugs in toast to the beginning of the planting season as the first green shoots rise from the earth. The transition into the full bloom of spring was a welcome distraction from the otherwise tedious lives of peasants.

In fact, peasants had no real possessions and few rights save taxation, and the realization of such had prompted more than one scythe-wielding farmer to wonder what exactly they were paying taxes for. Fortunately, the preparations and lingering aftereffects of May Day celebrations kept commoners occupied until summer crops and harvests demanded more of their time. For this reason, the monarchs of Offerdell threw quite a party on May Day, as did most authoritarian governments across the globe.

The social pinnacle of the May Day celebration was, of course, the Royal Banquet in the Great Hall of the Palace of Offerdell. An uncountable number of candles were lit in the immense chandeliers by an uncountable number of servants. Flags and banners draped the walls. In their efforts to fully decorate the room, the servants had even hung the one musty tapestry in the back corner showing Hubert, the second King of Offerdell, falling off his horse multiple times.

Princess Maryan swept into the hall, her black skirts trailing, her ailing wyverns clanking against her wrists as she strode towards the high table. She nodded to the left and right as various members of the nobility and merchant elite greeted her, and kept her eyes off the other end of the table where Prince Mikhail sat in shadow, despite being under a large chandelier.

The noble families and rich merchants of Offerdell filled the hall, voices and laughter competing in volume with the clatter of plates and glasses. An admiral from the fleet passed by her with a brief bow, the lady's white uniform bedecked with many ribbons and badges from service. Maryan navigated around a small crowd surrounding Merchant Gonzalez, the large man dazzling in a blue suit with ruffled cuffs and extravagant gold rings.

"Excuse me, Your Highness." A man in fine but faded clothes bowed before her, his black hair and mustache neatly trimmed.

She recognized him as a knight from the northern provinces. "Good evening, Sir Humphrey."

"I apologize, ma'am, but I can't find my place." He waved his arm around the many tables in the hall, where cards with gold calligraphy declared who would take each seat.

Maryan bit her lip. Sir Humphrey had fallen on hard times, and it was entirely possible that a poor knight, out of favor with the king and queen, might not be invited at all.

"Perhaps you mortgaged your place setting along with your family home, Sir Humphrey," said Merchant Gonzalez with a sneer, waving dismissively with a bejeweled hand.

The knight's eyes flashed. "Why, you—"

"I forgot to tell you, Sir Humphrey, that you were assigned as my personal guard for the evening. We have a spot for you at the high table."

The knight bowed. "An honor, of course, ma'am."

Maryan sighed. Knights were famous for dueling with each other, but it was unwise to duel with merchants who had the ability to buy off judges and arrange "accidents." She distracted Sir Humphrey by asking him to fetch her a glass of Offerdell's famously over-sweet spring punch, then ordered the frazzled chamberlain to arrange an extra seat at the end of the high table.

Much to her chagrin, the king and queen intercepted her at the corner of the table, where they could interrogate her without being overheard.

"How did it go with Prince Mikhail, my sweet?" asked the King, his bushy eyebrows raised.

"Dad, I can't marry a warmongering vampire."

"Please, Maryan, most people would consider themselves lucky to be married to someone even half as ambitious." He spread his hands. "You must admit, he has large territories which act as a great buffer state. And marriage is really just an exercise in game theory."

"Oh honestly, Albert, how unromantic." The queen frowned at him, then turned to Maryan with a wide smile. "Marriage isn't game theory, dear. It's about avoiding recessive genes. The two of you can produce fantastic grandkids."

"Mom, I can't marry him. He's using us for our iron mines."

The dulcet tones of a mighty bell echoed in the hall, and the many guests moved to take their seats as the banquet began.

Her father nodded at her. "I trust you to make the right choice for the security of Offerdell."

Her mother squeezed her hand. "Great talk, dear. And don't forget the grandkids."

Maryan followed the king and queen to the center of the high table. Fortunately, she was sat at the queen's left, while Mikhail was further on the King's right, so she could focus on the first course.

On her left sat Ambassador Flotsam from Southport, who reveled in the dish. "It's a delight to get fresh vegetables," he said. "To be honest, in Southport we're happy to get fresh *anything*."

The ambassador told a story about his brief encounter with pirates on the southern seas. She appreciated the respite from her own worries, and thrilled in the man's description of the floating villages of the Wayward Archipelago. But anxiety stirred uneasily inside her, much as a condemned prisoner stirs uneasily inside a cage hung from a tree outside a mountain castle. Would she ever be able to travel herself? Or would she be stuck in a loveless, suspiciously short marriage?

Her anxiety leapt to the fore when her father rapped his glass with his fork, shattering it. "Oh, bother," he muttered. "Sally, do you mind?"

The queen tapped her glass with her fork, and the hall quieted as the ringing crystal reverberated.

King Albert stood at the head table, a fresh glass raised high. "Citizens and friends of Offerdell, welcome to the May Day Banquet!"

The hall resounded with several calls of "hooray" and "huzzah."

"Let me be the first to welcome our most distinguished guest, His Royal Highness Prince Mikhail of the Tangled Heights."

More cheering followed, as well as several "oohs" and "aahs", and Prince Mikhail stood.

Next to Maryan, the ambassador pointed at the Prince's red-cloaked honor guard. "A most impressive display, don't you think?" he whispered.

The six soldiers stood in a row against the far wall, unmoving, staring at her with wide black eyes that never blinked. "They're Death Knights, Ambassador Flotsam."

"Most impressive," he repeated.

"Your Majesties King Albert, Queen Sally, good citizens of Offerdell, and most especially, Her Royal Highness Maryan," began Mikhail.

The hall rang with happy murmurings as the well-fed and reasonably punched audience absorbed the warm greetings.

"And an absent welcome to Maryan's older brother Prince Bryce as well, who I understand is away at sailing camp."

"Prince Bryce!" echoed the King, raising his goblet.

The Prince continued. "I am a simple man. I tend to my harvests, bow my head in humble worship, and inflict ancient evils upon any who oppose me."

The audience nodded again, with someone in the back of the hall shouting, "You tell it like it is, Prince Mikhail!"

The Prince leaned over and gestured at Maryan. "And when I saw yonder maiden, I was smitten immediately. Does she not sit like a delicate crocus, that fine harbinger of spring amidst the snow?"

Maryan did her best not to roll her eyes.

Many in the audience breathed "aahs" at this, and a lady at a table in front fluttered her fan with a great sigh, a tear upon her cheek.

"I first saw her, or at least, first saw her roughly sketched likeness, just a month ago. I remember the day vividly. My squire had jotted down a few scratches depicting the royal family. I was standing amidst the high-grade ore of Offerdell's mines, and when my squire explained that the scratches on the right side of the drawing were her Royal Highness, and not a tree, I knew right then and there that I should dedicate my life to having her at any cost." He regarded his goblet. "My cost, or anyone else's."

More clapping and sighing.

Queen Sally leaned into her with a whisper. "Oh, isn't he a

charmer?"

Maryan shrank back into her chair. Clearly, Mikhail was either going to propose to her at the banquet, or at least tell them all that he'd already proposed. She decided to pretend to choke on something, but then noticed that the efficient waitstaff had silently removed her dish. What accident could she improvise with only a napkin?

But her wits fled her, leaving a dry taste in her mouth. She was cornered, stuck at the high table, stuck in her role as Princess, a gilded cage which would soon transport her to stand next to the other, considerably less-gilded cages at the Prince's mountain stronghold. Maryan could only watch, unmoving, as he uttered the words she'd been fearing all evening.

Mikhail raised his glass, jewels glittering from the eye sockets of a skull-shaped ring on his finger. "And now, in front of Offerdell's finest families, I will repeat the question I posed to Princess Maryan earlier this evening."

"Who will defeat the Lich King in the east?"

The hall quieted for a moment as everyone wondered why Mikhail would ask *that* question, and also why, when he asked it, his voice switched from a smooth tenor to a raspy, quavering alto.

The Prince himself stared at the back of the hall with his eyebrows raised, mouth agape.

Heads turned until everyone stared at the old lady standing there in a dirty gray peasant's dress and a bright red shawl. "Who will defeat the Lich King?" she repeated. Her voice was like paper tearing, but not a nice, even tear that follows the seam, but more like a jagged, unruly tear that cuts away from the seam and you have to crumple up the whole page and tear out another one.

"Who are you?" demanded King Albert, his bushy eyebrows knitted together.

The peasant lady curtsied, her joints creaking. "Your Majesty, I come from afar, bringing a prophecy of utmost concern to your and all other lands."

The King rubbed his eyes. "Oh, why does this happen to *my* banquets?" he muttered, but only Maryan and her mother could hear.

"The prophecy states that the Lich King will devour all before him in a rising tide of the undead, unless the chosen one recruits a fearless band—"

"No prophecies!" roared King Albert, and the chandeliers shook.

"Sire, this is a prophecy of the highest order, with great dangers and a romance that spans the ages—"

"No prophecies." The King pointed to a large sign to the side of the door, where "NO PROPHECIES" was engraved in large letters on varnished wood.

Ambassador Flotsam whispered to Maryan. "I'm so glad you have one of those signs. We should get one in Southport."

The peasant looked from the sign back to the King. "Sire, there are terrible repercussions to all if the prophecy is not followed. Also, it has this clever rhyming scheme—"

"No." King Albert turned to a large knight in shining plate mail. "Sir Otto, what happened to the last person that tried to tell a prophecy?"

"Hah!" Sir Otto's voice boomed through the hall, and his ceremonial armor reflected the lights of the chandeliers like an unfortunate glitter accident. "Sire, I believe that so-called soothsayer is *still* running from our hounds, though we set the dogs upon him over two years ago."

"And that was punishment for telling a *short* prophecy," said King Albert. "You don't want to know what we do to anyone that tries to tell us a long one."

The peasant swallowed. "What about a terse, cautionary tale?"

"No deal." King Albert crossed his arms.

"Very well, Sire. May I amuse the guests with a dirty limerick?"

"A dirty limerick?" asked the King. "Of course!"

"Cheers to dirty limericks!" echoed Sir Otto with a toast.

The peasant touched a finger to her cheek. "Let me see..."

King Albert frowned. "You're not making it up, are you?"

"Not at all, Sire. Just one second more..."

"You're making it up!"

"All set!" She clapped her dirty hands together, releasing a small cloud of dust. "Here we go."

> *There once was a big evil lich*
> *Whose bad plans we needed to switch*

CHAPTER TWO: PROPHECY

With a Mage and a Ranger
And an Axe against danger
We can stop that son of a witch

Scattered, uncomfortable applause broke out when she had finished.

Sir Otto squinted. "I think it could have been dirtier."

Prince Mikhail cleared his throat. "Well, that was an intriguing bit of poetry. A real window into the mind of a commoner, was it not?" He raised his glass again, and faced Maryan. "Anyway, as I was saying—"

A bell rang, the high tones cutting through Mikhail's speech.

"Ah, dinner is served!" bellowed the King. "Good Prince Mikhail, we'll have to save your toast for another course."

Mikhail sat again with a pained smile as the waitstaff brought out large platters of roast boar.

Maryan took a deep breath. She'd been granted a reprieve, but only a short one. After the main course Mikhail would surely relay his proposal, and she'd be forced to publicly refuse him, and then there would be a huge row with her parents, and diplomatic repercussions, and who knew if her refusal would ultimately stick?

Sometimes being a princess really sucked.

Even so, the mood in the hall had changed. The peasant lady remained standing under the "NO PROPHECIES" sign, her hands clasped before her as if waiting for something. No one took any steps to remove her, unusual for commoners who entered the hall uninvited, but Maryan didn't mind.

Prince Mikhail's red-clad honor guard had not moved, but now their unblinking attention was on the peasant. They no longer appeared quite so menacing, and in fact leaned away from her as if about to run.

Mikhail himself had only two bites of his main before standing and wiping his face with his napkin. He shot a single furtive glance at the peasant, then approached the King.

"By your leave, Your Majesty, I must depart for my homeland again."

"So soon, good Prince Mikhail? You'll miss dessert."

"My apologies, Sire, but there are urgent matters to attend to back in my kingdom."

"Very well, Mikhail. We'll see you in a few weeks, I trust?"

"Oh, yes." Mikhail's eyes glittered. "I promise."

King Albert didn't look up from his plate. "Good."

Maryan kept her face impassive as Mikhail approached her and kneeled.

"Princess." He gathered one of her hands and clasped it, and her fingers chilled.

"Prince."

"Do not fear marriage so, good Maryan. I'm sure your parents explained it. Game theory and recessive genes."

"I've already given you my answer, good Prince."

"You have until the next full moon to accept my proposal. I beg you to consider your kingdom's best interests, as well as your own."

With that, the Prince swept from the hall, his honor guard turning and following him one at a time in synchrony.

Queen Sally sighed. "It's so nice that his honor guard moves with such precision."

"They're Death Knights, Mom. They're undead automatons powered by the souls of the tormented."

"Well, they must practice, don't you think?"

"Most impressive," agreed Ambassador Flotsam.

Maryan picked at her plate, but she wasn't hungry. Prince Mikhail was intent on taking her hand in marriage whether she was interested or not, and her own family wasn't concerned either. What options did she have?

A dirty hand tapped at her shoulder. "Princess?"

Maryan turned and found the peasant lady with the red shawl sitting behind her. Oddly, no one else at the high table took any notice.

"Where did you get a chair?"

"Prince Mikhail wasn't using his anymore."

"He seemed to be, well, *afraid* of you."

"Not afraid, my dear, although that would be nice. *Inconvenienced* is probably a better word."

"Why?"

"Princess Maryan, I don't have much time, so I'll get to the point. Did you like my limerick?"

"It was very unique."

"How would you feel about fighting the Lich King?"

"I'd rather avoid it."

"And finding legendary romance?"

"I'm discovering that other people's idea of romance doesn't necessarily match my own."

"What if your only other option was to marry Prince Mikhail?"

"How exactly does one fight a Lich King?"

"You'll figure it out." The peasant lady stood, her eyes focused on the far distance. "I need to go now. And you, too. The first step to fighting the Lich King is to leave immediately."

"Now?"

But the peasant lady was gone, and Mikhail's chair was back at his empty place setting at the other end of the high table. Maryan blinked under the bright candlelight of the chandeliers.

After all, why *shouldn't* she leave? Nothing remained for her here, except for continual pressure from her parents to marry. If she didn't leave now, she'd be boxed in by their expectations for the rest of her life.

"Everything all right, dear?"

"Yes, Mom, I'm fine. I'm going to step out for some fresh air."

"That's a wonderful idea, dear. Make sure you're back in time for dessert."

Chapter 3
Knight

> *There is nothing more important than one's honor.*
> *Well, food is important. You can't go too far in life without food! And shelter. And money. Money is nice!*
> *Now that I think about it, honor isn't super-high on the list of important things. But for some people it is a currency nonetheless.*
>
> — *Considered Revelations, Book 22 "More About Knights", Chapter 2, Verse 15*

When a noble flees a palace at night it is important to pack all their travel clothes ahead of time, have their horse fresh and rested with saddle bags ready at the stable, and cute travel meals prepared in small paper boxes with monogrammed napkins. If pressed for time, one can do with simply packing an extra cloak and hose, dumping travel blankets helter-skelter into the saddlebags as they run out of the stable, and grabbing a few apples from the kitchen for meagre sustenance on the way.

Under no circumstances should a noble flee the palace with no horse, food or extra clothing.

"Oh, my," said Maryan as the fair towers of the capital receded in the distance behind the three travelers, "I seem to have fled the palace with no horse, food or extra clothing."

"I have some food with me, Your Highness. But can you remind me why we have fled at all?"

"I was chosen to fight the Lich King..." Maryan paused. In the great hall, surrounded by dazzling chandeliers and piles of roast boar, it had been easy to believe in prophecies and hear the call of the open road. Once on the road, which, let's face it, was terrifyingly *open*, the prophecy seemed somewhat less relevant and the prospect of encountering a Lich King at night a great deal less prudent.

"May I hazard a guess, ma'am?" The knight pulled at one pointy end of his mustache. "I suspect that the prospect of marrying a conniving vampire of a Prince has motivated thee to seek other lands, until such time as thine parents come to their regal senses."

CHAPTER THREE: KNIGHT

"I fear that may be a long time."

"Indeed."

"I appreciate you coming with me, Sir Humphrey, but why?"

"Well, ma'am, you did appoint me your guard. I am bound by honor to assist you, wherever you go."

"Ah." She'd appointed Sir Humphrey her guard only as a temporary ploy to get the man a seat at the May Day Banquet. But having a knight accompany her now struck her as reasonably good fortune. "And how is it you already have your horse packed and ready for the journey?"

Behind them strode Humphrey's sturdy gray mare, Daisy. She moved silently, like the evening breeze, except for the constant creaking of the knight's plate mail, bundled into two large sacks across her flanks, and a long scabbard which whacked against the mail now and then, and a pot and a pan which clanged against a dangling helmet with every step.

Sir Humphrey hung his head. "This is all I own, ma'am. I've been living off Daisy's back since I was forced to mortgage my estates last week."

"Oh, I'm sorry to hear that, Sir Humphrey."

"Nay, ma'am, 'tis a tale known to all of Offerdell, so I don't see why it should be a secret to you. My father was a brave man, and passed to me the importance of maintaining one's honor, no matter the situation. Sadly, he also passed to me a considerable sum of gambling debts, which the merchant houses of Bluntworth demanded I pay."

"So you have lost your family estates?"

"For all practical purposes, yes." The knight spared a glance back behind them, where his former estates lay far away to the north, lost in the darkness below the Teeth of Janks. A single tear glistened in the corner of his eye. "Only two weeks remain to pay off the debts, or else the merchant houses will auction off my lands."

"Oh, my."

The knight shook himself, then set his shoulders to face away from Offerdell. "You see, ma'am, I'm happy to join you and see what fortune awaits. The road is my home now."

"You are quite welcome, Sir Humphrey," said Maryan with earnest warmth in her voice. She turned to the third traveler, who walked next to Sir Humphrey. "And who, good sir, are you?"

The man turned, as if startled to be addressed. "Oh, good evening, Your Highness, Sir Humphrey. I am Cornelius. Please, carry on and don't mind me."

"A pleasure, Cornelius. But I am curious about who you are, and why you are here."

"Of course, ma'am." He took off his beaten cap, exposing a thick head of silvery hair, and bowed deeply on the path, his cloak billowing around him. "I am Cornelius, a Chronicler, at your service."

"A Chronicler? Here? What for?"

"Word has it, ma'am, that a prophecy is about to unfold. And I suppose if a prophecy unfolds, *someone* has to go along to Chronicle it."

"Please forgive me, good Cornelius, but you seem less than excited about it."

"I'm sorry, Your Highness. But I was recently demoted to prophecy work. I'm still getting used to it."

"Demoted? What did you Chronicle before?"

Cornelius stood a bit taller, his chest puffed out a bit more. "I was a ghost Chronicler for celebrities."

"Oh, 'tis no finer tale than a celebrity memoir! I have lost many an hour in such novels, good Chronicler." The knight lunged forward with an invisible sword. "Mayhaps you wrote the story of Sir Oswald, the famous knight from the southern wastes?"

"Not that one, Sir Humphrey."

"Did you write any of Lady Mollywhop's books? I loved how she could fight off goblin raids and serve high tea all on the same afternoon."

"Not those, ma'am."

"Pray tell, Chronicler, what celebrities did you write for?"

"Well, sir, probably the most famous was Kyle of Hoddlestam." The Chronicler faced the blank stares of the others. "The small-town cheese sculptor? No recollection?"

The knight frowned. "A small-town cheese what?"

"Which town?" asked Maryan.

"You misunderstand me, ma'am. He sculpted dioramas of small towns out of soft cheese. He also placed highly in a local baking competition. Er, top five. Still not ringing any bells?"

Sir Humphrey raised an eyebrow. "Forgive my prying, good Chronicler, but why were you demoted?"

The Chronicler let out a long sigh, filled with such sadness that Daisy's ears drooped. "I'm afraid I clashed with the Guild on editorial discretion."

Sir Humphrey gasped. "'Pon my word, sir, that strikes me as most serious for a Chronicler!"

"Aye, brave knight! I foolishly spoke out against the publication of Prince Mikhail's upcoming book."

"Oh?" Maryan's ears perked up. "I wasn't aware he was writing a book."

"It was mostly ghost-written by another Chronicler, ma'am. You know how these things work. It's yet another book where an up-and-coming noble expounds his values."

"Prince Mikhail is known for his charm and wit, sir!" Sir Humphrey gestured broadly. "I can only imagine his values are as chivalrous as he presents!"

"Well, sir, I guess I took issue with one of his values."

"Which one?"

"The one where he kidnaps innocent people, puts them in cages, and suspends the cages from trees on his property."

The knight looked unsure of himself. "Mayhap he cages innocents for the good of his country?"

"Aye, sir, that's what he says."

"He puts innocent people in cages?" Maryan frowned. "What's the name of his book?"

"*My Values*," replied the Chronicler.

Maryan put her hands on her hips. "That's it? He doesn't mention putting innocent people in cages at all?"

"That's the subtitle. The full title of the book is *My Values: Dangling Kidnapped People in Cages for the Good of the Country.*"

Maryan gasped. "You can't publish a book like that!"

"Yes, that's what I told the Guild."

The knight scratched his head. "I wager such a book would sell."

"Yes, that's what the Guild said when they demoted me."

Maryan sighed. "I'm so sorry to hear that, Cornelius."

"It is all in the past, ma'am. Now I am a Chronicler of prophecies."

He looked around the dark horizon. "Where are we going, by the way?"

"I'm not entirely sure," admitted Maryan. "But based on the limerick—"

"*Prophecy*," corrected the scholar.

"Based on the *prophecy* we need to find a Mage, a Ranger, and an Axe."

"We could buy an axe at the next town," said Sir Humphrey. "And rangers are easy to find. If you throw a stick in these lands, 'tis as likely to land on a ranger as a rabbit. But a mage, now, that's a different prospect."

"That's what I was thinking. The mage is the hardest part, so perhaps we should look for that first, and we can pick up the axe and ranger on the way."

"Very well, ma'am. And why are we on this road?"

"The old lady at the banquet said the Lich King was east, so I took an east road."

Cornelius swallowed. "East? Doesn't that lead into the Forest of Madness? Is that wise?"

"As you say, good Chronicler, I didn't want to venture into those dark woods. So I picked a road further south."

The scholar near jumped out of his cloak. "The Flower Hills? Are they not infested with trolls and ettins and... and skunks?"

"I'm taking the road that cuts *between* the Forest of Madness and the Flower Hills. So as to avoid the perils of either."

"Or encounter the perils of both," said Cornelius, looking from side to side.

"This is odd," said Sir Humphrey. He knelt by the side of the road, inspecting the leaves of a camellia.

Cornelius leaned over the man's shoulder. "What is it? A spider?"

"Aye, Chronicler, but unlike any spider I've seen before. See? This spider is shriveled, as if dead for days, yet moves still. Egads!" The knight jumped back, and Cornelius yelped as he moved out of the way.

"Did you see that? The accursed beast leapt at me." The knight crushed the crawling spider with his boot, then regarded the shadowed forests and hills around them. "'Tis a strange thing. The peasant lady at the banquet spoke of a rising tide of the undead.

CHAPTER THREE: KNIGHT

Could such a curse begin with the insects?"

"Arachnids, Sir Humphrey."

"Them too, Chronicler. Where is Princess Maryan?"

"Here." Maryan called out from behind them, where she peered into the hills further south. "I thought I heard something."

Sir Humphrey tapped the hilt of his sword. "I was about to propose that we make camp for the night. But now I bid we make haste further east before halting."

"Yes." Cornelius looked in all directions, eyes wide.

Sir Humphrey faced him. "And tell me, good Chronicler, when and how exactly did you join us? I don't remember seeing you at the May Day Banquet."

"Well, that's an interesting story—"

"There's no time!" Princess Maryan dashed back from the west, breathless. "An undead skunk has caught our scent! It's right behind us!"

For reasons that have never been explained, Daisy decided that the safest direction was off the road, straight into the Forest of Madness. The three travelers froze in shock as the clanking horse disappeared into the dark trees, then they all scrambled after her.

The ground was uneven, with grasping roots and vines, and thorny branches stuck out at odd heights to scratch them, and everything was enveloped in a darkness as thick as soup, though a rather leafy and cold soup, perhaps a gazpacho with hints of pine and dread.

Maryan chased after the others who ran ahead of her, unseen amongst the dark shadows. Yet she followed them easily based on the noise of Daisy's metallic crashings and frequent yelps from Cornelius.

"Wait!" she called, but in vain, for the clamor of the horse faded into the distance. Following the prophecy wasn't going anything like she'd expected. Wasn't she supposed to be bravely leading a band of adventurers to battle a Lich King? Instead, she was running after everyone, flying headlong into darkness.

She stole a glance behind her. A small creature with a black-and-white furry face squinted at her in the moonlight, then went back to rooting for food beneath the shrubs by the road.

A large crash sounded directly ahead of her, and Maryan slowed, but not quite in time, and she tumbled off a ledge. Maryan decided to scream in terror but fell into a bush of thick brambles before she could even open her mouth.

"Ouch," she said.

"Your Highness!" Sir Humphrey's voice was close and sharp with concern. "Are you hurt?"

"I'm fine." She extricated herself from the brambles with some effort, her black dress somewhat the worse for the experience, with several loose threads along the sleeves and small rips along the hem. Some of her hair had come loose from her bun, and dangled over her face with bits of twigs and dead leaves.

The Chronicler huddled nearby, under a large oak tree. "Oh, this is horrible, *horrible*."

"I'm afraid Daisy ran around this hollow, ahead of us on higher ground." The knight faced the direction they had come from, waving his fists. "I am without my sword or armor, but I can best any skunk with fisticuffs."

"Not just a skunk, but an *undead* skunk." The scholar shrank further, his arms curled over his head.

"That's why I was calling out to you to wait. I think perhaps it was not undead after all." She swallowed. "Or even a skunk."

The knight turned his head to her, his fists frozen in mid-wave.

"In fact," continued Maryan, "I think now it was just a raccoon. Probably a juvenile, by the size of it." She let out a long sigh. "I'm so sorry. But it was dark and you'd been assaulted by an undead spider..."

Sir Humphrey lowered his arms. "No fisticuffs tonight, or not yet, it seems. Still, all's well that ends well, no?"

"No," wailed the scholar. "For now we have wandered deep into the Forest of Madness, and at night, no less."

The knight raised his fists again, and waved them at the darkness. "Let any fell beast in this forest attempt to harm the Princess, and it'll feel the wrath of my knuckles."

Maryan took a step back, which wasn't the best of decisions given that she stood in front of thick brambles. But she ignored the pricks of the vines. What monsters would come at them now that they'd ventured unarmed into the Forest of Madness at night? She was a princess, wasn't she? Shouldn't she have a plan or something?

CHAPTER THREE: KNIGHT

A hoof clicked against a small rock somewhere east of them, a small noise accompanied by the clanking of armor and pots and pans. "Is... is that Daisy?" she breathed.

They clambered up out of the hollow on the other side, and after only a few steps they ran into the horse, calmly nibbling at the grass in a small clearing.

Maryan appraised the ground, lit by silvery moonlight filtering through the trees. "Daisy has found us a camp site. Maybe we can start a fire here?"

"Indeed, ma'am, I have to agree." The knight rummaged in his packs for flint.

In no time they'd built a small fire, and the light and the warmth helped soothe their unsettled spirits, although Cornelius kept staring into the darkness between the nearby trunks.

Maryan put her palms towards the fire, feeling the heat run up her arms. "Perhaps Daisy's mad flight was a boon."

The knight raised an eyebrow. "How so, ma'am?"

"My parents will have realized by now that I've left the castle grounds. They're sure to send out scouts along the major roads. This camp site is far enough from the road that I doubt even the fire is visible."

"Indeed, ma'am. And yet, you raise a point I hadn't considered. I could now be accused of kidnapping your royal person."

"Come now, Sir Humphrey. I'm doing this of my own free will, and you are accompanying me as my guard."

"True, ma'am." He took a deep breath, staring into the fire. "And while I would prefer to undertake this mission with the blessing of the king and queen, I can serve you with honor."

"Not a mission. A *prophecy*," said Cornelius.

"Of course, good Chronicler. I wouldst fain understand your role in this. What is it you do?"

"I Chronicle, of course! Ages from now, when people want to hear of this prophecy unfolding, it will be *my* account they read."

"So you will be the author of the tale?"

"The same."

"What is your method?"

"I keep careful notes." Cornelius raised a large tome, thick leather boards containing hundreds of bound pages, plus many more stuck in at odd angles. "I accompany the major actors on their journey, and I interview dozens more people during and after the fact, and assemble it all into a narrative in the seasons following."

The knight's eyes narrowed. "Please excuse my observation, but it strikes me that you have the ability to write a rather embellished account of your own actions in any such narrative."

"Sir!" Cornelius reared back, his hand on his heart. "I have sworn holy oaths to the Chronicler's Guild to recount all events faithfully and without bias. Even a hint of impropriety and I would be cast from the ranks of Chroniclers, my reputation ruined, and all royalties from past works forfeit."

Maryan cut in. "Isn't it dangerous work, Chronicling prophecies?"

"No, no, not really." Cornelius waved vaguely. "Of course, accidents do happen, ma'am. No one knows of the prophecy of the Stomping Manticore of the Seven Hills. The Chronicle was never written."

"What happened to that Chronicler?"

"Stomped. Nor have the peoples of this earth been graced with a retelling of the prophecy of the Cursed Ninja Troll."

"Oh my, what happened to that Chronicler?"

"Diced. And the prophecy of the Two-Headed, Fire-Breathing Dragon of Gutsworth likewise remains untold."

"Let me guess what happened to that Chronicler," said the knight. "Roasted and toasted?"

"No, he also was stomped by the manticore." Cornelius sighed. "All in all a tragic incident."

"Ah." Maryan looked over. "Sir Humphrey, whatever are you doing?"

"Standing on my head, of course, ma'am. It's long been a favorite exercise of mine. I find it relaxing, especially when facing anxious circumstances."

Cornelius rubbed his chin. "I have to confess, I know of no recent surviving Chroniclers of prophecies. But it is imprudent to draw conclusions from a paucity of data. A scant dozen fatal accidents do not define a trend, wouldn't you agree?"

The upside-down knight squinted. "Have you ever been in mortal peril?"

"It didn't come up much in past assignments."

CHAPTER THREE: KNIGHT

Sir Humphrey righted himself in a single, smooth motion. "Many newcomers to battle find it frightening. I've known more than one squire that wet their breeches at the first sign of danger."

"Honestly, sir, no one wants to read such a thing. And I can assure you that *I* will keep my wits about me, however novel the circumstances." Cornelius waved in irritation. "I would never write 'Squire Robert screamed in fear and cowered in a trembling ball of terror.' Instead, I would write around it, something like 'When danger suddenly appeared, Squire Robert was indisposed, but his friends fought bravely,' or other such phrasing."

A single, lonely howl rose from beyond the light of the fire, and all three travelers stood, Cornelius with some effort and much groaning. Sir Humphrey pulled his sword from out of its scabbard, and Maryan picked up a nearby bough.

"It's just a wolf," Cornelius said.

"Where there is one, more will follow," said the knight in a low voice. "Especially in the Forest of Madness."

They waited, two weapons and one pen at the ready, but no more howls greeted them.

Cornelius shrugged. "Perhaps the pack is elsewhere."

The night erupted in howls, and great furry beasts charged out of the darkness from all around them, eyes glowing and jaws open and full of glistening teeth.

"Crazed night wolves!" cried the knight. "Fight them with blade and fire!"

Cornelius was indisposed, but Maryan and Sir Humphrey fought bravely. A gray wolf leapt at the knight, but he thrust at it with his family sword, and the beast jumped away with a growl. Another snapped at the Princess, but she deftly side-stepped and brought her heavy bough down on its flank with a loud thump. The wolves retreated with yelps and more howling.

She pulled a burning stick from the fire, and held it aloft. "More approach! Prepare!"

But what stepped out of the darkness now was not a wolf, but rather a man in furs, shoulders broader than Sir Humphrey and Cornelius put together. The four of them stood staring at each other in the firelight as the wolves circled.

Chapter 4
Barbarian

> *There is no greater threat than a barbarian with an axe.*
> *Except maybe a dragon. Or, worse yet, a dragon with an axe.*
> *But a dragon with an axe is very unusual so it is more practical to fear the barbarian.*
>
> *— Considered Revelations, Book 32 "Travel Hazards", Chapter 2, Verse 5*

The man in furs glared at them, arms akimbo. "What are you doing, riling up the wolves at this hour?"

"What? We're not—" Maryan faced the man. "We're protecting ourselves."

Sir Humphrey stood between the newcomer and the Princess, sword held low. "And who are you who walks the Forest of Madness at night, good sir?"

"I don't walk the forest at night. I prefer to sleep, unless people start shouting and waving swords at me."

"I asked you your name, sir."

"I'm not deaf, you know. I'll give you my name when I feel like it. And who are you?"

"Sir, if you won't tell us who you are—"

"I'm Cornelius." The scholar shuffled forward, favoring one foot. "I'm a Chronicler."

The newcomer's eyes went wide. "A Chronicler? Here? What for?"

"Well—"

"Look," interrupted Maryan, "I don't think we have time for introductions. The wolves are circling."

"Bah. Once they see that we'll hold our ground, they'll seek easier prey. Shoo!" The large man waved his hands at the trees, and the glowing eyes of the wolves disappeared as the animals turned away. "You can see, they're not that big. They mostly scare people with their freakishly red eyes."

"I say," said Cornelius after the animals had left, "have you been in the forest long?"

CHAPTER FOUR: BARBARIAN

"Over a year, Chronicler."

"Oh, my!" Maryan couldn't help the outburst. "How did you survive the Forest of Madness for over a year?"

"Oh, it's not as bad as it sounds. Most of the Madness is aimed at armies and larger concentrations of people. If you're quiet and respectful, the forest mostly leaves you alone."

"You should address her as Your Highness," cut in Sir Humphrey. Then he covered his mouth in shock as he realized what he'd done.

The man in furs stared at Maryan in shock for a moment, then bowed. "Greetings, Your Highness." His eyes narrowed when he straightened. "Princess Maryan of Offerdell, I'd guess. What brings you here, ma'am?"

Maryan glanced at Sir Humphrey in irritation. "I'm fulfilling a prophecy, mister, ah..."

"I'm Gunthar, a barbarian." The man bowed again, then bit his lip. "Well, a *former* barbarian."

Maryan regarded him in the firelight. The former barbarian had long blond hair and an unkempt blond beard. He wore a kilt and cloak of bear fur, all bound by thick bands of leather and iron, with a shield and something else slung over his back. "What is that over your shoulder, Gunthar?"

"My axe, ma'am."

"An axe!" exclaimed Maryan, her hands to her cheeks, which was awkward when holding a large branch and a flaming stick.

"An axe!" shouted Sir Humphrey, his sword up as he backed away, keeping himself between the large man and the princess.

"An axe! The prophecy unfolds! Where is my pen?" The Chronicler shuffled back to his spot by the fire and dug in the leaves by his book. "Oh, curse the thing. Where did I put it?"

"What's so special about an axe?" asked Gunthar.

Maryan peered around the knight. "I think you could be in our prophecy. 'An Axe against danger.' We thought it meant a weapon, but now I wonder if it's referring to you."

"No unfolding!" Cornelius dug furiously through piles of dead leaves near his notebook. "No unfolding of prophecies until I find my pen!"

Sir Humphrey lowered his blade a hair. "You think *he* could be in the prophecy, ma'am?"

"Maybe."

"Found it!" Cornelius held the pen triumphantly aloft, then shuffled back with a great scattering of leaves as he juggled his stick, the notebook, and his pen. "Right, now unfold."

"I think we're done," said Maryan.

"Oh, bother. Well, I'll make notes anyway." Cornelius started scribbling.

"Pray join us, Gunthar," said Maryan as she put the burning stick back onto the fire. "We don't have much food, but you're welcome to share what we have."

The barbarian sat opposite, with Sir Humphrey sitting near the princess, his eyes never leaving the large man.

"And what does a prophecy have to do with the Forest of Madness, ma'am?" asked Gunthar.

"Very little," she sighed. "We are heading east to find what we need to battle a Lich King."

"A Lich King! Why would you mess with one of those?"

Sir Humphrey bristled. "Do you doubt our courage, barbarian?"

"Not at all, sir. Merely your sanity."

"Gentlemen, please," said Maryan.

Sir Humphrey sat back in a sulk.

"My apologies, ma'am," continued Gunthar. "What is it you are looking for?"

"The limerick—"

"—*prophecy*—" interrupted Cornelius.

"—states that we need a Mage, an Axe, and a Ranger."

Gunthar scratched at his beard. "What exactly is this prophecy?"

"A peasant lady in a red shawl broke into our banquet—"

"Nay, ma'am!" said Sir Humphrey. "'Twas a soothsayer, and she delivered the prophecy to us:"

> *There once was a big evil lich*
> *Whose bad plans we needed to switch*
> *With a Mage and a Ranger*
> *And an Axe against danger*
> *We can stop that son of a witch*

Gunthar made a face like he'd sucked on a lemon. "That's a prophecy?"

CHAPTER FOUR: BARBARIAN

Sir Humphrey hesitated. "Methinks it sounded better when the soothsayer said it."

"This so-called soothsayer," asked Gunthar, "was she a Prophecy Scholar? Because I might believe it then."

The knight shook his head. "She did not present herself as such, no."

"I know it's not a very good prophecy," said Maryan. "I think she made it up on the spot."

"Huh." The barbarian waved it away. "The hills are infested with rangers. Finding one of those wandering rogues will be easy."

"Yes," said Maryan. "And we appear to have found our Axe."

"Maybe, ma'am." Gunthar shifted uncomfortably.

"What is it, sir?" Sir Humphrey leaned in. "Will you not respect the wishes of the princess, and join us?"

Gunthar nodded to Maryan. "Beg pardon, ma'am. But I'm not really in the barbarian business anymore."

"What business are you in?" The knight gestured at the forest around them. "And how did you end up here?"

Gunthar settled back with a sigh, crossing his heavy fur boots. "That's a sad story, sir."

"Wait, wait," called Cornelius. "I need more paper."

The barbarian glared at him, but waited for the Chronicler to pull out a fresh sheet. "I was a successful barbarian in my youth. Axe-throwing tournaments, coastal raids, sieges, fishing derbies, that sort of thing."

"In your youth?" Maryan tilted her head. "You don't look that old, Gunthar."

"About two years ago, I was battling mountain giants near the passes of Raknor when a strange group marched down the road. All in red armor, with unblinking eyes."

Maryan frowned.

"They came at us without so much as a 'Nice battle' or 'Who might you be?'," continued Gunthar, staring into the flames. "They chopped through the giants and took me prisoner."

"Barbarians live beyond the Teeth of Janks," noted Sir Humphrey. "How did you get here?"

"That's just the thing, sir. Those red-armored fiends brought me back across the pass, and then through the northern part of the

Forest of Madness. I think they were going to bring me back to their mountain stronghold. But the beasts of the forest attacked, scattering them, and I was able to free myself and escape here." The barbarian waved around them. "I've stayed in the southern end of the Forest of Madness since then."

"Oh, curse that Prince Mikhail."

"I'm sorry, ma'am?"

"The people that captured you. I'm pretty sure they were Death Knights, serving Prince Mikhail of the Tangled Heights. He's my betrothed."

"What? Your fiancé did this?"

"Technically, I have rejected his hand in marriage, so I'm not sure if he's really my fiancé or not. But it's not clear that my opinion matters. Marriage among noble families is all game theory, you know."

"Don't you also have to watch for recessive genes?" asked Cornelius.

"Yes, that too," snapped Maryan. "Anyway, Prince Mikhail seems to have been behind your capture."

"'Tis a sorry predicament, truly." Sir Humphrey squinted at the large man. "But why were you battling giants alone anyway? Don't barbarians operate as a tribe?"

Gunthar's face turned even redder in the firelight. "That's my business."

Maryan stood. "It's late. Let's gather more wood for the fire, then get some sleep. We can figure out next steps in the morning."

"Yes, ma'am," said Sir Humphrey, standing with her. The knight watched Gunthar stand, but kept his hand off his sword.

"Ouch!" The Chronicler tried to stand, but fell back to the ground again. "My ankle," he said, holding a hand to his left foot. "I did something to it when those cursed wolves attacked. I'm sure it's broken."

"Egads!" The knight reeled in horror. "We've lost our Chronicler! 'Tis the curse of chronicling prophecies!"

"Wait." Maryan knelt by Cornelius. "You were walking before, so it is unlikely to be broken. The ankle is a bit swollen, probably a light sprain. I'll bind it. Sir Humphrey, please find a suitable stick he can use as a crutch."

The Chronicler had an extra shirt, which Maryan used along with some short sticks to form a splint. He complained and whimpered with every adjustment that Maryan made, but appeared satisfied when done. "You've set splints before, ma'am."

"Field training with Sir Otto," said Maryan as she sat back. "That should hold for a while."

The knight returned with a particularly gnarled stick, with a small, leafy green branch sticking out the side.

Cornelius eyed it with disdain. "Is there nothing straighter to be found?"

"Beg pardon, Chronicler, but the selection at the moment is somewhat limited. Perhaps you would prefer to look in the woods yourself?"

"Let's turn in," said the princess. "I'm sure everything will be clear in the morning."

Chapter 5
Dunswell

Hie thee to the fair lands of Dunswell!
Dunswell, where the great dunes meet the sea!
Dunswell, where the mead flows in rivers!
Dunswell, where no one's dairy products are ever entirely safe!

— Considered Revelations, Book 63 "Places to Hie For", Chapter 12, Verse 443

The coals of the fire burned hot in the morning, though Gunthar recommended not adding any more wood, since the smoke would be visible and who knew what sort of men or creatures that would attract.

The barbarian promised them a breakfast of spiced fiddleheads. He foraged for the bright green shoots in the many ferns of the area, and returned with a sizeable harvest carried in his cloak. "May I borrow your pan, Sir Humphrey?"

The knight grumbled but handed over his battered tin cooking pan, which Gunthar put on the coals.

"Not too fast!" Cornelius furiously scratched in his notebook, attempting to keep up with the barbarian's cooking. "I'm trying to capture all the details."

"The details?" Gunthar shot him a sideways look. "Who cares what we had for breakfast?"

"Details matter! You'll see, when this is all written, that your account in this prophecy will be much richer—"

"Whoa, there, Chronicler. You can write your book if you want, but I'm not joining any prophecies."

Maryan leaned in. "What will you do?"

"I'll stay here a bit longer, ma'am. I'm quite comfortable in the forest now."

Sir Humphrey snorted. "Comfortable? You sleep upon tree roots with a mad forest hanging over you."

"It's far better than the world of people beyond the eaves."

"Sir, I think you might be better served by facing your fears."

"Don't think that the amateur psychotherapy of knights will somehow spur me to join your cause. I'm happy how I am."

Sir Humphrey bristled. "Amateur what? Sir—"

"Um, please stop?" Maryan waved at the arguing men from the side, worried that things would escalate. "Gunthar, you don't have to join us. But could you escort us to the edge of the forest? We're trying to find our Mage."

"Of course, ma'am."

They broke camp. The Chronicler's ankle was still swollen, so they distributed most of the knight's belongings among the other three walkers, and put Cornelius on Daisy. The scholar complained about the special treatment, saying it wasn't fair to the others that he should ride while they carried everything, that he wanted to pull his fair share, and could they tighten the strap on the left side, and pass him the rest of the fiddleheads, and could someone take the helmet since it was rubbing against his leg?

Maryan followed the barbarian, who carried the knight's armor in two great sacks on his back, pans dangling, though he moved as if unburdened.

They walked for hours, Gunthar somehow finding his way through the dense trees and thick undergrowth. No wolves returned, though they did see several deer, bounding away through the brush, and countless birds twittered above them. Despite the name, Maryan found she liked the calm of the Forest of Madness.

They entered a grove of birch trees, the tall white trunks scattered around them. Sir Humphrey threaded through the columns. "Good barbarian, I am curious. What is your style move?"

Maryan frowned. "His what?"

"His style move. Each barbarian has a unique strike with their axe, which they use in battle against their fiercest opponents. 'Tis a wonder to behold, or so it is said!"

"Well, I think axes and so-called *style moves* are a little overrated." Gunthar's cheeks turned scarlet. "And that's kind of a personal question."

Maryan decided to change the subject. "Is it far to the edge of the forest?"

"No, ma'am, we're very close to the Golden Plains now."

"And whither from there, ma'am?" The knight waved ahead. "Do we continue east?"

"There isn't much east of the plains, except more plains," noted Gunthar.

"We have a decision to make." Maryan stepped over a tree root. "I've heard there is a wizard's school of some sort to the northeast. Or else there is another further south, along the coast, in Dunswell."

"Northeast?" Gunthar shook his head, the sacks of armor creaking. "That's dangerously close to ogre territory."

The knight pointed to the right. "In that case, mayhaps our course is decided. South into Dunswell. That land has fair roads, and their inns are famous."

"And their king!" Gunthar nodded in appreciation. "It is said that no one can match the King of Dunswell's skill at hunting. Or, for that matter, spends as much time doing it."

"And he's rich," said Sir Humphrey. "*He* never has to worry about his estates being mortgaged! Not with all the gold he has, or the gold he takes from his people. And all their dairy."

"Yes." Cornelius frowned. "Is that why his people have been rioting so much of late?"

"And burning down the king's many hunting lodges," added Gunthar.

Maryan shook her head. "I don't think we should venture into Dunswell. They've been having political troubles lately."

"I guess we won't be trying their famous inns any time soon." Sir Humphrey sighed.

"Northeast it is then, though it means traveling across the plains, exposed to wild beasts and ogres. You might need to use that." The barbarian pointed at the knight's sword, now swinging from his waist.

Sir Humphrey tapped the hilt. "Old Gwendoline here has served my family for many generations. She's got some fight in her yet."

"You name your sword?" Maryan looked at the scabbard, a steel sheath covered with silver and gold detail.

"Of course, ma'am. Though I'm not sure if my family named her, or if she came to us with a name already. Gwendoline is a magic sword from long ago."

"Magic?" Gunthar raised an eyebrow.

"She used to be." The knight sighed. "Time was when a knight of

CHAPTER FIVE: DUNSWELL

the Happenhouse family would raise the blade in battle, cry 'Onwards, Happenhouse,' and it would blaze with lightning. Many a foul beast fell to the electrical charms of fair Gwendoline in olden times, I can tell you."

"Really?" said Gunthar. "Just shout 'Onwards, Happenhouse,' and the blade lights up?"

"You have to push the button, here." Sir Humphrey tapped a knob near the hilt. "Then it turns on."

Maryan regarded the scabbarded sword with interest. "But it no longer works?"

"No, ma'am. I don't know why not. I've heard it worked for my grandfather. But it didn't work for my father, nor for me. If I turn it on now, it will only hum and maybe give a single spark."

Gunthar shrugged, and all the armor he carried clanked together. "Perhaps it is as they say. The relics of the old world are fading."

"Maybe." The knight hung his head. "Certainly the Happenhouse fortunes are fading."

"Don't despair, Sir Humphrey." Maryan couldn't help but speak up. "We'll see if we can get Gwendoline fixed. Maybe at the school of wizardry."

The knight straightened his shoulders again. "Thank you, ma'am. And don't worry—Gwendoline still has a fierce bite, even if she can't do the lightning thing anymore. She'll stand strong against any opponent that challenges us, even ogres."

"You'll soon find out." Gunthar pointed ahead. "The Golden Plains."

Chapter 6
Plains

Hie thee to the fair Golden Plains!
The Golden Plains, where the long golden stalks wave in the wind!
The Golden Plains, where, well, that's about it.

— *Considered Revelations, Book 63 "Places to Hie for", Chapter 12, Verse 448*

The forest ended abruptly, like a bad haircut, and the tall grass of the plains swept before them, waving in the spring breeze.

"Oh," said Maryan. "I thought there'd be more cover. And maybe a path."

"I ventured a ways out of the forest once. There's a trail near a stream, not far ahead." Gunthar pointed an indeterminate distance into the grasses. "I'll take you that far."

They walked into the plains, the grasses coming up to their waists. Insects buzzed and clicked, and birds swooped around them.

The sunlight warmed Maryan's cheek. "It's nice to be in the sun again."

"Maybe, ma'am, but as for myself, I'll be happy to return to the forest."

"Are you sure, Gunthar? I think we could use you."

"Sorry, ma'am." He stopped at the top of a small rise, below which a stream ran in a gravel course. "The stream. And here is the trail."

Sure enough, a worn footpath lay next to the rushing water.

"Do you think the trail will lead us to our Mage?" asked Sir Humphrey. He held a hand over his eyes as he looked up and down the stream.

"I have no idea," said Gunthar. "But if you go upstream, it takes you northeast. That's the direction of the wizard's school you mentioned."

"Thank you, Gunthar." Maryan held out a hand. "I wish you'd come with us, but I appreciate all your help in getting us this far."

"You're welcome, ma'am." He shook her hand vigorously. Maryan

CHAPTER SIX: PLAINS

had trained with enough knights to return the firm handclasp.

The barbarian stepped back. "And take care. With luck you'll avoid any ogres."

"Oh, horsefarts," swore Cornelius, staring north. "Ogres."

The travelers swiveled their heads to follow the Chronicler's gaze. Three large green humanoids strode towards them, the grasses only coming to their mid-thigh. Two carried thick clubs of wood with large spikes sticking out of them, while the third had a sword nearly the height of a man, but a man made out of steel with really sharp edges, a steel man an ogre could swing in battle without the man screaming the entire time.

The knight swallowed, his hand on his hilt. "I've only read about ogres. They're bigger than I was expecting."

Gunthar's face went pale, his jaw dropping. "Oh, no."

"What is it?" asked Maryan, looking between the ogres and the barbarian. "Is all hope lost?"

"It's worse than that." The barbarian dragged a hand over his face as he grimaced. "I'm two years out of date. Look at what they're wearing. No one wears furs anymore. It's all oiled leather now."

Maryan looked back at the approaching ogres. Like the barbarian, they wore light armor of banded iron, but their kilts and shoulder braces were made of shining leather. "Does that matter? I didn't think ogres cared about fashion. Or barbarians, for that matter."

"Where did you hear that barbarians don't care? Style is everything." Gunthar took a deep breath, straightening himself. "Look, don't mention the leather, all right? Best not to give them a leg up in any negotiations."

"Negotiations?" The knight spoke out of the side of his mouth, all of his focus on the ogres. "We're not going to fight?"

"We'll see. They probably just want to trade information." Gunthar stepped forward. "Look, let me do the talking. I speak ogre."

The three ogres stopped in front of them, glaring down. Maryan caught glimpses of small black eyes over thick tusks that curled up over their green cheeks. The one in the middle stood tallest, carried the non-screaming man-sized sword, and had steel caps on his tusks. She marked that one as the leader.

Fortunately, the sword remained sheathed, slung across the lead ogre's back, and the other two ogres had their spiked clubs dangling from straps at their waist.

"Oh my," whispered Cornelius. "I think that one could knock me clear back to Offerdell with a single swipe of its club."

"Courage," the knight whispered back, his face pale.

The barbarian strode out and stopped a few paces in front.

"Don't worry," Maryan whispered back to Sir Humphrey and Cornelius. "I'm sure Gunthar knows how to put them at ease."

"Ho there," called Gunthar in a loud, barrel-chested voice. "What are a fat lot of piss-drinking sons of goblins doing out on my plains?"

Everything went quiet for a moment, except for a squeaking noise from the scholar which Maryan figured was a hyperventilating scream of terror.

Then the lead ogre sneered, which is even more frightening when done by someone with large tusks topped with sharpened steel. "We were looking for worthy prey, but seem to have found ****-covered scrapings from a dung troll."

Gunthar didn't flinch. "I don't think you could find ****-covered scrapings from a dung troll if you got down and buried your nose in its—"

"I can't write this," complained Cornelius, but Maryan shushed him.

"If I did bury my nose in a dung troll's ****, I wouldn't **** your **** even if I **** **** with a ****."

Cornelius gasped from his seat atop Daisy. "My pen is well-nigh smoking. Where on earth did they learn this language?"

"From your mother," said the nearest ogre.

"Oh, deary me," said Cornelius, fanning his face.

"I find their dialect refreshing," said Sir Humphrey.

"Let me do the talking," hissed Gunthar. Then he addressed the ogres again. "While you were **** each other with that **** stick, did you happen to see a school of wizardry? It's like your ****, only not as tiny."

"If I did see a **** school, why would I **** tell a **** like you?" retorted the ogre. "I **** turds with more backbone. If you're so keen on that sort of ****, why don't you drag your **** on the path for a few days and get what's coming to you."

CHAPTER SIX: PLAINS

"Good news," Gunthar whispered back to the travelers. "This is a scouting party on reconnaissance. And they say there's a school of wizardry three days up the path."

"What?" Cornelius' eyes went as wide as dinner plates, though more like eyeball-sized dinner plates, or perhaps regular dinner plates seen from some distance away. "We're turning around and running the first chance we get, aren't we?"

"Shush," said Maryan, then turned to Gunthar. "Why are they scouting here?"

"I'll check, ma'am." The barbarian faced the ogres again. "Why don't you ****s go bugger off to whatever dark **** you came from?"

"Even the darkest **** has less **** then that **** mouth of yours. And you can **** with a **** with **** **** **** undead ****."

Cornelius made a sort of retching sound.

"Tried that, but the **** said you were too ****." Gunthar turned back to Maryan. "It's troubling, ma'am. There's some sort of disturbance with the undead further east. I think the ogres may be scouting potential avenues for retreat."

Maryan inhaled, then looked over the plains farther east. "The Lich King and his rising tide of the undead. It's like the peasant lady said." She nodded to Gunthar. "Wish them well, and let them know we'll be heading to the school of wizardry as fast as we can."

"Aye, ma'am." The barbarian turned and boomed out again. "I, Gunthar son of Gudmund, will be going wherever the **** I want, even if that's straight up the path into your **** ****. And you can **** yourself in the meantime."

The lead ogre bent forward, spittle flying from between his tusks. "And I, Huknar son of Kurk, will **** your sorry **** wherever I see it. Don't get any **** ideas."

Then he beckoned to the other two ogres to follow him, and walked around the travelers.

"Nice kilt," said the last ogre as he passed, giving Gunthar's furs a disdainful glance.

"Go **** yourself," said Gunthar with a forced smile and a faint wave.

They watched the broad-shouldered, green ogres continue further south along the path.

"I think that went amazingly well," declared Maryan.

"Indeed, ma'am, I feared the worst, but instead we seem to have gained valuable information." The knight looked over at Gunthar. "Is that right, sir? Are we free to follow the path?"

The barbarian jerked his head up, as if pulled out of his thoughts. "Eh? Oh, yes. We're allowed to venture across the plains, so long as we hunt only what's necessary for ourselves."

"*We?*"

"Well, ma'am, it's like this." Gunthar smoothed his fur kilt a bit sheepishly. "I think I've been out of touch with civilization for too long. I'm behind the times."

"So you'll join us?"

"At least as far as a major town. Someplace I can pick up better clothes."

Chapter 7
School

How mighty and powerful are the wise!
They who can break mountains, and travel through time itself.
To what use are their legendary powers applied?

— *Considered Revelations, Book 55 "Why Wizards Are the Best", Chapter 8, Verse 3*

They spent three days crossing the Golden Plains. It rained, then cleared up, then rained, then cleared up, then cleared up again, which surprised them but Cornelius said that was common in this area.

Daisy ate from the many grasses, and if anything seemed to be a half-hand taller, as if the stout grains had worked a mysterious magic on the horse. The others ate whatever human fare Gunthar and Sir Humphrey managed to find, inevitably a tough and sour-tasting plains rat.

Despite the unpleasant food, they were happy to see no signs of anyone else, no travelers or ogres or undead. "In fact, the view is entirely monotonous," complained Cornelius. "Waving grass in every direction. I'm glad we have a stream to follow, otherwise we'd just walk in circles."

"*We'd* walk in circles, but *you'd* stay comfortable on *my* mount," grumbled Sir Humphrey as he shifted the large pack on his back.

"I'm still gravely injured from my ferocious battle with those demon wolves." Cornelius pointed to his wrapped ankle.

"Don't worry, Chronicler. You should stay off that ankle for a few more days." Maryan didn't enjoy the two bickering, but it did take her mind off the bitter aftertaste of plains rat.

Gunthar was in the lead, and although his head was obscured by the bags of armor piled on his shoulders, they could hear his voice. "There's not much forage here on the plains. Most people take the road along the southern end. It's faster and has many inns and taverns."

"Perhaps, but I'm glad we're not on the road. I'm sure my parents will have scouts on it by now, looking for me. We can avoid them on the plains."

"Even so, the description of the road striketh a chord within me," said Sir Humphrey. "How better to mark a prophecy than by having the compatriots gather in a tavern, eh, Chronicler?"

"I think it would be expected," said Cornelius.

"Speak for yourself. I'm just looking for a tailor."

Maryan caught the desperation in his voice. "Come now, Gunthar, don't worry about that. I think your kilt looks very dashing."

The barbarian turned, the bags of plate mail swinging around with clanks and squeaks. "I know what you're really thinking, ma'am. I'm a sad, out-of-date, backwoods barbarian with no fashion sense."

Maryan was taken aback. "Not at all. Besides, look at what I'm wearing. A dirty, frayed funeral gown."

Gunthar faced forward again, striding off with redoubled vigor. "Let's get to this school of wizards as fast as we can. Maybe they've got a seamstress or something. The sooner we're all outfitted the better."

"Truly, good barbarian, I'm surprised you care at all. And what's the hurry?" The knight half-jogged to keep up.

"I'll be honest, sir. The furs are a bit hot in the spring sun."

"I tire of this scenery," complained the Chronicler. "What wouldn't I give for something to break the monotony of the plains!"

"Behold!" The knight pointed northeast. "Something to break the monotony of the plains!"

They had crested a small rise, and from the top they discerned a compound of many buildings ahead, all enclosed by a tall white wall. "The school!" exclaimed Maryan, and they all descended with increased energy.

Soon, the dirt track became a path of smooth stones, winding towards the walls. The compound lay in a valley where the harsh cliffs of the north met the grasslands.

"What exactly is this place?" asked Gunthar as they approached.

"I'd say it was the North Hills School of Wizardry," said Cornelius, pointing towards a large sign by the side of the path that claimed the same.

CHAPTER SEVEN: SCHOOL

"It's very impressive." Maryan stared up at the buildings looming above the walls. The nearest hall was made of gray stone, blackened at points as if it had withstood fire and lightning, and other arcane assaults besides. Flying buttresses rose with slender power, peppered with gargoyles, the stone beasts staring down at them, frozen in mocking cries.

"It's a school, and there are wizards inside," said Sir Humphrey. "What else is there to know?"

"Wizards are very secretive. But from what I've read, they use these schools to train promising apprentices in the magical arts." Maryan took a deep breath. "Who knows what arcane secrets lurk behind this forbidding wall?"

"'Tis a forbidding wall indeed, ma'am, but with pleasant tulips and daffodils and roses." Sir Humphrey pointed at the rows of flowerbeds.

"And what topiary!" exclaimed Cornelius. On each side of the gate stood a tall boxwood, carved in the shape of a spiral. They stopped in front of great oak doors which remained closed, despite it being the middle of the day.

"One supposes that a knock will suffice." Sir Humphrey rapped sharply on the stout wood doors, then stepped back. "Do you think they might teach us some spells, ma'am?"

"Ha!"

Everyone jumped, and then peered to the side, where a young woman in a white robe stood near the spiral boxwood, under the shadow of the wall.

"We don't train just anyone, you know." She stepped forward into the light, her long black hair shining. "Apprentices must train for years to become a Mage. Most don't learn their first spell until they enter their fifth decade."

"Mercy!" Sir Humphrey looked back and forth between her and the wall.

"Sorry, I'm trying to take notes here." Cornelius leaned in from atop Daisy. "Does 'entering their fifth decade' mean when they turn forty, or fifty?"

"Sounds like fifty to me," said Gunthar.

"Nay, good barbarian, 'twouldst be forty."

"Oh sure, sir, if you go strictly by the math," said Gunthar. "But

I'm sure the lady was speaking metaphorically."

"Or would it be forty-one?" Cornelius tapped his quill feather against his temple as he thought.

Maryan addressed the robed lady. "Are you an apprentice here?"

"I study here," she answered. "So I guess you could say—"

"She's our gardener." The oak doors now stood wide open, and in the middle of the archway towered a man with long gray hair in a light blue robe. His hand clasped a tall staff of onyx, with a cage-like carving at the top holding a glowing white gem.

"Yikes." Gunthar staggered back, his bags of armor creaking and clanging.

"Indeed, sir. Ah, begging your pardon, of course," Sir Humphrey said to the man in blue. "We didn't see you open the doors. Or generally notice your appearance at all."

The man in blue spoke with a voice like molasses, but warm molasses so it could flow and looked good but you would be careful about touching it. "I am Thristletoramallicus, Keeper of the Gates of Orst, though you can call me Thristletoramallicus, Keeper of the Gates for short."

"I am Maryan, of—"

"I know who you are."

"We are here—"

"I know why you are here. Please follow me." With that, Thristletoramallicus, Keeper of the Gates walked up the path to the center of the compound.

The companions followed, the gardener following behind. She leaned towards Sir Humphrey. "Do you see his staff?"

"Indeed, it is hard to miss given its height and luminescence."

"It is said that when he touched it, he had a vision of the rock melting in primeval times, hardening into a vein of pure onyx, and then the crystal is a piece of star that fell from the skies, and a gnome mystic trapped the star piece within the onyx cage."

"Really?" Gunthar scratched his head, which set all the armor he carried to clanking again. "I've never heard of gnomes doing anything useful."

"Well, that one did."

"How long have you studied here?" Maryan asked her.

"Around two years—"

CHAPTER SEVEN: SCHOOL

"Yang doesn't study here." Thristletoramallicus, Keeper of the Gates had stopped noiselessly and they all awkwardly reared up in a cluster to avoid running into him. Daisy piled into them and sniffed at Maryan's hair—which was quite fragrant after several days travel—so the princess absently stroked the horse's nose.

"This way." Thristletoramallicus, Keeper of the Gates walked off to the right where a large outbuilding squatted, with smoke drifting up from multiple large chimneys.

"I think they're worried I might not have enough magic."

"I'm sorry?" Maryan turned back to the gardener Yang.

"They don't yet let me study here because they're having problems determining the extent of my magical capabilities—"

"There is no problem," intoned Thristletoramallicus, Keeper of the Gates. "You have no magic. None."

"Well, I think it was hard for them to get a good read on it—"

"We tried five different times, five different ways. You have no magic. This is why you do not train."

Yang lifted her chin. "The seer in my village said I was destined for greatness, so they sent me here."

"You are destined to be a great gardener." Thristletoramallicus, Keeper of the Gates, stopped at the steps leading into the lodge. "You may refresh yourselves here. I will return in a few hours with the Master of the School."

"Thank you," said Maryan, but the man in blue was gone.

Yang put her hands on her hips. "I think he prefers to zap himself around. He only walks when he's leading visitors into the grounds."

The lodge was a pleasant wood structure, with entire tree trunks acting as beams spanning the length of the building, supporting a large roof atop at least two stories. They tied Daisy to a post outside, then helped Cornelius off the horse's back. He limped after them, using the leafy bough from the Forest of Madness as a crutch.

"How is your ankle?" Maryan asked.

"Much better, thank you, ma'am," he replied. "It's still a bit stiff and swollen, but much better than three days ago."

"Here, I'll show you around," said Yang. "They let me use the lodge in return for all the gardening I do. You know, until they admit me as an apprentice."

They followed the gardener through the tall doorway, into a large interior room filled with light. "The Hall of Refreshment," she declared.

Light filtered down from above, the warm wood walls glowing in sunbeams, long white curtains fluttering lazily in a breeze. A balcony above looked down on a great room with several couches and tables and a plush blue rug decorated with stars and unicorns.

"'Tis a pleasant sight after days on the road!"

"I was expecting... I don't know. Maybe something darker and more erudite?"

"Indeed, ma'am, it's not what I was expecting of wizards."

A man with long gray hair walked by in a plush white robe, with matching white slippers. He carried a steaming cup of coffee with a cookie on the saucer.

Gunthar frowned. "Shouldn't wizards be doing something else? Something more wizardly?"

"Don't believe everything you hear about wizards. For every hour of study, there are many more hours of *this*." Yang waved her hand around the room.

A short, plump man in a white uniform hurried up. "Ah, today's guests. The Gatekeeper said you'd be here."

In short order, each of the companions bathed and wrapped themselves in thick white robes, then filed out to a dining hall in the east wing. Light filtered down from high windows as they helped themselves to food from a central table.

Maryan looked around for waitstaff. "No one serves the food?"

Yang picked large fronds of salad onto her plate. "No servants, except those you conjure yourself. That's the rule."

Gunthar piled his plate high with roast boar. "Suits me fine."

Sir Humphrey's eyebrows went up. "Are you allowed to take that much?"

"No one complained about my first plate, sir, and it was bigger than this."

"In that case..." The knight took another helping.

They sat at a side table with a bright silver tablecloth with gold-stitched runes and stars and cutlery. Cornelius sat down with a modest plate of greens and gnocchi. He hummed and hawed as he sniffed at it, then cut one open and inspected it. "They make it themselves, apparently." Then he popped it in his mouth.

Sir Humphrey shifted in his seat. "I've never seen wizards before, Your Highness. 'Tis most unusual to share their canteen."

"Who knows what they're capable of?" Gunthar looked at one green-robed form at a table on the other side of the room. The salad levitated over the table, and the wizard extracted the raisins and walnuts from the floating constellation of herbage.

"That's my favorite part of the salad, too," noted Maryan.

"Oh, it's Warlock Tyrheus." Yang pointed out the man they'd seen earlier with long gray hair. He sat at a table across the room, chatting with a woman whose mass of thick curly black hair was contained in a bright headband. The two wizards' staffs leaned against the wall next to them.

The gardener leaned over the table, and they all huddled in to hear her whisper.

"The long metal staff belongs to Tyrheus. When he first held it, he had a vision of the iron being smelted and forged into a rod, and every hammer blow of the smithy drove magical power into the metal."

They regarded the staff, which to Maryan looked like a tall candlestick with spikes at the end, where a glowing red gem floated above. "What does the red orb do?"

"He added that later. I don't think it does anything." Yang pointed to the other staff, made of bright crystal that refracted the sunlight. "And that's Mage Niane's staff. When her fingertips first brushed it, she saw the crystal running as liquid in the furnace. When it was made, the skies darkened for a day, as all of the sunlight was drawn into the heart of the staff."

"Pray tell, lady Yang, do mages always have visions when they touch things?"

"Only when they first touch *their* staff. No one knows who each staff is destined for. Sometimes a mighty staff is made but then sits unused for hundreds of years, unable to find its mage."

Gunthar snorted. "Seems inefficient to me."

Yang shrugged. "That describes a lot of what mages do."

"I'm in awe of their power," said Maryan. "They can bend the very laws of nature. Why aren't they off curing world hunger, or banishing disease?"

"I don't know. Mostly they relax here. Or play sports." Yang leaned in again, making swooping gestures. "There's one game where they chase a ball in the air. It's very thrilling."

"Oh."

Gunthar sat back, then flinched. "Holy snow sheep!"

Next to him stood Thristletoramallicus, Keeper of the Gates. Once again the mage had somehow appeared without a sound.

"I hope you have refreshed yourselves." He tipped his head slightly. "I have brought Headmaster Morozov."

A man in a lush red robe loomed over the other side of the table, right behind Maryan and Cornelius. A red cap peppered with black and gold symbols perched on his head, and a bushy gray beard tumbled over his chest. They turned in their seats and made to rise, but the Headmaster held up his hand.

"Your Highness, Chronicler, all of you. No need to get up." He scratched his nose. "You've caused enough inconvenience already. Don't make more of a fuss. Besides, heaven knows when you'll eat next."

Maryan raised her eyebrows. "Headmaster? Does this mean we'll be traveling again?"

"I should think so. Your plight has the energy fields of the entire hemisphere wound up like the guts of a fire beetle. As if I don't have enough to worry about already. It's like this big ball of bundled fire beetle guts that could explode at any moment."

"Ah," said Maryan, her appetite gone.

The Headmaster shook his head. "I've got a faculty meeting now, but after that, we'll hold a proper Council of Great Wizards to discuss what to do."

Cornelius gasped.

"A Council?" Maryan asked.

"Look, I don't have time to answer questions. I've got to prepare for a Council on short notice." He leaned on his staff, a hollow shell made from dozens of thick steel wires. "Gardener Yang, why don't you take them to the Meeting Hall."

"Of course, Headmaster." She cleared her throat. "And when can I start my own training?"

"Like I said before, I'll be happy to take you as a student once you show even a glimmer of magic. At the moment, we can't find any."

He peered at her. "You're kind of a bottomless pit of no-magicness, actually."

"That's not much of a timeline, Headmaster."

"I'm sure we'll discuss it again and again. I'll see all of you at the Council in an hour." He straightened himself. "Now if you'll excuse me, I'm going to grab a snack before the faculty meeting." The red-robed mage shuffled off to the central table.

Cornelius stared after the Headmaster, mouth agape, his eyes lit with wonder. "A Council of Great Wizards," he whispered.

Chapter 8
Council

> *Few mortals have had the privilege of experiencing the majestic spectacle that is a Council of Great Wizards.*
>
> *— Considered Revelations, Book 22 "Majestic Spectacles Worth Writing Home About", Chapter 3, Verse 11*

The plump master of the Hall of Refreshment returned their clothes to them, cleaned and mended.

"This is so dated." Gunthar held up his fur kilt in disdain. "It's like it's from the last ice age."

Maryan sighed. "At least you can walk in it. I've got to wear my black dress again."

"Indeed, ma'am, good barbarian. But your other option 'twoudst be to face the Lich King in your robe and slippers."

"At least that ensemble would be from the current century," grumbled Gunthar.

But they each went off to change and returned to the Hall of Refreshment, Cornelius gamely hobbling along on his crutch.

Gardener Yang clapped her hands together. "Oh my, what a day. We're going to see a Council of Great Wizards!" She led them out the door, towards another large building with a round, peaked roof.

"What is so special about a bunch of wizards meeting?" Sir Humphrey asked. "Don't they meet all the time here?"

"A Great Wizard is someone who has unlocked one of the Secrets of the Ancients," said Yang. "It's not just a regular Wizard. There are only a handful of Great Wizards in the entire world."

"Only a handful?" Gunthar raised an eyebrow. "And they're all here?"

"I guess," said Yang. "I thought the Great were scattered all over the globe, but Headmaster Morozov said they'd all meet now."

"What are the Secrets of the Ancients?" asked Maryan.

"No one knows." The tall iron door swung open noiselessly at the touch of Yang's hand.

"'Tis as dark as a cave."

CHAPTER EIGHT: COUNCIL

"Come in, and close the door," called the Headmaster from further inside. "There, that's better."

Maryan blinked. As her eyes adjusted, she could make out the soft glow of thousands of candles dotting the perimeter of the room, at many levels. Large flagstones composed the floor, a stone bench encircling most of the room. Statues stood interspersed around the wall, Great Wizards of the past looming over them with hands outstretched as if frozen in mid-spell, their faces shadowed beneath stone cowls. Several paintings depicted past glories of the School, the nearest one showing five mages battling an angry dragon with four arms being ridden by a furious goblin who also had four arms.

"Actually happened," whispered Cornelius, pointing at the painting.

"Don't huddle in a quivering mass by the entrance," snapped Morozov. "Get over there by the monks." He waved them to an open spot near a group of dark-robed men and women on raised tiers. Thristletoramallicus, Keeper of the Gates, stood nearby.

Across the room sat a barrel, with many small round staffs sticking out of it.

"Are those for training?" asked Gunthar.

"Those are initiate staffs," said the gardener. "You get one when you are ordained an apprentice."

"Oh," said the barbarian, losing interest.

"I don't see any Great Wizards here," Yang whispered to them. "But several of the school faculty are here."

"I can hear you, gardener." The Headmaster glared at her, and even in the dim firelight Yang's ears turned red.

Morozov turned to the gathered faculty. "As our perceptive gardener has pointed out, the Great Wizards are not here. Yet we need their wisdom, for Princess Maryan has come on an urgent quest regarding the greatest peril our age has seen. We require the counsel of the wisest sages on earth, though they are untold leagues distant." The Headmaster raised his hands. "But we are not talking about regular mortals, bound by the rules of space and time. Distance is not an obstacle. These are *Wizards*. With them, we shall work ancient magic today to bring all of the wise here together in a great, ah, Council of the Great!"

"A Council of the Great." Yang repeated the words, her eyes wide in the candlelight. "I can't believe it."

Cornelius turned in all directions, his wooden crutch creaking as he attempted to take it all in. "Few Chroniclers have had the fortune to see a full Council assembled," he whispered to Maryan.

The Headmaster strode to a wide, round podium at the center of the room. Then he yanked a cloth off the podium with a flourish, revealing a dark crystal ball.

"Behold," he said, "a Seeing Jewel of Kohinoor!"

Gasps echoed in the room.

"One of the Seeing Jewels." Cornelius whispered as he furiously wrote in his notebook. "An artifact from the time of the Elder Gods."

Morozov folded the cloth reverently, his eyes on the crystal ball. He nodded to Thristletoramallicus, Keeper of the Gates. "Thristletoramallicus, Keeper of the Gates of Orst shall be our master of ceremonies. Gatekeeper, prepare."

Thristletoramallicus, Keeper of the Gates raised his hands, and all of the monks raised their chins in attention.

"I've never seen so many in one place," noted Gunthar.

"Yes," said the blue-robed man. "We get better audio if I add a few extra monks."

"Now, Gatekeeper," intoned the Headmaster.

Thristletoramallicus, Keeper of the Gates directed the monks, who began to chant in exquisite harmony. They started softly, like someone whispering next to you, but then raised their volume in gentle steps, as if the person whispering next to you was worried that you weren't paying attention and they had to speak louder and louder, until they had your full attention but they kept getting louder anyway because after all it was a lot of monks and they were here to get some serious chanting done.

As the chanting grew, the crystal ball rose and levitated above the podium, then flickered into life, at first just with the glow of another candle, but as the monks continued the light grew stronger and stronger until it was a blue-white star in the center of the room, illuminating all.

Morozov raised both hands and called to the blazing crystal. "In the name of Kohinoor, first Archmage of the World, I call a Council

CHAPTER EIGHT: COUNCIL

of Great Wizards."

The monks changed their timbre, from a growing major chord to a suspended seventh, or maybe even a seven-and-a-halfth, and with the increased tension new stars of light appeared, floating in the air in a line across the far side of the room. Maryan held her breath in rapture. The chorus elevated her, as if her very soul rose to join the levitating orbs, golden white light glimmering in every direction.

The chanting resolved back into a major chord with deep harmonies, and in that instant the orbs were replaced by the flickering images of the Great Wizards of the world. They were bedecked in flowing robes of silk. Some had finely carved staffs of wood, others had staffs of iron or precious metals, and the mage on the far left appeared to have a staff made out of clouds. Maryan stared at them, her mouth open, and the Great Wizards in turn regarded each of them in the chamber as if they too could see everyone here. She swallowed and smoothed out her dress.

The Wizard in the middle stepped forward, her black robes billowing around her.

"That's Archmage Nayantara, the head of the Council," Yang breathed next to her.

Nayantara carried herself more regally than any king or queen. She moved as if conquering the center of the room, and once she held that position she stared down at them with a cold glare, haughtily royal but tinged with a buzzing sparkle that hinted at untold powers. The Archmage raised her hand, and the monks' chanting grew in power, thundering harmonies that shook the bones of the room, but also with soprano overtones that focused attention like a lens.

Everyone in the room had stopped breathing, all eyes on the Archmage, waiting with anticipation, and Maryan would swear that even her heartbeat paused in deference.

Nayantara began to speak, looking at them in turn as she moved her lips in slow deliberation, each word a gift unto itself.

However, the words themselves were silent. Other than the monks' quiet chanting, no voice sounded in the room. After a second or two, Maryan looked around in confusion, and found her companions doing the same.

Thristletoramallicus, Keeper of the Gates, leaned in. "Archmage Nayantara, I think you're on mute."

The flickering image of the Archmage cursed silently, and she fiddled with something they couldn't see.

"Y'all froze for like five seconds." The loud, clear voice startled Maryan and she looked over at the furthest image on the right, a Wizard with a long gray beard and a green cashmere scarf. Snow fell behind him, through a window with frosted panes. "Did y'all see it? Or was it just me? I—" Then he froze in mid-sentence, his face looking as if he was coughing up a stone.

The second Wizard from the left was just a large nose, with several gray hairs poking out of its nostrils.

Headmaster Morozov spoke out. "Master Vicente, you need to move your Seeing Jewel back a few feet. All we can see is your nose."

Thristletoramallicus, Keeper of the Gates, directed the chanting monks with one hand while he waved at Nayantara with the other. "Archmage, you're still on mute. I can't unmute you from here. I can only mute people. You can use the second jewel on the left to adjust your audio."

Nayantara continued swearing, her mouth now moving rapidly and with visible but unheard venom as she continued to work a contraption out of their sight.

Morozov cleared his throat impatiently. "While we're waiting—"

"While we're waiting—" The Headmaster's voice returned to them in a mocking contralto.

"Oh, honestly—"

"Oh, honestly—" The contralto repeated him again.

Morozov waved at Thristletoramallicus, Keeper of the Gates, and the blue-robed man directed the monks into a brief staccato.

"I've had to mute everyone. We're getting an echo. Master Haruto, there's a homunculus in a cage behind you. I think it's repeating everything we're saying."

The Wizard in question, a man with cropped dark hair and a crisp white robe, looked behind him and then sighed in silent exasperation. He stood and took a cage off the wall, which indeed contained a small imp-like form, and carried it away and out of sight.

CHAPTER EIGHT: COUNCIL

"Right," said Morozov. "You can unmute yourselves again. Master Vincente, can you hear me? You need to move your Seeing Jewel back a few feet."

The nose scrunched, but otherwise didn't change.

"Why are these Councils always a complete ****show?" asked an imperious-looking Wizard on the left with a frown.

Morozov opened his mouth to answer, but shrieking monks interrupted him. Several of the robed forms began screaming in soprano discord, and everyone covered their ears.

Gunthar's face wound up in pain. "Why are they screeching?"

Headmaster Morozov stepped forward, wincing. "We're getting feedback from someone. Master Nuwa, do you have *two* Seeing Jewels of Kohinoor?"

Wizard Nuwa stood on Nayantara's right. She shifted her eyes slightly. "Uh, no, of course not."

The monks continued their screaming, and Maryan kept her hands over her ears as the Headmaster bellowed.

"*Someone* here has two Seeing Jewels. How else would we be getting feedback?"

"Excuse me for a moment." Wizard Nuwa stood and walked out of sight with something hidden in her hand, revealing a bookcase behind her cluttered with leather-bound tomes and bottles of all shapes and sizes.

The monks abruptly stopped shrieking, and Maryan dropped her hands from her ears with relief as Wizard Nuwa returned to view.

Nayantara waved her hand. "Can you hear me now? Hello?"

"Yes, Archmage Nayantara, you're unmuted now."

"Oh, by the corrosive tears of the gods. Do I have to start all over again?"

Morozov blushed. "Ah, no, Archmage. Let's just say the Council has been formally opened."

Archmage Nayantara glared down at them. "Headmaster, why have you called us together?"

"Well, Archmage, the princess here—" he waved at Maryan "—is caught up in a prophecy which might require one of our scholars."

"Good lord, I hate prophecies." She sighed. "Which one is it?"

"Ah, The Lich King in the East. The Teapot, and all that."

The Archmage's eyes widened. "Oh, my. That one."

Wizard Haruto whistled in astonishment.

Headmaster Morozov looked between the both of them. "What? Is it as bad as the one with the two-headed dragon?"

Haruto shook his head. "Worse."

"Worse?" Morozov fell back a step. "Worse than the four-headed demoness?"

"No, not that bad."

"Right. Maybe a three-headed thing?"

"Something like that."

Nayantara frowned. "Does anyone have a copy of the prophecy at hand?"

The nose, Wizard Vincente, moved as his owner apparently spoke. "I gave my copy to Wizard Halfdan." Everyone looked over to the Wizard in the snowstorm, who remained stuck in mid-cough.

"Uh, he's still frozen," said Morozov.

The Archmage waved her hand in irritation. "Don't worry about it. These prophecies tend to be poorly-written and vague as hell anyway. Is there a Prophecy Scholar who can explain it?"

"Ah, not really, Archmage." Morozov fretted with his hands. "We're having problems finding any Prophecy Scholars at the moment."

Nayantara rolled her eyes. "We appear to have very little to go on. Do we at least have a Seer who can provide a Reading?"

"Yes, Archmage." One of Morozov's faculty stepped forward. She had a robe of deep azure, and carried a brazier containing a slight amount of a shimmering blue liquid. "I can perform a Reading."

"Very well." Morozov nodded to Thristletoramallicus, Keeper of the Gates, who shifted the monks into a low rumble.

The Seer placed the brazier near the central podium as the monks chanted ominously. She waved her hands over the surface, speaking in words that Maryan couldn't hear, and the water began swirling and glowing, sending a ray of illumination up into the Seer's face.

"I see!" she declared. "The Lich King stirs, bringing an age of the undead, lasting seven years and ten."

People gasped in the room.

"Would that be seventeen years, then? Or just seven years and ten

CHAPTER EIGHT: COUNCIL

months?" Cornelius waved his pen. "Anyone?"

The Seer bent further over her brazier, the light illuminating her face changing from blue to red. "His minions are beyond counting, and even now march to his banner. He must be thrice-beaten, or will be victorious everlasting."

Sir Humphrey whispered nearby. "*Thrice*-beaten?"

The Seer shrieked, and everyone in the room jumped. "I see a rent in the fabric of magic. I see a vast army of the undead. I see a barbarian in pants. And, oh no, the princess..." She paused, but the brazier promptly flickered out.

Morozov paced over. "What is it?"

"Sorry, I ran out of juice."

"What?"

"I was teaching a class on Readings right before this, and didn't have time to refill the brazier."

"We were just getting to the interesting parts."

"Not to worry." The Seer held up her hands. "I only need some curdled elderberry syrup with a pinch of myrrh. I brought extra with me."

"Oh, good."

The Seer walked to a shelf on the wall and lifted a small pitcher. She looked at it in astonishment. "It's empty!"

"Empty?"

Gunthar burped, then looked at the two of them. "Curdled what?"

Headmaster Morozov pulled his own hair. "Oh, by the gods..."

Gunthar shrugged to his companions. "I thought it was a help-yourself thing, like that Refreshment place."

"We can stop the Seeing. I think we know enough as it is." The Archmage waved the seer away. "Princess, I'm familiar with the prophecy. You can only defeat the Lich with a bishop. And you'll need to donate one of your students, Morozov. The prophecy seems worthy of an apprentice, at least."

Wizard Haruto nodded in agreement.

"An apprentice?" The Headmaster took a step back. "I've been training my apprentices for over twenty years. I can't just throw one into the jaws of a vicious Lich King."

The Archmage put her hands on her hips. "You heard the Seer. This is serious. Sacrificing an apprentice is a small price to pay."

"But—"

"It is decided. Princess Maryan, you must journey to Bluntworth, acquire there a bishop, and then enter the Badlands to defeat the Lich King."

Several of the assembled faculty gasped at this.

"Uh, very well, Archmage." Maryan's mouth felt full of cotton. The Great Wizards seemed to think following the prophecy was dangerous. And what vision had caused the Seer to cry out?

Nayantara raised her hand. "And Headmaster Morozov will send one of his apprentices with the princess."

"Great. Bye, everyone." Wizard Haruto waved and blinked out.

"Archmage Nayantara, are you sure?"

"Sorry, Morozov, I don't have time. I've got to jump to another meeting. We can talk later." She also disappeared.

"Quick!" Morozov hissed to Thristletoramallicus, Keeper of the Gates. "End it. I don't want to be the last one."

The blue-robed man dropped his arms, and the monks wound down their chanting as the other Wizard images blinked out one by one.

The last image remaining was Wizard Halfdan, who unfroze. "Hello? What did I miss?" But the Seeing Jewel in the middle of the room abruptly switched off and fell back to the podium with a thunk, and the image of the snowy Wizard disappeared.

Some of the faculty pulled cords on the walls, lifting shutters, and the room brightened with daylight. Morozov remained unmoving in the middle of the room, lit by a sunbeam. His brows knit together as he stroked his beard, deep in thought. "I can't believe I have to sacrifice one of *my* apprentices..."

Maryan approached him. "Headmaster?"

The red-robed man strode across the room, grabbed an initiate's staff from the barrel, and tossed it to the gardener. Yang caught it with one hand, then looked at the Headmaster in confusion.

"Congratulations," he snapped. "You're an apprentice now."

Chapter 9
Hills

What is sweeter than a garden gnome?

— Considered Revelations, Book 207 "Things You Think Are Harmless, and Truly Are", Chapter 14, Verse 3

"Please, outside as fast as you can. The prophecy waits for no one," said the Headmaster as he ushered them out of the Meeting Hall. "Also, we have a banquet here in an hour. The room needs to be turned over."

They stood in the late afternoon sunlight, and Sir Humphrey wandered over to untie Daisy from the Hall of Refreshment.

"I can only imagine how happy you must feel. Your prophecy demanded an apprentice, and the North Hills School of Wizardry delivered!" The Headmaster pointed to the gardener.

"Thank you." Yang held the simple, wooden staff in her hands as if it might bite her. "But shouldn't I be trained somehow?"

"But you *have* been trained, Gardener—er, *Apprentice* Yang. You've been at the school for two years now."

"But in that entire time, I've only been gardening."

"You see? The North Hills School of Wizardry rewards good work." Morozov stroked his beard. "You'll be facing a demonic Lich King from the mists of time. Don't worry about your performance, which I'm sure won't last long. It's not like my other apprentices could do any better in that situation, trained or not. Speaking of which, Princess Maryan, *how* exactly do you intend to overcome the lich?"

"We have an Axe, and a Mage, or near-Mage, and a knight with a magic sword." She gestured at each in turn.

"My, that *is* brave," he said. "I'd also recommend a ranger. They're everywhere, and sometimes come in handy."

"Yes, we'll get one of those too."

"Headmaster, if you don't mind, 'twouldst be a boon to me if you could take a look at Gwendoline. The sword hasn't worked for a generation." Sir Humphrey proffered the scabbarded sword at his waist.

"If it will make you feel better," said the red-robed man. He pulled the blade out and ran his hand over it, runes glittering in the light. Morozov squinted, as if peering inside the metal itself. "Oh yes, one of the early elvish models. Solidly made, though these can get a bit twitchy around Ultimate Dragons. I'd watch out for that, though we don't tend to see them much anymore." The Headmaster checked the edge, then returned the sword to the knight. "I don't see anything wrong with it. As far as I can tell, it's still functional."

Sir Humphrey stared at the sword in his hands. "Indeed, Headmaster? But it hasn't worked for me."

"While I know a great deal about magic, I unfortunately know very little about swordcraft. Who knows? Magic swords often have their own personalities."

The knight put the sword back in its scabbard. "I was hoping I could get it working again, to protect us from the vicious creatures of the wilds. Not to mention the undead."

The Headmaster laughed. "You have little to fear here, Sir Humphrey. Few creatures can breach our defenses. You won't have to worry about your desperate fight for survival until you are outside our walls." He turned. "Speaking of which, Gatekeeper..."

Thristletoramallicus, Keeper of the Gates, nodded and the travelers once again stood in the high grass outside the walls.

Maryan looked around. "We're on the east side of the school now."

"Aye, ma'am." Sir Humphrey scanned the horizon ahead, then yelped. "Where is Daisy?"

The horse suddenly appeared next to them. She raised her head, regarding each of them in turn, then went back to grazing.

"Good luck to you!" Behind them, the Headmaster waved down from the top of the wall. Thristletoramallicus, Keeper of the Gates, stood next to him.

"Thank you for all of your help, Headmaster!" Maryan called back.

Gunthar snorted at this.

"It's better to be polite," she told him. "No sense making enemies."

Cornelius hobbled up to her, using his leafy stick to steady

CHAPTER NINE: HILLS

himself. "Where is the apprentice, ma'am?"

Indeed, the gardener-turned-apprentice was nowhere to be found.

"Mayhaps she decided 'twas better to avoid this prophecy?" speculated Sir Humphrey.

"Headmaster—" Maryan started to call, but the wall was deserted. "They've gone." A breeze picked up, stirring her hair, and the tall grass rustled around them.

Gunthar put his hands on his hips. "I thought our apprentice might last a bit longer."

Cornelius scratched his head. "Maybe there is another school of wizardry further along we can check?"

Maryan shook her head. "Let's wait a minute. I can't imagine Yang would abandon us without a word."

The knight shook his head. "I don't know, ma'am. I'm not sure if I trust these wizardly types. They often have their own agenda."

"Hey! Wait for me!" A form in a white robe waved at them from the south end of the wall as it picked its way along the path.

"Ah, good. I knew she'd make it," said Sir Humphrey.

Apprentice Yang reached them a moment later, out of breath. She carried her initiate staff and a canvas knapsack.

"The Gatekeeper wouldn't teleport you along with us?" asked Maryan.

Yang shook her head. "He was very upset. He and the Headmaster thought I was being difficult."

"Why?"

"I don't know. I guess they tried to teleport me, and it didn't work? Anyway, I grabbed my pack and ran here as fast as I could." She took another deep breath. "Sorry it took me so long. The only gate is on the other side."

"I'm glad you are with us, Apprentice Yang," said Maryan. "Let's get going again. We can cover a league or two before sunset."

They got Cornelius up on Daisy again, then trudged along a faint path through the grasses, winding its way east with more hills to the north.

Maryan brushed the sleeve of her dress. "It's nice to have clean clothes, at least briefly."

"Indeed, ma'am. Those schools of wizardry certainly know a

thing or two about laundry."

Yang looked at the barbarian. "Is that real fur?"

Gunthar's brow furrowed. "What kind of a question is that?"

"I thought I heard some of the school's laundry staff talking about it—"

"You should know better than to listen to laundry staff," he grumbled. "Even if they have legendary surfactants and a deep understanding of fabrics."

"What did they say?" asked the knight.

Yang shrugged. "They thought the furs were fake."

"Fake furs?" Sir Humphrey stopped, his eyes wide.

"Fine." Gunthar himself stopped and turned to face the others. "You should know. I'm not very good with an axe, and I don't have a style move, all right? I'm a joke among barbarians." He tugged at his kilt. "They dressed me in fake furs and cast me out of the village. Happy now?"

The knight stared at Gunthar's outfit in wonder. "Fake furs?"

"No style move?" The Chronicler scratched his head. "Do you think he still counts as the Axe from the prophecy, Your Highness?"

"Look, I didn't ask to be in your prophecy—"

"Please, Gunthar, it's fine," said Maryan. "Archmage Nayantara said that prophecies are vague. Why would we have met you unless you're in the prophecy?"

"How come *he* gets to be in the prophecy?"

"It's not a choice, Sir Humphrey! The prophecy is foretold by, well, by prophecy people."

"'Tis odd that a *fake* barbarian is in the prophecy, but not a proper knight."

Gunthar rolled his eyes. "You know where you can stick your prophecy?"

"Ah, excuse me, Gunthar, Sir Humphrey. Can you stop?" Both men turned to glare at her, and Maryan dropped her eyes. Why did they have to bicker all the time? She just wanted them to stop so they could get on with the journey. The princess tried to think back on all the times when knights and generals had argued in court. How had her parents managed that?

Cornelius spoke up in the silence. "Do you know this land at all, Apprentice?"

CHAPTER NINE: HILLS

"Not very well," she said. "I've never been this far in this direction. From what I've heard, there are gnomes and ogres in the hills to the north, and further east is the wide river Goldswell, which runs south to Bluntworth."

"Gnomes." The barbarian said the word like it was a foul-tasting stone in his mouth.

"What's wrong with gnomes?" asked Maryan. "They stay out of everyone's way and are super cute, in my opinion."

"I don't know, ma'am. I find them creepy."

"In sooth, good barbarian? We march towards a Lich King, but 'tis the gnomes that disturb you?"

"Oh, don't get me wrong. I don't hate gnomes. But something about their smile, I don't know..." Gunthar shuddered. "They just seem a little off, sometimes."

"I love gnomes," offered Yang. "I had several small gnome figurines in the gardens at the school of wizardry. I can't get enough of them. Why do you call them creepy? Are you sure you aren't projecting your feelings of inadequacy on an entirely unrelated culture?"

"Enough about gnomes!" thundered the barbarian. "Besides, we should worry more about the undead. Is everyone prepared for battle, should they come?"

"Of course, sir. I have Gwendoline here, and if she fails me, I shall stand my ground and mow down my opponents with fisticuffs." The knight waved his fists in front of him.

"I'm carrying Cornelius' stick," said Maryan, waving the leafy branch. "I can use it to defend myself if need be."

"And you, apprentice?" Gunthar looked at Yang.

"I'm not sure." She blinked at them. "I guess I hadn't thought about it."

"So you have no magic?" asked Sir Humphrey.

"None."

"You look like you're from East Kathandar. Don't you know whack-fu?" Gunthar made a cutting motion with his hand.

Yang glared back at him. "You think I know whack-fu, just because I'm from East Kathandar?"

The barbarian swallowed. "Oh, I'm sorry. That was an ignorant thing to say."

"Whatever. Look, I don't know magic—yet—and I'm not much of a fighter. But I guess I can use my staff." She waved her initiate staff in front of her.

"I'm sure it will be fine," said Cornelius. "As for me, I'll stay on Daisy, so I can scout for everyone, and support the group from somewhere very far back in the rear."

"I've been meaning to ask," said Yang. "How did you come to join the group, Chronicler?"

"Yes," agreed Gunthar. "I never heard how you came across the princess and the knight."

"Well, it's quite an amusing story—"

"There's no time!" shouted Sir Humphrey, pointing south. "Undead chickens!"

Several small forms waded through the tall grass, most of their feathers having fallen off, their skin ashen. The clucking was ominous and a tad gurgly.

"To arms!" shouted Gunthar, hefting his axe.

"Onwards, Happenhouse!" Sir Humphrey raised his sword and pushed the button. A single spark popped out of the handle, then the blade remained silent.

Maryan and Yang held their sticks in front of them, while Daisy sensibly carried the cowering Chronicler behind the knight. All the while the fowl undead bore down upon them.

Maryan shifted her weight, shrugged her shoulders, then shifted her weight again, readying herself for the upcoming battle. She calmed her breathing, holding her stick up at the ready, then plucked a handful of grass and let it fall, judging the direction of the wind. Her left arm felt awkward, dangling there, so she shook it and held it back at an angle.

"I say," said Sir Humphrey after a minute, "they aren't terribly fast, are they?"

"Stay at the ready!" Gunthar stayed in a wide stance, axe held back. "Battle is imminent."

"Couldst we not make battle *more* imminent? Mayhaps if we charged them, to save time?"

"We have the stronger position," Gunthar countered, his eyes ablaze. "We do not go to them, they come to us."

"Perhaps we can meet in the middle?" suggested Maryan. "We

could take a few steps forward."

Gunthar rolled his shoulders. "Aye, ma'am. My arm is getting tired."

They strode into the low grass south of the path, then stopped after closing a little more than half the distance to the undead chickens.

"Prepare!" cried Gunthar, hefting his axe again.

Sir Humphrey raised his sword. "Onwards, Happenhouse!"

Maryan brought the leafy stick to the ready. A breeze stirred the grasses again, bringing a scent of dry grains and wildflowers. Birds called from some distance away.

Gunthar threw up his hands. "Oh, by the icy gods of the wind-swept tundra. Let's charge them, all right?"

"Indeed, sir! If you couldst but give the word, ma'am."

Maryan counted to three, then the four of them surged forward in a ragged charge, weapons raining down on the still-approaching undead poultry.

Sir Humphrey lunged and stabbed with Gwendoline, and Gunthar's axe was a blur, although he dropped it once. Maryan used the brief melee as an opportunity to practice her skills, swinging the branch with smooth strokes. Next to her, Yang chopped furiously, beating their opponents as if with a club, as fast as she could.

In a moment, the undead were no more, reduced to a set of rotting gray puddles amongst the tall stalks.

Gunthar waved a hand under his nose. "Ugh. Let's get back to the path."

"Pray, describe the smell!" pleaded Cornelius from atop Daisy, some distance away. "This is for posterity."

"Fine," said Gunthar. "It smells like ****."

Cornelius paled. "Never mind."

Sir Humphrey cleaned and sheathed his sword, then twirled the end of his mustache. "A fine first skirmish, was it not?"

Yang breathed heavily, her initiate staff dangling from her fingers. "Wow. We did it, didn't we?"

They rejoined Cornelius and Daisy on the path, then continued on their way east.

"We have met the first of the rising tide of the undead. That didn't seem so bad."

"Indeed, ma'am. But I fear we will see more dangerous foes ere long."

"And faster," said Yang.

"'Twouldst be nice."

Gunthar cast a suspicious glance northward. "At least we haven't had to deal with any gnomes."

"Come now," admonished Yang. "Gnomes are harmless."

Cornelius pointed further out into the tall grass. "Gnomes."

Gunthar rubbed his hand over his face. "Oh, great."

Only a minute later, several blue-clothed gnomes approached them.

"Hello, Your Highness," called the lead gnome, waving his hand. His long white beard hung over his portly belly, and though he wore a tall red cap, it barely came to the adventurers' waists.

"Hi," said Maryan.

"We don't often see visitors out here," said the gnome, "so we thought we'd come out and greet you personally."

"That's very nice of you." Yang bowed.

"Hi, I'm Buttercup!" A gnome in a blue dress stepped forward, hopping from foot to foot. "Is there anything we can get you? We have food!"

"And water," added another from behind.

"Ah, that's very kind, of course," said Maryan.

Sir Humphrey saluted them. "I say, it's not often one meets such gracious hosts out in the wilds!"

"Oh, we're only too happy to share. Charity is a gnome virtue." The lead gnome gestured back to the north, then coughed. "Terribly sorry to ask this, but you are all *innocent*, is that right?"

Sir Humphrey put his hand over his heart. "Indeed, sir, my code of honor demands nothing less!"

The gnomes all smiled at this, bright wide smiles that revealed many teeth.

Daisy whinnied, and a breeze blew between the two groups as they stared at each other.

"Not to get too theoretical here," said Yang, "but if your offer of assistance is contingent on a subjective assessment like *innocence*, then it's not really charity, is it?"

Buttercup blushed. "Oh, I may be behind on the latest arguments on the ethics of philanthropy. Why don't you have some dinner, and explain it to us?"

Gunthar frowned, pointing into the tall grass behind the gnomes. "Is that a cage back there?"

Indeed, a large iron cage stood among the waving stalks some distance away. One might have mistaken it for a bird cage, except that it was over eight feet tall.

Maryan put her hands on her hips and faced the lead gnome. "You're not kidnapping people, putting them in cages, and dangling the cages from trees, are you?"

"It's for the good of the country—" began one gnome, but the others shushed him.

The lead gnome spread his hands with another overly-wide smile. "Not at all, ma'am! We just happen to carry all our food in cages. I mean, the food we carry for innocent people to eat."

"And water!" added Buttercup.

Sir Humphrey took a step forward. "I *am* hungry—"

"Sir Humphrey, it's a trap." Maryan glared at the gnomes. "They're trying to lure us back into the cage so they can kidnap us."

"Put us in a cage?" The knight's face drained of all color. "No!"

"Well, maybe," said the lead gnome.

"Hey!" Cornelius pointed to a spot near the cage. "Is that Editor Larsson? Why are you hiding back there?"

A tall woman in clothes strikingly similar to Cornelius stepped out from behind a low bush. She looked up to the Chronicler as he sat on Daisy. "Oh, hello there, Cornelius. I thought we reassigned you to prophecies now. How is it you're still alive?"

"What are you doing back there?" asked the Chronicler.

Editor Larsson waved vaguely at the bush. "Oh, you know, I was, um, gathering mushrooms."

"And who is next to you?" asked Gunthar.

A man in a bright flowered shirt stepped out next to Editor Larsson. He clutched a clipboard to his chest. "Hi there, adventurers! I'm Kwento, here to study the gnomes. I research different markets for the Chroniclers Guild."

Sir Humphrey squinted. "You what?"

Cornelius pointed at the gnomes. "You see, Editor Larsson? This is exactly why we shouldn't be publishing drivel like Prince Mikhail's book."

"Nonsense! In fact, it's exactly why we *should* be publishing drivel like Prince Mikhail's book!" Kwento held up a graphic with several bar charts. "The message resonates with many demographics."

Editor Larsson waved an advance copy of the book. "*My Values: Dangling Kidnapped People in Cages for the Good of the Country* is going to sell like garlic at a vampire invasion!"

"Oh, yes!" The excited Buttercup did a gnome dance involving small hops, twirls, and one dab. "I only saw a preview of the cover, and even if I buy it that's probably as far as I'll read it, but Prince Mikhail is so handsome and sincere I can't imagine why anyone is upset about his book at all!"

"We're going to love his book," agreed the lead gnome.

Maryan frowned. "Editor Larsson, I must agree with the Chronicler. You can't publish Prince Mikhail's book."

"Now, now, Your Highness," she said. "The public needs to hear *all* voices on the important issue of dangling innocent people in cages."

Buttercup nodded. "Some people don't realize it's a controversy at all!"

Maryan addressed the researcher. "Why are the gnomes blindly accepting Prince Mikhail's hideous idea?"

"Gnomes love authority figures. They don't even care who or what the authority figure is." Kwento hugged his clipboard. "I'm sure we'll sell fifty thousand units in the northern plains alone."

The lead gnome took another step forward. "It would be a shame for innocent people to go hungry when we have food to spare!"

Yang leaned over to Maryan. "How does one escape gnomes, ma'am?"

Kwento overheard, and flipped to a piece of parchment on his clipboard. "Based on my research, you can outrun them. Gnomes have very short legs, you know."

Maryan bowed. "Editor Larsson, Researcher Kwento, it's been a pleasure." Then she turned to her compatriots. "Run!"

They dashed off to the east, the gnomes in pursuit. Just as the researcher's notes indicated, the short legs of the gnomes couldn't keep up with the desperately running adventurers. Maryan ran, the

CHAPTER NINE: HILLS

sun casting her shadow long in front of her, while Buttercup wailed behind them and promised a pleasant dinner and a second helping of dessert if only they'd get into the cage. In only a few minutes the pleading voices of the gnomes faded into the distance.

Maryan turned to Gunthar, who ran next to her. "Are there any other creatures who follow authority figures as blindly as the gnomes?"

Gunthar shrugged while running, which is harder than it sounds. "I'm sure it's just the gnomes, ma'am."

The adventurers ran for at least an hour longer, because who wouldn't? Finally they collapsed in a small dell, all energy spent, the trail too dark to follow. They fell into a deep slumber.

Chapter 10
River

> *There is very little you can't accomplish if you have ancient magic, duct tape, and a forge that can reach eleven hundred degrees.*
>
> *— Considered Revelations, Book 9 "Famous Sayings from Ancient Elvish Swordcrafters", Chapter 17, Verse 2*

In the morning, the sun rose in a blaze of red and pink behind high clouds.

Maryan yawned and stretched her arms. "I hope we don't see any gnomes today."

"It's unlikely, Your Highness," said Yang. "Gnome territory is further north."

"Even so, we should keep our eyes open. I don't trust that Editor Larsson." Cornelius scanned the horizon. "Or researchers of markets."

"A foul omen ahead." Gunthar pointed at the bloody clouds. "I wonder if we shall face more of the undead today."

"Mayhaps, sir, but we will remain victorious nonetheless." The knight tapped the sword at his belt. "Gwendoline's spark may have dimmed, but she cuts as well as ever."

Maryan eyed the scabbard. "The Headmaster thought the sword should work."

"Perhaps, ma'am, but Gwendoline seems to be ailing still."

Yang tilted her head. "Is there anything else about the sword besides the button to turn it on?"

"Gwendoline has many charms, and many surprises. You can see the runes here on the blade. Their purpose is a mystery, but they are striking to look at. And there is convenient storage in the hilt."

"Storage?" Maryan peered at the intricate grip.

The apprentice stood and leaned over them as Sir Humphrey unscrewed the pommel.

"You see here, ma'am? 'Tis a curious thing, that the hilt is larger inside than out."

"Ooh," cooed Yang. "A Hilt of Holding. You don't see that very

CHAPTER TEN: RIVER

often."

Maryan squinted. "What's in there?"

"Oh, there's a lot, really." He turned the sword up and shook it, and many items tumbled out of the opened hilt, including several sewing needles, hobnails, three dice, and a lockpick. "One second, ma'am." The knight used his pinky finger to fish around in the opening, and finally pulled out a large piece of clothing. "I keep a spare cloak in there for emergencies. There's plenty of room for it, though 'tis tricky to stuff it through the opening."

"So the hilt is empty otherwise?"

"Not really, ma'am. There are shelves or something further back." He held up the opened hilt again.

"Oh my," said the apprentice. "Not shelves, but several rows of capacitor banks. Those ancient elves didn't mess around. Swords aren't built like that anymore!"

"I'm sorry, apprentice? My knowledge of the magic arts is limited."

"What's that?" Yang pointed inside.

"That's my father's lucky gold sovereign." He sighed. "It's all I have left of the family fortune."

Maryan whistled. "A gold sovereign is a fair amount of money!"

"Aye, ma'am, but not near enough to buy back my estates."

"But where is it placed?"

"Apprentice?"

"The gold coin. It's wedged in there, between two capacitor stacks."

"My father didn't want to lose it, so he jammed it in there—"

"I think it's shorting out the stacks. Have you tried removing it?"

Sir Humphrey tried reaching in with a finger, but frowned. "I can't reach it. Does anyone have a stick?"

"Here, Sir Humphrey." Maryan found a long stick near their fire.

"I'm indebted to you, ma'am." He stuck the stick inside and stabbed a few times, then tried pushing it to one side. The stick broke with a crack, and he pulled it out with a grimace. "Nay, the sovereign is wedged in there like a goblin in a mountain giant's jaws."

"Oh, wait, you can use my knife." Apprentice Yang offered a small dagger.

"This may do, apprentice, although I don't know if it's quite long enough." Sir Humphrey pushed the knife in all the way to the hilt, and started twisting it. "I think I might be able to reach the coin—"

"The undead!" Cornelius shrieked and pointed east, where several low forms shambled towards them on the path.

Gunthar shielded his eyes. "What are those?"

"Demons!" Cornelius hobbled back towards Daisy. "They come crawling on all fours, like the hellspawn they are."

The Chronicler grabbed the saddle, then tossed his stick to Maryan, who caught the leafy branch as she stood.

Yang stood next to her and pulled out her initiate staff. "Are they... Are they *pigs?*"

Gunthar lifted his axe and rolled his shoulders. "I think so, apprentice. And faster than the chickens, it would seem."

The undead pigs lurched towards them, filthy gray skin tinged red with the dawn, some showing large open wounds, with one having an exposed rib cage. They snorted through greasy, slimy snouts.

Yang scrunched up her nose. "Gross."

Maryan stepped forward. "Let's stay in a line again."

"Ha! I've freed the sovereign!" Sir Humphrey shouted triumphantly behind them. "Wait for me!"

"Ready," said Maryan. She brought back her stick, preparing to strike, as did Gunthar and Yang.

The knight arrived, standing between her and Gunthar, and raised Gwendoline above his head. "Onwards, Happenhouse!"

Lightning played at the periphery of Maryan's vision, then a large explosion boomed over the grasses, and Sir Humphrey was gone.

Yang's jaw dropped. "Did the knight just blow up?"

"Eyes forward, apprentice!" cried Maryan. "The undead are here."

A shambling pig tried to gnaw on her, and Maryan shoved the stick at it, then brought the bough back and whacked it solidly on the side. The undead swine oinked as it staggered sideways, then Gunthar smashed it before it could recover its balance.

Next to her, Yang whacked repeatedly at an advancing, decaying hog.

"Apprentice Yang, slow down," said Gunthar, walking over. "You're doing too much work. You need to use your opponent's momentum against them, like this." He demonstrated by stepping in front of the hog, which charged him. The barbarian smoothly stepped aside with a turn, bringing his axe across and toppling it.

Yang panted. "How is that?"

Another of the porcine undead menaced to her left, and Maryan turned to face it. She tripped it, then whacked it.

"This is absolutely disgusting," she said.

To her right, Gunthar finished off the last of the undead pack with a smooth backstroke. "You see, apprentice? I let the fiend walk into that. Do it like that, but don't drop your weapon like I did. That wasn't on purpose."

"I guess I was too focused on hitting things before. I'll think more about positioning." Yang tried a slow strike with her initiate's staff, adjusting her footwork.

"It just takes practice." The barbarian waved a hand under his nose with a frown. "What's that smell? It's not the undead."

"It's ozone." Yang clapped her hands to her cheeks, her eyes wide. "Oh my. I forgot about Sir Humphrey."

They looked further back on the path, where a large black circle of scorched grass sent tendrils of smoke in the air.

"Oh, no..." Maryan knelt by the grass.

"He was a fine companion." Gunthar also knelt. "We mourn his loss. He fought bravely and defended us all, even though he seemed to harbor some resentment about me being in the prophecy."

The knight sat up in the grass nearby, smoke rising from both ends of his mustache. "I harbor what?"

Maryan jumped up with relief. "Sir Humphrey! You're alive!"

"What hit me?" He rubbed his head. "I remember raising Gwendoline, then a flash, and then... Well, then I woke up here."

"It's like I said. The gold sovereign was shorting out the capacitor banks. Now that you've pulled it out, the electric bits work again." Yang put her hands on her hips. "But I think the sword's voltage is *way* too high."

"Once again, apprentice, I don't understand your magic arts." The knight stood up and dusted off his trousers, which were covered in charred grass.

"Can I look in the hilt again?"

Sir Humphrey opened the pommel and handed Gwendoline over to Yang, who peered inside. "I don't see any way to adjust it at all. There is an obscene amount of voltage going through the blade." She handed the sword back to the knight. "It's really not safe."

Gunthar shrugged. "Isn't that the whole point?"

"Indeed, sir!"

"I think you're likely to get a bad shock whenever you use it, unless we can find a way to insulate you."

"Apprentice?"

"For now, at least wrap the hilt with a bit more leather. You don't want to touch any of the metal bits. Do you have a glove you can wear?"

Cornelius looked down at them from atop Daisy. "We've been attacked now by chickens and pigs. What's next?"

Gunthar rubbed his beard. "The rising tide of the undead seems to be starting with farms. Maybe cows?"

"Not horses, I'd hope," said Maryan.

"Goats," proclaimed Cornelius.

"'Tis more likely to be cows."

"No, I mean, goats!" The Chronicler pointed eastward, where a group of undead goats staggered up the path towards them, bleating maliciously.

"Oh, for heaven's sake," said Maryan. "I really don't like hitting farm animals."

"Maybe we can go around them?" Yang pointed to a faint side trail to the south.

Gunthar shrugged. "We aren't really killing them, ma'am. They're undead, after all. Mostly we're helping them return to their eternal slumber. And if we don't handle them, they could be a danger to someone else."

"Even so, it creeps me out."

"Death Knights?"

"Kind of like that, yes."

"No, I mean, Death Knights!" Now the Chronicler pointed north, where six red-robed forms marched towards them in a synchronized line, led by a man dressed in black and white.

"Oh, holy snot," swore Maryan. "It's Prince Mikhail."

CHAPTER TEN: RIVER

Yang looked back and forth. "We're caught between Death Knights and unhappy goats."

"The goats, right?" Gunthar pointed down the path. "We're better off taking our chances with them."

"No such luck. The prince and his Death Knights are much faster." Maryan sighed. "With luck he'll just kill us, rather than try to make awkward conversation."

The approaching man waved. "Princess Maryan!"

"Prince Mikhail!" Maryan put on her best fake regal smile. "What a surprise to run into you here on the plains. I didn't think anyone knew where I was."

"I heard as much of the prophecy as you did, Princess. I figured you'd head to the nearest school of wizardry, then cut east to the river."

Maryan took a step back. "I guess I hadn't realized how obvious my path would be. Why haven't my parents already caught me?"

"Let's face it, Princess. Parents love us, but they have no idea how we really think. I doubt it's occurred to them yet that you are trying to follow the prophecy."

"Indeed, Prince. You have some insight into the parent-child relationship. I'm curious. Whatever happened to your parents?"

"Do you really want to know?"

Maryan thought of all the things that Mikhail may have done to his parents. "No."

"You are as wise as you are beautiful, Princess Maryan." He gave a mock bow, then extended his hand. "Now, let's stop this foolishness. It's time you joined me, forever."

"I'm sorry, good Prince, but we've already had this conversation. I'm not going with you."

Mikhail stepped forward, and his Death Knights followed with a synchronized step of their own. "No, it is I who am sorry, Princess. I'm not asking for your hand now. I am commanding you."

Gunthar hefted his axe. "I'd choose your words carefully, Your Highness. The princess goes where she wants."

Prince Mikhail laughed, the first sincere laugh she'd ever heard from him. "Is this your guard, Princess Maryan? A demoted Chronicler, a bankrupt knight, an apprentice with no magic, and an outcast barbarian? Nice furs, by the way."

Gunthar's ears turned red.

Sir Humphrey raised his chin. "Though we may be low mortals, yet we will fight for the princess still. Step away, sir."

He raised his sword, and clicked the button. Lightning blazed from the sword, chains of sparks dancing around it. Yang's hair spread out in a big globe, and Maryan's skin tingled with static electricity.

Prince Mikhail took a step back, and his Death Knights did the same, their unblinking eyes now fixed on the electric blade.

"I suggest you return home," said Sir Humphrey. "Unless you'd like a taste—"

An explosion cracked over the plains, and the knight went sailing over the heads of the goats, who ignored him.

Yang's hair settled down again. "Oh, no," she said, following Sir Humphrey's arc.

"For a moment there, I was worried you might be able to stop me. But your knight appears to have blown himself up in a short-circuit." Prince Mikhail smiled broadly as he walked forward again. "Princess Maryan, my love for you is so great that I will slaughter your friends and leave their remains to be eaten by reanimated goats."

"Bison."

"Nay, Chronicler, they are quite clearly goats."

"No, I mean, *bison!*" The Chronicler pointed north, where several large bison skeletons bore down on the Death Knights from behind. The beasts retained a semblance of shaggy coats, the ground shaking with the pounding of their mighty hooves.

"By the fangs of the night mother!" Prince Mikhail drew his sword and faced the undead bison, as did his Death Knights.

"Quick!" shouted Yang. "Run around the goats! Let's get to the river."

Maryan and Yang sprang onto the side trail, Gunthar following. Daisy trotted after, bouncing Cornelius on the saddle. "Ow ow ow ow ow," he called as the horse passed them.

The undead goats ignored them, and kept bleating as they limped towards Prince Mikhail. One grabbed a mouthful of grass, but kept marching.

"What will we do at the river?" Maryan shouted to Yang as they

CHAPTER TEN: RIVER

ran. "Won't Prince Mikhail trap us there?"

"We can get a boat," the apprentice replied. "There's a lot of river traffic."

"A boat will just happen to be there when we arrive at the river? Isn't that unlikely?"

"Well, maybe a boat won't be waiting for us. But we shouldn't have to wait long."

"How long?"

"I don't know. Maybe a few days."

"A few days?" Maryan slowed down.

"It's all I can think of," said Yang. "What else can we do?"

"These are horrible odds. There's no way a boat will show up right when we need it."

Cornelius called from further ahead, still bouncing on Daisy. "I see a river barge!"

They ran ahead and gathered a dazed Sir Humphrey, and Gunthar carried him down a long slope to the river Goldswell, which rushed before them.

A river barge floated just upstream, and Cornelius waved to it from atop Daisy at the water's edge.

"You see?" said Yang triumphantly. "We'll be at Bluntworth in no time."

Chapter 11
Haffleton

Haffleton.

> *— Considered Revelations, Book 171 "List of Places That Are Totally Hip", Chapter 1, Verse 1*

The barge captain was suspicious at first, but happily escorted them on board once Maryan offered him some silver. In no time at all the barge carried them downstream, the wide current of the Goldswell carrying them swiftly away from Prince Mikhail and the Death Knights.

Maryan cast a glance upstream. A flash of red caught her eye, far off in the distance, but then the river swept the barge around a bend, and all of the north disappeared from view.

Gunthar sat in the front of the barge, his back to several large sacks of grain. He kicked his feet out in front of him and clasped his hands behind his head. "Now *this* is the way to travel."

"In sooth." Sir Humphrey appeared much recovered from his second electrical explosion. He gestured at the broad expanse of water surrounding them. "'Tis far better to have a moat around oneself when traveling amongst the undead."

A tall sail extended over the wide, flat-bottomed river barge. The wood gunnels were worn with use, smooth and bleached a pale gray by sun and water. Barrels and crates piled around them.

"I'm going to talk to the captain, see what he knows," said Maryan.

"I'll go with you, ma'am," said Cornelius.

Yang followed them as Maryan threaded her way amongst sacks and barrels to the rear of the boat, where the pilot stood at a tiller on the quarterdeck.

Maryan grabbed the low rail at the side. "Thank you again for taking us, captain."

"Always happy to take an extra fare, so long as we have room, and you stay out of the way of my crew."

"Of course, captain." The crew consisted of two teenagers, the captain's niece and nephew. "How far is it to Bluntworth?"

CHAPTER ELEVEN: HAFFLETON

"It's well-nigh fifty leagues from here, give or take a few furlongs. But Goldie runs swift these days, with the spring rains. We'll get there by this time tomorrow, I shouldn't wonder."

"Are there any dangers? Rapids? Serpents?"

The captain kept his eyes on the river, his hand guiding the rudder with smooth, gentle movement. "There's but one danger on the river this time of year, and that'd be the hipsters in Haffleton."

"Pardon?"

"They're a right pretentious lot. A bit snooty about most everythin'."

"Oh."

"But we'll skip Haffleton altogether." He took his eyes off the river momentarily to flash her a big smile with a few missing teeth. "I'll land you at the quay in Bluntworth, or my name's not Captain Marco!"

The next day at noon, they pulled into a large wooden dock on the east side of the river. Behind it stood merchant buildings built of wood and stone, and rows of brightly-painted homes stretched down the roads further in.

Yang pointed at a house further downstream, bedecked with tangles of lavender flowers. "Oh, look at all the wisteria!"

"Is this Bluntworth?" Maryan asked.

"Nay, lass, the quays of Bluntworth are choked up with river traffic. This is Haffleton. We'll have to unload here." He flashed her another half-toothed smile. "But we'll have the barge unloaded by sundown, or my name's not Captain Marco!"

A bearded man in skinny trousers waved from the dock. "I'm afraid not, captain! We're busy unloading other cargo ahead of you, and the dock crew has a hot yoga session in the afternoon. We'll get to you tomorrow."

A castle and a cathedral jutted above the rooftops further down. "Is that Bluntworth?" Maryan pointed at the tallest tower.

"Aye, lass." The captain spat into the river. "That's the mayor's palace."

"Perfect. We can walk from here." Maryan thanked the captain and his young crew, then led the group down the gangplank.

The dock master watched them approach. Next to him stood a young lady with blue hair and a matching blue cloak, in a suit of patchwork armor.

"I'm the customs officer," she explained, sweeping back her blue hair. She pulled a small slate tablet and chalk out of her handbag. "Names and places of origin?"

"I'm Mary from Offerdell." She inspected the officer's shoulder pieces, smaller than usual with scaly imprints. "Is that *kobold* armor?"

The officer lifted her chin. "It's a mix of goblin and kobold armor that I salvaged from three different consignment shops. And look..." She turned and stuck her hand in a chain mail sleeve at the waist. "It has pockets."

"Oh, wow." Maryan pointed to her own outfit. "No pockets. I have to carry a satchel for everything."

"Even so, I love what you're wearing. Funeral dress with boots. I'm getting a goth-on-holiday vibe, is that right?"

Maryan looked down at her black gown. "Something like that."

"Love it," echoed the dock master.

"Right, Mary of Offerdell, welcome to Haffleton. Next!"

The barbarian took a step forward. "I'm Gunthar, from the Northern Wastes."

The customs officer glanced at his outfit, then turned back to her slate with wide eyes. "Right, ah, Northern Wastes..."

Gunthar put his hands on his hips. "I'm wearing these furs ironically."

"Oh, oh, *right*." She laughed in relief.

The dock master grinned. "Wow, you really had me there." He whistled. "Furs! I haven't seen an ensemble like that in a while."

Gunthar smiled through gritted teeth. "Yes, well, I..."

The customs officer waved him on. "Next!"

Once they'd all disembarked, the dock master found them a high-walled gangway, and Daisy walked off the ship. Sir Humphrey stroked the horse's mane. "She's a well-travelled horse, is Daisy, and she can handle gangplanks when needed, but I think she appreciates a more solid platform."

They hefted Cornelius onto Daisy again.

"How is your foot, Chronicler?" asked Maryan.

"Better, thank you, ma'—Mary." He passed his leafy walking stick to the princess. "I think it will be right as rain in another day or two."

"Good to hear you are mending." Maryan walked up the docks to shore. "We can be in Bluntworth by early afternoon."

Gunthar shouldered his large packs, the knight's armor jangling, and turned to the customs officer. "Is there a tailor in Haffleton, by any chance?"

The blue-haired officer chortled. "We don't have any of that bourgeoisie capitalism in Haffleton. That's something you'd find only in Bluntworth."

"Got it, thank you!" Gunthar turned to follow Maryan.

The dock master called after him. "There's a very good thrift store on Elm Avenue, next to the organic chai shop!"

Yang kept turning around, admiring the homes they walked by. "Look at all the gardens! Isn't this beautiful?" She stopped at a flower box with bright purple blooms. "Oh, I just love tulips."

A bearded young man poked his head out of the window. "They're North Hinterland tulips, from the marshes by the Sea of Wisps. They're not *common* tulips."

"Very nice," said Yang, retreating to the street.

A gaggle of Haffletonians walked by Sir Humphrey. "Methinks my trousers are too baggy," he said when they'd passed.

"I don't think they can run in those," said Cornelius, looking at the narrow styles favored by the locals. "Nor sit."

"It's definitely a very *trendy* suburb," noted Yang.

A nearby couple watched Gunthar walk by, their mouths agape.

"Ironic," he explained, pointing at himself.

"Oh!" the couple exclaimed, then smiled at him and went on their way.

"I told you, furs are at least two seasons out of date," grumbled the barbarian. "As far as I'm concerned, we can't get out of Haffleton fast enough."

A large man with flaring leather shoulder pads and artfully dangling goblin skulls stepped into the road before them with a sneer. "By the cold winds of the northwest passage! If it isn't Gunthar the Pacifist. Have you gotten any real furs yet?"

Gunthar sighed. "Hello, Rangvald. Here for some shopping? Or just traveling further from home to brag about your style move?"

"The last I heard, you got captured and dragged out of the tundra by a poncy bunch of southern wimps." Rangvald chuckled, then tapped the large axe strapped to his back. "And yes, everyone here is impressed by my amazing style move. How could they not be?" The man addressed the other adventurers. "It's this amazing jump and spin thing, where I bring the axe down as I touch down again. I've also got this cool yell. People go wild for it. But of course, you wouldn't understand that, would you, Gunthar?"

"It's great to see you again, Rangvald. Thanks for all of your efforts to, you know, ostracize me from the clan and everything." Gunthar made to step by the other barbarian. "Maybe we'll bump into each other again."

"Not likely. I don't rub shoulders with weak captives with no style moves." Rangvald snorted and walked away.

Sir Humphrey watched the other barbarian leave. "'Tis an acquaintance?"

"Distant relative. Barbarians sometimes venture this far south for work, or just to hit things." He shrugged. "Right, now I'm *really* ready to get out of Haffleton."

"The gates must be around the next corner," noted Maryan, seeing the town wall of Bluntworth above a shop selling hemp sandals. "Remember, let's not use my name or title. I'd like to keep my parents off my trail a while longer. With luck, we can slip in unnoticed."

"Of course, ma'am," said the knight. "'Tis a great advantage of cities, that a noble may walk incognito amongst the commoners."

They rounded the corner, and faced the large northern gates of Bluntworth, tall doors wide open under a crenellated wall. In front of the gates lay a small square, deserted except for a boisterous crowd standing at the side of the road and on bleachers. A band started playing polka, and guards at the top of the gatehouse unfurled a "Welcome Princess Maryan" banner that fluttered happily in the afternoon breeze.

"Welcome to Bluntworth!" called the Mayor from a raised dais nearby.

Chapter 12
Bluntworth

> *Times of legendary crisis call for leaders of legendary smartness.*
>
> — *Considered Revelations, Book 112 "Leaders Who Are Very Smart", Chapter 53, Verse 2*

The Mayor led them through the gates and up the broad promenade into the administrative district of Bluntworth with the palace at its heart. Citizens of the town had thrown open their windows, and garlands of flowers hung from many homes. The crowd from the gate followed them, as did the polka band, with Daisy and Cornelius bringing up the rear.

"Of course, Your Highness," said the Mayor as he waved to each side of the street, "we'd received an urgent missive from your parents a few days ago, letting us know you might be traveling. So when we received word that you'd landed in Haffleton, we set up a welcome for you right away."

"My parents knew I'd be coming here?"

"Their message was a little unclear. It seemed they might expect you anywhere." He laughed, but without making eye contact, as he still waved at the crowd. "Almost as if they didn't know where you were!"

"I suspect they know now."

The Mayor gave a thumbs-up to a merchant in rich green robes as they passed. "Oh, yes, ma'am. You'll be happy to hear that we sent messenger pigeons to your parents right away."

"Wonderful."

Well-wishers lined the street, citizens of Bluntworth who cheered and waved garlands of blue and yellow flowers. Windows opened above them, with more townspeople leaning out and calling, eager to see the spectacle of visiting royalty. They passed through the gates into the palace, the Mayor waving behind them to the crowd, which was not allowed to enter. No sooner had Daisy walked through than the guards closed the gate, and the polka music and cheering of the crowd suddenly dimmed.

The Mayor dropped his arms. Though tall, he sported a large paunch that strained the buttons of his doublet. "I can't stand parades, you know. A lot of non-stop waving and smiling. Still, it's the sort of thing voters expect."

"Mayor, we need to enter the Badlands and confront the Lich King."

"Out of the question, ma'am."

"I'm sorry?"

"The Badlands are closed." He gestured around them. The slender towers of the palace cast shadows across the courtyard, which contained several fountains and statues and marble-lined rows of flowers. "This is why Bluntworth is so prosperous! All commerce in this region is squeezed to the edges of the Badlands, and Bluntworth has a strategic position here. We take a fifteen percent cut of all trade on river and land." He raised his chin. "The Lich King and his cursed Teapot are of course a blemish on the land, a most unfortunate event with horrible repercussions for us all, yet we have made it work."

"But we can put an end to the Lich King and his Curse—"

"I'm sorry, ma'am, that would be catastrophic for our tax revenues. I mean, it's too dangerous."

"Mayor, if we *don't* stop the Lich King, he will engulf your city in a rising tide of the undead, killing everyone."

The Mayor's eyes widened, and he put a hand to his head. "Oh my, Your Highness. That would be even worse for tax revenue."

"Indeed, Mayor."

He exhaled in a long, ragged sigh. For a moment, he looked as if the weight of the world had come crashing down on his narrow shoulders. But then he straightened and raised his fist. "This is the sort of news that would crush a lesser mayor. But I have developed a sure-fire strategy to deal with unpleasant facts."

"Oh? What's that, Mayor?"

"I refuse to believe them."

"Mayor, I don't think you can choose to ignore hard facts—"

"On the contrary, ma'am, I do it all the time."

"Mayor, the Lich King and his minions will lay waste—"

"No, they won't. All this talk of Lich Kings and Teacups and widespread death are rumors made up by my political opponents.

CHAPTER TWELVE: BLUNTWORTH

There, see, ma'am? I made it a political thing."

"Mayor—"

"It was a prophetic fact, but I turned it into politics, and now I can deal with it on my terms." The Mayor wagged his finger. "Trust me, voters are also desperate to disbelieve bad news. They'll happily prefer my political distortion to the unpleasant reality."

"But thousands of people will die—"

"Nope, I don't believe you, ma'am. See? It's easy."

Maryan opened her mouth to reply, then closed it again. What was she supposed to say when the leader of the town refused to acknowledge plain facts? Nothing in her royal education had prepared her for someone like this. She swallowed, then pointed to the tops of the cathedral towers, just visible over the palace walls. "Can I find the bishop at the cathedral?"

The Mayor opened a door at the side of the courtyard. "There is no bishop of Bluntworth. And I'm sorry, ma'am, but no one enters the Badlands." He walked off, and the door closed behind him.

Sir Humphrey whistled in disbelief as he looked at the closed door. "In sooth, ma'am, I have never come across a more disagreeable leader."

A councilor in gray robes approached them. "The Mayor is a formidable political force. He didn't win four elections by accident."

Yang frowned. "I thought he'd only been elected once."

The councilor nodded. "He had to keep recounting the ballots until he got the result he wanted. He likes to win, even when he loses."

"Ah."

He bowed at Maryan. "Ma'am, if I may suggest."

"Yes?"

"The Mayor will keep you here until your parents come to collect you, probably four days or so. He'll probably refuse to meet with you in the meantime. But there will be a feast to celebrate the spring tax receipts in the town square tomorrow night, and he'll have to invite you for reasons of protocol. You might be able to force his hand then."

"Oh? How is that, councilor?"

"If you can find a Prophecy Scholar who can attest to the danger facing the city, and convince other leading nobles, then the Mayor may be forced to allow you to enter the Badlands."

Sir Humphrey snapped his fingers. "Of course! 'Tis well known that Prophecy Scholars are guided by knowledge and holy insight. Who better to convince the skeptical?"

"We'll get a Prophecy Scholar, then. And councilor, what did the Mayor mean by Bluntworth not having a bishop?"

The councilor bowed again. "I'm sorry, ma'am. The previous bishop passed three months ago, and the Mayor does not approve of the candidate proposed by the seers of the church." He smiled apologetically. "The candidate can be found near the cathedral most days, although he isn't allowed inside."

"The Mayor can stop a bishop from being appointed?"

"It's part of the history of Bluntworth, ma'am. Bishops are selected by the church, but must be approved by the Mayor."

"So why doesn't he approve this candidate?"

"It's all part of the political theater, Your Highness. The church elders nominate a corrupt and compliant bishop, and the Mayor is expected to pay them a hefty bribe in return. But this time, the Mayor offered too low of a bribe, and so the church elders have nominated a most unsuitable candidate until he agrees to increase the bribe. The current candidate will never be approved."

"Oh, my. Bluntworth is much more complicated than I expected."

The councilor bowed a third time. "Of course, ma'am. But be aware that there are some who would prefer that the city *not* be consumed by a rising tide of the undead." He gestured to another doorway. "Now, please allow me to show you to your rooms."

The councilor led them to guest quarters in the south wing of the mayor's palace. The rooms had balconies overlooking the city, and opened to a central courtyard with a fountain. Everyone looked in their rooms, then returned to the courtyard.

"My room has silk curtains and a malachite desk," said Yang. "I've never seen the like!"

Gunthar frowned. "My bath contains some sort of torture device."

The councilor laughed. "It's not a torture device, it's a... Well, it's something you use after you..."

Gunthar's frown deepened.

"You can ignore it." The councilor turned to Maryan. "Ma'am, I trust everything is to your liking?"

CHAPTER TWELVE: BLUNTWORTH

"Indeed, councilor. I am overwhelmed by the luxury. I had thought Bluntworth was a small, poor town on the hinterlands."

"Once it was, ma'am. But over the generations, the curse of the Badlands has channeled all the region's trade through our ports." He gestured west, where the sun approached the horizon. "If you need anything, just ask for me, Councilor Wilson. Now please, make yourselves at home for the night. I am sure tomorrow will be a busy day."

* * *

In the morning, a rooster crowed from the palace gardens, and Maryan woke to find sun streaming in from the eastern window.

After dressing in her black outfit again, she went out to the guest quarters courtyard, where the others were already eating from a bowl of fruit. Sir Humphrey held up a chunk of bread. "That Mayor may have the character of a toad's ass, but he knows a good breakfast."

Maryan grabbed an apple and polished it absently. "We need a Prophecy Scholar to attend the feast tonight. Any ideas where to find one?"

Everyone looked at each other.

Gunthar shrugged. "Well, Your Highness, I'll ask questions while I'm in the garment district."

"The garment district?"

"Aye, ma'am. That councilor chap told me it was on the south end of town. I'll find a tailor there, I'm sure."

Maryan frowned. "Perhaps you're right. We could split up and ask in different parts of the city."

Sir Humphrey stood. "I'll take the north end, ma'am. 'Tis the merchant district, and I mean to see about extending my timeline."

"Your timeline?" Yang asked.

"I have to pay back the merchant houses in one week, or lose my family estates forever."

"Oh." Yang blanched.

"Very well. I'll take the east side of town."

"I'll go with you, Your Highness," said Yang.

"I think I'll try walking more today," said Cornelius. The scholar hobbled around the courtyard with his stick. "My ankle feels better."

Maryan regarded his foot. "It's been a week since it was injured. Don't overdo it."

"Chroniclers never overdo things, ma'am."

Maryan washed her hands in a small bowl. "Why don't we all meet at the palace entrance at noon?"

"Right," said Gunthar. "See you then."

"Aye, ma'am. I'll see you at noon." Cornelius hobbled after the departing barbarian, the knight following.

Maryan and Yang walked out of the palace and headed away from the large parks and graceful manors by the river, towards the hot and dusty side streets by the town's eastern wall. After a few hours of exploring alleys, ramshackle dwellings, and dead ends, they gave up and returned to the neighborhoods by the palace.

"That was a waste of time," grumbled Maryan.

"And the gates on the east side of the town wall are all barred," complained Yang as they walked back towards the cathedral. "It's like they never want to open the doors to the Badlands at all."

"Perhaps the Mayor keeps them closed so no one wanders out and gets hurt."

"I think he's more interested in protecting his precious tax revenue, ma'am."

"That too." Maryan looked up at the two towers of the cathedral, rising far above the square in front of the church's great front doors. The doors were shut, with chains and a sign hung in front saying "Closed until appointment of a new bishop." Dust and grime covered the doors and sign.

Maryan sighed. "It appears this standoff won't end any time soon. There won't be a bishop appointed for a long time."

"I guess." The apprentice put her hands on her hips, looking at the chained door. "What do people do without their bishop? Isn't that the spiritual leader for the entire region?"

"Oh, we get by, you know," drawled a lazy voice next to them.

Maryan and Yang turned and saw a young man in a tattered sackcloth robe sitting in the shadows of the cathedral's wide front steps.

He nodded at them and stood. "One merch asked me, 'Hey, how

CHAPTER TWELVE: BLUNTWORTH

will we get by without a bishop?' And I was like, 'You don't need a bishop to live righteously, merch.'" The man absently pushed his unkempt black hair out of his eyes. "But he was totally after an indulgence, you know?"

"An indulgence?" Yang asked.

"Yeah, those merchants used to come in before every deal. It was a thing. They'd pay a small fee to the bishop, then lie to their customers. Utterly bogus."

"You seem to know a lot about the workings of merchants and the church," noted Maryan.

"You catch on to this stuff once you've lived here long enough. People ask me, 'Why aren't you more angry about it? Why don't you lay into those wicked merch types?' And I'm like, 'I'm not into the whole judging thing.' We need to let people find their own way, you know?"

"Have you lived in Bluntworth long?"

"Yeah. Hey, aren't you that noble lady who's visiting town, Your Highness? I saw the crowds yesterday. You're Maryan of Offerdell, right?"

Maryan straightened automatically. "Yes."

"Well, ma'am, I've lived on these streets my whole life. My name's Onkar." He bowed.

"Good to meet you, Onkar." Maryan studied the man in front of her. He had a simple rope for a belt and his robe looked like it had spent more than one morning sitting on steps. Perhaps he was a dissolute monk? "Do you know of any Prophecy Scholars in town?"

"Oh, yeah," said the man, scratching his belly. "Prophecy Scholars used to hang out here all the time. One taught me to read, in fact. Some of them are a good laugh, you know? I'd be like, 'Is the sun prophesied to rise tomorrow?' And they'd be like, 'It's totally in the stars.' Get it?"

"The Prophecy Scholars *used to* hang out here?"

"Yeah, ma'am. They're all gone now. They all took off in October, before the winter rains. Like something in the Badlands totally freaked them out, you know? I was like, 'Hey, where are you all going?' And they were like, 'We're just leaving for a quick walk.' And I was like, 'Really? With all of your stuff on your back?'" He looked sadly out to the west, where the river Goldswell ran by the town.

"That was the last anyone saw of them. Round these parts, anyway."

Yang put a hand to her forehead. "All the Prophecy Scholars have gone? What will we do?"

"We'll think of something," Maryan said, although her heart fell. The distant river flowed past the docks at the waterfront, and she imagined the scholars fleeing on fast ships.

"If all the scholars left, why did you stay?" Yang asked the black-haired man.

Onkar spread his hands out and flashed a toothy grin. "I'm not going anywhere. These are like, *my* people, you know? Bluntworth is a family."

Maryan raised an eyebrow. "Do you know anything about the candidate to replace the bishop?"

"Of course, ma'am. That's *me*." He laughed, then looked back and forth at the two of them. "Whoa, you both look like your brains just fried."

Maryan tried but failed to close her open mouth.

Yang stammered politely. "Yes, well, that's wonderful, I'm sure..."

Shouting carried across the square, an angry voice echoing back from the cathedral. Maryan frowned. The voice struck her as familiar, though she couldn't make out the words.

Onkar tilted his head. "If you don't mind, Your Highness, I'd better check on that. There's a tavern there, and sometimes hot-headed folk need a calming."

"We'll go with you." Maryan fell into step beside Onkar, who walked swiftly despite wearing frayed sandals.

They rounded the corner of the square and arrived at a tavern which faced the main palace road. In front of it stood a man with long blond hair, wearing a dazzling leather kilt and matching banded armor. He shouted at his two compatriots near the tavern door.

"Wow, that guy's got some serious duds." Onkar studied the shouting man for a moment. "Like, a noble from the west?"

"No," sighed Maryan. "That's our barbarian. He appears to have found a tailor. And he's upset about something."

Chapter 13

Tavern

> *What says "prophecy tale" better than adventurers meeting in a tavern?*
>
> — *Considered Revelations, Book 113 "More Reasons to Love Taverns", Chapter 22, Verse 7*

Maryan stepped up to where the barbarian stood, shouting at Cornelius and Sir Humphrey. "Gunthar, what's wrong?"

"Oh, Your Highness." He suddenly looked a bit sheepish. "Sorry, ma'am, I lost my temper for a moment. But these two were trying to force me to do something utterly ridiculous."

"It's not ridiculous." The Chronicler leaned on his leafy stick as he waved behind him. "We suggested having lunch."

The knight shrugged. "Indeed, ma'am, we merely suggested that we enter the tavern. But the barbarian objected—"

"I'm *not* going into a tavern. It's a cliché."

"Sir, be reasonable. 'Tis a respectable venue." Sir Humphrey took a pleading tone. "And a bard plays there now, a rogue who earns his keep by song, but also travels through hardship—"

"*No.*" The barbarian gestured angrily. "You see what I'm talking about, ma'am?" Then he faced the knight and Chronicler, his voice rising again. "I did *not* give away all my last possessions for a fashionable outfit, only to be dragged into the most pathetic cliché imaginable—"

"Whoa there, compadre, whoa." Onkar raised his arms, his wide sackcloth sleeves falling back to his shoulders, revealing pale, skinny arms. "Like, take a deep breath, maybe count to five. Your buddies just wanted to include you in what they thought should be a shared experience, right?"

Gunthar looked away. "Well, maybe..." he muttered.

"And you worthies," said Onkar, addressing Sir Humphrey and Cornelius. "You should know that a group of adventurers entering a tavern is totally cliché, right?"

The Chronicler's ears turned a bright red.

The knight kicked at a small pebble in the gutter. "Mayhaps."

"May I suggest a compromise? Why don't we have them serve food here?" Maryan pointed to a large table outside the tavern, shaded under an arbor with flowering vines of purple clematis. "So we can eat, but don't have to go in and deal with singing bards or any of the owning family's drama."

"Of course!" Cornelius took a seat happily. "I spent all morning walking around the palace. I'm hungry."

Gunthar and Sir Humphrey sat down with some grumbling, but soon fell into discussing the barbarian's new armor and the tricky clasps at the shoulders. Yang sat next to them.

"You're welcome to join us, Onkar," said Maryan.

"Thank you, ma'am, but I should get back to the cathedral. I need to be there. If I'm away too long, people are like, 'Hey, why weren't you at the cathedral?' And I'm all, 'Well, I had this errand,' but then they're like, 'Yes, but I have this really big problem and I need to talk to you about it.'"

"Of course, well, maybe next time."

"Good day, ma'am." Onkar squinted at Gunthar. "You're not related to Scholar Markus, are you?"

The barbarian looked up at him. "Who?"

"The Prophecy Scholar, Markus. No? You're like a younger version of him. It's uncanny." Onkar shrugged, then waved at the table. "Enjoy your meal, everyone."

Yang watched the robed man walk back to the cathedral square. "He's not what I'd expected of a bishop candidate."

Maryan sat at the table, and in short order a serving boy brought them wooden bowls of beef stew and big rounds of crusty bread. "I see you traded the furs, Gunthar."

"Aye, ma'am." He brushed a speck of dust off the shiny black pauldron at his shoulder. "They had this set of oiled leather. It's much more fashion-forward, like formal wear you can take to the battlefield."

"I thought the furs looked fine," noted Yang.

"No, this is much better." Gunthar shifted in his seat with a wince. "Though the tailor did tell me these can chafe a bit."

"Oh, please," said Cornelius. "Can we talk about something else?"

"I sympathize, sir," said Sir Humphrey. "I've had to send more than one codpiece back to the smithy due to chafing."

Cornelius leaned over. "Not to change the subject, but have you tried the stew, Gunthar?"

Gunthar held up his empty bowl. "I made short work of it."

"And you, Sir Humphrey? Any luck with the merchant houses?"

The knight shook his head. "They weren't interested in any sort of extension, ma'am. I have one week remaining to come up with the money, or they'll auction off my lands."

"Oh, no," said Yang. "I'm sorry."

"We didn't have much luck either," said Maryan. "According to Onkar, all the Prophecy Scholars left town months ago."

"That's what the tailor said too, ma'am." Gunthar spoke around a large chunk of bread in his mouth.

Maryan pushed her half-eaten bowl of stew away, her appetite fading. "We're stuck in Bluntworth, there's no bishop, and we don't have any Prophecy Scholars to convince the Mayor to let us into the Badlands. So he won't let us leave, and my parents will take me back to Offerdell soon. The whole journey here was for naught." She buried her face in her hands. "I don't think this day could get any worse."

"Princess Maryan of Offerdell?" A page in the livery of the mayor's palace stood next to her.

Maryan looked up "Yes?"

"A message has arrived for you, ma'am." The page handed over a small rolled-up piece of parchment, then bowed and left.

"Who could it be from?" Yang looked at the parchment in Maryan's hand.

"The wax is stamped with the royal seal of Offerdell." Maryan unrolled the parchment, then sighed. "It's from my mother, of course." She read the letter aloud.

> *Dearest Maryan-*
>
> *We were beside ourselves with worry when you disappeared after May Day. So you can imagine our joy at hearing that your royal person was identified at Bluntworth. I'm sure you are missing the comforts of home, but please avail yourself of the sparse luxuries of the palace there. You will be delighted to hear that we are on our way to fetch you as I speak.*

Prince Mikhail and your father have had a bit of a falling out, I'm afraid. Something about a sneak attack and a border raid and a lost caravan of iron ore. I know you liked that dashing prince in black and silver, though you tried to hide it. Parents can always tell these things, honey.

But cheer up! As it turns out, my sister's friend's cousin's half-brother is also in Bluntworth. What a chance coincidence! He's a wonderful young man, a real salt-of-the-earth type, which I know you adore. And he's due to inherit almost half of the borderlands east of Southport, so your father approves of him.

I've asked the Mayor to invite him to the feast, so that you two can get acquainted. Isn't that just the most perfect thing?

Anyway, we'll arrive on Monday. Much love-

Queen Sally of Offerdell, First Lady of the Realm, &c.

PS. We hope you are having fun and enjoying the local culture and ask that you never leave the confines of your room in the palace tower, since nowhere else is safe.

"Monday," groaned Maryan. "And today is Friday. That doesn't give us much time."

Gunthar squinted over. "What's that?"

"Maryan's parents have set her up with a blind date for tonight's feast," said Yang, grinning.

Cornelius looked up from writing in his folio. "You adore salt-of-the-earth types?"

"I don't remember saying that particularly. I must have made a throw-away comment at some point that my mother interpreted as undying love for salt-of-the-earth."

Yang absently curled a lock of hair around her finger. "I wonder what your mystery man looks like? And what will Prince Mikhail think?"

"Oh my, ma'am. You're caught up in a love triangle." Sir Humphrey shook his head.

"No." Cornelius jumped up from the table, and slammed his pen down on his notebook. "I *refuse* to write any love triangles with vampires. I know I was demoted to writing prophecies because I disagreed with the Guild's editorial direction but even though this is my final probation as a Chronicler a person *must* retain some personal dignity. I've fallen so low that I'll write prophecies, and by the seven gods of grammar I'd even contribute to the travesty of children's books by celebrities, but I have to draw the line. *No vampire love triangles.*" Tears welled in his eyes.

Maryan stood and put her hands on the table. "Everyone, please calm down. I am *not* in a love triangle with a vampire, nor will I be."

Cornelius exhaled a long, shaky breath. "Very well, ma'am." He sat again.

Gunthar reached across the table and patted the Chronicler's shoulder supportively.

Maryan addressed the table. "We need to stay focused. Our goal is to get into the Badlands and confront the lich king before he can overwhelm these lands with vicious undead."

Sir Humphrey pounded his fist in front of him. "Hear, hear!"

"To do that, we need to convince the Mayor to let us leave. And that means we need a Prophecy Scholar."

The table fell silent. Gunthar chewed bread absently, while Yang contemplated the palace towers.

Sir Humphrey left the table and stood on his head.

"Is he all right?" asked the serving boy as he cleared their empty plates.

"He's fine," said Maryan. "He likes to stand on his head when he thinks."

"Ah." The serving boy took their plates inside.

"Could we create a Prophecy Scholar?"

Everyone looked at Yang.

"Is such a thing even possible?" Sir Humphrey returned to his feet.

The apprentice spread her hands. "The bishop candidate said that Gunthar looked a bit like one of the famous departed Prophecy Scholars. Couldn't we claim he is the son of a scholar?"

Now the table turned to Gunthar, who frowned. "I'm hardly the scholarly type."

"Well, sir, you do cut an imposing figure in your new leathers," noted Sir Humphrey.

Gunthar straightened. "That's true."

"And imagine how imposing you'd look in Prophecy Scholar regalia," said Yang. "They usually wear these cool robes with necklaces, and they get to talk down to everyone."

"Hmm..." The barbarian rubbed his chin.

Maryan bit her lip. "What I most appreciate about Gunthar is his straightforward style of speaking. Mightn't that detract from the illusion of being a Prophecy Scholar?"

"I could make a Potion of Erudition." Yang thrummed her fingers on the table. "It's not hard. It's just overpriced carbonated water with a few herbal ingredients."

Gunthar's eyes narrowed. "It won't make me gassy, will it?"

"No more so than most scholars."

Maryan raised her hand. "Does anyone have any better ideas?"

Again, the table went silent.

"Well then, let's try that. Apprentice Yang will make a Potion of Erudition, and Gunthar will be a new Prophecy Scholar come to warn the city of impending peril. And then we'll convince the Mayor to let us in the Badlands."

Chapter 14
Feast

Nothing raises the spirits of the weary better than heartfelt song.

— Considered Revelations, Book 352 "Heartfelt Things That Raise the Spirits of the Weary", Chapter 2, Verse 8

They returned to the Mayor's palace, where the councilor met them at the door with a broad smile. He walked with them up to their quarters. "You adventurers went to a tavern, didn't you?"

"No." Gunthar's eyes blazed. "We had lunch on the terrace of a gastropub. It's totally different."

"Ah." The councilor turned to Maryan. "Any luck finding a Prophecy Scholar, Your Highness?"

"We may have found one," she said.

The councilor's eyes widened.

"But," she continued, "do you think that will be enough? We need the mayor to let us into the Badlands, and appoint that candidate Onkar to be the bishop."

The councilor spread his hands as they reached the courtyard by their rooms. "It's worth a try, ma'am."

"Wait, Your Highness," said Apprentice Yang. "Don't we also need a ranger?"

Maryan took a drink of chilled water from the pitcher at the table. "Councilor, we are also looking for a ranger."

"We thought we'd find a ranger on the way here," noted Gunthar. "Normally, rangers are everywhere. But we haven't seen any."

Princess Maryan realized that they'd come all this way without seeing a single ranger. Not in Offerdell, or the Plains, or the river, or in Bluntworth. Where were all the rangers? A cold feeling settled in the pit of her stomach. "Uh-oh. A cold feeling has settled in the pit of my stomach."

Yang pointed to the pitcher at the table. "Well, ma'am, it's probably because you are hot from walking around town all day and climbing the stairs, and then you took a drink of chilled water."

"Oh yes, that must be it. But why haven't we seen any rangers?"

"They're all at the great Ranger Convention, of course. It happens once every five years." Councilor Wilson pointed out to the west. "This time, it's in Southport. I'm sure you can find one if you go there."

"They're all at a Ranger Convention in Southport?" Maryan frowned. "That's weeks from here. What if we need a ranger here in Bluntworth?"

"Then you're out of luck, ma'am."

The princess heaved a long sigh. "Nothing in this prophecy is really going to plan. Still, we'll make do with what we've got."

That evening, they assembled in the courtyard again.

Gunthar looked positively regal in a subtly patterned maroon robe with gold trim. Maryan had managed to rent it from the merchants in the northern quarter of town, although there had been a last-minute snafu when Gunthar had declared the sandals they'd supplied didn't match the fringe, and they'd had to swap them out right as the merchants closed for the day.

His long hair flowed in long, golden braids. "Oh, my," exclaimed Maryan. "Your hair looks amazing. Where did you get that done?"

"The knight." Gunthar jerked his head over at Sir Humphrey, who adjusted a necklace.

"I have a younger sister," explained the knight. The necklace was another rental item, a large ruby pendant hanging from a gold chain. He placed it around Gunthar's neck.

"Ah, good, I see you got a ruby one. The emerald one clashed." Gunthar nodded approvingly, then tapped the pendant with a frown. "No, not that tight. You saw pendants in Haffleton. People are wearing them with longer chains this year."

"Of course, good sir, my apologies." Sir Humphrey adjusted the necklace.

Yang entered the courtyard, carrying a small flask. A thin blue mist cascaded out of the open top. "The Potion of Erudition," she declared.

"When should Gunthar take it?" asked Maryan.

"Around now, Your Highness." Yang looked at the long, golden sunlight bathing the rooftops near them. "The potion takes about an hour to start working, then lasts for three or four hours."

"Very well," said Maryan.

CHAPTER FOURTEEN: FEAST

Gunthar took the flask and sniffed at it suspiciously, then his eyebrows went up. "Smells like pine needles."

"I added that," said Yang.

"Here goes nothing," said Gunthar. He drank from the flask in a single big gulp, then belched. "Tastes like a horse took a **** in my mouth."

Cornelius paled. "It's not working. He still talks like a barbarian."

"Like I said, the potion needs an hour to take effect."

"Let's get going," said Maryan. "We need to get down to the town square for the feast."

They descended the staircase, and Councilor Wilson joined them at the palace gates. "Good evening, Your Highness, adventurers," said the man with a bow. He also wore a formal robe, with a large gold medallion on his chest. "I'd heard all the Prophecy Scholars had left the city, but you seem to have found one." He gestured at Gunthar. "Are you related to Scholar Markus, by any chance?"

"A nephew," said Yang.

"Whatever," said Gunthar. He belched again, then addressed Yang. "I thought you said I wouldn't be gassy?"

"I can't help it. I had to use carbonated water."

"Wait, do I know him?" The councilor raised an eyebrow at Maryan.

"He's feeling a little rough right now," she explained. "But I'm sure he'll be fine in a few minutes."

"Very well, ma'am. If you'll follow me..."

The councilor led them down the street to the square between the Mayor's palace and the town cathedral.

Earlier, when they'd met Onkar, the square had been deserted. But now tables filled the area, townspeople milling around with large platters of food and tankards of rich ale. The surrounding buildings were festooned with lanterns and flowers and garlands of green ivy, banners hanging from the palace and the cathedral. The walls echoed with the sounds of people talking and joking and toasting.

A few large tables stood above the rest, on the landing in front of the cathedral. The mayor sat in a large chair at the center table, with several of the town worthies around him.

"This way," said the councilor, leading them up the steps.

A nearby table of townspeople quieted, and they pointed at Gunthar, eyes wide.

"Can't we grab some grub?" complained Gunthar. "I'm hungry enough to eat a mule."

"Where exactly did you find this Scholar?" Councilor Wilson squinted at Gunthar again.

"He's new to the Scholar business," said Maryan, taking the councilor's arm and propelling him ahead. "But don't worry. He'll hit his stride soon."

"Yeah, right," snorted Gunthar.

"Ah, of course," said the councilor. "Here is the table you'll be sitting at." They had arrived at a large table on the edge of the landing, next to the mayor's table. Servants bustled around them and laid out plates of food.

"Now that's more like it!" exclaimed Gunthar, seeing a roast boar laid out nearby.

"Indeed, sir, 'tis a feast worthy of the name."

"I'll leave you here then, Your Highness, adventurers." The councilor bowed, then walked up to his seat at the Mayor's table.

"So when do I do the Scholar thing?" asked Gunthar. He held a large, greasy boar leg in his hand.

"Um, well, I think we'll wait for a chance to address the high table later. We need to convince the Mayor and other councilors that the prophecy is real."

"Great." He took a bite, then talked through a mouth full of roast boar. "So maybe after the second course?"

"Oh, this is a disaster." Cornelius shook his head.

"I know I should have asked earlier, but are there any side effects of the potion?" asked Maryan.

"None, really," said Yang. "It's pretty safe, as far as potions go. However," here she wagged a finger at Gunthar, "you shouldn't mix it with mango juice."

"Mango juice?" A piece of boar meat fell out of Gunthar's mouth, and he stuffed it back in. "I *love* mango juice."

"Yes, well, it's not likely to come up anyway."

Cornelius looked around the party with concern. "What if the Mayor serves mango juice?"

"That would be most improbable, respected Chronicler. We are in a northern latitude, well above the fortieth parallel. Transporting tropical fruit would pose severe logistical challenges. Transporting juice even more so." Gunthar stopped speaking, his face white with shock. He looked down to his hands, which were carefully cutting the boar leg with a knife and fork. "By the sparkling prose of Saint Gertrude!"

"It looks like the potion has taken effect." Yang looked up at the darkening sky. "Just under an hour, as expected. The pine needles helped, I think."

"Wow, it really works!" Maryan's eyes went wide.

Gunthar raised a goblet, his pinky finger extended. "Indeed, Apprentice Yang, we toast both your proficiency and your perspicacity."

Sir Humphrey raised his goblet uncertainly. "Is that an appropriate toast for mixed company?"

"I like this new barbarian!" Cornelius toasted the table, then drank.

"More roast boar, sir?" asked a servant.

"Nay, but thank you, good man." Gunthar waved at the common table. "Earlier, I described a most delightful incorporation of lettuce, apple, and pecan. If you have it, a moderate amount of such would tide me until the final course."

The servant nodded and retreated.

Maryan sat back with her goblet. "It looks like the feast might go well after all."

"Hello, Your Highness, is this seat taken?" A tall young man in fringed leathers sat next to her, his dark hair cropped short and a small diamond glittering from a piercing in his ear. "It is now!"

"Oh, hey, look! Goblets!" Another young man sat next to him, also in leather, his short blond hair in a similar cut.

"Excuse me?" asked Maryan.

"Of course!" The man with the earring swept a hand back across his chest. "I am Sir Chad, of the Southport Borderlands."

"Ah," she sighed, her shoulders slumping. "You are my mother's friend's cousin's half-brother."

"The same!"

"And I am Squire Brock, at your service, Your Highness." The blond man leaned over at her, as if bowing, his goblet extended.

"My wingman!" exclaimed Sir Chad, and they exchanged a complicated fistbump-handshake-elbow-bump.

"Wingman!" echoed Squire Brock.

"Wingman?" asked Cornelius.

"Oh, hey there, yeah. It's a term we picked up from the estuary. There're these big fat gray swan things that always fly in pairs." Sir Chad made a flapping motion to illustrate.

"Anser's gray goose, as noble a wayfarer as one will find in the western basin. Seasons ago, I would observe the flocks on their annual migration north across the tundra." Gunthar raised his goblet. "O, the sight of it! To see an entire acre of geese, congregating and discoursing through the day, soaring together in the evening thermals. As if an entire civilization had peregrinated at once to the northern shores."

Sir Chad laughed, then hesitated. "Is he all right?"

Yang leaned over to address him. "He's a Prophecy Scholar."

"'Tis always a pleasure to meet a fellow knight," said Sir Humphrey. "To which liege are you pledged?"

"I am pledged to the Lord of *Party!*" roared Sir Chad.

"Party!" echoed Squire Brock, and they exchanged their complicated fist bump again.

"I don't know those lands," said Sir Humphrey with a frown. "Is Party further south?"

"I'm just kidding, bro," said Sir Chad. "I am a knight under the Lord of Southport."

"So there is no land of Party?"

"How did you enjoy the estuary?" interjected Maryan.

"It's cold and wet, ma'am. But we rocked it anyway, didn't we?" He went to fist bump his squire again, but Brock had his goblet up and intently gulped down its contents, so he turned back to Maryan. "We rocked it."

"Rocking? By which you mean geological investigation? Not many scholars appreciate it, but the southern estuaries contain many mineralogical surprises. Whilst most of the wetlands are sand or peat, past episodes of glaciation have deposited several boulders, carried from beyond the Teeth of Janks. More than one geologist has stumbled across geodes in the reeds! To say nothing of the wonders of the hydrology, of course."

CHAPTER FOURTEEN: FEAST

Sir Chad stared intently at the barbarian, his smile fading. "What's he saying?"

"More wine!" The squire raised his goblet, and one of the servants ran over with a large pitcher. "And no need to water it down this time."

"I'm sorry, sir," said the servant. "All the wine is watered. It's tradition at the feast." The man filled both Brock and Sir Chad's cups again.

"Oh, all right then." Brock waited until the servant had finished pouring, then fished a small flask out of his jacket. "Your wingman saves the day!" He poured a small amount of whatever was in the flask in his and Sir Chad's goblets.

"We should get to know each other, right, Your Highness?" said Sir Chad with a grin. "Why don't I spend the time telling you all about myself?"

"Indeed, Sir Chad, I can't imagine the evening going any other way."

Sir Chad launched into a rambling story about how he and Brock had bumped into a troll's hut in the estuary, a telling slowed down by the squire's constant interruptions to back up and explain his contributions in more detail. Maryan lost track of the thread.

"And so, ma'am, there we were, hungry and in our underwear, when the troll returned with a deer—"

Brock shook his head. "No, Sir Chad, it wasn't a deer. It was an elk."

"An elk? Are you sure?"

"Had to be. It looked like a deer only because a troll was carrying it."

"Sorry," interrupted Yang, scratching her head. "Why were you in your underwear?"

"Go back, bro! Tell her about the goblins in the hollow log again." Squire Brock lifted his goblet with an unsteady hand.

"Excuse me, Your Highness." The councilor stood in front of their table. "Now would be a good time to address the Mayor and the rest of the town council."

"Of course!" Maryan stood. "Gunthar, please join me."

"Fine folk of Bluntworth!" The Mayor stood at his table, a hand raised, and the square quieted a moment as everyone turned to hear what he said. "We have a special treat at tonight's feast. Merchant Connor is a close and personal friend of mine." The Mayor waved at a fat man in a greasy green robe, who beamed back. "As a gift to the town, and a sign of support for my administration, he has shipped an entire cargo of mango from the southern continent at his expense. Tonight, we are providing everyone a glass of mango juice!"

"What?" Yang's mouth hung open. "That's not possible."

"Mango juice!" Sir Chad and Squire Brock exchanged their complicated fistbump again.

Gunthar heaved a great, longing sigh. "Ah, that heavenly nectar. If one were to bottle a daydream and infuse it with honey, would it be any sweeter?"

Sir Chad lifted his goblet to the barbarian. "Right on, bro!"

"Your mango juice, Your Highness," said a servant as he placed a small glass of the golden liquid in front of Maryan.

"Don't drink it, Gunthar," warned Yang as another servant placed a similar glass in front of the barbarian.

"Of course, Apprentice Yang. This is a parable regarding temptation, is it not? Whether to abstain and endure a wasting sense of loss in service of one's duty to abstract objectives, or to capitulate to physical desire and sample passion incarnate?"

"Don't drink it," the apprentice repeated.

"Come, Gunthar, now's our chance." Maryan walked over to the Mayor's table.

"Aye, ma'am, it is our highest ideals to which I remain steadfastly committed." The barbarian followed her, upright in his regalia.

A councilor in a blue gown noticed Gunthar's approach first, and she fixed her gaze on him as the barbarian strode with calm, deliberate steps to the front of the table. The lady's companion stopped talking, also fixed on Gunthar, and one by one the other worthies quieted and stared, until even the Mayor himself turned and regarded the regal Prophecy Scholar.

Maryan raised her chin. The plan would work, after all. Gunthar had their undivided attention, and the aura of a Prophecy Scholar would lend more authority to their request. Certainly, they could convince many of the council of the need to confront the Lich King, and win the popular backing of the townspeople as well. The

CHAPTER FOURTEEN: FEAST

Mayor would have to let them go at that point.

"Mayor, councilors, worthies of Bluntworth." Maryan bowed. "I am Princess Maryan of Offerdell, and I have come with a Prophecy Scholar, a nephew of the respected Scholar Markus."

Several of the councilors gasped, and the councilor in blue leaned forward. If anything, the focus of the worthies only increased.

Below the steps, the tables of townspeople quieted. They also stared up, curious to see what Maryan and Gunthar would say.

Maryan raised her voice so that all in the square could hear. "We have come a great distance, and endured many perils, to speak with you today." She gestured to Gunthar and backed up to give him center stage. "The Prophecy Scholar has information of utmost consequence to you and your future."

The square fell deathly quiet, and Gunthar stepped forward.

He nodded to the worthies and the Mayor, then jumped spryly atop their table and turned to face the square, his arms spread wide. "Who wants to hear a song about a horny dragon?" he yelled.

"Yeah!" Sir Chad and Squire Brock raised their goblets in unison. Several of the townspeople cheered.

Maryan turned to the apprentice with a look of shock, and both dropped their eyes to the barbarian's place at the table.

His glass of mango juice stood empty.

Yang raised a hand to her face. "Oh, no..."

Cornelius went white. "I hope he's not referring to Plucky the Dragon from Huck. That song is banned in most of the east, and for good reason."

"This is called Plucky the Dragon from Huck!" Gunthar began singing in a loud and clear voice, kicking up his sandals and making hand gestures to illustrate.

> *There was a young troll from Halden*
> *He had a big **** but his **** were stuck*
> *He **** them and **** them but they just wouldn't *****
> *What did he need? He needed a ****!*

Sir Humphrey approached the princess uncertainly. "'Tis a most unusual introduction. Mayhaps he will introduce the prophecy after the rude song?"

"No," said Maryan, her mouth dry. She considered tackling the barbarian, but it would take multiple people to drag him off the table, and that would make even more of a scene. "I think we've lost our chance to convince the Mayor."

> *I'm Plucky the Dragon from Huck!*
> *I'm plucky and I'm lucky and I just love a good ****!*
> *In Huck we're all happy and **** ducks galore*
> *And lucky for you, I have come to your shores*
> *I know what you want and I have what you need*
> *You need love and to give is my creed*
> *And most of all you need a good *****
> *Nothing says love like a **** **** *****

The Mayor strode over and confronted Maryan, his face beet-red. "What is the meaning of this..." He waved at the boisterously singing and rudely gesturing Gunthar, words failing him for a moment. "This *insult?*"

"I do apologize, Mayor. I think he is exhausted from travel. Perhaps if we could meet tomorrow, he can explain—"

"Tomorrow? Tomorrow you will all be confined to your quarters."

> *So the troll left with a smile on his face*
> *His **** was **** and his **** were *****
> *Plucky the Dragon gave him a crazy good ****!*
> *He got himself a crazy good *****

Maryan pleaded. "Mayor, it's more of a song about friendship, isn't it?"

"'Tis a sing-along, good Mayor," added Sir Humphrey. "See how the barbarian asks 'What did he need?' And the crowd yells back 'He needed a—'"

"Enough!" roared the Mayor.

Behind them, Gunthar finished singing, and many townspeople clapped and cheered. Squire Brock had his head down on the table, apparently asleep, but Sir Chad applauded with gusto.

"Oh, heavens me," said Cornelius, his hand on his heart. "That was atrocious. Still, it could have been worse. At least he didn't get to the second verse. As bad as the first verse is, the second is quite unfit for human ears. Absolutely scandalous."

CHAPTER FOURTEEN: FEAST

"Second verse!" shouted Gunthar from atop the Mayor's table.

There was a young goblin from Howe
*With **** **** and a **** with a buck*
*But her deer kept begging for **** **** ****
*What did she need? She needed a ****!*

Chapter 15
Visitors

After many observations I have concluded that any end to a drum circle must be, by necessity, awkward.

— *Considered Revelations, Book 182 "On Winding Down Drum Circles", Chapter 4, Verse 37*

Maryan led the group back into the Mayor's palace of Bluntworth. Although darkness settled over the town, a waning but nearly full moon rose to the east. Behind them, the town feast was going strong, with other citizens having taken up Gunthar's challenge to sing rowdy songs.

"That was a disaster." Maryan flopped down onto a bench in the small courtyard by their rooms.

Yang sat down next to her. "I'm so sorry, ma'am. The pine needles helped the Potion of Erudition work faster, but made the mango reaction worse."

"What happened, anyway?" Gunthar rubbed his head. "I was about to tell the Mayor about the prophecy, but the next thing I remember was Sir Humphrey pouring his drink on my face."

"Well, sir, you had laid down on our table after singing your song about the dragon. I thought the watered wine might awaken you."

"Aye, it did!"

Yang leaned in. "What happens now, ma'am?"

"I don't know." Maryan rubbed her temples. "The Mayor was very upset. He said we'd be confined to quarters. He'll keep us well-fed but locked in here until my parents arrive, I'm sure. And then I'll have to go home again."

The knight frowned. "But what about the prophecy?"

"It could be worse!" Cornelius strode to the center table, which still had two fresh apples in a bowl. "We can stay here in comfort. 'Well-fed,' you say? It's not all bad, right?"

"Hey, why so glum, everyone? You look like an ettin just farted on your pancakes!" A man in fringed leathers hopped into the courtyard from the low parapet at the side, then helped another

CHAPTER FIFTEEN: VISITORS

man over as well.

"Sir Chad?" Maryan stood, her jaw open. "How did you—"

"We climbed up the side of the palace, of course, Your Highness!" He bowed with a flourish.

"Lots of gargoyles everywhere on the south face. That helps." Squire Brock pulled his flask out of his jacket. "Let's get this party started!"

"Party!" Sir Chad and his squire exchanged the fistbump handshake again.

"Sir, this is not a time for merriment." Sir Humphrey gestured back at the princess. "Her Highness has been confined here indefinitely, along with all of us."

"Really?" Sir Chad looked at each in turn, then smiled. "We'll join you!"

Maryan recoiled. "Sir Chad, that's not necessary. We were hoping to have some time for quiet contemplation—"

"Drum circle!" shouted Sir Chad, and Squire Brock pulled a small drum out of his pack and began slapping his palms on it.

"Only Squire Brock has a drum, but the rest of you can circle up, you know, and maybe beat on furniture or something." Sir Chad tapped out a rhythm on the center table with his hands.

Maryan stepped forward. "Ah, Sir Chad, I appreciate the gesture, but we're not—"

"C'mon, everyone!" Sir Chad whacked on the table with a frenzy, then noted Cornelius standing nearby. "Hey, you're the Chronicler, right? You should write this down!" And he increased his table-pounding, accented with whoops and calls.

"Ah, well, Sir Chad, I'm not sure if I can really capture the, you know, the *spirit* of this—"

Sir Chad quieted his drumming and squinted at him. "Wait, how did a Chronicler join the group in the first place?"

Yang perked up at this. "That's right, Cornelius, I never heard how you joined Her Highness and Sir Humphrey."

"Well, that's actually kind of a funny story—"

"There's no time!" cried Maryan, pointing over the parapet. "A banshee!"

A shadowy form flew out of the night, its wings tinged silver by the low moon. Ragged wounds on its gray skin revealed decaying flesh beneath. It reached out to them with large, grasping claws, and screeched from a wide mouth full of sharp teeth.

"To arms!" Gunthar grabbed his axe.

Sir Humphrey raised his blade. "Onwards, Happenhouse!" He clicked the button at the hilt, then an explosion of lightning played across the landing, and the knight disappeared.

Yang grabbed her initiate's staff, then looked around in confusion. "What happened to the banshee?"

"And where is Sir Chad?" Squire Brock stood in horror, his small drum falling to the courtyard stone with a thump.

Cornelius pointed out across the parapet. "Oh no! The undead banshee has taken Sir Chad." He squinted. "I think he's being eaten."

"Ah, I've found Sir Humphrey." Gunthar pointed up at the roof above the courtyard, where Sir Humphrey lay above the gutter.

The knight raised a smoking hand. "Ouch."

"What is the meaning of all this racket?" The Mayor burst into the courtyard, accompanied by the councilor and two burly palace guards.

"The prophecy! It has struck!" Maryan pointed out where the banshee could be seen flapping away with its meal.

"What?" The Mayor squinted, then waved it aside. "I already told you. I've chosen to not believe the prophecy."

The councilor coughed. "Mayor, this is concrete proof of the rising tide of the undead."

The Mayor opened his mouth to retort, then closed it, staring after the departing monster.

"And it ate Sir Chad!" wailed Squire Brock.

"Get ahold of yourself, man," snapped the Mayor. "It's only one person dead. That's not a high mortality rate."

Gunthar pulled over a wooden chair from his room, and stood on it in an attempt to reach Sir Humphrey in the gutter.

"What happened?" asked the dazed knight as Gunthar worked to get the knight's leggings unhooked from a gargoyle.

"You need a grounding wire, I think," said Yang, looking up at him. "That sword is dangerous to hold. Like an electric eel."

"A serpent?"

"A bit like that, Chronicler, but underwater, and with electricity."

"No, a serpent!" Cornelius pointed to an undead boa constrictor

CHAPTER FIFTEEN: VISITORS

slithering over the parapet, leaving a trail of gray slime.

"Protect me!" screamed the Mayor, cowering behind his guards.

Sir Humphrey fell on top of Gunthar, and both crashed to the courtyard stone.

Yang raised her initiate's staff and stepped in front of Maryan, but the serpent coiled around Squire Brock in a flash, then heaved the man and itself over the parapet again.

Everyone stood in shock, staring at the abandoned drum at the edge of the courtyard, then Cornelius dashed over and looked down. "The undead boa constrictor has taken Squire Brock. I think it's eating him too."

"Oh, no." Maryan put her face in her hands.

"I'm sorry about your blind date, Your Highness," said Yang.

"And his wingman," added Cornelius.

Gunthar knelt. "We mourn their loss. Sir Chad was a free spirit, unfettered by convention or awareness of basic social cues. And his wingman, Squire Brock, was a faithful companion to the end."

"Will you let us enter the Badlands now, Mayor?" Maryan gestured east. "It's the only way to stop the undead."

"I told you, Your Highness, I've chosen not to believe the prophecy."

"But thousands of people could die!"

"It's a sacrifice I'm willing to make for the good of the economy."

The councilor stood by Maryan. "Mayor, I think it would be wise to listen. Their path will be perilous, but with the bishop they may be able to put an end to the undead attacks."

"Perilous, you say?" The Mayor surveyed the group in the courtyard, his eyes gleaming.

"It's very dangerous," said Maryan, "but according to the prophecy, we can defeat the Lich King with the bishop."

"I'm not appointing that Onkar person to be bishop. It's out of the question." The Mayor held up his hand. "However, I am a compassionate man. Even though I have chosen to not believe in the prophecy, I can see that it means a great deal to you. I will allow you to enter the Badlands if you insist on going."

"Without a ranger or the bishop?" Yang looked back and forth between Maryan and the Mayor.

"We'll go." Maryan turned to her followers. "We have to do

something, even without a ranger or the bishop."

"Very well! You can enter the Badlands tomorrow." The Mayor leaned forward. "I hope you appreciate that we are making an exception to our policy out of consideration for your feelings, Your Highness. And *no* bishop!"

Chapter 16
Badlands

Wish you were here, leading me out of this accursed place.

— *Considered Revelations, Book 322 "Collected Badlands Postcards", Chapter 27, Verse 2*

The morning broke cold and gray, a light mist rising from the packed earth of the Badlands. Dark clouds hovered on the eastern horizon.

"May be storms today," noted Gunthar.

"No, good barbarian." The councilor stood to one side. "There is always a cloud over that part of the Badlands. Tradition holds that the Castle of Terror used to stand there."

"Charming," said Cornelius, swallowing.

"'Tis nothing to be afraid of! Indeed, the tools of fear work against the foul demons there. The storm clouds act as a beacon to guide our way." Sir Humphrey patted the hilt of his sword.

"Well, Your Highness, here you are. Entering the Badlands as you requested." The Mayor put his hands on his hips. "And there's no shame in turning right around and heading back inside the walls."

Maryan looked back. The companions stood twenty paces beyond the town's eastern gatehouse, the walls of Bluntworth stretching out to the north and south. "Thank you, Mayor. But I won't return until we have defeated the Lich King."

"If you say so, ma'am. Since you remain determined to go, I am sending an observer on behalf of the city." The Mayor beckoned to someone behind him. "Bookkeeper Andi."

A woman in a crisp gray outfit stepped forward, holding a small book. "Of course, Mayor." Though about the same height as Maryan, she looked down, her lips pursed. "Greetings, Your Highness."

"Um, hello, Bookkeeper Andi."

Bookkeeper Andi regarded each of them in turn. "Are you the knight? Why are you here?" she asked Sir Humphrey.

"I'm bankrupt."

"I'm an accountant. I'm not impressed by bankruptcy." Her gaze rested last on Cornelius, who stood watching her as he leaned on his stick. She harrumphed at him and made a note in her book.

Maryan sighed. "Mayor, why do you need an observer?"

"Not my idea, I assure you. But it's been a while since anyone has gone into the Badlands, and the City Council insisted on sending someone to see what's out there." He bowed at her. "And to report back on how you fare, of course."

"We're going to fight a Lich King. I'm sure Bookkeeper Andi is a very good observer, but it will be dangerous."

"Of course. That is why we have also hired a guard for her." The Mayor snapped his fingers.

A man in dirty, rust-colored robes stepped forward. He carried a tall staff of blackened iron, with a glowing red orb on top. A worn satchel hung across his back, and a studded leather eyepatch covered his left eye.

The Mayor gestured at him. "This is Wizard Ignacio, the fiercest battlemage in these parts. He'll be protecting Bookkeeper Andi."

Ignacio's eye fixed on the distant thunderclouds over the Badlands. It shifted to meet Maryan. "Your Highness." His voice was like gravel being crushed by larger gravel in a land that was generally known for sharp rocks that crushed other sharp rocks. The wizard walked past her, his staff thumping on the hard ground.

The Mayor clapped his hands together. "Well, I'm sure you're all eager to get going. Best of luck, ma'am." With that, the Mayor turned and headed back into the gates, his entourage following.

The councilor half-turned as he left. "Good luck, Your Highness."

The Mayor's party walked back into Bluntworth, the palace and cathedral visible in the distance through the doorway. Then the gates closed, and Maryan was left staring at the hard town wall, a few guards on top glaring down at them.

Maryan shrugged. "Right, everyone, on we go."

They helped the protesting Cornelius atop Daisy again.

"Really, Your Highness, this isn't necessary. My ankle feels fine."

"I know, Chronicler, but I want to make sure you're fully recovered. We'll do a lot of walking today."

Gunthar hefted the large sacks containing Sir Humphrey's armor, which clattered and clanged as they shifted. "Do you think you'll

CHAPTER SIXTEEN: BADLANDS

wear this armor soon?"

"Indeed, I expect I will. Though 'tis awkward to walk in." The knight shouldered his large backpack. "And in all honesty, I haven't worn that set yet. That's the family armor."

Bookkeeper Andi raised her eyebrows as they walked east. "You've never worn the family armor?"

"No, ma'am. It's a basic set of knight's armor, but with some fiddly bits I didn't really understand."

Andi *harrumphed* again and made another note in her book.

Yang looked at the sacks of armor on Gunthar's back. "You wear plate mail while carrying an electric sword?"

"Of course!"

The apprentice shook her head. "I don't recommend wearing a suit of armor while holding that sword. You'll have conductors touching your skin the whole time, with a lot of voltage in play."

"Again, apprentice, I am ignorant of the magical arts. But this is how my ancestors always went into battle."

Ignacio stared at Yang. "You are an apprentice." His voice was now like gravel rolling uphill, which Maryan took to mean he was surprised.

"Yes." Yang held up her initiate's staff.

The battlemage shook his head. "Yet I can see no magic in you. None at all."

"I know. All the wizards tell me that."

Gunthar looked back over his shoulder. "Apprentice Yang, if all the wizards say you have no magic, what led you to the School of Wizardry in the first place?"

She shrugged. "I come from a small village in East Kathandar. Not long after I was born, the village seer said I was destined to become a great wizard. And when I turned eighteen, she said I should join the school. That was her dying request, so I went." Yang frowned. "Sometimes I wonder if she was mistaken. I mean, I can *see* magic. I can see magical items, spells, and even the magic in other wizards. But I can't see any in myself."

Ignacio rumbled next to her. "You've got the vision, perhaps. But not the power." Then he walked off.

The apprentice hung her head.

"Don't worry, Apprentice Yang. You must have some power.

Otherwise, why would you be in the prophecy?"

Yang raised her head again. "Thank you, ma'am. I sure hope you're right."

"You're lucky, apprentice." Sir Humphrey snorted. "You get to be *in* the prophecy, at least."

They walked on through the Badlands, the ground unyielding and gritty beneath their boots. Few plants lived here, save for one or two hardy sagebrush that clung to small cracks with their roots. Wind occasionally rose up and cast dust in their eyes, so the group became accustomed to raising a cloth over their face at the first sign of a breeze.

"I'm curious, Battlemage Ignacio." Gunthar caught up with the fast-walking man. "I've heard wizards see the origins of their staff when they find them. What did you see when you first touched your staff?"

"I saw the Caves of the Cursed," growled Ignacio. "I heard the screams of the damned. Within, goblins forged the iron, and quenched its fire in the blood of—"

The barbarian's face paled at the description. "Never mind." Gunthar let the wizard walk ahead.

In the early afternoon they reached a broad basin in the plains, where dusty hills rose across from them, sparse weeds fluttering in the breeze. The Badlands stretched in all directions, the high sun painting everything the color of bone. A wide stream burbled before them, flowing across their path.

"The Moonflow." Ignacio looked up and down the stream. "And no way to cross."

"No way to cross?" Gunthar laughed and removed his boots. "Only you southerners would need a bridge. Look how shallow it is. We can ford it here." He strode across in great steps.

"None can cross this direction except at the invitation of the Lich King himself. Do you have an invitation, barbarian?" Ignacio cackled, an unpleasant dry sound.

"Ouch!" Gunthar recoiled mid-stream, as if he'd run into something. He took out his axe and swung it, but the blade whistled through empty air. After a few more attempts with his hands and blade, he returned to the party, shaking his head. "Indeed, Your Highness, there's some sort of barrier there which I cannot pass, though my axe can't bite it."

Bookkeeper Andi made another note in her book.

Maryan took off her boots and waded out to the middle of the stream. The cold, clear water chilled her skin, and rocks and pebbles sparkled at the bottom. Just as Gunthar had said, a hard barrier ran down the middle of the stream. To her hand it felt spongy, though it resisted more and more as she pushed at it. But she could see nothing, and when she threw rocks at it, they sailed right through.

She returned to the others on the bank. "It is as Ignacio says. We can't pass this way."

"Can't pass this way?" Bookkeeper Andi raised her eyebrows. "You realize that the stream cuts through the Badlands entirely? There is no way around."

Maryan raised her chin. "The prophecy led us this far. I don't think a stream will stop us."

Ignacio chuckled again. "It appears to have stopped us for now."

The princess looked north, where flat plains receded into the distance. But to the south, the plains gave way to jagged canyons and plateaus. "Let's go that way."

"The Broken Heath?" Ignacio shrugged. "It's your call, Your Highness."

They spent the remainder of the afternoon walking south, following the stream. Though they could not cross it, the Moonflow provided fresh water and was a reliable guide.

"What are we looking for, ma'am?" asked Yang as they hiked.

"I don't know. The stream may be constricted to canyons further down. Someone may have built a bridge there."

"Maybe." Yang gazed further downstream to where the Broken Heath rose, low cliffs now visible in the evening sun.

In another hour, they reached the first of the bluffs, the stream's course continuing in a wide and eminently unbridged basin.

"Let's camp here," said Maryan. "We can continue our search in the morning."

They set up camp against the face of the bluff.

"There's no wood to be had for miles around," said Bookkeeper Andi. "So what will we do? Freeze here?"

"You think this is cold? Try the tundra sometime." Gunthar

brushed his leathers. "Just wrap your cloak around you."

The battlemage cackled unpleasantly at this, and the bookkeeper pressed her mouth in a thin line and made another note in her book. No one said anything after that, and they all huddled up in their cloaks and blankets and shivered through the night.

The morning broke silent and cold.

"Ah, that feels good," said Cornelius as the first rays of dawn struck them.

Bookkeeper Andi stretched her hands out to the sun as if warming herself at a fire.

"We've got another day of food, maybe," noted Gunthar as they broke camp. "There's no game here for us to hunt."

"Well, let's spend the time looking for a way across the Moonflow," said Maryan.

"Are you sure that is wise?" asked Ignacio. The wizard pointed northeast, where a dark cloud hung over the Badlands. "We're getting farther away from the Castle."

"The castle still stands?" asked Sir Humphrey, shielding his eyes from the sun.

"No longer," rasped Ignacio. "It fell when Archmage Omondi was betrayed. Now its secret chambers lie under the Badlands." His one eye peered into the dark shadows under the stormcloud.

"I for one am all in favor of going south," said Cornelius, pointing along the stream, away from the Badlands and the castle ruins. "That seems to be a very sensible direction."

Bookkeeper Andi made another *harrumphing* noise and added a note to her book.

Cornelius bristled. "Madam Bookkeeper, there is already a Chronicler here. You don't need to write anything down."

Andi looked at him, shook her head and wrote in her book again.

"Well, I never," said Cornelius, making a note of his own.

"Come now, good Chronicler," said Gunthar. "She's just doing her job. Let's not hold grudges."

They spent the morning clambering over rocks and chasms as the stream wound its way further into the Broken Heath. Sometimes the stream would drop into a narrow canyon on its own, leaving the adventurers to scramble and attempt to find their own way to follow, like an uppity Bookkeeper making futile attempts to assemble a coherent sentence despite an obvious lack of Chronicler training.

They had lunch on a small plateau, baking in the sun. By late afternoon, the company was hot and tired and no closer to crossing the Moonflow. They had reached a wider canyon, able to approach the stream again.

Maryan waded in and pounded on the invisible barrier. "It's still here! How far does this barrier go? All the way to the ocean?"

"Perhaps it stretches from one end of the earth to the other." Gunthar looked further downstream.

"Nay, good barbarian." Sir Humphrey wiped his brow. "'Twouldst be most awkward for coastal traffic. Can you imagine being on a sailing ship, and then *thwack*, you and your companions are flung back by the barrier while the ship keeps going?"

Ignacio chuckled, but with more malice than mirth. "Indeed, the barrier ends many days from here. The stream grows to a river, then dissolves into the Salt Marsh, a more formidable barrier than anything magic can construct. Getting around the Moonflow is many weeks travel, north or south, and both routes are perilous."

"That's wonderful." Maryan glared at the stream.

"Wait," said Yang. "If people can't cross the barrier, even on a ship, why do we think we can cross a bridge?"

Maryan shrugged. "I don't know. Does anyone have any better ideas?"

That night, they camped in a south-facing canyon, the earth still warm from the sun. The stream taunted them all night, chattering and gurgling as it flowed past, again shallow and wide, but remained impassable with its magical barrier.

Maryan got very little sleep. She huddled in a thin blanket, staring at the Moonflow. What could they do? They had come all this way, and she didn't intend to give up. But there was nothing here she could fight, no army or beast to overcome. The bewitched stream stood as a dispassionate, impenetrable obstruction.

In the morning, Gunthar asked the question on everyone's mind. "We're about out of food, Your Highness. Where to now?"

Maryan shook her head. The stormcloud over the castle was now too distant to see, far to the northeast. "We need to find a town. Is anything closer than Bluntworth?"

"No, ma'am," said Ignacio. "Bluntworth is the only town within several days walk."

"Let's head back to Bluntworth, then. We'll cut across the Broken Heath, and follow canyons north to the Badlands if necessary."

Gunthar nodded. "Very well, ma'am."

"Let me add," said Cornelius as he climbed up on Daisy again, "that I think you've done the best you could. You kept pushing for a way to reach the castle ruins, and were turned back only by lack of provisions."

"Thank you, Chronicler." Maryan fought to keep her voice even, though she felt as if she had been punched in the gut. "But I think the Badlands have won this round."

They filled their waterskins at the Moonflow and cursed the invisible barrier a final time, then turned away. The next several hours were a grueling clamber back to the northwest, trying to cut as directly to Bluntworth as possible to save time. But the Broken Heath worked against them, with canyons and deep ravines blocking their path at many points. Usually they'd turn north when the way became impassable, knowing that eventually they'd reach the flat Badlands, but sometimes even that path required scrambling up steep inclines or broken steps of fractured ground.

At noon, they had an unsatisfying meal of the remaining crumbs on hand, then set off again under the sun with empty stomachs. The Broken Heath was like the top of a great cake, its crust cracked by baking, appearing as a handsome plum loaf with a light dusting of sugar.

"You look hungry, Chronicler," said the knight, looking up at him.

"I am, sir!"

An hour later, they found the way north and west impassable, and went further south to go around, but after a few minutes another steep drop blocked their path.

"Oh, by the cursed wolves of the wild wastes," said Gunthar. "Why won't the Heath let us escape?"

"There may be a way down this way," pointed out Maryan. Sure enough, the cracked ground of the Broken Heath had crumbled into the canyon at the edge, leaving a tenuous path down along the cliff face. The adventurers descended in single file, a hand on the sheer wall to their right for balance.

CHAPTER SIXTEEN: BADLANDS

Near the bottom, an ominous crack of thunder rang from the top of the cliff, and pebbles rained down.

"Quick, everyone!" shouted Maryan. "Run!"

They dashed madly down the broken steps, Cornelius complaining as Daisy jumped down the boulders, more rocks crashing down next to them. A large boulder bounced near Maryan, and she had to duck to avoid being smashed. Behind her, Ignacio screamed as the path collapsed beneath his feet, but Gunthar grabbed the man's arm and pulled him back up. By some luck, the party made it safely down and hurried further up the canyon, the route behind them dissolved into a creaking pile of rubble and dust.

The adventurers stood in the sun, panting and gasping in shock. Daisy stared at them before finding some brush to graze.

"We're not getting back that way," noted Gunthar dryly. "I hope there is another way out of the canyon."

"It narrows ahead," said Maryan, walking north. "Let's see if there's a way out there."

They followed the princess, the canyon narrowing as they went, the walls closing in above them. Just as they thought they'd hit a flat wall at the end, Maryan discovered that the final stretch of the canyon crooked to the right.

"Oh my." She stopped and stared ahead once she'd made the turn.

"What is it, ma'am?" Gunthar stepped forward with concern, then stopped himself. "Oh my."

The wizard stepped forward, his eye scrunched up in irritation. "What are you fools stopping for?" Then he also stepped back. "By the unholy chants of the dark order!"

The rest of the party rounded the bend in the canyon. Ahead of them, the canyon ended at a sheer wall, but a large opening loomed at the base, topped with an arch of carved stone blocks.

They had stumbled upon a secret passage under the Badlands.

Chapter 17
Caverns

Heed the warnings.

— Considered Revelations, Book 74 "Why Heeding Remains Relevant, Even Today, Especially in Caverns", Chapter 19, Verse 2

The adventurers stood in the shadows at the base of the narrow canyon. Cool air flowed out of the opening ahead, chilling their boots.

"What does that say?" Maryan pointed to the keystone of the arch above the opening, where weathered characters formed a single word.

Wizard Ignacio stepped forward, reading the inscription. "It says 'Beware' in the lost tongue of the ancients."

"What do you mean, lost tongue?" asked Cornelius. "If it's lost, how can you read it?"

"It's not really lost, just abandoned." Ignacio waved his hand. "Very vague and torturous syntax, so no one uses it anymore."

Bookkeeper Andi paled. "A passage underground! Could it lead under the barrier?"

"Let's hope so." Maryan tightened her gauntlets. "It's certainly heading the right direction."

"But that would mean reaching the castle!"

"Aye, 'tis the point of this entire expedition." Sir Humphrey peered into the darkness ahead. "Indeed, there does seem to be a passage here."

The Bookkeeper pointed at the inscription. "But it says 'Beware'!"

"Not to worry, Madame Bookkeeper." Sir Humphrey shrugged it off. "'Tis likely an admonition to watch your step. There's a ledge here at the opening. Mayhaps the ancients were warning us of a tripping hazard."

"Could it be a message for those *leaving* the passageway?" Gunthar looked back down the canyon. "As in, 'Beware, for the Broken Heath sucks.'"

"What? It's clearly warning us not to go in." Bookkeeper Andi

CHAPTER SEVENTEEN: CAVERNS

looked back down from the inscription, but everyone else had already walked into the opening. A rock clattered somewhere in the canyon far behind, and she hurried into the passage herself, stumbling over the ledge at the opening.

"It's dark," noted Gunthar.

"Quiet, fools." Then Ignacio whispered to his staff and its red orb brightened, casting a torch-like light around them.

"The passage does head northeast, as far as I can tell." Maryan put her hands on her hips. "Who knows if it leads to the castle, but there's a good chance that it cuts under the Moonflow, at least."

Ignacio's eye fixed on the shadows ahead. "After you, Your Highness."

Maryan led them further into the passageway, with Gunthar and Sir Humphrey next. Ignacio strode in the middle of the party, his staff raised to provide light, the Bookkeeper cowering after him. Yang and Cornelius walked in the rear, leading an as-usual unconcerned Daisy.

The flat and dusty floor remained featureless, and the walls and ceiling curved over them. Fortunately, the passageway was wide, easily enough for two to walk abreast, and the roof stayed out of reach above. Their footsteps echoed around them, every small noise amplified in the enclosed space.

After some time, the walls gleamed with water, and the air became moist.

Gunthar turned to Sir Humphrey. "Are you humming?"

"Nay, good man, I thought mayhaps *you* were attempting a tune."

"It's not us." Maryan put a hand to the cold, wet wall. "It's something else."

"We pass beneath the Moonflow. Its water is seeping through the walls." Ignacio scanned the ceiling overhead, which occasionally dripped onto them. "The noise we hear is the barrier. Perhaps it is angry that we have escaped its reach."

"What?" Bookkeeper Andi furrowed her brow. "We can't have reached the Moonflow this quickly."

"We walked away from the stream for several hours on the Broken Heath, but we had to keep backtracking, climbing and cutting away from our heading. The passageway is leading us straight," noted Maryan. "It's much faster."

A large drop of water fell on Bookkeeper Andi's face, and she shook her head with a curse.

"We're past the barrier now!" Maryan walked onwards again.

"Indeed." Ignacio followed, peering into the blackness.

They pressed on for an untold amount of time, though Ignacio claimed it was only a few hours. The passageway had minor twists and turns but mostly carried on unerringly ahead.

"What if it's just leading us in a big circle?" asked Gunthar. "We'd never know."

"Aye, sir, or even a wide spiral down into the depths of the underworld." The knight looked around them with a shiver.

"Bah." Ignacio waved his hand. "By my arts, I know our location, and the time. The passage leads us true."

"I hope you're right, Wizard Ignacio," said Maryan.

Only a few minutes later, the passageway opened into a wide and round chamber, with many stalactites and stalagmites and more than a few natural columns. On one side lay a dark, still pool.

"Water!" said Gunthar, approaching it.

"Hold, barbarian!" Ignacio's staff flared brighter. "Do not touch it. We are near the Castle of Terror, or its remains. Water here will be polluted."

"Very well." Gunthar frowned and took a small sip from his waterskin instead.

A growling noise echoed from the distant ceiling.

"What was that?" Yang held her initiate staff in front of her.

Gunthar hefted his axe. "Goblins, maybe?"

"Nay, sir, it sounded smaller. Likely kobolds, or other vermin." Sir Humphrey lifted his hands. "Mayhaps a denizen of the cave will face the wrath of my fisticuffs."

"Ah, sorry, that was my stomach." Cornelius' face shone redder than normal in Ignacio's red light. "I'm starving."

"No shame, good Chronicler." Sir Humphrey dropped his fists. "I also feel the keen bite of hunger."

"I'm sorry, everyone. I know it's dinner time. But I think we should press on while we have some energy left." Maryan gestured ahead, where the passageway continued out of the cavern.

Gunthar tightened his belt. "Lead on, ma'am."

The passageway continued ahead, but now started climbing. At times it made sharp turns, and the footing became uneven.

"I see something!" exclaimed Yang.

"Where, apprentice?" Gunthar peered around in the dim red light. "I see nothing."

"It's ahead. A glowing fog."

Maryan squinted. "I don't see it."

"I do. Dark magic, which only the Apprentice and I can see." Ignacio's growl echoed around them. "The Castle lies but a short distance ahead."

"We're close, then," said Maryan.

Only a minute later, the passageway opened into another chamber, though smaller than the last one. It was round, with a ceiling far above them in shadow. The passageway continued ahead through another opening in the chamber wall, but everyone stopped and stared.

A skeleton leaned against the far wall, shreds of clothing stuck to its frame.

"Oh my," breathed Bookkeeper Andi. "Another warning."

Gunthar's eyebrows went up. "A warning? How so?"

Andi pointed at it. "Can you not see? The path is marked by a skeleton. The meaning is plain. It says, 'This is what happens to those who continue.'"

"I don't know." Gunthar rubbed his chin. "The pose seems far too casual."

"To me, it speaks of ennui." Yang looked around the small, plain chamber. "Maybe the meaning is, 'You'll die of boredom if you stay here.'"

Andi looked back and forth between the apprentice and the skeleton. "What?"

"Nay, 'tis clearly a warning about posture!" Sir Humphrey pointed at the skeleton's elbow, sagging against the wall. "Those who slouch will end up skeletons in a forgotten cave. My mother used to tell me that all the time."

"There's nothing here," said Maryan. "Let's carry on."

Andi remained behind as everyone else left through the next opening. "We can't keep going. It's a warning!"

Daisy looked at her, snorted, and continued after Cornelius.

"Fine," said Andi, following them.

In a moment, the passageway opened into another similar chamber. Again, the party halted. A skeleton lay curled up on the floor against the far wall.

"Oh my," said Bookkeeper Andi, pointing. "You must admit, this is a warning."

"What?" Gunthar waved it off. "They died in their sleep. That's hardly a warning."

Yang peered at the dusty bones. "Or maybe someone was tidying this cavern? They may not have wanted another skeleton lounging against a wall."

"This is ridiculous." Bookkeeper Andi put her hands on her hips, facing Gunthar. "Two skeletons in a row. These are clear signs of danger."

The barbarian raised his eyebrows. "I find the meaning ambiguous at best."

"Ambiguous?" Andi's voice rose, her words echoing in the room. She pointed at the skeleton. "How could impending peril be made any more obvious?"

"Well, if I was going to make a statement about impending peril, I'd make it much more plain. It would have to be more than just an abandoned skeleton. You'd want a pose that conveyed complete desperation." Gunthar illustrated with broad gestures. "Like, maybe the person was stabbed in the front, so, you know, they'd have this expression of surprise and anguish"—here Gunthar demonstrated with an expression of his own—"and then they'd turn to run away, but then they'd be stabbed in the back, and they'd fall to the ground with an even bigger expression of fear." The barbarian crouched with an expression of anguish and surprise and terror.

"That makes no sense." Andi glared at him. "A skeleton can't show an expression."

He straightened. "It could be mummified, then."

"Mummified?" The bookkeeper turned away, exasperated.

"'Twouldst be difficult to see both wounds, sir," noted Sir Humphrey. "For if the mummy lay on its back, you wouldn't see the wounds there, and likewise if it lay on its front, the opposite problem."

"It would have to be lying on its side," said Gunthar.

The knight nodded. "That might work."

CHAPTER SEVENTEEN: CAVERNS

Bookkeeper Andi rolled her eyes.

Ignacio stared into the dark passage ahead. "We must continue."

Yang swallowed, following the man's intense stare. "We're very close. The magic is almost overwhelming."

"Let's go," said Maryan, and she led them ahead through a natural stone opening.

The passageway climbed again, then opened into yet another chamber. In the middle of the floor a mummy lay on its side, a spear in its belly and an arrow in its back, the dry face a mixture of anguish and surprise and terror.

"A mummy that's been attacked from the front and back," breathed Andi.

"See?" said Gunthar. "That's much clearer."

"One wonders, why were the earlier skeletons there?" Sir Humphrey stroked his mustache as he thought.

"Maybe they were practice attempts?" Yang pointed to the mummy. "It'd be hard to get this right the first time."

"We're turning back, right?" Andi looked at them.

Maryan's gaze was steel and fire, together, but not so hot as to melt the steel, more like a fire that showed how hard and sharp the steel was, without actually damaging it. "We're confronting the lich king."

Gunthar dropped the large sacks of armor with a crash. "Get ready, everyone."

"Right." Sir Humphrey pulled pieces of armor out of the sacks.

"You can't be serious." Andi pleaded with them. "Look, we've seen enough. Clearly, the prophecy is real. We've found a way under the barrier. We can go back and report—"

"If the prophecy is real, that's all the more reason to confront the Lich King now." Maryan tied her hair back. "Before things get worse."

"Now, where do you think this goes?" Sir Humphrey held up a clasp.

Gunthar squinted down at the pile of metal plates and small ceramic discs scattered on the floor. "What kind of armor is that?"

"'Tis my family armor, sir. Though I know not how to assemble it."

Yang crouched nearby, then held up one of the ceramic pieces.

"An insulator!"

"What?" The knight regarded the armor pieces again. "Is it magic?"

"Not quite, but look, this piece goes here"—she placed a ceramic plate on Sir Humphrey's shoulder—"and then the armor piece goes on top." She tightened the strap, binding the metal pauldron against the ceramic, a good inch above the knight's skin. "See? You can wear the whole suit, without the metal touching you. You're insulated."

"In faith, good apprentice! I see now what you mean. Ha!"

Gunthar, Yang, and Sir Humphrey assembled the rest of the armor with gusto.

Maryan put a hand to her forehead. "Oh, by the gods of afternoon tea. I came all this way, and I don't even have a weapon."

Bookkeeper Andi made a note in her book.

Maryan swallowed. She'd been so fixed on their destination that she hadn't thought much about what they'd do when they got here. Why did she think she could skip across the Badlands and battle a Lich King?

Nonetheless, she was here to fulfill a prophecy. The strange peasant lady had seemed to think she could do it. And it wasn't like she could turn back now.

Casting about the chamber, Maryan noted the mummy on the floor. She strode over and put a foot on its shoulder, and pulled the spear out with a dry creak. The cold steel glinted as she inspected it, then tested it with her finger. "Still sharp."

"Your Highness, you can't be serious..." Andi's voice trailed off. The bookkeeper stepped back, apparently giving up on further protest.

Maryan walked back to the group, the spear at her side. "Is everyone ready?"

Sir Humphrey stood, now in full armor. The plates were decorated with scrollwork and the letter 'H.' He tapped the hilt of his sword. "All set, ma'am."

Gunthar raised an eyebrow. "It's assembled, but... Well, it seems a bit *puffy*, doesn't it?"

Indeed, the knight's armor appeared a size or two too large, his head almost lost between the large plates hovering over his shoulders. "Puffy?"

"Don't worry about it, Sir Humphrey." Yang studied the ceramic-backed layers of metal. "The insulators make it look big, but I think this is reasonably safe."

"Are you fools ready?" Ignacio stared at the dark entrance to the passageway with his one eye. He licked his lips. "The Teapot awaits."

"We're here to stop the Lich King, Ignacio," said Maryan. "Not to take the Teapot."

"Speak for yourself." Ignacio walked ahead, the light atop his staff now blazing.

"Hey, you're supposed to be guarding me!" complained Bookkeeper Andi.

"Quick, everyone, follow him!" Maryan pointed after the departing wizard. "He's our light source."

The battlemage walked swiftly, and they all jogged to catch up, Sir Humphrey creaking in his oversized armor.

"Wizard Ignacio, please wait for us!" called Maryan. "We need to work together to defeat the Lich King."

"You idiots will only get in my way," he called back. "Best flee while you can. You don't have the skill to stand up to him."

"He's gone mad." Gunthar made spinning motions with a finger by his head.

Andi sputtered angrily. "He's supposed to be my bodyguard. I have a receipt!"

"'Tis clear that the battlemage has decided to strike out on his own," said Sir Humphrey. "But fear not, Madame Bookkeeper. We will protect you."

Andi pushed past him. "I don't want a puffy knight with outdated ideals of chivalry. The city paid for a battlemage!"

A bright light ahead lit the passageway now. A set of large steps lay before them, and Gunthar and Sir Humphrey stayed back to help Daisy and Cornelius get up.

Maryan and Andi rounded a corner and emerged into a final chamber. A large column of rock partially screened the entrance, and they peered around it cautiously. Unlike previous chambers, this was a massive space, large enough to fit a small village, as if enormous bubbles had formed in the rock and merged, creating a moonscape of raised platforms and low dark pools, the entire place dotted with columns and spikes of hard rock. Glowing orbs at scattered points along the walls lit the room, almost as bright as daylight.

And against the distant far wall of the chamber, a large chest sat on a raised dais, glowing with a golden light.

"Is the Teapot in there?" wondered Maryan.

Certainly Ignacio appeared to have no doubts. The battle mage strode across the broken ground towards the chest, his staff raised high, bathing him in red light.

"No one else seems to be here. That's good." Bookkeeper Andi barely breathed, then ducked back behind the column of rock. "I'm afraid to make any noise. I don't want to disturb anything."

"Don't worry, Bookkeeper," whispered Maryan.

A metallic crash erupted from the passageway behind them, followed by a knight's swearing.

"I'm so sorry, Sir Humphrey!" called the Chronicler from the darkness.

"Pay no mind, Chronicler. 'Tis most awkward to walk in this armor."

"Cornelius, throw me that rope!" shouted Yang. "We can pull Sir Humphrey back up with Daisy's help."

"Oh, by the small gods of irritation! Are we there yet?" Gunthar yelled from further back. "These leathers are chafing like tundra heather."

The others exited the passageway, blinking in the light of the chamber next to Maryan and Andi.

"Wow, it's bright in here!" exclaimed Gunthar. "That's a nice change."

All at once, the lights around the chamber dimmed, plunging it into twilight. One great table of rock ahead of Ignacio brightened, lit by a falling rain of glowing white drops.

Ignacio stepped back, his staff held before him.

In the midst of the glowing rain, a figure materialized. One moment there was empty air, but the next there stood a creature in flowing purple robes, a cowl over its face, the air around it crackling with sinister energy.

Maryan's face was grim. "The Lich King."

The purple form turned to face them, its skin a translucent gray.

"Who," it intoned, the rocks shaking, "who disturbs my domain?"

Chapter 18
Lich

Lich Kings.

— *Considered Revelations, Book 87 "List of Things Which Are So Scary That, If You Meet One, You Will Pee", Chapter 1, Verse 1*

Maryan and the others crouched behind the large pillar of rock, observing the scene in the great chamber before them. The lights in the walls flickered, as if dim white torchlight, while luminous threads bathed the Lich King, standing on a raised shelf of rock.

Before him stood a robed form with a blazing red staff. "I am Wizard Ignacio, and I have come to take that which you have held for too long."

"What's he doing?" hissed Andi.

"He's taunting a Lich King," said Gunthar.

"He's after the Teapot." Maryan shook her head.

"At least he's left us out of it," said Cornelius. "That's nice."

"And I bring you a sacrifice," said Ignacio to the Lich King. "You can have the lives of those behind me."

The Chronicler sighed. "Or maybe not."

The Lich King leaned towards Ignacio with a sneer. "I don't make deals, *wizard*."

Ignacio raised his chin. "Then I will end you."

A hacking laugh echoed in the great room. "You sad mortal. None can defeat me." Quick as a squirrel, or maybe faster, the Lich shot out a skeletal hand, releasing a blast of fire.

The wizard raised his staff, and the fire rolled past him, as if deflected by an invisible shield, though he staggered back a step.

Maryan's face warmed with the fire, though it burned several paces away.

"Ooh, that's a nice fire blast," said Yang. "He's good."

Ignacio returned a fire blast of his own, though the Lich King parried it in a similar way.

"Why do you smile, mortal?" asked the Lich King, his voice

CHAPTER EIGHTEEN: LICH

dripping with malice.

"Because I know something you do not!" cried Ignacio, and he tossed his staff to his other hand. "I am *not* left-handed!"

He released another, larger fire blast, and the Lich and the rock shelf were consumed by fire.

"The left-handed trick!" exclaimed Gunthar. "Works every time!"

Then the fires faded, revealing the shelf and the Lich, both completely unharmed.

"Oh," said Gunthar.

"I also am not left-handed," said the Lich. "I'm ambidextrous." With that, he released a double-barreled fire blast, both hands extended in a super-squirrel move.

The adventurers turned away from the bright flash and cowered from the heat. A studded leather eyepatch flew between Maryan and Andi, struck the wall next to them and fell to the ground, on fire. Further in the chamber, Ignacio's scorched iron staff fell with a clang in a burned-out pit, the red crystal cracked and dark.

"The battlemage has fallen." Sir Humphrey shook his head.

"Oh, no." Bookkeeper Andi pursed her lips. "I hope the city can get a refund."

Gunthar knelt. "We mourn his loss. Though we knew Wizard Ignacio for only a short time before he betrayed us, he was a guiding light in the darkness. And he died doing what he loved best, backstabbing other people in pursuit of treasure."

"Now," said the Lich, his voice like broken glass scattering on a floor, "where are my sacrifices?"

"Running, right?" said Bookkeeper Andi. "We're leaving."

"Uh-oh." Gunthar pointed behind them. Skeletal forms appeared in the passageway, shuffling towards them, bony arms raised with swords and spears.

"It has been so long since I've had guests!" The Lich King laughed and spread his arms. "I extend to you the *full* hospitality of the Castle of Terror."

The great chamber rumbled, and small rocks and dust pelted them from the ceiling. More skeletons rose from the ground, all over the room.

"Ha!" Gunthar shrugged and hefted his axe. "It's just a bunch of skeletons. We can take these."

"Indeed, sir. These undead fiends shall taste Gwendoline's edge!"

"What are those?" Bookkeeper Andi pointed past the column.

"Blight it all." Yang shook her head. "He's got *two* undead wizards."

Robed forms flanked the Lich King, each on their own rock platform. Their robes were tattered, their dry skin cracked and flaky, their eye sockets empty, yet they leered at the adventurers with a vicious focus.

"You have to applaud the planning," noted Gunthar. "See how he's got himself and his wizards up high like that? Hard to reach, and they've got overlapping, unobstructed fields of fire."

The nearest wizard flicked his wrist, and a small speck of crackling blackness wobbled in the air towards them.

"A Hawking Hole!" cried Yang. "Duck!"

They all fell to the floor, except for Daisy, who shuffled some distance away, and Sir Humphrey, who followed her. The Hawking Hole hit the wall and exploded, rock spraying everywhere. A high-velocity pebble ricocheted off the knight's breastplate with a clang.

"By the deficits of the export department!" swore Andi, lifting her head from the ground. "We're finished!"

"Mind the undead!" called Gunthar.

The skeletons were upon them, a stumbling mass of bones and sharp edges. Some charged from the passageway, others from one side of the rock column, and more swarmed from elsewhere in the chamber.

"To the princess!" cried Sir Humphrey. He swung his sword, cutting down an advancing line of undead.

"Take that, spawn of the underworld!" Gunthar hewed through another rank, bones falling in a clatter. "Look at that." He pointed to one dismembered skeleton. "No one's worn collars like that in at least six hundred years."

"Are those *ruffles?*" asked Yang, peering over.

"I know, right?" Gunthar hacked through another group of undead. "This place is like a time capsule."

Another Hawking Hole exploded, not far from Bookkeeper Andi and Daisy, and she bolted. Not Daisy, but Bookkeeper Andi. She screamed and fled for a far end of the huge chamber.

Daisy watched Andi run by, then trotted after her.

CHAPTER EIGHTEEN: LICH

"Bookkeeper Andi!" called Maryan. Then a skeletal warrior charged the princess, and she cut and smashed it with her spear.

"I'll help," said Gunthar, but then he dropped his axe again, and it went clattering away on the hard ground. "Oh, bother. One second." He chased after his weapon, dodging another skeleton.

"Stay here, ma'am, barbarian. I'll save her." Sir Humphrey careened after the Bookkeeper in his oversized armor, Yang following him.

Cornelius also hobbled after with his leafy stick. "Daisy!"

Bookkeeper Andi reached a far corner and, finding nowhere further to run, turned and screamed again. Before her advanced many skeletons, weapons raised.

Sir Humphrey charged forward, holding his sword high. "Onwards, Happenhouse!"

The mighty blade of Gwendoline shot through with lightning, and the knight cut through the skeletons in one stroke, dry bones shattering and splintering with the energy.

A great warrior from an age long past charged Yang, and she turned and caught its blade on one end of her initiate's staff, continued her spin and whacked its jaw with the other end. The jawbone went flying, but even before it landed, she had turned again, sweeping the skeleton's legs out from under it, then smashed its skull.

"You've got it, Apprentice!" called Gunthar from across the room. He flashed her a thumbs-up sign, then slashed through another rank of advancing warriors.

Sir Humphrey raised his blade to strike an advancing horde, but a bolt of lightning from the sword shot over his chest and arms. A thundering boom echoed in the chamber, and Sir Humphrey flew back into the wall. "Ouch!"

Yang frowned. "That blade arcs like crazy. I don't know what those ancient elvish swordmakers were thinking."

"Sir Humphrey?" Cornelius hobbled up to the knight.

"Look out!" called Yang. A Hawking Hole flew over towards the Bookkeeper. Yang jumped up and stood before it, holding up her initiate's staff.

The tiny black dot touched her staff and exploded, and the nearby skeletons fell back. The blast shattered Yang's staff, and threw the apprentice to the side.

For the moment, no skeletons approached. Cornelius tossed his leafy stick away.

Sir Humphrey blinked at him. "Chronicler?"

"My ankle's fine now. Quick!" Cornelius grabbed Sir Humphrey, who blinked but appeared to recognize him. He put Daisy's reins in his hands. The knight wobbled compliantly after the horse as she led him back to Maryan. The Chronicler found Bookkeeper Andi amidst the dust and falling debris and pulled her with him.

Two skeletons stepped forward, blades raised.

"Ah!" The Chronicler tripped and fell backwards, and Andi shrieked.

Sir Humphrey leapt forward with a cry, and with gauntlet-clad fists punched their bony faces. Both skeletons toppled back, their skulls split.

Sir Humphrey stood his ground before another advancing rank of enemies, waving his fists before him. "Are there others who wouldst fain touch the Bookkeeper? You shall taste the wrath of my fisticuffs!"

"Come on, you fool," said Andi, but she said it less coldly this time, and she pulled him and Cornelius after her. They reached Maryan and Gunthar before any skeletons could touch them.

"Whew," said Cornelius. "That was close."

Maryan beheaded a skeleton with a sweep of her spear, then pushed another back and sliced off its arm. "Wait. Where's Yang?"

All color drained from the Chronicler's face. "Oh, no, ma'am. I forgot."

They looked back to the far end of the chamber in horror, where the apprentice lay unmoving on the ground, pieces of her initiate's staff scattered around her. Between them and Yang stood many ranks of skeletal warriors.

"Apprentice!" called Gunthar.

Sir Humphrey staggered forward, his mustache smoking. "I'll save her."

"It's too late." Bookkeeper Andi's eyes went wide, and she put a hand over her mouth.

"Stay together!" cried Gunthar. "This is our last stand!"

The party stood in a circle facing outward as masses of skeletons

CHAPTER EIGHTEEN: LICH

descended upon them.

Across the chamber, the apprentice woke and groggily raised her head from the brittle ground. Her ears still rang from the near-miss with the Hawking Hole. Her vision blurred, and everything sounded far away.

Yang could hear her compatriots calling, but they were unseen, at some distance behind ranks of oncoming skeletons. She staggered to her feet and felt her face, sticky from blood. A cut on her forehead stung, and her nose bled. Wiping her face with her sleeve, she went to pick up her initiate's staff, but of course it had been destroyed, leaving pieces not much larger than toothpicks.

"Oh," she said. While she had always wanted to be an apprentice, the ruined staff seemed to be a final statement on the matter, a chapter in her life that was now completely closed.

She blinked and looked over the oncoming masses of skeletons. Raised on a platform of rock, the nearest undead wizard smiled at her, a full set of teeth behind dry skin, a pallid glow shining through empty eye sockets. It raised a hand and sent another Hawking Hole at her, as if tossing her a bouquet of flowers.

The incoming singularity crackled and hissed, the small black dot distorting space around it.

Looking down, she spied the stick which Cornelius had discarded. It was a lumpy, awkward stretch of oak, with a leafy shoot still growing out of the top. She'd sometimes wondered why the Chronicler had bothered to bring the bough all the way from the Forest of Madness. But now, all that mattered was that there was something she could grab, and perhaps use as a weapon, or a shield.

She reached down and picked it up.

The entire chamber disappeared, as if a painting that someone had suddenly yanked away. Everything went quiet, and Apprentice Yang found herself staring at an acorn.

The acorn lay on a grassy hill, and it had fallen beneath its parent tree. The parent was a quiet, unassuming oak on the east side of the forest, and everyone had always thought that it and its offspring would never amount to much more than firewood.

But everyone was wrong.

A chipmunk dashed up, spotted the acorn, and placed it in its cheek. Then it scrambled to the top of the hill and started digging furiously. Once a proper hole had been dug, the chipmunk placed the acorn within and covered it all up again. Then, satisfied that it had a cache of food it could return to later, the chipmunk dashed off to another part of the forest.

Now, chipmunks being what they are, with many caches to keep track of and an entire forest to explore, this particular acorn was abandoned. And so, rather than being eaten in the winter by a hungry chipmunk, it sprouted and grew.

All the seasons flashed by Apprentice Yang in a dizzying sequence. The acorn grew and grew, from a taproot to a shoot to a sapling, then to an oak tree, and became taller and wider and stronger. In time, it towered at the top of the hill, its branches great and numerous and it was known within the forest as a *good* tree, a friendly tree, a place you could shelter or even live.

Multiple generations of robins nested in the upper canopy, and many other chipmunks and squirrels made homes lower down. During storms, the wind would blow and rain would drive in hard sheets, but the tree kept its branches spread, stoutly protecting the deer that would often shelter under its boughs.

And so it lived for almost two hundred years, its fame spreading throughout the forest, until the mighty storm of New Year's Eve four years ago.

The storm blew in from the south, some said spurred by a god of the winds, jealous of the attentions of the sea, and the gale howled across all of the Flower Hills and the Golden Plains and especially the Forest of Madness. It was a vicious storm, and it shredded houses and boats and dashed at least one ship to splinters near Southport.

At the Forest of Madness, it was an evil storm, and it shot bolts of lightning into innocent trees and attempted to bring boughs down on top of the animals. The mighty oak at the top of the hill fought back, waving its branches, blocking the attacks of the storm, as deer and other beasts huddled near the trunk.

In a last desperate act of malice, the storm spent its final energy on a great bolt, arcing downwards with roaring thunder, intent on destroying all the animals massed there. But the tree sacrificed itself instead, placing its boughs before the bolt, and shattered into a smoking ruin.

The storm ended, the clouds melting away, leaving a ruined stump at the top of the hill. The animals of the forest sadly abandoned the place, having lost a warrior and friend.

But in its last breath, the tree channeled all of its energy and spirit into one misshapen bough, flung far away by the final blast. The leafy branch lay on the side of the hill, until wind and at least one curious bear carried it further down, where it rested on a pile of decaying leaves for four winters.

Then the staff was chanced upon by a knight, one Sir Humphrey Happenhouse, and given to a Chronicler who unwittingly carried it halfway across the continent as his crutch, all so that ex-Apprentice Yang would have it when she needed it.

Hello, Yang, it seemed to say. *I have been waiting for you.*

The chamber returned, all at once, as if someone had placed the painting back on the wall, and Yang blinked at the commotion, skeletons still advancing, the deadly Hawking Hole now only a few yards away, flying towards her.

Just as before, she could see the magic in the room. The Lich King blazed as an intense bonfire of power, the two magicians appearing as smaller flames, the flying Hawking Hole a sparkling ember. And just as before, she could sense no power in herself.

But the lack of her own power no longer concerned her. Instead, having no power seemed to be *part* of her, as if the absence of magic was magic in its own right.

She was meant to mold the magic that was already here, rather than add her own.

Out of the corner of her eye, she saw the barbarian, battling hordes of the undead. As he'd taught her, he did not swing blindly or furiously, but moved fluidly and with intent, using his opponents' attacks against them.

Yang snapped her attention back to the Hawking Hole bearing down on her. She considered the bundle of magic, crackling threads of power wound together so tightly that space and time were squeezed beyond the breaking point. But every knot that can be tied can be untied, if you pull in the right places, and Yang saw more than one loose thread in the undead wizard's construction. With a sharp intake of breath, she reached out and inspected the buzzing projectile, cocooning it in her hands, stroking the thrumming fibers. She pulled and threaded and re-stitched and tossed the bundle back at the legion of advancing skeletons right in front of her, who promptly disintegrated.

The great chamber went quiet, and the air chilled as the Lich King fixed his attention on her.

"What was that, *Apprentice?*"

"I'm not an apprentice anymore." She wiped more blood from her face, then raised the leafy stick. It thrummed in her hand. "I had my vision. My staff and I have found each other. I'm a wizard now."

The Lich's evil laughter echoed in the chamber. "You're not a wizard. I can *see*. You have no magic, only emptiness. You're nothing." He snapped his fingers. "End her."

Both undead wizards stretched forth their hands and unleashed death upon her. One sent a Hawking Hole, fast as an arrow, and the other shot a raging bundle of green wraith fire.

This time, she welcomed the missiles, inspecting and prodding the clusters of magic filaments. She tamed them as they orbited around her, then re-spun them as sparkling seeds and sent them back with a push from her hands. Both undead wizards crumbled into piles of dirt. The dirt hummed and buzzed, and everyone stepped back in trepidation. With a sudden *pop*, both piles of dirt sprouted flowers and butterflies.

"Ooh, geraniums!" exclaimed Bookkeeper Andi.

"You'll need more than party tricks to defeat me, *Apprentice*. I've studied the dark arts for over five hundred years." The Lich King stepped back and raised his hands. "Goodbye."

He cast forward a furious torrent of energy, fire and lightning and arcane curses in a twisted cable that roared at her, larger and stronger than anything she'd ever seen before. Just before it reached her, it took the shape of a raging dragon, a tremendous beast filling almost a quarter of the chamber, its wings and neck swept back. Then it lunged forward, all of the energy striking Yang at once.

She swept her arm and reflected it, a raw stream of vicious energy surging forth like an angry river that has broken a dam meant to contain it.

CHAPTER EIGHTEEN: LICH

The stream slammed into the Lich King, and he attempted to shield it. For a brief second he appeared to succeed, the stream breaking around an invisible barrier in front of him. But the barrier began to crumble and the Lich leaned forward on his staff, screaming against the oncoming current. The stream ripped away the last of his barrier, then tore away his staff and his robes, leaving him stumbling, a lich in yellow silk boxer shorts with blue stars, and then he was overwhelmed, and when the energies faded away there was nothing left, not even ash.

"You *pantsed* him!" cried Gunthar triumphantly, raising his axe. "*Style move!*"

All of the skeletons in the room collapsed to piles of bones, lifeless once again. A rumbling noise began in the far distance, then grew louder, the room shaking around them, until with a great *crack*, the ceiling between Yang and the others collapsed in a cataclysm of falling rock and golden sunbeams.

When the dust cleared, an opening led up out of the cavern, into the fading sunshine far above.

"'Tis a blessing!" said Sir Humphrey. "I didn't look forward to walking back in the passageways in the dark."

"Ah!" Bookkeeper Andi screamed, and everyone turned.

The princess had fallen, a skeleton's spear piercing her side. The Bookkeeper knelt, cradling Maryan in her arms. "The princess!" she cried. "What do we do?"

"Quick," said Gunthar, "get her bandaged and on Daisy. We'll run to Bluntworth overnight."

Chapter 19
Healer

> *True healing is only accomplished by achieving oneness with the motions of the heavenly bodies.*
>
> *— Considered Revelations, Book 165 "Medicine in the Age of Ignorance", Chapter 8, Verse 7*

The adventurers scrambled out of the collapsed cavern and chased the fading sunset. Almost immediately, they ran into the Moonflow, the wide stream reflecting the dim light.

"The magic wall!" Bookkeeper Andi looked up and down the stream. "How will we cross?"

"Let's try going through," said Gunthar. "The battlemage said it only blocks one direction."

Indeed, now that they headed west instead of east they crossed the stream easily, the slow waters only coming to their waists at the deepest point. Gunthar stopped mid-stream and tested the path back towards the Castle again. "Ha! The barrier resists this way. Yet we are free to continue west."

They led Daisy across the stream, the unconscious Maryan on top.

"It is most encouraging that no magicks bar our path," said Sir Humphrey. "Yet I am concerned for the princess. She has not stirred, though she breathes still."

"Let's get to Bluntworth," said Gunthar. "There will be physicians at the palace who can bleed her."

Yang winced. "I know bleeding people is a super-popular cure, but I don't think it does much good."

"In sooth, Apprentice—er, *Wizard*—I am inclined to agree with you, yet I know no other path." Sir Humphrey helped Daisy up the western streambank.

Gunthar shrugged. "What else can we do?"

"I'm no physician," said Yang, "but I don't think bleeding will help. I think we need to carefully clean and stitch the wound and check for broken ribs."

CHAPTER NINETEEN: HEALER

Bookkeeper Andi walked behind them. "*Not* bleed her?" She snorted. "You're right. You're no physician. Bleeding is the only way to help your princess now." She frowned at Yang in the dim light. "Honestly, who doesn't believe in bleeding people? You sound like that crazy mystic healer south of Bluntworth."

Gunthar stopped. "The who?"

"The crazy mystic..." Andi looked at each of them. "Oh, no. You're not seriously considering taking the princess to the crazy mystic, are you?"

Gunthar waved them forward. "Come on. The moon will come out in another hour, and we can move faster. Let's get to this healer as fast as we can."

"We shall press on with alacrity, good barbarian! 'Tis night, but now we are on the open Badlands, with nothing in our way."

"Whoooooo?" called a voice in the darkness.

"'Twas a reference to all of us, of course," said Sir Humphrey.

Bookkeeper Andi huddled up against the knight, grabbing his arm as she surveyed the cracked, starlit ground. "Please, Sir Humphrey, keep your voice down."

"Yeah, put a cork in it," agreed Gunthar, his hand on his axe. "What was that?"

"Whoooooo?" called the voice again, closer this time.

"Well, that time we were referring to you," answered Gunthar.

"Yes," replied the voice, floating ethereally above them. "I knowwwwwwwww. I was asking a rhetorical questionnnnnnn."

Andi squinted up in the darkness. "Is something glowing up there?"

"Look," said Gunthar, "you obviously know we're here, so you can drop the eerie voice bit. It won't scare us."

"It might," countered Andi, still gripping Sir Humphrey's arm.

"It's a fairy!" Wizard Yang pointed. "I can see her hovering over us, with bright, gossamer wings."

"We do not share your wizard's vision," said Sir Humphrey, looking above, "but I, like the good Bookkeeper, see *something* glowing up there."

Andi released her grip on his arm. "Oh, it's Inga! The pretty fairy queen that haunts the Badlands at night."

The fairy zipped down to hover in front of Andi. Now everyone could see a person-sized apparition with large, shining butterfly wings. The ghost fairy pointed a long, luminous finger. "*Pretty* is not an adjective you should use when referring to someone. It suggests you value appearance more than other qualities."

"Sorry." The Bookkeeper huddled behind Sir Humphrey again, then whispered to him. "Everyone in Bluntworth has heard of Inga. She's very mean. Legend has it that she was jilted at the altar, centuries ago, and withered away to a bitter spirit that haunts—"

"*And* you should know better than to gossip."

"Ghost fairy Inga," said Gunthar, "we're not here to bother you. We're trying to get to a healer as fast as we can."

"For her?" Inga gestured at Maryan, unconscious atop Daisy. "I doubt she'll make it."

"We're trying anyway. We're looking for a mystic healer south of Bluntworth."

"Oh, that one? Good luck. Still, it sounds like you're trying to leave my domain as fast as you can, so I'll help. See the constellation of The Swan, there? Aim for that. Later, when The Awkward Wedding Toast touches the horizon, aim for that. You should reach the healer near dawn."

"Thank you, ghost fairy queen."

"Go awayyyyyyy." And Inga disappeared.

* * *

In the morning, the sun crested the horizon at their back, bathing the lands before them with a crisp yellow light. After a night of walking across the featureless Badlands, the appearance of trees and grasses made a welcome sight. The high plains fell towards the river here, the wide waters of the Goldswell winding south.

To the north, green farms and orchards dotted the riverside. Ahead lay a tangled hodgepodge of brackens and fruit trees.

Gunthar frowned. "What is this place?"

"This is the Mystic Forest. No one goes here." Bookkeeper Andi pointed upriver, where the spires of the Mayor's palace gleamed in the sunlight. "I told you we should have gone to Bluntworth."

"Look, there's a path." Yang nodded to where a trail cut through the bracken. "The ghost fairy's directions have been good so far."

CHAPTER NINETEEN: HEALER

"I beseech thee, please hurry!" The knight walked at the back of the party, a hand on Maryan's arm. "The princess is much weaker this morning."

Gunthar led them briskly up the path, pushing large branches out of the way. "What's in here? A village? A market?"

"I don't know." Andi peered through the thick undergrowth. "I've only heard of the mystic healer."

The trail wound up a wooded hill, then opened to a clearing. A small earthen hut with a thatched roof stood ahead, a lonely wisp of smoke winding up from a crooked chimney.

"Let's ask here," said Gunthar. "Maybe they know about this healer person." He strode up and knocked on the stout hickory door, then stepped back.

The door opened partway, revealing a rotund man with a thick head of brown hair, wearing a brown robe. He stared at them all. "Yes?"

Yang spoke up first. "Please, can you help us? We have a wounded friend and we're looking for a healer."

The man's eyes widened, and he threw open the door. "You've come to the right place! We are the healer's servants. Bring the wounded one to the table."

They lifted Maryan off Daisy and carried the princess into the hut. The dark and musty interior smelled of incense and freshly-cut grass. Strange implements and tools lined the walls, and herbs hung from the ceiling in long strands and bundles.

The adventurers crowded in, pushing their way through the hanging herbs, the hut now quite cramped with the five of them, plus the man in a brown robe and two others, also in brown robes. They placed Maryan on a large oak table in the center of the hut.

"Welcome to Nyala's hut, weary travelers," said the large man who had opened the door. "I'm Rob, this is Bob," he pointed to one of the robed men that looked like his twin, "and this is Bartholomew," he said, pointing to the other robed man that also looked like a twin. Rob considered Maryan on the table. "Now, what seems to be the problem?"

"Our noble compatriot has fallen in battle," said Sir Humphrey. "She was impaled on a spear from a skeleton chief."

"Ah," said Bartholomew, shaking his head, "a skeleton chief."

"Most serious," agreed Bob.

"Look," said Rob, gesturing the adventurers to lean in, "Healer Nyala is on her way, but we need to do something about the skeleton spirit first."

"Skeleton spirit?" Yang blinked.

"Oh, yeah, it's a thing." Rob nodded. "Bob, can you get some incense going? We're going to have to smoke it out."

"Sure." Bob rummaged through a shelf, then turned to the knight. "What kind of skeleton was it? Like, more of a lanky scout type? Or a thicker, heavier champion type?"

"Ah, well, good sir, it all happened very quickly, and the skeleton collapsed shortly after. I'd chance that it was on the heavier side?" Sir Humphrey looked to the others.

"Yes, more of a champion type," said Andi.

"Champion type, right, okay, I'll go with lavender."

Bob lifted a stick from a small jar, but Bartholomew stayed his hand. "Bob, are you sure? What about sandalwood?"

"Ooh, yeah, let's go with sandalwood." Bob swapped out the stick, then lit it in a small holder.

Andi coughed in the smoke, and everyone's eyes started watering.

"Gather in," ordered Rob. "Here, hands on each other's shoulders. No, Bob, that's too far on the arm—yes, that's it. Everyone good? Now repeat after me. Foul scout skeleton—"

"It was a champion, Rob," said Bob.

"Oh, right. Okay, foul *champion* skeleton, may your spirit leave this poor helpless waif—"

"She's not a helpless waif, my good man. She's a warrior princess," noted Sir Humphrey. "She led us across the Broken Heath and bested over a score of the evil soldiers herself."

"Across the Broken Heath?" Bartholomew's eyebrows went up.

"Yes," said Yang. "For two days."

"Oh, wow," said Bob. "That's not easy."

Rob spread his hands. "Foul champion skeleton spirit, leave this warrior princess, and return to your land of the dead, where rivers of fire run in obsidian canyons, and spires of glass dot the landscape—"

"Is that description supposed to entice the skeleton spirit to return to its home?" Bartholomew had a suspicious look on his

CHAPTER NINETEEN: HEALER

face. "Because it doesn't sound very attractive."

"I'm trying to remind him what his home looks like. Skeletons love the fire and glass thing."

Bob leaned in. "Are we supposed to be repeating these parts?"

"Oh, yeah. Okay, everyone with me. Foul scout, or champion—" Rob started coughing.

Andi waved at the smoke. "Can we open a window?"

They opened the door and windows.

"That's probably good enough," said Rob. "I'm sure the skeleton spirit is gone."

"I'm worried about the princess," said Yang. "Can we speed this up?"

"Of course!" said Rob. "Bartholomew will arrange the crystals, and I'll get the drink."

"Let's get these going." Bartholomew walked along the walls, adjusting small rocks with bits of crystal. "Oh, this is great. There's a lot of good energy in the room."

"Here." Rob had returned with some small cups of steaming liquid from a pot on the hearth, and handed them out to the adventurers.

"Wait," said Yang. "Maryan is the wounded one. Shouldn't she be getting the potion?"

"This is for us," insisted Rob. "We need to chant for the healing."

"Chant?" Wizard Yang squinted at him.

"Everyone got their cup? Good. Now take a sip."

"Ugh! What is this?" Andi made a face like someone had slapped her tongue with a bramble, which is a pretty good description of how the concoction tasted.

"It's an infusion of several roots, mostly chicory. Okay, hands on shoulders. No, Bob, higher up—yes. Now keep chanting. If you don't know the words, just hum. I'll get the star chart."

Bob and Bartholomew led with rumbling chants, while the others hummed as they stood over Maryan.

Rob returned with a large scroll. "Great, great. Can you all feel the energy? It's like, at a seven now, and we need to get it up to a nine or a ten. Next step—"

"What is going on?"

Everyone turned at the voice. A woman with long gray

dreadlocks stood in the doorway, frowning at them.

"Good morning, Healer Nyala!" Rob bowed.

"What is this?" Nyala looked around at them. She wore trousers with fine leather boots and a sharp green top, and if they'd seen her in town they'd likely have mistaken her for a noble on a hunt. "Crystals? Incense? Chanting? What are you doing?"

Rob swallowed. "Well, you know, we were getting ready..."

Nyala looked at the cup in Yang's hand. "Why did you give them my tea?"

"Ah..."

The healer strode over to the hearth and poured herself a small cup. "Thank goodness, there's still some left."

She walked back next to Yang, perched herself on a small stool, and took a sip. "Ah. Nothing clears the mind better than a shot of chicory." Nyala lowered the cup. "I was up all night with the centaurs. Great kids, but they'll talk your leg off. Always one more story about the constellations."

Yang cleared her throat. "Ah, healer, we were hoping you could help us."

"Of course, I'm sorry." Nyala turned to Cornelius. "Is it your ankle? It appears to have fully recovered."

The Chronicler opened and closed his mouth.

"Ah, no, Healer Nyala. It's her." The barbarian gestured at Maryan, lying on the center table.

"Ah!" Nyala screeched and handed her cup to Gunthar. "I didn't see her there." She put a hand to Maryan's forehead, then moved to the bandage, moving it aside so she could inspect the wound. "Ah!" she shrieked again. "She's got severe lacerations, a punctured kidney, an arterial contusion, and a secondary infection. We should..." Nyala backed up into a long string of garlic, then looked around them, her eyes wide. "Wait, why are we in the garden shed?"

Rob coughed again. "Well, you know, we were worried about bad energy—"

"What is it with this ridiculous mumbo-jumbo? What, were you going to read her horoscope next? You were, weren't you?"

Rob moved the star chart behind his back. "Not necessarily."

"I know it's the middle ages, but even in the middle ages, educated people don't believe in that crap. Move her into the

CHAPTER NINETEEN: HEALER

operating theater in the main house. Quickly now. And wash your hands. Wash everything, quite frankly."

Nyala watched Rob, Bob and Bartholomew carefully move Maryan onto a stretcher, then carry her out the door of the garden shed. "Sorry about them," said the healer, taking another sip of her tea. "It's their first day."

* * *

The next day, they all sat together at breakfast at a long table in Nyala's sun room. Light streamed in through large windows which looked down over the forest, the Goldswell churning far below.

Maryan sat at the middle of the table, her compatriots around her. "Thank you, Healer Nyala. I think I owe you my life."

"Indeed, Your Highness, I have never seen nor heard of a healer so skilled." The knight nodded to Nyala, who sat at the head of the table. "She treated and stitched the wound with a deftness that defies belief."

"You are very kind, Sir Humphrey, but I did little more than clean the wound and ensure no foreign objects remained. Most of your princess' recovery is due to the Elixir of Sakura." Nyala pointed to a large decanter in a glass case behind her, filled with a deep red liquid.

"What is that?" asked Yang.

"It's a recipe I picked up on my travels. Difficult to make, since it requires distilling several infusions for months at a time. If you make even the smallest mistake, you have to throw it all away and start over. But it is well worth it. I always keep some on hand, just for these emergencies." Nyala leaned forward. "Now, tell me how you got yourself injured, young lady."

They retold their adventures thus far, ending at the battle with the Lich.

"I thought that battlemage, Ignacio, had beaten him!" said Gunthar. "He did the 'I'm not left-handed' move."

"Oh, no!" The healer's eyes widened. "That won't work. Liches are ambidextrous."

"Indeed, healer, Ignacio paid a terrible price for his mistake."

"Honestly, he should have known better. That's like Lich 101."

Nyala sat back. "Thank you, Bartholomew. You can put that on the table."

The large, brown-robed man placed a heaping tray of bread, fruit, and vegetables before the adventurers, then nodded and left.

"Please, help yourself," said Nyala. "Fresh from our baker, and the garden."

"This is a beautiful house, Healer Nyala," said Yang as she broke apart a piece of bread.

"Oh, thank you. I bought it many years ago from a dryad who used it as a guest house. I knew I'd retire here!" Nyala gave the thick timbers a fond look. "Of course, it was much smaller then. I renovated it, added the operating wing a few years ago, and extended the living halls last spring."

"Are you from these parts, Healer Nyala?" asked Yang.

"No, Wizard. I'm originally from Adnam, but I liked this forest the moment I saw it. And it's in the middle of everything, you know?"

"You're from Adnam?" Gunthar clapped. "You must be a great dancer!"

Nyala looked at him with a wry grin. "Adnam is known for its dancers, but not everyone from Adnam is a great dancer, barbarian. That's kind of a generalization."

Gunthar swallowed. "Oh, I'm sorry. That was an ignorant thing to say."

"I saw the Argean vase in the hallway," said Maryan.

"And the Zalish saber!" Sir Humphrey waved a large carrot.

"Have you traveled much?" asked Yang.

"In my youth," said Nyala. "I crossed the known lands many times, and the unknown lands more than once."

"What did you do?" asked Maryan.

"I was a ranger."

The room went quiet.

"What is it?" asked Nyala, returning their sudden stares.

Maryan spoke first. "Healer Nyala, you heard the prophecy. *You* must be the ranger it speaks of!"

The healer chortled, then waved it off. "Prophecies. They're ridiculous. Horribly vague, and almost always with clumsy, adolescent rhyming." She sat back. "And I've never heard of a

CHAPTER NINETEEN: HEALER

prophecy with a ranger."

A large pigeon fluttered to a smooth landing at the window sill, then hopped inside to a small wooden box by the glass case. It dropped a piece of paper inside, then flew outside again.

Nyala frowned at the container, then stood. "I apologize. I don't like to read messages at the table, but I haven't checked my inbox since yesterday."

She rifled through the many tiny scrolls within. "Is this... Oh, yuck." She tossed a small, gilded piece of paper into the fireplace. "Somehow I got on the Mayor's mailing list. I can't get them to stop." The healer picked up a slightly larger scroll. "Ah, a message from Councilor Wilson."

Nyala read for a moment, then put a hand over her heart. "Oh, my."

"What is it?" asked Maryan.

"The council has discovered that the battlemage perished in the Badlands. Other wizards notice when someone's staff breaks, you know." She sighed. "So there is renewed fear that the rising tide of the undead will consume the town."

"Does the Mayor believe the prophecy now?"

"No, of course not, Your Highness. But some of the council aren't complete idiots. They're the ones who are worried." The healer brightened. "Good news at the end. Your parents have sent a young man to fetch you."

"To *fetch* me?"

"Yes. Councilor Wilson says, and I quote, 'he's the sweetest, most gracious young noble he's had the pleasure of meeting in many a year.'"

Maryan frowned. "I can't believe they send suitors after me. Honestly."

The knight sat back, having finally eaten his fill. "Didn't we solve the prophecy, ma'am? We defeated the Lich King."

"I thought we were supposed to defeat him three times," said Yang. "At least, that's what the seer at the School of Wizardry claimed."

Maryan bit her lip. "We seem to have many hints about the prophecy, but we don't really know what's true."

"You could always check the Archives, ma'am." Nyala returned to the head of the table.

"The Archives?"

"Yes, ma'am. They are in the basement of the Mayor's palace. They have copies of most of the world's prophecies, bad rhyming schemes and all."

Maryan stood, then bowed at the healer. "Lady Nyala, we—and I mean the royal *We*—are in your debt." She gestured to the other adventurers. "Come, let us venture to the Archives. We'll get to the truth of this prophecy."

Chapter 20
Archives

> *True lovers spend a significant amount of time simply gazing into each others' eyes.*
>
> — *Considered Revelations, Book 65 "Keeping the Spark Alive Whilst Fending Off the Undead", Chapter 417, Verse 1*

The party set forth again, the late morning sun peeking through leafy branches far overhead. They followed a wide trail that led northwest, where it would join the river road, the fastest path to Bluntworth.

"We should arrive by late afternoon," noted Maryan, catching a glimpse of the distant spires.

"'Tis a pleasure to have your company, Healer Nyala."

"Of course, Sir Humphrey. While I swore off traveling when I retired, I think a quick jaunt up to Bluntworth doesn't count." Nyala smiled. "And while I think prophecies are ridiculous, why not join it?"

Gunthar looked back over his shoulder. "I feel much better about heading back to face a hostile Mayor, and a possibly not-yet-completely-defeated-rising-tide-of-the-undead, with a healer in the party. Especially one with that Elixir."

"I'll do my best to look out for you all," said Nyala with a chuckle.

Maryan caught a glimpse of sunlight reflecting off the windows of Nyala's house behind them. "I really appreciate your coming with us, but aren't you worried about leaving Rob, Bob, and Bartholomew in charge?"

"Not really, Your Highness. This is their first time being left alone for any length of time, but how much trouble could they get into?"

A rumbling blast shook the forest, and bits of incense flaked down upon the adventurers.

Rob poked his head out of the house far above them. "Sorry about that! We were just starting our meditation session. I think Bob lit too many lavender sticks."

Bartholomew appeared next to him. "Master Nyala, how do you

turn on the fire sprinklers? Is it the big knob by the back door?"

Healer Nyala stared up at a dark plume of smoke rising over the trees. "You know, I should probably run back and check on things."

"Indeed." Sir Humphrey followed her gaze.

Nyala jogged back up the trail. "I'll join you in Bluntworth when I can!" she called back.

"Thank you, and good luck, Nyala!" Maryan waved after the departing healer.

"What now?" Gunthar watched Nyala disappear into the trees with obvious disappointment as he brushed bits of lavender incense off his shoulder.

"We continue to Bluntworth." Maryan walked down the trail again. "We need to get to the Archives."

In a short while, the trail brought them out of the forest and onto the river road, which they followed upstream past farms and orchards and pleasant river villas, until they finally reached the southern gates of Bluntworth.

"I hope the Mayor doesn't see us," noted Gunthar, studying the battlements above.

"Let's see if we can slip into Bluntworth without being noticed," said Maryan.

Sir Humphrey shook his head. "Methinks we can avoid having a group of musicians follow us this time!"

"Lady Maryan of Offerdell?" A young man in a crisp white shirt and green leggings bowed in front of her.

"Yes?"

"I am Prince Juan Martin Ramirez, at your service." He straightened and presented her a rose, bright red and with a fragrance so sweet and so strong that even a Chronicler in the back of the party beside a sweaty horse could smell it.

"Oh, my, well, yes, it is very nice to meet you, Prince Juan. I am Princess Maryan." She bowed in return.

"Please, milady, allow me to accompany you back into town." Prince Juan stepped next to her and extended his elbow. "You are returning to the Mayor's palace, I presume?"

"Yes, well, that would be very nice, thank you." Maryan gave a startled look back at Yang, who flashed her a thumbs-up.

"Of course, princess. This way." The prince gestured ahead, then led them through the gatehouse.

Four musicians stood just inside the city walls, wearing sharp white outfits with bright vests, guitars slung in front of them. They fell into step behind the party and sang a sweet song, which although in another language was almost certainly about a young man pining for the affections of a young lady, though he was not quite worthy of her love, yet he wooed her anyway, with many flowers and tears and at least one gifted donkey.

"I am curious, Prince Juan, how you knew to meet me here?"

"Well, my princess, your royal parents let me know that you were in the area. I asked the Mayor about you, and he and his staff were all in a tizzy, worried about you and wondering about your whereabouts. He and his councilors heard from the wizards that their battlemage had fallen, so they posted sentries at the edge of the Badlands, looking for any sign of your party. Yesterday a scout returned, breathless from running, and reported that he'd seen your party far to the south. The Mayor sent a search party along the river road, hoping to find you." The Prince looked back after them with a raised eyebrow. "Indeed, I was surprised that the Mayor's guards did not come with you."

"We didn't see them," said Maryan.

"I can guess what happened." Wizard Yang strode behind the nobles. "We were in the Mystic Forest, and the Mayor's guard probably continued south on the river road, well past us."

Prince Juan stopped and turned, raising his hands. "Ah, of course, most insightful wizard! They would have kept to the river, assuming that your party would make immediately for the Goldswell, and so they missed you." He bowed. "It is rare that a wizard possesses wisdom and beauty, as well as youth!" Then he turned back and swept up Maryan's arm again. "Come, my princess. I'm sure you are tired and looking forward to refreshment after such a long and arduous journey."

Yang stood in the road, fanning her face. "Oh, I could get used to him!" Then she had to hurry forward to avoid being bumped into by the trailing musicians. They briefly sang something in a minor key, as if the suitor in their song were hitting hard times, but then resolved again in a triumphant chorus of passion.

By now, the streets of Bluntworth bustled with the traffic of early afternoon. The party purchased food from the market while the musicians played a haggling song, then continued up to the palace.

Councilor Wilson stood at the gates, and he bowed as Maryan approached. "Good afternoon, Your Highness. We feared the worst after hearing of Wizard Ignacio's demise."

"Good afternoon, Councilor Wilson. The Lich King gave us a bit of trouble at first, but we were able to defeat him."

"And though we lost a treacherous battlemage, we picked up a wizard of our own." Gunthar gestured at Yang, who bowed.

The Councilor raised an eyebrow. "Let me be the first to congratulate you on your victory! The Mayor will be happy to hear that you have ended this threat, though he will be disappointed that the Badlands may open to overland travel, providing routes of commerce which avoid Bluntworth and its taxes."

Maryan leaned in. "We're a little unsure if the Badlands are safe or not. The prophecy is somewhat vague on this point. We were hoping to check the Archives."

"The Archives!" He shrugged. "It has been a while since anyone has ventured into those musty recesses of the palace, yet you have certainly earned the right. Please, follow me."

He led them to the palace's main staircase, then down several floors to the store rooms. No windows penetrated the gloom here, where a long corridor led them through the thick sandstone blocks of the palace foundations. Torches flickered at intervals, and they passed only a few doors. One had chains and locks and a large sign saying "Do Not Open Without Treats," but they walked right past it.

Councilor Wilson made a right turn, then a left, then stopped in front of a large wooden door with a worn brass ring on the front. "Here you are, ma'am. Librarian Banda will be able to help you." Then Councilor Wilson returned up the passageway, leaving the party in the torchlit hallway. The musicians sang a short thank-you verse, then returned to a more dramatic song, apparently involving the hero following his love through dark caverns.

"My princess, I would follow you through the darkest of caverns, anywhere so long as I could gaze deeply into your eyes," said Juan.

Maryan blushed. "Oh, well, that is very kind of you."

"'Twouldst also be most convenient to have someone else to carry baggage," noted Sir Humphrey approvingly.

CHAPTER TWENTY: ARCHIVES

"Doesn't this Archives place seem a tad creepy? And why put it so close to the dungeons?" Gunthar pointed down the hallway, where several cell doors stood closed with large padlocks.

Yang gripped her staff. "This could be a trap. It's suspicious that we've been led down here, then left alone."

"I don't think Councilor Wilson would betray us." Maryan's voice may have quavered slightly.

"Everyone stay sharp," said Gunthar, and he struck the door three times with the brass ring. The booming echoed throughout the hallway, shaking the very bones of the place. But when the final rumble faded away, the door remained shut.

"Very suspicious," repeated Yang, looking around.

"I would protect you through any battle, my princess," said Juan, "so long as I could gaze deeply into your eyes."

The musicians sang a peppier song, about a hero that defended his lady against insurmountable odds, buoyed and protected by her adoring gaze.

"Really?" asked Maryan. "You can engage with the enemy while gazing into my eyes the whole time?"

"Oh yes." Juan demonstrated by dancing around her while maintaining constant eye contact. "I've developed my own fighting style. I call it Juan-fu." He lit on a martial pose. "To be honest, it's mostly back kicks."

An ominous click echoed down the hallway, as some unseen locking mechanism shifted in the large Archives door. Maryan stood at the threshold, flexing her hands, while Gunthar and Sir Humphrey flanked her, hands near the hilt of their weapons. Juan crouched to one side, looking up at her. The musicians sang a plaintive song about a hero who went to a library but got lost and wasn't sure if he was at the right place and it was dark and scary and he wanted to run far away but he had a self-help book on hold and also had to return another book before more late fees accumulated.

The great door swung open with loud creaking and scraping, revealing a tall man with a broad chest in a black turban and a thick black beard just starting to gray. He returned their stares with his deep, brown eyes. "Yes?"

"Ah, excuse us," said Maryan. "We're looking for the Archives."

"Are you now?" He surveyed the group. "Many come to the

Archives, but few return."

Maryan swallowed. "Really?"

"Oh, I'm only kidding. Come in, come in." He stepped to the side and beckoned them further. "I don't get many guests down here."

Chapter 21

Teacup

Has anyone seen my cup? No, the one with the matching saucer. I thought I left it in the kitchen, but now I can't find it. What? You put it where?

— Considered Revelations, Book 133 "Known Utterances of the Elder God Marutuk", Chapter 41, Verse 2

Maryan stepped through the doorway onto a platform overlooking a large underground chamber. Tall bookshelves filled the space, with many stairways and balconies and bridges spanning the gaps. Torches flickered at many points on the walls and balconies, the light glittering on brass fixtures.

"I am Librarian Banda," said the turbaned man once they'd all entered. "Welcome to the Archives."

"It's beautiful," she gasped as she peered over the railing.

"Oh, you know, we keep it tidy," said Banda with obvious pride. "Now, how can I help you?"

"Well—"

"Wait, wait, let me guess what each of you is looking for." The librarian looked at Maryan. "Malwart's Books on Strategy?"

"Um, no."

He stepped before Wizard Yang. "The Greater Summonings of Mage Rehan?"

"Ah—"

"The Lost Arts of Double Entry Bookkeeping?"

Andi shook her head.

"Flatter Abs in Thirty Days?" he said to the barbarian.

"Oh, that's a great one," said Gunthar. "Already read it."

Banda stepped back and gestured at the stacks of books behind him. "Perhaps a book on crop rotation? How to prevent erosion? There is a lot of knowledge here, hard-won and ready to be applied."

"Well," said Maryan, "we're looking for information on a prophecy."

The librarian's shoulders fell. "Oh, why is it always prophecies?"

"I'm sorry," said Maryan. "But we're wondering—"

"Follow me, I'll take you to the prophecy room." Banda led them down one of the staircases to the floor and across towards a small door. "Honestly, I don't know why we even bother having a horticulture section, or animal husbandry, or metallurgy. People only want to read about prophecies."

"Well—"

"Why are prophecies so popular, anyway? Back in my day, we didn't need to make a prophecy any time someone sneezed or needed to make a bill payment. But now, everyone seems to think they can't cross the street without a freaking prophecy."

"I'm not sure—"

"You know what? I've got a prophecy for you. I'm going to scratch my butt." A second later, he raised his hands. "Lo! It has come to pass."

"Librarian Banda, if there's someone else—"

"No, it's fine." He pointed to a row of fine leather folios as they passed. "A twelve-volume set on the dwarven circulatory system. You know who reads that?"

"Librarian—"

"No one! No one reads it. I don't know why I bother."

They arrived at the small door, and Banda retrieved a key from his belt. The lock clicked and screeched, then the librarian kicked the door open with a snarl. "Here we are, the prophecy room."

"You know, Librarian Banda, I can see you're busy, we can probably take it from here."

"No, no, let me help you." He grabbed a lantern from a shelf outside the doorway, lit it and then went in. "Watch your head."

They entered a small room with dusty bookshelves along the walls and a large wooden table in the center, stacked with scrolls and many candles. There wasn't room for all of them, so the musicians stayed outside in the larger Archives room and sang a song about a hero who went into a really cool place but didn't bring all his friends, and the hero regretted it, especially when bad things started happening and his friends weren't there to help, and the hero felt guilty about it and vowed to make it up to them, until finally Juan shut the door.

CHAPTER TWENTY-ONE: TEACUP

"Thank you," said Maryan.

"I would gladly shut doors for you, my princess, so long as I could gaze deeply into your eyes."

"Will you do everything while gazing into my eyes? Like, all the time?"

"Yes, I have a schedule." Prince Juan held up a small scroll. "Just a few bathroom breaks."

"Don't you think it's important that people in a relationship have their own lives as well? You know, make meaningful contributions to their community and advance their careers independently, while also nurturing their mutual bond?"

"I would gladly and independently advance my career for you, my princess, so long as—"

"Hey, are we going to find this crappy prophecy of yours, or what?" Librarian Banda glared at them while holding up his lantern.

"Ah, yes, of course. It's the prophecy with the Lich King, and the Teapot of Valor, and the Castle of Terror."

"Oh, that one, half a second..." Banda ran a finger along a shelf, then cried out in triumph. "Here it is!" He handed his lantern to Sir Humphrey, then pulled a worn tome off the shelf and blew the dust off it.

Bookkeeper Andi coughed and waved the dusty air away.

"It was filed under 'H' for Horse Puckey," said Banda. He dropped the heavy book on the table, sending scrolls and more dust flying.

"Thank you so much. I think we can read it from here."

"Can you?" Banda opened the cover, revealing tight sentences written in a spidery hand. "It's in Ancient Akkalarian. Can any of you read Ancient Akkalarian?"

"Um, well, not as such, no—"

"Of course not!" Banda gestured around them. "Why bother to learn another language, when you can read a bunch of loser prophecies?"

"Librarian—"

"Look at this." Banda flipped through several pages. "Ridiculous amounts of tedious, amateur verse. Why can't these prophecy writers speak plainly?"

"Well—"

"Canst you find the interesting bits?" asked Sir Humphrey. "Concerning the end of the Lich King?"

"We know some parts already," added Maryan. "For instance, there's a Mage, and a Ranger, and a Barbarian. And the Lich may need to be thrice-beaten."

Banda frowned. "I don't see any of that. There's a Lich King, all right, but I don't see anything about needing to beat him three times. As far as I can tell, the Lich is invincible. And there's no mention of a mage, or a ranger, or a barbarian."

"An Axe, maybe?"

"No. This mentions a Protector, and a Wise One. Ring any bells?"

Maryan frowned. "No, not really."

Banda ran a finger along several rows of dense script. "This seems to be the end part. I'll skip the awkward rhyming and give you the summary. The Lich can only be defeated if he invites the bishop across the Moonflow for tea."

"That's it? Tea with the bishop?" Maryan peered at the text.

"What about if the Lich got pantsed?" Gunthar waved in conjecture. "Like, if he got seriously pantsed, could he be beaten then? Because that's pretty much what happened."

"No. He can only be defeated if he invites the bishop across the Moonflow for tea." The Librarian frowned. "It looks like the Lich King only comes back stronger if you kill him."

"What?"

Banda looked up at them. "If you kill a Lich King, it only comes back stronger. That's Lich 101. Don't you read anything besides prophecies?"

"'Tis there nothing else?" asked Sir Humphrey. "Anything we can use against him?"

"As far as prophecies go, this one is pretty fluffy," said Banda, flipping through the pages. "There isn't a whole lot of relevant content."

"What do we do?" Maryan turned to her compatriots. "I'm worried that the Lich may come back."

"Oh, here's one warning," said Banda, pointing to another page. "Under no circumstances should you bring the Teacup out of the Castle of Terror. It mustn't be separated from the Teapot."

"What?"

CHAPTER TWENTY-ONE: TEACUP

"Don't remove the Teacup from the Castle."

Maryan shrugged. "Sure, we'll avoid that."

"Ah, well, what would happen if you *did* remove the Teacup?" Yang winced and wrung her hands. "You know, hypothetically."

Banda returned to the text. "Let's see... You'd have to disable multiple magical locks and traps on the chest it was held in, and if you survived that, only someone immune to magic could actually touch it." He laughed. "I don't know why they even mention the Teacup. It appears to be impossible to remove it anyway."

Maryan's face went pale. "Just how hypothetical was your question?"

"Um..." Yang opened her satchel and pulled out a Teacup. Or rather, she pulled out a rent in the fabric of spacetime, a starry void the size of several galaxies, with nebulae and stars, all in the form of a Teacup on a matching Saucer. The relic pulled energy to it, as if made of the coldest ice Maryan had ever seen, and fog condensed around it and fell to a pool on the floor. The air filled with magical energy and a deep buzzing rattled the room.

"No one else touch that," said Banda flatly.

"I'm so sorry, Your Majesty. But we were all dashing to get you out of the cavern before it collapsed, and I thought it would be a shame not to at least look inside the chest before it was crushed, and when I saw what was inside, I thought it might be important." Yang shrugged. "So I took it."

"Can someone describe it for me?" asked Prince Juan. "I'm desperately curious but I don't want to stop staring into the Princess' eyes."

"Is it magic?" asked Gunthar.

Yang shook her head. "It's something older."

Maryan tore her gaze from the Teacup, and returned to Banda. "Um, so what happens if, hypothetically, we were to remove the Teacup from the Castle?"

"Yes, let's maybe skip ahead to that part." The librarian turned the page, scanning the text. Then he turned his head away from the page in horror. "Oh, my god."

"What is it?" Maryan's mouth went dry.

"Sorry, it's just some particularly awful prose. Why do all prophecies sound like they were written on a napkin in a tavern?"

He leaned in. "Right, here we go. If you remove the Teacup, the Lich King is no longer bound to the Castle of Terror, and is free to pursue his evil conquests to the ends of the earth." Banda looked up at them. "After over six hundred years of confinement, the Lich King is free."

"Wait, what? I thought we beat him." Gunthar looked around. "We beat him, right?"

"Oh, wait!" Banda held up his hand as he read the last page of the prophecy. "There is one piece of good news. The undead can be held at bay by sprigs of lemongrass."

"What?"

"Lemongrass." Banda pointed at a line of text. "Apparently the undead don't like it. If you wear a sprig of lemongrass, it doesn't protect you directly, but it protects other people near you." He looked up. "So if everyone wears lemongrass, everyone is protected."

"Is this even the right prophecy?" Maryan scratched her head.

Banda raised an eyebrow. "What prophecy did you hear?"

Maryan repeated the limerick.

> *There once was a big evil lich*
> *Whose bad plans we needed to switch*
> *With a Mage and a Ranger*
> *And an Axe against danger*
> *We can stop that son of a witch*

"Wow." Banda's eyes went wide and he staggered back. "What a load of drivel. You didn't pay for it, did you?"

Maryan stared at the thick book on the table. "Our soothsayer didn't mention a Protector, or a Wise One, or lemongrass. She spoke of an Axe, and a Ranger, and a Mage. That isn't in there at all?"

"Nope. And I can assure you, this is the only prophecy concerning the Lich King and the Teacup." Librarian Banda gestured around them. "It's the most relevant prophecy to Bluntworth. It's our history."

"What about a romance that spans the ages? The soothsayer mentioned that too."

Banda snorted. "There's nothing the least bit romantic about this

CHAPTER TWENTY-ONE: TEACUP

prophecy, ma'am."

Wizard Yang leaned forward. "Who was this soothsayer that talked to you, Your Highness?"

Maryan blinked. "I never got her name. She wore a peasant's frock with a red shawl, and she made Prince Mikhail uncomfortable."

Banda squinted. "Who is Prince Mikhail?"

"Her Highness is in a love triangle with a vampire," explained Yang.

"I am *not*."

"I would gladly extricate you from a love triangle with a vampire, my princess, so long as—"

"Did you say a red shawl?" Librarian Banda closed the prophecy book with a snap, and placed it back on the shelf. Then he gathered the lantern back from Sir Humphrey, and led them out of the dim and dusty prophecy room, and back into the airy and brightly-lit main Archives hall.

The musicians sang a song about a hero who rejoined his friends and vowed never to abandon them again.

The Librarian led them past rows of bookshelves, made a right turn and climbed up a stairway, walked along a balcony, then stopped in front of a glass case.

"Ancient history," he said as he unlocked the case with another key. "Not as popular as prophecies these days, but more relevant. Good knight, can you pass me the third tome on the left?"

Sir Humphrey pulled out a large, leather-bound book with gold lettering on the front, and handed it to the Librarian. Banda placed it on a small shelf and flipped through it.

"Let's see... a red shawl. Here we go." He read from the book.

> *Those great beings who made the earth were called titans*
> *After their labors, most of them returned to the void from whence they had come*
> *But some stayed, acting as guides and teachers to the new peoples of the world*
> *The titan Garash brought magic to the wisest of the new peoples*
> *The titan Ninkurra taught all how to till the land and provide food*
> *But the titan Ereshkigal was a trickster, and she misled many with*

false promises
She takes many forms, but always wears a red shawl

"There's a bit more, but you get the idea. Your so-called soothsayer was likely the titan Ereshkigal, and she's playing a trick on us." Banda tapped the book with a frown. "And the Teapot and Teacup are themselves artifacts made by the titans. I wonder what she's up to?"

"Oh, no." Maryan put her hands to her cheeks. "She told us a false prophecy. We annoyed a Lich King, only because a titan was playing tricks on us."

"We didn't just annoy the Lich King," said Bookkeeper Andi. "We've killed him, which apparently makes him stronger, and freed him now, too."

"I would gladly battle a titan for you, my princess, so long as—"

"Please, Prince, give it a rest for minute. I need to think."

"Why did you believe this random soothsayer anyway?" asked the Librarian.

"I don't know." Maryan shook her head. "She had a prophecy, and seemed very mysterious."

The musicians sang a song about a hero who really messed up and brought pestilence to the land by accident and felt bad about it but was also very hungry because it was getting close to dinner time.

"What do we do now?" Gunthar looked at Maryan, as did the others.

Maryan lifted her chin. "We need to talk to the Mayor again. He needs to be aware of the danger the town is facing."

Chapter 22
Peril

> *Great leaders who are known for their smartness trust their experts and learn from front line reports.*
>
> — *Considered Revelations, Book 112 "Leaders Who Are Very Smart", Chapter 23, Verse 7*

The adventurers returned up the stairs to the main floor of the palace, where Councilor Wilson met them. After some discussion, he led them back up to their quarters in the tower.

"But we need to see the Mayor," protested Bookkeeper Andi. "Why are we going here?"

"I apologize, but the Mayor is both busy and upset." The councilor spread his hands. "By returning to your quarters, you allow him to confront you and your uncomfortable news on his terms."

The barbarian growled. "He's going to lock us up here again, isn't he?"

"It is not my place to speculate on what the Mayor may do."

"It's all right." Maryan led them through the doorway, back to the small courtyard looking over the town below. "We're going to have to try to convince him to do the right thing for the good of the city. And if that comes at some cost to ourselves, so be it."

"If nothing else, the Mayor will be interested to discover what happened in the Badlands," noted Councilor Wilson. "I'm sure he'll be here shortly."

Bookkeeper Andi looked out the balcony, which had a partial view to the east. "Is that a storm?"

Councilor Wilson joined her. "It is the storm cloud over the Castle of Terror. Over the past day, it has gotten larger, and now appears to be moving this way."

"The Lich King and his legions approach." Maryan shook her head.

"I would gladly face this Lich King with you, my princess, so long as I could gaze into your eyes the entire time."

Maryan sighed. "Prince Juan, your idea of a relationship seems to involve a couple just sitting around staring into each others' eyes the whole time."

"Indeed, my princess, is this not what love is? To stare into each other's eyes all the time?"

"I don't think I'd be happy that way, Prince. I like the idea of being in a relationship, but I also need to live my own life."

"Well, what if your own life is hollow and unhappy, my princess? In that case, wouldn't you rather spend your time staring into someone else's eyes all the time, rather than confronting your own unhappiness?"

"I think if my life was hollow and unhappy I would focus on fixing it so I could be happy on my own, Prince Juan, and *then* maybe I'd consider a relationship with someone else."

Prince Juan blinked a few times. "Wow, my princess, that's a lot to think about. I'd like to turn my head and consider your words a moment, but I feel I must continue to gaze into your eyes as well."

"What in the name of the gods of poverty is going on?"

Everyone except Prince Juan turned at the Mayor's voice. He stood at the entrance to the doorway, flanked by his guards, with another councilor behind him.

"Good evening, Mayor. We have returned from the Badlands, and the Castle of Terror, although the battlemage you hired did not survive."

The Mayor frowned. "So we heard. The loss of Ignacio is most unfortunate."

"It's all right, Mayor." Andi held up a piece of paper. "I kept the receipt. I think we can get at least a partial refund."

The Mayor brightened again. "That's better."

"Mayor, time is pressing." Maryan pointed to the approaching storm cloud. "The Lich King is free, and stronger than ever. Even now he advances with his legions of the undead."

The Mayor rolled his eyes. "I already told you, Your Highness, I don't believe in the prophecy."

"We found the correct prophecy in the Archives this time."

"Nope, I don't believe in that one either, ma'am."

Yang stepped forward. "Mayor, do you know if there is any lemongrass in the city?"

CHAPTER TWENTY-TWO: PERIL

He raised his eyebrows at the question. "Lemongrass isn't native to these parts, but I believe there are some who grow it, yes."

The wizard breathed a sigh of relief. "That's good news. Wearing a sprig of lemongrass will deter the undead. It won't directly protect the wearer, but it protects others nearby. So everyone should wear one."

"Now we're supposed to wear sprigs of lemongrass?" The Mayor waved it away.

"Mayor, I observed and recorded the whole thing." Bookkeeper Andi held up her small book. "What the princess and the others say is true. The Lich King exists, and he has a fearsome horde of undead soldiers. And he is free now to attack the city."

The Mayor frowned at her. "Bookkeeper Andi, your words carry some weight. You were sent by the city to observe the happenings in the Badlands. Do you swear that everything the princess has said is true?"

"Yes, Mayor."

"Right, then, my choice is obvious." The Mayor pointed to Bookkeeper Andi. "You're fired."

"What?"

"Your observations run counter to my political narrative, ex-Bookkeeper. We can't have so-called experts contradicting my claims."

"But Mayor, the city faces an imminent and deadly threat—"

"I've already told you, ma'am, I have chosen not to believe what you say. It's just too inconvenient."

"But thousands of people will die!"

"People die every year. This is nothing different. And voters don't like to hear bad news." He glared at Maryan. "You are all confined to these quarters, *again*. And this time, you'll stay here until your parents arrive."

"This is fantastic news, my princess. We can spend the time gazing into..." Prince Juan trailed off, and looked away.

Maryan blinked, feeling oddly free now that she was no longer under the young man's gaze. "Prince Juan?"

"I've had an epiphany," he said. "My quest for romance was all a form of denial, wasn't it? I was using my love for you as a way to avoid facing my own fears. Rather than attempting to look for meaning in my own life, I was ignoring my own needs, using emotional attachment to others as a flimsy surrogate for deeper personal introspection and self-acceptance." The prince took a deep breath. "I need to get comfortable with myself before I start a relationship."

"I don't recommend that," said the Mayor. "Trust me, it's better to stay shallow, avoid introspection and instead reflect your fears and insecurities back on other people."

"Ignore him, Prince Juan," said Maryan.

"It's an easy problem to solve," said the prince. "I can just accept that I'm never going to have the confidence or curiosity to face my own demons. And then I can go back to blindly attaching myself to potential romantic prospects instead."

"Prince Juan, you said you were going to get comfortable with yourself—"

"No, the moment has passed." Juan stared at her with wide eyes. "And we can go back to gazing deeply into each other's eyes as I repress other meaning in our lives."

Maryan's shoulders slumped. "Oh, bother."

"That's my boy!" said the Mayor.

Yang sighed. "Shoot, for a second there, I thought the prince might face his own fears."

"Demons," said Cornelius.

"Well, *facing one's demons* is a common metaphor—"

"No, I mean, *demons!*" cried Cornelius, pointing out over the balcony.

With a horrible screech, three large winged figures landed in the courtyard. They had the hooves of goats, the horns of rams, and their massive arms ended in sharp talons, which also carried long swords with glittering runes of fire.

Sir Humphrey drew Gwendoline, Gunthar hefted his axe, and the musicians played a cautionary song about some demons who ate musicians and then got terrible indigestion.

"Onwards, Happenhouse!" Sir Humphrey raised his blade and pushed the on switch.

A blinding flash strobed in the courtyard, but this time Wizard Yang absorbed all the energy of the errant electrical arcs, and sent it blazing out at the advancing demons. The explosion knocked the

CHAPTER TWENTY-TWO: PERIL

adventurers—and the Mayor and his entourage—off their feet. Echoes of the blast rumbled over the town as everyone stood up again.

"What is that smell?" complained the Mayor.

"It smells like burnt hair... oh." Ex-Bookkeeper Andi looked at two smoking forms on the balcony.

"That's two of them," said Gunthar, kicking at a charred hoof. "But where is the third?"

The musicians played a suspended chord.

"And Prince Juan," added Gunthar. "Where is he?"

"Oh, no!" said Cornelius, pointing out over the town. "The third demon escaped with Prince Juan. I think he's being eaten."

"I'm so sorry about your suitor," said Yang.

Gunthar knelt. "We mourn his loss. Though we knew Prince Juan Martin Ramirez for only a short time before he was consumed by literal demons, he was a well-intentioned man who used romantic attachment to avoid confronting his own anxieties. He will be missed."

Maryan pointed at the distant flying fiend. "You see, Mayor, the hosts of the underworld are at hand. You must prepare the town for battle."

"No, Your Highness, that's just too horrible to comprehend. I frankly don't have the mental capacity. So I'm going to ignore the problem, or maybe even interfere with any attempted solutions and make the problem worse." The Mayor paused at the threshold. "Remember, you are all to stay here until Princess Maryan's parents return." Then he left, his guards and councilors following.

Everyone tipped Prince Juan's musicians, then they left as well, the door closing behind them with a clang and an ominous click of the lock.

"This is great," said Gunthar, flopping down onto a bench.

"Wait, why am I locked in here?" asked Andi.

"I'm sorry, good Ex-Bookkeeper," said the knight. "'Tis your punishment for presenting the Mayor with facts."

"Oh, curse me!" Andi sat down and put her face in her hands. "Why didn't I just ignore reality and pretend the threat to the city didn't exist, like the Mayor wanted? That's what everyone else in the administration is doing."

A knock rang at the door, and it opened. A palace page handed Maryan a note. "We received this via carrier pigeon," he said, then closed and locked the door again.

"What is it?" asked Yang.

"It's from my parents." Maryan read the note aloud.

Dearest Maryan-

We hope this missive finds you well.

I'm sure you are wondering why we are not already in Bluntworth! We stopped at our good friend King Girard's territories by the ocean. Do you remember King Girard? Good man, came to our wedding and one of our border clashes. He's always ready with a funny joke or a cavalry charge.

Listen, times being what they are, we were captured by bandits on his northern border. I'm sure you are busy, what with the spring festivals and all, so don't worry about us. But we wanted to let you know why we were delayed.

With luck the bandits won't kill us, and we'll somehow pay the exorbitant ransom they are demanding.

Much love-
King Albert of Offerdell, Lord of the Northern Realm, &c.

PS. On the off chance that you find yourself in the area, the bandit tower is just up the third tributary on the right as you head downstream from Bluntworth.

Maryan lowered the paper. "They're trying to guilt me into rescuing them from bandits."

"It's nice that they found time to write," said Ex-Bookkeeper Andi.

The princess looked out over the balcony. The sun lay close to the western horizon, casting long shadows over the landscape. In the east, the sky darkened with shades of purple, and torches and lanterns shone through windows in the many homes below.

What was she supposed to do? The Mayor ruled here, though obviously incapable of meeting any challenge at all. And her parents weren't helping.

The authority figures in her life had failed her, and all the while the Lich King advanced upon the town. Her heart jumped into her mouth and her body tingled with weightlessness, as if falling from a height, and she almost put out her arms to steady herself.

But a thought kept nagging her. *She* knew what to do, even if the people in charge didn't. And why should she let them stop her from doing what needed to be done?

"All right," she said, "this is what we'll do. Based on the Mayor's behavior, we are no longer ethically bound to remain prisoners here. I'll go and rescue my parents."

Sir Humphrey stood. "Indeed, ma'am! And I shall accompany you."

"I'll go," said Gunthar. "I'm sure it will be dangerous."

"Sir, do you doubt—"

"Stop it." Instead of feeling intimidated or powerless, seeing the two large men bicker only made her angrier. This was just another example of something that wasn't helping. "I'll go alone."

The knight and the barbarian blinked at her, unable to say anything.

"The rest of you, scour the local area and see if you can find any allies who will stand with us against the army of the undead." She looked at the group in the courtyard. "Then we'll meet tomorrow on the edge of town and face the Lich King again."

"Uh, yeah, sure, right," said Gunthar.

With that, Princess Maryan swung over the balcony and climbed down the palace wall.

Chapter 23
Bandits

> *In the far future, when our primitive sailing ships and horse-drawn carriages are replaced by more miraculous forms of transport, our natures will be similarly elevated, such that the decadent spectacle of royal affairs will be ignored in favor of more virtuous intelligence.*
>
> — Considered Revelations, Book 83 "The Miraculous Future of Media", Chapter 17, Verse 5

Maryan climbed down the palace tower, alighting on the cobblestones of the town square as the sun set. Then she ran down to the docks, where a fisherman sold her a rickety boat for a handful of copper coins.

"You should wear a sprig of lemongrass," she told him as she cast off. "It can protect others."

"I don't want to believe in the rising tide of the undead," the fisherman called after her. "Also, it's uncomfortable. So I won't wear one."

Then the current swept her away, and she had to row furiously to cross the swift Goldswell. Large trees and other floating debris rushed by in the river, and she had to peer through the fading light to avoid having her boat smashed. At the third tributary, she rowed to shore and tied the boat up to a tree.

By now the darkness of night had fully settled upon the forests around her, although enough starlight glimmered to follow the stream east. She made her way over uneven ground, dodging tree roots and brambles as she oriented herself by the gurgling of the water.

She thought of the army of the undead, advancing upon Bluntworth far behind her. "I should be building my own army to defend the city," she said to herself through gritted teeth, "not rescuing my parents from bandits. Why didn't they bring more guards?"

Just before midnight, three bandits attacked her, which did nothing to improve her mood. She knocked one unconscious with

CHAPTER TWENTY-THREE: BANDITS

her walking stick, cut the other with his own sword, and the third ran away in terror.

"Please don't kill me," pleaded the second bandit, holding his cut arm.

"Hand over your satchels," she said. "I'm hungry."

She tied his hands, bound his feet in a short stretch of rope so he could walk, then bandaged his wound.

"So sorry about attacking you," he said. "We meant to kill you at the time, of course, but now I feel bad about it."

The satchels contained a slim amount of stale bread and dried meat, which she washed down with water from the stream. "Right," she said, "lead me to your tower."

"Well, it's not *our* tower. We don't really own anything," he said. "We're anarcho-communists. We don't believe in social constructs like private property."

"Whatever. Just walk in front of me."

A few minutes later, the quarter moon rose behind them, and by its light she could see a tall tower by the stream, lights shining from windows.

"We don't have private property," repeated the bandit. "This is a good example of what should be collectively-owned property."

"What do you mean, *should be?*" Maryan looked at him. "This isn't your tower?"

"Not yet. We keep trying to appropriate it, but they won't let us in."

"Fine." Maryan strode up and pounded on the gates.

"Who's there?" called the sentry.

"It is Princess Maryan of Offerdell, and I have come with a bandit who needs to be arrested. And I want to see my parents."

"Oh, wow, that's great," replied the sentry, and the portcullis rose and the gate opened.

Maryan stepped into the torchlit glow of the inner yard. "Where is the master of the tower?"

"He's right inside the main hall," said the sentry, pointing ahead.

"Here's the bandit." Maryan handed over the rope attached to the bandit's bindings.

The main hall at the base of the tower sparkled with opulent decorations, with many rich tapestries and fine furniture. Torches flickered on the walls and a large candelabra hung overhead with dozens of candles. A young man stood to one side of the room in front of an easel. He held a mirror at arm's length with one hand, and sketched on the easel with the other.

"Hello?" Maryan walked up to him.

The man turned, then smiled. He had the most fashionable clothes she'd ever seen, putting even the most trendworthy Haffletonians to shame. A laced flower pattern accented his dark leather pants, and he wore an equally detailed wool jacket over a crisp white shirt. As he turned, his bright boots rang on the stone floor.

"Princess Maryan!" He sauntered over to meet her.

"I'm sorry, I don't think I've had the pleasure—"

"I am Prince Hugo, at your service." He bowed. "Your parents said you might turn up."

Princess Maryan raised an eyebrow. "My parents?"

"Oh, yes. They're upstairs now."

"Upstairs?"

"I'll take you to them. They'll be delighted to see you, I'm sure. But first, join me at my easel."

She followed him back to the easel. The prince swapped in a new piece of paper, then clipped the mirror to the frame and stood back.

Maryan frowned at their reflection in the mirror. "What—"

"Smile, my princess!" he said as he took her in a one-armed hug. "More! A little less! Yes, like that!" With his other hand he sketched their reflection. In a few quick strokes he'd captured their faces, and spent most of his time detailing their clothes. "Is that a funeral gown? Delightful!"

"What is this?" she asked as he released her.

"I'm an influencer." He rang a bell by the easel, and a page hurried into the room. Prince Hugo handed the man the sketch. "Send copies of this to all the cities within a day's pigeon flight, and have it posted in each town square next to my other sketches."

The page nodded and dashed away with the sketch.

Prince Hugo flipped his hair. "It's not easy, you know. I have to constantly post new updates to keep my followers interested. How fantastic that you should come by tonight!" He winked at her. "My

CHAPTER TWENTY-THREE: BANDITS

followers love it when I pose with other royalty. Love it!"

Maryan thought quickly. She'd come to rescue her parents, but fate had given her an opportunity. "Prince Hugo, I'm very glad to have run into you. Bluntworth is facing an army of the undead, led by an invincible Lich King, and I'm looking for allies to stand against him."

Hugo squinted at her. "I'm not sure why you are asking me about it. Unless..." His eyes widened. "Of course! My followers will *love* to hear about a battle, and this is the perfect time to introduce my summer collection."

"Could you introduce your summer collection by leading an army to the defense of the city?"

"Ha! You have a flair for the dramatic, Princess Maryan." He shook his head. "I can't leave this tower, of course. It's too dangerous for me to leave."

"Prince Hugo—"

"I have a better idea, Princess Maryan." He gestured at his easel. "Why don't we have an awkward romance which we chronicle in my postings? We could have over-the-top displays of affection, then a tumultuous elopement, and then a falling out later where we trade scandalous recriminations." He rubbed his hands together. "It's a good ten months of content, at least, and we could cover the fall and winter collections. Then, in the middle of our messy breakup, we could promote the spring collection as a renewal of hope."

"Prince Hugo, I think you underestimate the danger of the Lich King."

"And I think you underestimate the appetite of commoners for a royal engagement! Seriously, Princess, I'm talking about hundreds of thousands, maybe millions of followers, and several sponsorships."

"Why would anyone care about two spoiled people in a dysfunctional relationship?"

"I know, right? It's like magic." He snapped his fingers. "We should start with a beach getaway."

"Where are my parents? Upstairs, you said?"

A scream from outside interrupted them, then a resounding shatter of wood and stone, and the sentry dashed in. "The undead have risen! Monsters have stormed the gates!"

Close on his heels followed two undead trolls with large clubs. Their decayed and gray skin bore as many rips and tears as their ragged clothes. But the huge monsters swung their clubs with fearsome power.

"Happening now!" cried Prince Hugo. He held up his mirror and sketched himself with an approaching troll over his shoulder.

Maryan backed up against the far wall. She used the knife she'd taken from the bandits to hack through a rope there, and the large chandelier fell onto the head of one of the undead fiends, smashing its skull and bringing it to the floor.

"Where's the other troll?" she asked the cowering sentry.

"It took Prince Hugo and ran away!" cried the man. "I think it's eating him."

"Get the other guards and fix the gates," she told him. Then she climbed the stairs up the tower.

Two floors up, she came across the ornate entrance to the guest quarters. She knocked on the hard wood.

"Come in," called a voice inside.

She opened the door and found her mother and father, the Queen and King of Offerdell, seated by the fire.

"You're still up," was all she could think to say.

Her mother put down her knitting. "It's past our bedtime, dear, but that Prince Hugo is a bit of a night owl."

"It's great to see you," said her father. "Can you bring the grapes over here?"

Maryan put a hand over her face. "Oh, no. You pretended to be captured by bandits so that I'd come and meet Prince Hugo, didn't you?"

"Isn't he the sweetest thing?" asked her mother. "And so fashionable."

"He's got like a million followers," said her father. "I'm not sure what that means, but many of my peers are impressed. And he's in line to inherit all the southern territories."

Maryan glared at them. "Mom, Dad, you need to stop sending suitors after me. They keep getting eaten by servants of the underworld."

Her father spread his hands. "A relationship requires work *and* sacrifice, Maryan."

"Honey, I know dating can be uncomfortable at times, but we want grandkids." Her mother picked up her knitting again. "I mean, we want what's best for you and your future."

"Well, I'm sorry, but Prince Hugo was eaten by an undead troll a minute ago."

"Oh, bother, another one fallen?" Her father stroked his regal beard. "We're running out of eligible nobles."

"What about that nice sailing boy from the islands?"

King Albert looked at the queen. "Reginald the Merciless?"

"Mom, really, a second rate pirate?"

"He's got a large fleet, dear, and those dashing boots with the large cuffs that I know you like."

"When did I say I liked—"

"And he controls most of the shipping routes east of Karrutha," said her father. "That's nothing to sneeze at."

"Look," said Maryan. "I'm heading back to Bluntworth. I need to help defend the city."

"Oh, yes, dear, how's that going?"

"Not great, now that you ask. We accidentally freed the Lich King from his desert imprisonment, and he's coming to kill everyone. And the Mayor won't help because he doesn't want to believe it's all really happening."

"We're always here if you need to talk, dear."

"Thanks, Mom." Maryan stopped at the doorway. "Mom, Dad. You need to stop sending suitors, all right? When the time is right, I'll find someone. But it will be up to me."

The queen glared at her. "Maryan, I'm sure you have strong feelings right now, what with your boyfriend having been consumed by an undead ettin—"

"It was a troll, Mom. Only one head."

King Albert folded his arms. "Trust us, Maryan. We know politics, and we know *you*, so we can pick—"

"You don't know me as well as you think, Dad. It's not your fault. But I'm my own person now."

The queen harrumphed, but Maryan held her gaze without blinking.

Her mother shook her head and returned to her knitting. "Well, dear, if it's so important to you, we could give it a rest until the fall."

Maryan turned to her father.

King Albert finally shrugged. "I'll do what your mother says, of course."

"Thank you. Now, you should leave in the morning and get back to Offerdell. It's not safe here."

"And there's little reason to stay, since your undead friends seem to have eaten the prince anyway," muttered the King.

Her mother waved at him. "Oh, honestly, Albert, don't be such a grump. It wasn't Maryan's fault."

Maryan waved. "See you."

"Right you are, dear, and remember, we love you."

"Love you, too."

Princess Maryan walked down the winding stairs to the base of the tower. The journey back to Bluntworth awaited her, long and difficult. But now that she'd gotten her parents to respect her own choices, just a little, she felt as if she could cross the distance in only a few great bounds.

She entered the courtyard, where guardsmen repaired the damage to the gates. The captured bandit helped to nail the large planks together. "See, I'm contributing to the common good," he explained. "Also, they said they'd hit me if I didn't help."

She waved good-bye, then started back for Bluntworth, the moon now directly overhead.

Chapter 24
Defenders

> *I should clarify Verse 27, where I said 'Great leaders show their smartness by seizing easy opportunities to protect their citizens from catastrophe.'*
> *Seizing and destroying doesn't count.*
>
> — *Considered Revelations, Book 112 "Leaders Who Are Very Smart", Chapter 72, Verse 28*

Maryan began the long hike back to Bluntworth. The sky brightened, dawn imminent when she reached the river and untied her small boat. The Goldswell rushed even wider and stronger here, downstream of the city. She rowed as fast as she could, avoiding debris and the occasional bit of early morning river traffic, and made it to the eastern shore, now even further downstream. But the river road awaited her, a fast and easy walk along the smooth ground. Far to the north she could see the bright morning sun glinting off the spires of the Mayor's palace.

After a few hours, about when she reckoned she was halfway there, an overgrown trail cut off to the right to climb a forested hill. "Healer Nyala's house," said Maryan to herself, looking up the hill. Should she detour and see if the healer was still there?

Nyala walked down the trail and waved to her. "Oh, hello, Your Highness. Fancy meeting you here!"

"Good morning, Healer Nyala! I was heading to Bluntworth."

"Perfect, ma'am. I'll join you, if that's all right."

"Of course. I hope your house is in good shape?"

"Oh, yes. A bit of cleaning up to do, but nothing too bad."

A large plume of smoke wound above the city as they approached the southern gate. Maryan frowned. "I hope nothing is wrong!"

"It seems to be near the palace," said Nyala. Indeed, the smoke rose beside the towers of the palace and the cathedral.

They hurried through the city streets, and finally reached the central square. The Mayor and many townspeople stood in front of a bonfire.

"That's odd," said Nyala. "They're burning a big pile of lemongrass."

"Mayor, what are you doing?" Maryan pointed to the crackling flames. "Why are you burning all the city's lemongrass?"

"I already told you, I don't want to believe in the rising undead or any threat to the city. It's a situation I'm not capable of handling, so I've decided to ignore it."

"But why burn it all?" Maryan waved her arms. "It makes no sense! Even if you don't believe a sprig of lemongrass can help, it doesn't hurt to wear it, and by wearing it, the citizens can protect each other."

"The very existence of lemongrass threatens my narrative that the prophecy is fake." He raised his chin. "And also, I find wearing a sprig of lemongrass to be uncomfortable. It's kind of scratchy on my shirt. It's not worth it, even if it does protect other people from death."

"Yeah!" One of the town coopers held up a torch, and a sign that said *Burn the Lemingras*. "We won't live in fear!"

Maryan groaned. "It looks like we can no longer deploy lemongrass for our mutual protection. Where are my compatriots?"

"We threw them out of the city," said the Mayor. "They're in the Badlands."

"Do you mean they escaped the palace and are now facing the Lich King on their own, because you refuse to?"

"We threw them out of the city," repeated the Mayor.

"Citizens of Bluntworth!" called Maryan. "We face a threat greater than any the city has seen in generations. The armies of the undead are massing outside our gates. Our only chance to defeat them is to stand together now. Who is with me?"

The square remained quiet, except for the crackling fire of lemongrass.

"I told you," said the Mayor. "The problem is too big and scary, so most people would prefer to ignore it. And I've been telling everyone for days not to believe you. No one will go with you."

"Oh, hey, I'll go." Onkar the bishop candidate shuffled forward in his brown robe. "Wow, Healer Nyala, you're here too? That's most

CHAPTER TWENTY-FOUR: DEFENDERS

righteous of you."

"Normally, I'd refuse any citizen who asked to use the eastern gate." The Mayor spread his arms. "But since you clearly want to face certain death, and are bringing the troublesome bishop candidate with you, how can I say no? You are free to enter the Badlands."

"Thank you, Mayor." Maryan walked away.

"Oh wow, like, everyone is here. Good to see you all." Onkar stood on the cathedral steps and waved at the crowd, none of whom waved back. "I can see you're angry now, that's all right. Sometimes I get angry too. But you can't give in to that." He looked east, shielding his eyes with his hand. "So I'll go with the princess now, and maybe I'll come back, maybe not. I'd be happy to see others of you join us outside the wall to defend our town. But I won't demand it of anyone. It's a choice everyone has to make on their own, you know? Anyway, I'll miss you all. Take care of each other."

Onkar walked down the steps, townspeople moving out of his way. The town cooper glared at him and threw another bundle of lemongrass on the fire. But several others in the crowd lowered their gaze to the ground and shifted uncomfortably as the bishop candidate passed them.

The sackcloth-robed Onkar joined Healer Nyala, and they followed Maryan out of the square.

Outside of the city gates, the Badlands remained as hot and flat as Maryan remembered. Above, darker clouds invaded the blue sky, a boiling dark mass that occasionally crackled with thunder and lightning. Further east, darkness obscured the plains, and she bit her lip. The shadows could easily conceal several armies, only an hour's march from the city walls.

Right in front of her stood five people and a horse. "Hello, everyone!"

Gunthar broke into a broad grin. "Good to see you, Your Highness!"

Maryan surveyed the small group. "So no one else agreed to stand against the Lich King?"

Sir Humphrey shook his head. "We tried, ma'am. The townspeople just laughed at us and said they didn't want to believe in the Lich King. Haffleton didn't want to risk fighting unless Bluntworth was fighting too. We sent messages farther out, but..." He shrugged. "No one has turned up."

"We'll see what we can do," said Maryan.

"If you don't mind, Your Highness, I'd like to contribute as well."

They turned at the voice. Councilor Wilson stood there with several servants in tow. "I brought you this," he said, as his servants scurried around the flat ground.

In a few minutes they had assembled a grand tent, striped with blue and white, with a small gold flag on the top. "This is all I can do, but I think it's better than nothing."

"Thank you, Councilor Wilson."

"My pleasure, ma'am." And he and his servants returned back inside the gates.

Maryan and the others inspected the tent. They found a large table, several chairs and pillows, some food and water, and a chest full of maps.

"Well, we have no armies to stand against the Lich King, but we do have a tent." Yang tapped the center pole. "That's something."

"What do you think will happen next, Your Highness?" Ex-Bookkeeper Andi looked at her with wide eyes.

"If I was the Lich King, I'd use that storm cloud to good effect. I'd bring my armies as close to the city as I could, then reveal my forces all at once, to scare any defenders."

"Hey," called Onkar. "Something is happening out here. It's, like, really weird."

The adventurers emerged from the tent and stood near the bishop candidate. Ahead of them, the plains dipped slightly, then rose to a high point less than a league away. The storm clouds there churned, an eerie howling noise echoing on the flat ground.

All at once, the storm clouds dissipated, condensing and falling to the ground as drops of black ink. With the clouds gone, the entire ridge across from the city was visible, and lined with an undead host. Vast legions spanned the horizon. Mighty giants stood tall above the horde, their dirty cloaks waving in the breeze. Mounted cavalry stood in the front, armored riders leering at them with empty eye sockets, ripped gray flags flying on the tips of sharp lances. Skeleton troops leered at them everywhere they looked, an uncountable mass of undead soldiers.

And across the plains stood a tattered tent, with the Lich King sitting in front atop a large throne of skulls. He regarded them as if considering a bug on a chessboard.

"Oh, shoot." Gunthar shook his head. "I really thought Wizard Yang had destroyed him."

"I did." She frowned. "But he has returned, stronger than before."

"The Lich King has brought his armies for the final assault, just like I thought." Maryan's expression was grim.

"And then what?" asked Ex-Bookkeeper Andi.

"If I was him, I'd also keep several forces in reserve."

"Indeed, ma'am, I see the spears of many companies behind the main lines," noted Sir Humphrey, peering across the plains.

"Then, seeing that I was opposed by less than ten people, I'd send out a skirmishing force to eliminate the defenders."

"Skirmishing force, straight ahead!" cried Gunthar, pointing at an advancing mob of undead. "Looks like mostly skeletons, with some undead trolls."

"This is it, everyone." Maryan pulled out the sword she'd taken from the bandits.

Gunthar and Yang helped the knight into his armor, and he pulled Gwendoline out of her sheath.

"Wait, Sir Humphrey, I got you something." Wizard Yang dug in her pack, then straightened. "Ta-da!" She held up a long ribbon.

The knight squinted at it. "What is that?"

"It's a grounding ribbon," she said. "I couldn't use wire, since your sword has too much current. Regular wire would be vaporized. So this is a wide ribbon of chain mail." Yang attached the long stretch of flexible metal to Sir Humphrey's right wrist.

The knight raised his sword. Even with his arm fully extended, a considerable length of ribbon dragged on the ground. "'Tis very long," he noted.

"Yes." Yang grimaced. "You'll have to be careful not to trip over it. But I think it's better than being shocked all the time."

"Onwards, Happenhouse!" he cried, and clicked the switch at the hilt. The valley lit with a blazing flash of light, and Gwendoline sparkled with blue-white energy bolts. Once in a while a particularly bright bolt would crackle, and the ribbon would light up, scorching the dirt where the chain mail touched the ground.

"It seems to work," said Yang.

"Indeed, Wizard!" He took a practice swing, and the blade arced and crackled, sending a jolt into his arm. The knight staggered back. "Ouch!"

"I'm sorry, Sir Humphrey. I don't think you can wave the sword around that much. Just hold it in front of you like a torch."

"Like this?" He shuffled forward in his oversized armor, holding his arm out straight, the sword sticking straight up, energy bolts occasionally zapping the ground.

Yang nodded. "Yup."

"Methinks it is, well... Less badass."

"I know, but it's all I could think of."

"Heads up!" cried Maryan. "The undead approach!"

The oncoming horde had reached the low point of the slight valley ahead, and now climbed the slope towards them. Many ranks of skeletons advanced at the front, long spears at the ready, with trolls marching behind.

Gunthar hefted his axe, and dug his heel into the dirt. "We won't sell this ground cheaply."

But only a few steps later, the approaching force stopped. The skeletons and trolls stared at them, then turned around and walked back.

"What's happening, ma'am?" Ex-Bookkeeper Andi didn't take her eyes off the departing soldiers.

"I'm not sure." Maryan lowered her blade a fraction of an inch.

"Sorry we're late."

The princess turned, and saw a mass of town militia behind her. Men and women stood in lines, carrying swords and spears and wooden shields.

The leader stood in front of them in a leather vest and pauldrons, and raised a knuckle to his forehead in salute. "Your pardon, ma'am. The Mayor wouldn't let us use the eastern gate, so we had to go around the south."

"Who are you?" Maryan blinked at them all.

"We're about half the militia from Bluntworth, ma'am. Not everyone listens to the Mayor." He nodded to Onkar. "Candidate."

"Oh, hey there, Vikal. Wow, you all showed up at the right time."

CHAPTER TWENTY-FOUR: DEFENDERS

"Yes." Vikal stroked his short black beard uncertainly. "Ah, ma'am, where should we..."

Maryan gestured in front of the tent. "Set up your companies there, Captain. And start digging lines of stakes immediately."

"Aye, ma'am." Vikal turned and shouted to the militia forces. "You heard Her Highness! Set up smartly, now."

"What are they doing, ma'am?" Andi pointed out across the valley. The undead skirmishing force had stopped retreating, and now stood motionless, staring at them.

Maryan frowned. "If I was the Lich King, I'd order a cavalry charge to catch us off-guard. The heavy cavalry could scatter our lines before our defenses were prepared."

"Cavalry incoming!" Gunthar pointed out, where a line of armored, undead knights charged on bony steeds.

"Look alive, now!" Maryan raised her sword.

The militia stopped their preparations and instead huddled in groups, spears at the ready.

"Do you have any archers, Captain?"

"No, ma'am," answered Vikal.

They were both very surprised when a swarm of arrows whistled overhead, plunging into the advancing cavalry. The arrows punched through armor, sending many skeletal knights to the ground. The few riders that made it through the wave of arrows were brutally dispatched by the militia, while a second wave of arrows decimated a following rank of horsemen.

The remaining cavalry wheeled and staggered back to the lines of the undead, leaving piles of bones in their wake.

Maryan looked back. Ranks of archers stood behind them, in rows before the walls, led by the blue-haired Customs Officer.

"Hello, Your Highness," she saluted. "Haffleton reporting. Where should we set up?"

"Welcome, Captain. How about there," said Maryan, pointing to the ground above and behind the militia companies.

"Right." The Customs Officer winced. "Can we set up a bit higher? Then we'd line up with both the militia and your command tent. It's better Feng Shui."

"Sure."

The Customs Officer directed the archers to set up, then waved at

Gunthar. "Nice leathers, Barbarian!"

"Thanks! Though they do chafe a bit."

"If you think that's bad, you should try kobold armor!" she called back.

Ex-Bookkeeper Andi stared with wide eyes at the assembled troops. In front, the militia completed lines of stakes and a trench, while the archers had set up ranks behind, their longbows ready at their sides. "What happens now, Your Highness?"

Maryan looked up. "It's late in the day, and now the Lich King has realized we have more defenders than he thought. I think he'll wait, adjust his forces, and then try a new move in the morning."

Chapter 25
Champion

> *Remember Verse 15, where I disparaged a knight's sense of honor? I need to make an update: honor is even more of a liability than I thought.*
>
> — *Considered Revelations, Book 22 "More About Knights", Chapter 2, Verse 34*

Princess Maryan slept deeply, having missed the previous night's sleep. Low clouds obscured the moon, leaving the valley in absolute darkness. Occasionally, a scream or ragged laugh would carry across the plains, and several sentries reported distant footsteps and the sawing of wood, but no attack came.

In the morning, the sun rose behind gray clouds, and the small defending force could finally survey the undead host again.

"Interesting," said Maryan, pointing across the plains. "He's shifted more of his forces to the center, as I suspected, so as to apply more pressure here. But what is *that*?"

Right between the armies, in the no-mans land at the bottom of the shallow valley, stood many wooden bleachers around a flat square, marked with stakes and rope.

Maryan squinted. "He's up to something."

Something in the foreground caught her eye, and she recoiled in horror. "Gunthar, what happened to you?"

"Aren't these great?" He turned around so they could see his outfit. His leather vest had been replaced with a crisp blue collared shirt, which in turn was tucked into his trousers, girded at the waist with a braided leather belt. And the trousers themselves were a pleated wonder of tan fabric and sharp creases.

"I've never seen anything like it before," said Yang. "What are they?"

"They're *pants*. And of a new material, and a color, suitable for both battles and leisure." He put his hands on his hips, and raised his chin. "I found a better tailor."

"Oh, my," said Maryan, staring at the pressed trousers.

"They're called *khakis,* and they're the latest thing." He did a stretch, extending one foot far forward, lowering himself near the ground. "And no chafing!"

Several carts creaked along the flat ground in front of the walls.

Healer Nyala approached. "Councilor Wilson has organized provisions for the army," she said, pointing back at the wagons.

"Oh, good," said Maryan.

"Let's get breakfast ourselves," said the healer. "It won't do to be hungry."

They moved into the tent, and Maryan surveyed a map on the table as she ate. "The Lich King is clearly up to no good. Based on the stakes and the makeshift arena, I'd say he's going to propose single combat."

Wizard Yang blinked. "Why? What good does that do?"

"Probably a ploy to keep as much of his army intact as possible. I'm sure he has other conquests in mind after Bluntworth. He's likely to propose single combat, with the winner determining the course of battle. Given how outnumbered we are, he probably thinks we'll accept the challenge."

Gunthar spread his arms. "Well, why not? Single combat does strike me as better odds than facing his entire army."

"We can't accept any challenge. First, I don't trust him to honor the deal. If, by some chance, our champion wins in single combat, the Lich King would just attack with his armies anyway." She frowned at the map, which depicted the newly-built arena in the middle. "And even for single combat, I think he'd cheat somehow. It's guaranteed death for our champion."

Cornelius nodded. "I agree, Your Highness. It can only be a trick."

"None of us will accept any challenge to single combat from the Lich King, are we agreed?"

Gunthar muttered under his breath, but finally threw up his hands. "Fine, ma'am. I will agree *not* to accept any challenge, out of respect for your wishes." He wagged his finger at them. "But I want to be in the front lines when we do smash that son of a witch."

"Agreed," said Maryan.

"Your Highness!" One of the sentries dashed into the tent. "An undead messenger has approached under flag of parley. We have been challenged to single combat, with the outcome to determine

CHAPTER TWENTY-FIVE: CHAMPION

the fate of Bluntworth!"

Maryan gave the others in the tent an *I told you so* look.

The breathless sentry stood straighter. "The match is set for thirty minutes from now, and if our Champion wins, the Lich King and his armies will quit the field!"

"Go and tell their messenger that we decline the challenge." Gunthar waved at the sentry. "We'll battle this out, army to army, carnage upon carnage, like civilized peoples."

"Sir?" The sentry blinked.

Maryan leaned over the table. "Out of curiosity, what is the contest? Swords? Knives?"

"Fireballs?" asked Yang.

The sentry shifted his gaze from Gunthar. "Uh, no, ma'am. It is a contest of fisticuffs."

"Fisticuffs?" Maryan's mouth went dry, and she frantically scanned the tent. "Oh, no. Where is Sir Humphrey?"

"Do we know anything about the other Champion?" Healer Nyala pursed her lips.

"Just his name." The sentry looked at the scroll in his hand. "Grom."

"Grom." Nyala stared at the ceiling of the tent, tapping her cheek with one finger. "Do I know that name?"

The sentry turned back to Gunthar. "And sir, the challenge has already been accepted. Our Champion is preparing." He bowed to Maryan. "By your leave, ma'am, I need to return to my post."

The sentry left the tent, almost bowled over by a man coming the other way in oversized armor.

Sir Humphrey spread his arms. "Good news, everyone. I've solved our undead problem!"

Gunthar pointed angrily at the knight. "How come *he* gets to accept the challenge, and *I* don't?"

Sir Humphrey's jaw dropped as he stared at the barbarian. "By the trousers of the saints, sir, whatever are you wearing?"

"I get to accept the next challenge, right? Since Happenhouse here got to accept this one."

"Sir Humphrey, why did you accept the challenge?" Maryan sputtered as she tried not to shred the table with her bare hands. "What were you thinking?"

"What was I thinking, Your Highness?" He smiled and raised his fists. "No one can beat me at fisticuffs!"

"Have you ever beaten anyone in a fisticuffs contest before?" asked Yang.

"Er, no, good wizard. This would be the first time. But I truly enjoy the sport."

"Quick," said Maryan. "Let's decline the challenge anyway."

"I don't think we can, Your Majesty." Ex-Bookkeeper Andi crossed her arms. "If we decline now, that's a forfeit, and we'd give up Bluntworth to the undead marauders."

Sir Humphrey looked at all of them. "Why are you so worried?"

"Come on," said Maryan, striding out of the tent. "Let's see what we can find out about this opposing champion."

Outside, the bleachers around the contest square began to fill up. Skeletons stood around their side of the field, with many more in the stands, while the men and women of Bluntworth gathered on the other side. Flags from many nations past and present flew at the corners, and more food carts had come in from the city.

"Councilor Wilson!" Maryan spotted the man nearby. "I see the Mayor has opened the eastern gates. Has he decided to join in the defense of the city?"

"Good morning, Your Majesty. And no, the Mayor still refuses to believe the prophecy. He's asking people to simply ignore the massed ranks of the undead." The councilor pointed to the food stalls and performers nearby. "But the people rose up as one and demanded to be able to see the fisticuffs contest. And the street merchants wanted to be where the party was."

"Ah." Maryan pointed at a group of richly-dressed men and women behind a counter with tallies of numbers on it. "Who is that?"

"Ma'am, those are the famous Merchant Houses of Bluntworth. They're here to run the betting."

"Betting?"

"Hey, look!" Gunthar pointed at the table of numbers, then smacked Sir Humphrey on the shoulder. "You're getting even odds. Ha!"

"And who is the other champion?" wondered Maryan.

"There he is," said Ex-Bookkeeper Andi, pointing over at the lines

CHAPTER TWENTY-FIVE: CHAMPION

of the undead. A large, decaying man sat on the ground, surrounded by other undead who wrapped his knuckles in thick cloth.

"Wow, he's big," said Wizard Yang.

"Methinks that is an illusion," noted Sir Humphrey. "The skeletons around him are short in stature."

"No, he's definitely big." Yang held up her hand. "He's *way* taller than any person, and he's sitting down."

"Their champion isn't human," gasped Cornelius. "He's an undead giant."

Murmurs of surprise rippled through the gathered Bluntworth citizens as they beheld the Lich King's champion.

"Of course he's undead," said Sir Humphrey. "That goes without saying."

"Hmm, the odds seem to have gone down." Gunthar stared at the betting board. "You're a bit of an underdog now, Sir Humphrey."

"Aren't you worried about a contest of fisticuffs with a giant?" asked Ex-Bookkeeper Andi.

"Nay, lady. Giants are big, but move slow and think even slower. He'll get a taste of my knuckles before he even knows I'm there!"

"Is it *King* Grom, I wonder?" Healer Nyala squinted over at the undead champion. "He's been dead for over three hundred years."

"*King* Grom?" Gunthar looked at her.

"Yes, that's him, I'm sure of it. Grom, the king of the frost giants. He was big and fast and utterly ruthless. Grom the Slaughterer, they used to call him. Under him, the frost giants conquered most of the northeast. They would have taken the whole continent, I shouldn't wonder, but then Grom choked and died on an oxen bone at a feast, at the young age of sixty-three." Healer Nyala whistled. "He's well-preserved, given that he's been buried so long, but maybe that's an advantage of always being frozen. Seeing King Grom in action will be an amazing sight!"

Across the plain the undead champion stood up, towering over everyone and everything else. He flexed his muscles and his tattered sleeves ripped further as biceps the size of bears moved around. His undead flesh had a slightly blue cast to it, with patches of ice glinting in the sun. Fog condensed around him and pooled at his feet.

"By the gods of extra-large clothing!" exclaimed Cornelius. "I don't think a more fearsome giant has ever strode the firmament."

The town cooper fainted in fear, and had to be carried away on his *Burn the Lemingras* sign.

"Oh, my." Gunthar shook his head, looking back at the merchants. "I've never seen odds that low."

Maryan put her hands on her hips. "Sir Humphrey, you can't have a contest of fisticuffs with a twenty-foot-tall undead frost giant king. He'll smash you to pieces."

"*If* he doesn't freeze you first," said Wizard Yang.

"Methinks you could show more confidence in my skill," huffed the knight.

"Well, sir, I'd have to agree with them," said Gunthar. "Why don't we withdraw from the fight? The Lich King is going to attack afterward anyway."

"Withdraw?" Sir Humphrey stood taller, his eyes searing holes in each of them. "A Happenhouse *never* turns away from a challenge."

"Please, please." Healer Nyala waved the others a few steps back. "This isn't what he needs to hear right now. Let me handle this." She put a hand on Sir Humphrey's shoulder and spoke in her calm healer's voice. "Do you have a will?"

"Milady, please!" The knight waved vaguely in the direction of the opposing champion. "I can assure you that I have this fight in hand."

"We'd better get to the field, ma'am," said Councilor Wilson. "The referee will specify the rules."

"Referee?" Maryan looked around. "Who can be an impartial judge between mortals and a host of vicious undead?"

"I hope it's someone nice," said Ex-Bookkeeper Andi.

"Let's get this over with." Inga floated down, her butterfly wings shimmering in the sunlight. "I can't stand being out in the daytime."

"Who is that?" asked Maryan.

"We didn't get a chance to introduce you in the Badlands, because you were unconscious," said Andi. "That's Inga, the ghost fairy queen. She's always angry and bitter at everyone because she was jilted at the altar centuries ago, although I'm not supposed to gossip about that."

"Keep calm," said Maryan. "Jilted or not, I'm sure she cares about the town."

"I need a representative from each army to join me by the field," called Inga. "This fight will be run fair and square, even though nothing matters because we're all going to die alone, betrayed by those that claimed to love us."

Chapter 26
Fisticuffs

> *A considerable number of fisticuff matches are won on a technicality.*
>
> — *Considered Revelations*, Book 43 *"Ways In Which a Considerable Number of Fisticuff Matches are Won"*, Chapter 68, Verse 2

Councilor Wilson stepped forward. "Your Highness, it would be best if you were the representative for Bluntworth."

"Of course." Maryan walked down to the field, the councilor following.

A short, wide skeleton approached from the Lich King's lines. He had a helmet with long, curved horns, and golden riding armor with a large mace swinging at his side.

Councilor Wilson whispered to the princess. "That's Grom's representative, ma'am. The Bandit Prince Tuguslar. He and his band of merciless riders terrorized the northern plains a century ago."

"Hurry up, representatives." Inga hovered near the field in the no-man's land, waving at them impatiently. "My goodness, it took you long enough. Please introduce yourselves."

Maryan nodded to the skeletal bandit prince. "Your Highness. I hope we can conduct this contest of champions in a manner befitting the honor of both our houses."

"I **** on your grave," said Tuguslar.

"Right, that's over with." Inga floated higher, and called out across the gathered armies. "I'll repeat the rules, since some of you have half-rotted brains, and the rest of you are undead. This is a contest of fisticuffs lasting three rounds. If a champion is knocked from the field, he forfeits the round. Best of three rounds wins the contest. Killing the other champion wins the contest. If you put a hand on a weapon, you lose the contest. Did you idiots get that?"

The field and its thousands of gathered spectators were deathly quiet.

"I'll take that as a *yes*. Are the champions ready?"

The undead frost giant had been sitting at the far end of the field,

CHAPTER TWENTY-SIX: FISTICUFFS

and now stood. He towered over the spectators in the highest bleachers, his gargantuan icy muscles rippling and shining in the sun. "King Grom is ready!" His voice rolled over the Badlands like a peal of cold fisticuffs thunder.

"Grom! Grom! Grom!" The undead warriors across the field began chanting, pounding the ground and bleachers with skeletal feet, shaking the earth.

"Objection!" cried Maryan. "King Grom emits a cold aura, freezing everything within five paces. That's not fair to his opponent."

"Well, I can't turn it off," said Grom. "And I have to suffer that human's stinky breath."

Inga shook her head at Maryan. "Objection overruled. A deadly cold aura isn't technically a weapon."

The skeletal bandit prince smiled a toothy grin, showing several gaps.

"Grom! Grom! Grom!" The chanting and shaking continued.

The knight stood only a few paces away, and waved at them. "I say! It's hard to hear myself over all the noise, but Sir Humphrey Happenhouse is ready!"

"Happenhouse! Happenhouse!" cried Ex-Bookkeeper Andi, but no one else took up the chant.

"Oh, my." Councilor Wilson paled as Grom rolled his shoulders, sending chunks of ice falling to the ground with loud *thunks*. "Ma'am, I've never seen a more fearsome opponent. What can Sir Humphrey do against that?"

"He has several tactics." Maryan considered the field. "His best approach is to stay mobile, far away from Grom so he doesn't freeze. With luck, he can stay warm and tire Grom out. Maybe then Grom will make a mistake."

"Mistake? Like what?"

An undead troll in an iron helmet threw a boulder across the field at Sir Humphrey, but from the side, where the knight couldn't see it in time to dodge. The humongous rock hit his left shoulder with a crunch, bowling him over.

"Ouch!" Sir Humphrey staggered to his feet again, his left arm dangling and bleeding.

"Objection!" cried Maryan. "The undead armies

sucker-bouldered our champion!"

"Sorry, dear," said Inga. "I didn't see it."

"Sir Humphrey!" Ex-Bookkeeper Andi screamed, but the knight couldn't hear her over the chanting of the undead armies.

"Champions!" Inga raised her hand, then brought it down. "Begin!"

"Right," said Maryan, "we'll see—"

There was a metallic crunch, and Sir Humphrey's ragged body flew over them, smashing into a fruit stand.

"By the gods of the subcommittee, that's one fast frost giant," noted Councilor Wilson.

"Round one to Grom, by field infraction," called Inga. "The Bluntworth champion was thrown from the marked area."

"Hurry!" Maryan ran towards the mangled knight, but Healer Nyala sprinted ahead of her and reached the man first. The healer tilted up Sir Humphrey's unconscious head and poured in some red Elixir of Sakura.

The knight coughed, then yelped. "Ouch! That hurt worse than being punched."

"The Elixir is designed to remind you of the pain," scolded Nyala. "You're not supposed to get yourself hurt in the first place."

"'Twasn't that bad," said Sir Humphrey, sitting up.

"Your rib cage had collapsed and punctured both lungs, your spine was broken in three places, and your pelvis was crushed."

"It could have been worse."

Maryan surveyed the knight's armor. The metal plates had buckled inwards in places, and thick frost encased every piece. "Gunthar, can you pop the worst of the dents out of Sir Humphrey's armor?"

"Aye, ma'am." The barbarian went to work, fixing and re-attaching the imploded metal panels.

"Oh, thank you." Sir Humphrey took a deep breath. "'Twas difficult to move with the dents pressing into me."

Inga hovered above the field. "Are you ready over there? If you take much longer, you'll forfeit the match."

"We're coming!" Maryan waved at her, and helped Sir Humphrey to his feet. The knight stumbled over to his corner of the field again.

CHAPTER TWENTY-SIX: FISTICUFFS

Cornelius wrung his hands together, seeing Grom standing three times taller than the knight. "I don't see any way that Sir Humphrey can win."

"Indeed, Chronicler, I think many citizens share your sentiment." Councilor Wilson gestured at the gathered townspeople, who watched the combatants with quiet dread. Only the undead made any noise, pounding the bleachers and chanting Grom's name over and over.

"Champions, are you ready for round two?" called Inga.

Grom waved, the air filled with undead chants of his name. Sir Humphrey waved as well, though no one took much notice.

Again, the undead troll threw a boulder at Sir Humphrey from the side, and again, it shattered his left shoulder and sent him crashing to the ground. "Ouch!" he repeated as he stood.

"Objection!" cried Maryan. "They—"

"Sorry, dear," said Inga. "I didn't see it."

"I can't look." Ex-Bookkeeper Andi turned away, sobbing.

"Grom! Grom! Grom!"

"Champions!" Inga raised her hand, then brought it down. "Begin!"

Maryan leaned in. "Now this time—"

There was a great metallic crash, and once again Sir Humphrey flew overhead, smashing to the ground amongst the food carts.

"Round two to Grom," called Inga, "by field infraction."

The adventurers dashed over, and Nyala administered the Elixir. Sir Humphrey coughed and wheezed as he opened his eyes again.

"He's doomed!" wailed a merchant. "We're *all* doomed!"

"What can we do against a horde of invincible undead?" asked a cobbler. "Maybe the Mayor's right. Maybe we should stick our heads in the sand and pretend the undead don't exist."

"I worry about the effect of this fight on the town's morale, Your Highness." Councilor Wilson shook his head. "Perhaps that was the impact the Lich King intended. I fear our militia will abandon the field without a fight, should it come to that."

"Let's do what we can for Sir Humphrey right now," said Maryan.

They rejoined the knight, who sat in the midst of their companions. Wizard Yang affixed armor plates again as Gunthar popped the dents out.

"I almost had him that time," said Sir Humphrey, pulling chunks of ice out of his mustache.

"Can't we do something?" Ex-Bookkeeper Andi wrung her hands. "It's not fair! And they keep cheating!"

"We can't interfere." Maryan's face was grim. "If we do anything, the match will be forfeit."

"I don't know if you're keeping score, but we're about to lose the match anyway." Wizard Yang frowned. "Why don't I channel some of the frost giant's aura into a shield, or something?"

"No cheating!" Sir Humphrey's eyes lit up. "We will never stoop to their level. A Happenhouse always fights fair!"

"But it's not right that you get beaten just because you play fair and they don't!" Ex-Bookkeeper Andi had tears in her eyes.

"I'm sorry, good Bookkeeper. Honor is paramount. Even if it costs me everything." He took a deep breath. "I guess that's kind of the point."

"Oh..." She looked away.

"Are you ready yet?" Inga's angry voice rose over the constant *Grom, Grom, Grom* chants of the undead.

Meanwhile, the townspeople waited sullenly in the bleachers for the contest to continue. No one waved Bluntworth flags anymore. A soldier in a green vest near Maryan hung his head in his hands.

"Coming!" Maryan walked with the knight back to the field. "Sir Humphrey, we can still call off the fight." Maryan said it quietly so the others wouldn't hear. "The fight doesn't mean anything, since the Lich King will assault the city no matter what happens."

How could she get the knight out of the suicidal third round of the contest? They had lost the first two rounds of fisticuffs, meaning they could only win if the knight knocked out the undead frost giant king in this final round, which would take a miracle. And in some sense, the damage was already done. The town's morale was shot.

"I appreciate your concern, ma'am, but the fight means something to me." The knight looked up at the undead frost giant king, towering above the other end of the field. "I thought maybe I had a chance. But perhaps this is just as well." Sir Humphrey spoke in low tones as he took his corner. "This way I can go out with some note, ma'am. The Merchant Houses will foreclose on my family estates in a few hours. And I'm not in the prophecy anyway."

"The prophecy doesn't—"

"Sir Humphrey, please accept this as a token from me." Ex-Bookkeeper Andi approached and held out a mug that said *I'm billing you for this*. "It's not much of a token, and I'm not an accountant for the city anymore, but it's all I have now." She looked down at the ground and kicked at a small pebble. "You're very brave for doing this. I know you're supposed to only get favors from nobility. And I'm sure knights usually get something nice, like a silk handkerchief or—"

"Lady." Sir Humphrey stood a good inch taller, the mug held reverently in both hands. "I can assure you, no knight has *ever* received a gift that meant more to them than this." He brought the mug in and held it close, so Maryan could only see *billing*. "I will treasure it."

"Right." Ex-Bookkeeper Andi stood on her tiptoes and kissed Sir Humphrey on the cheek. "Good luck." She dashed off, wiping at her eyes.

Maryan peered at the knight. "Sir Humphrey?"

He stood at the corner of the field, staring at the mug in his hands. The Badlands echoed with continuous chants of *Grom, Grom, Grom,* the sky loomed with ominous clouds, and his once-bright armor showed many scratches and dents, but for a moment the knight's entire world appeared to be a single, slightly chipped accountant's mug. Color returned to Sir Humphrey's face as something more powerful than the Elixir restored his strength.

"Sir Humphrey?" she repeated.

He looked up, as if surprised to find anyone else there. "I'm sorry? Oh, yes, of course, ma'am." He hooked the mug to his belt and looked over at Grom, who preened for his adoring undead fans. "You know, Your Highness, I think you're right. There are other things in life besides prophecies." He stepped up to his corner, a hand to his head. "*Now* what do I do? I need to think about this."

Sir Humphrey knelt and flipped himself up to stand on his head, his new mug clanking against his breastplate. He still had Gwendoline strapped to his back, and the sword slid out of its scabbard. The knight gasped and reversed course. He righted himself in a fluid motion, deftly using the grounding chain mail ribbon to catch the naked blade and tie it tightly to himself, finishing the wrap with a big bow at his waist. The knight stood and stared up at the mighty frost giant king across the field.

Maryan sighed. "I'm sorry, Sir Humphrey, it's not possible to stand on your head while armed and armored, is it?"

"Not really, ma'am." The sword stuck out behind his shoulder, sheathed no longer, bound to his armor with the grounding ribbon. He cocked an eyebrow. "But mayhaps 'twas enough." He called out with his hands cupping his mouth. "Ho, barbarian! How stand my odds?"

Gunthar winced. "You don't want to know."

"Put a sovereign down on me. I'm good for it." And he tossed over his last coin, the Happenhouse lucky gold sovereign.

Gunthar caught it and approached the merchants, who competed with each other to give him even more ridiculous odds, eager to claim the easy money.

"Why the smile, mortal?" Grom sneered down at the knight from across the field. "Prince Tuguslar already told me. You aren't in the precious prophecy. You're nothing!" The frost giant king roared in laughter, while the undead armies chanted behind him. *Grom, Grom, Grom.*

Inga called out to them. "Champions, are you ready for the final round?"

The knight kept his eyes on the mighty giant. "'Twas a revelation, my dear Grom!"

"Oh?" The giant kept laughing, then waved to Inga.

Sir Humphrey waved his readiness to Inga, then turned back to Grom. "You're not in the prophecy either."

The undead king chuckled, but his eyes narrowed.

The knight raised his mailed fists. "Onwards, Happenhouse!" The motion shifted the chain mail grounding ribbon, tightening it around the hilt of the naked sword, and Maryan heard a tiny *click* as the button there depressed.

Instantly, the sword lit with electric arcs, which now swirled across his armor, the grounding ribbon channeling the current all over the metal plates. The whole of the knight blazed as a bright blue star in the field, and Maryan had to step back from the heat, shielding her eyes.

CHAPTER TWENTY-SIX: FISTICUFFS

Sir Humphrey waved his gauntleted fists in front of him, crackling with blue lightning. "Let's dance, Grom!"

The soldier in the green vest raised his head and stared at the knight, his jaw open.

The undead troll threw a boulder at the knight once more, but Sir Humphrey raised his hand and lightning arcs caught the huge stone midway, shattering it into harmless gravel which pinged and sparkled on his armor. The knight flicked his wrist, and another wild arc of blue electricity caught the troll and vaporized it in a plume of greasy smoke, its iron helmet falling to the ground with a hollow *plonk*.

The townspeople in the bleachers roared in appreciation, the Bluntworth flags flying again.

The soldier in the green vest stood and stomped his feet, clapping his hands. "Happenhouse! Happenhouse!"

"Objection!" cried the bandit prince Tuguslar. "The Bluntworth champion atomized an innocent bystander!"

"Sorry, dear," said Inga. "I didn't see it."

The unceasing chants of *Grom, Grom, Grom* ceased, and Grom himself took half a step back, eyeing Sir Humphrey uncertainly.

"Champions!" Inga raised her hand, then brought it down. "Begin!"

"What?" King Grom pointed at the knight. "He cheated! He touched his sword!"

"Technically, the knight never laid a hand on a weapon. He used that metal ribbon thingy instead." Inga rolled her eyes. "You always were a whiner, Grom, even when you were alive. Get on with it."

Grom stared with horror as Sir Humphrey stepped towards him, more arcs of lightning zapping the ground with loud *cracks* and puffs of smoke. The undead king grabbed the twin axes at his belt. "I'm through playing with you, mortal. Now, you die!" And he brought both axes down upon the knight with a ferocious roar.

But Sir Humphrey stood with both fists upraised, and the axes shattered before striking, consumed and incinerated by furious bursts of electricity.

"Ah!" Grom stepped back again, waving his hands against the smoke.

"Happenhouse! Happenhouse! Happenhouse!" chanted the

townspeople, waving their flags.

"Grom cheated there, Your Highness," noted Councilor Wilson. "He laid hands on his weapons."

"No objection."

Sir Humphrey launched himself up at the giant with a tremendous leap aided by crackling blue energy, landing a punch just above the belt.

A great explosion shattered the Badlands, smoke and blue arcs flying in all directions. The blast knocked Maryan off her feet, and she could hear shouts and thumps as many townspeople fell in the bleachers. Dust obscured everything, and she blindly pushed herself back up as echoes of the blast reverberated. Bits of bone and frozen frost giant chunks fell from the skies, pelting the armor of the armies with metallic clanks. Next to her, Councilor Wilson clambered to his feet, coughing and waving at the dust. Further away, Cornelius gathered sheets of paper from the ground and stuffed them back in his folio.

A breeze cleared away the dust, revealing a blazing Sir Humphrey standing alone amidst a blasted patch of ground.

"Round three and contest to the knight," said Inga, "by controlled detonation."

"You did it, Sir Humphrey!" Maryan couldn't help but cheer.

Gunthar roared in appreciation, his axe held high. "*Style move!*"

"**** this!" exclaimed Tuguslar, and he charged at Sir Humphrey with his mace.

Ex-Bookkeeper Andi stepped in front of the charging bandit prince and slapped him. "Stop cheating!"

The skeletal Tuguslar stood in a daze, staring at her with empty eye sockets.

Andi grabbed the mace from him and thwacked his head, sending it sailing over the town walls while the rest of the bandit prince collapsed in a pile of bones. Then the Ex-Bookkeeper ran over to Sir Humphrey, who had the good sense to turn off his sword before she jumped on him and gave him a furious hug.

"Happenhouse!" cried the townspeople, waving their flags again.

"Oh, spare me," said Inga with disgust. "Anyway, the contest is over, so I'm leaving." She called out to the robed figure sitting on the distant hilltop on his throne of skulls. "Remember, Lich King,

CHAPTER TWENTY-SIX: FISTICUFFS

you promised to quit the siege if their champion won." The ghost fairy queen vanished in a small puff of glitter.

"Oh my." Gunthar smacked the knight's armored shoulder with a friendly punch. "Your wager is sure to have a healthy return."

"Ah, about that." The leader of the merchant houses rubbed his hands together with a wince. "You see, it's a funny thing, the odds we gave your wager were a little too high, so there's this liquidity problem at the moment—"

Sir Humphrey grabbed the man by the lapels of his rich jacket. "Merchant Schmidt, are you saying you don't have the funds to pay me my winnings?"

"Ah yes, well, normally, of course—"

"Just a moment." Andi waved at them. "Don't forget, Merchant Schmidt, you can deduct Sir Humphrey's debt from the total first."

"That's a good point, Ex-Bookkeeper, a very good point, but you see, even with Sir Humphrey's estates fully restored, we're still a small amount short."

The knight glared at the groveling merchant. "The Happenhouse estates are mine again, and furthermore, you owe me a debt you cannot repay?"

"Well, ah, there are several interpretations—"

"Methinks, sir, you have three weeks to pay the debt, or I'll foreclose on your property."

"Now, sir, there's no need to be hasty—"

A long, evil horn cut off the merchant, the foul tone echoing off the walls of the city.

Gunthar narrowed his eyes. "What's that?"

"The Lich King is calling his armies back." Maryan stared across the field, where the undead legions re-assembled into companies.

Wizard Yang followed her gaze. "Maybe he's retreating?"

"I doubt it." Maryan put her hands on her hips, watching the lines of cavalry and heavy infantry raising their spears. "Captain Vikal, recall your companies."

The leader of the Bluntworth militia saluted back, and soon the city's own horns rang back in challenge.

Maryan kept her eyes on the Lich King. "Now the battle for Bluntworth begins in earnest."

Chapter 27
Negotiations

O, for the silver tongue of a diplomat!

— Considered Revelations, Book 183 "Things that Make You Say O", Chapter 33, Verse 4

"That's an awful lot of undead."

Ex-Bookkeeper Andi looked across the lines to the great host of the Lich King, arrayed in the mid-morning sun. There were ranks of skeletons, undead horsemen, giants, and four mummified but still surprisingly spry ocelots.

"Where did he find ocelots?" wondered Yang. "They live much further south."

Sir Humphrey squinted at the distant small cats. "Mayhaps they were shipped?"

"No," said Andi. "The tariffs on those things are crazy high."

"Some sort of portal? Like, maybe a small one?" Gunthar indicated an opening maybe a foot wide.

"A bigger problem is the *non*-ocelot contingent," said Maryan. "He can overwhelm us with sheer numbers."

"He's been able to construct a huge army by accumulating everyone who has ever faced him and failed." Wizard Yang shook her head. "Over the centuries, that's added up to quite a multitude."

"'Tis Wizard Ignacio, unless my eyes deceive me." Sir Humphrey pointed out a skeleton in a burned robe further south.

"What? He showed up here, after abandoning us while he was supposed to protect me?" Andi started walking over. "You owe me a refund!" she cried.

Maryan jogged over and stopped her. "Save it for the battle, Ex-Bookkeeper."

"Your Highness!" The bishop candidate hurried over, breathless in his sackcloth robe.

"What is it, Onkar?"

He pointed further north, where a green-tinged force held a hilltop overlooking the armies. "Ogres, ma'am."

CHAPTER TWENTY-SEVEN: NEGOTIATIONS

Maryan frowned at the many spears glinting in the sun. "What are they doing?"

"It's King Bofor. He got our messages, asking for assistance. He's brought the entire ogre army here."

"Yes, but why is he set up in the middle?"

"That's exactly what I asked him, ma'am. I was like, 'Why are you set up here, King Bofor? Why not set up with us on the Bluntworth side?' And he was all 'Well, we haven't decided which side we're on yet.' Only he used more colorful language."

"Oh, that monster." Ex-Bookkeeper Andi put her hands on her hips. "He's using this conflict to enrich himself and his people."

Yang raised an eyebrow. "Isn't the Mayor refusing to fight the Lich King for similar reasons?"

"He's sacrificing his citizens for the good of the economy. It's totally different."

Maryan strode towards the ogre encampment. "Let's go treat with them. Gunthar, we could use your help in translating."

The barbarian shrugged and followed her.

"The Mayor is already talking to their king, Your Highness." Councilor Wilson fell into step beside her. "I'm sure he's making a good offer."

"Oh, yes." Onkar hurried to keep up on the other side. "Bofor asked him 'What can you do for us?' And the Mayor was like, 'Well, we can give you a twenty percent cut of the river taxes on cutlery and tableware.' And Bofor was like, 'You can stick that up your—'"

"It sounds like the Mayor doesn't really know how to negotiate with ogres," said Maryan.

"The Mayor is negotiating from the weaker position, ma'am." Councilor Wilson gestured at the seemingly endless horde of undead staring at them from the eastern ridge. "He's essentially asking the ogre to die with us in a last-ditch defense of the city."

"Oh, yes," said Onkar. "That's what the Bofor dude said too."

They reached the front of the encampment, where King Bofor sat on a raised chair of intricately carved ebony, with several officers around him. Bofor sported heavy armor, iron plates seemingly an inch thick, with large gashes here and there. His helmet gleamed next to him, of similarly heavy iron construction with large horns.

"Is that the ogre we met on the Golden Plains?" Maryan pointed out one of the officers who sported steel tips on his tusks.

"Good eye, ma'am." Gunthar waved and called out. "Hey Huknar, did you get your **** kicked by a pack of **** rabbits?"

The ogre flashed them a rude hand gesture. "Go **** yourself, humans."

Gunthar leaned in. "He says 'Hello.'"

King Bofor glared at them. "Keep quiet, or I'll rip your **** off." Then he turned back to the Mayor. "Carry on, you little ****."

The Mayor bobbed his head meekly. "Ah, yes, well, as I was saying, Your Majesty, forty percent is my final offer, and I'd point out, that's a pretty good deal, what with the increasing volumes in fine tableware this season."

"I **** in your tableware!" roared King Bofor.

The Mayor looked around in confusion. "Did he accept my offer? I don't speak ogre very well."

"It's a bit ambiguous," noted Gunthar, "but his body language says 'no.'"

"Oh." The Mayor's shoulders drooped. "Forty-five percent?"

King Bofor waved in irritation and turned away from the Mayor, facing the Lich King's delegate. Instead of a giant or a warlike king, the undead ambassador was a tall skeleton in rich robes.

"That's Merchant Korloff," whispered Councilor Wilson. "He ran a pyramid scheme in Bluntworth two hundred years ago."

Onkar shook his head. "It's sad when merchants feel they need to defraud investors by faking returns. I'm always like, 'Why are you just taking money from new investors and pretending it's investment gains?' And they're all, 'Because otherwise everyone wants their money back.'"

"You misunderstand me, candidate Onkar." Councilor Wilson gestured out to the Badlands. "He started a company to build a large pyramid in the desert. But then he realized there was no way to make a profit, so he ran out of town with everyone's money."

"Wow," said Gunthar. "Look at that. That undead merchant has an entire legion wearing red capes."

"You like that?" The skeleton gestured further back into his lines. "There's a separate contingent there, with togas."

The barbarian whistled. "You have the coolest-dressed undead."

CHAPTER TWENTY-SEVEN: NEGOTIATIONS

Merchant Korloff smoothed the front of his robe with a skeletal hand. "I'm a collector."

"Did you come here to trade **** with the humans? Or are you going to make this **** worth my time?"

The undead merchant bowed low. "Deepest apologies, King Bofor, which you can stick up your ****. I've come to offer you **** so amazing, your **** hair will turn straight."

Gunthar winced. "Oh, he's good."

Bofor and the skeletal Korloff discussed the offer, while the Mayor frowned at Gunthar. "Why are you trading pleasantries with the enemy?"

"That undead merchant? Look, he's got all the best old fashions. How could I not? And how come you didn't make a better deal with the King?"

"Sorry," said the Mayor. "I already told you. I'm incapable of meeting this undead challenge to the city. All I can do is blunder around and make things worse. It's in my nature. And I admire the Lich King. I kind of hope he wins the ogre king's loyalty."

"What?" Maryan looked between the distant Lich King and the Mayor. "Why do you admire him?"

"I admire despots." The Mayor sighed in longing at the tyrant. "The more undemocratic they are, the more I love them. The way he suppresses free speech, and crushes opposition by a combination of lies and brute force, it's just..." He shrugged. "I find it incredibly sexy. Brutality is the same thing as strength, right?"

Maryan turned to Councilor Wilson. "Why do people vote for this man?"

"Most people *don't* vote for him, ma'am, but he fixes that by endless recounts."

King Bofor roared in laughter, and they all turned to face the large ogre.

"Ambassador Korloff here promised me some great ****, Mayor. The Lich King will offer us ogres most of the north, including the **** bits by the marshes, and he's not going to kill us for a while. Can you top that, you worthless ****?"

The Mayor scratched his head. "Well—"

"I'd remind you," said Ambassador Korloff, "that the Lich King is mighty and wise and regularly uses his territory's legal system to intimidate and suppress his political opponents."

"Oh, wow," said the Mayor. "Perverting the justice system to attack your own citizens... I'm so turned on right now." He bowed to the undead merchant. "You win."

"What?" Gunthar waved his hands wildly. "You can't capitulate like that. The Lich King's offer wasn't even that good."

"Sorry, everyone. The Lich King's brutal rulership is too seductive for me to try to stand in his way." The Mayor hustled back to the walls of Bluntworth. "And I don't want to acknowledge the existence of the undead anyway."

Councilor Wilson stared after the departing Mayor. "Truly a fascinating study in leadership, ma'am."

"We're up goblin creek without a paddle now," said Gunthar. "The undead horde was bad enough. And now we have to face an army of ogres in addition?"

"Well, Your Highness, why don't you make a better deal? You're, like, not really from Bluntworth either."

"Of course! Candidate Onkar is correct, ma'am." Councilor Wilson put a hand to his head. "As a foreign noble, you represent a political power separate from Bluntworth and the Lich King. I don't know why I didn't think of that before."

"But all I can really offer is a last stand," said Maryan, gesturing at the undead horde.

"That's true." The councilor frowned. "We don't have anything better to offer."

Onkar raised his hands. "The ogres aren't like, stupid, you know. The Lich King is a threat to them, too."

"All right," said Maryan. "It's worth a try. Gunthar, can you make an offer?"

The councilor winced. "Sorry, ma'am. The representative needs to be of the nobility or upper merchant classes or the offer could be perceived as an insult."

"What? Why is that even material to the offer? Isn't that just classism writ large?"

"Oh, sure. But the point is that out of all of us here, only you qualify to make the offer."

"You can do it, Your Highness," said Gunthar encouragingly.

"Very well." Maryan steeled herself to make what was, on the face

CHAPTER TWENTY-SEVEN: NEGOTIATIONS

of it, a fairly pathetic offer that involved the ogres fighting for the city with no reward at all.

"And remember to speak ogre," he added.

"Speak ogre?" She blanched. Making a weak offer to a powerful king was bad enough. But how did one speak ogre?

"Can you ****s make an offer, or not?" King Bofor leered at them, then pointed at the undead merchant. "Otherwise I'm going with this ****'s offer."

"Ah..." Maryan bit her lip. How did one compete in diplomacy with a smooth-talking, two-hundred-year-old negotiator? What could she say?

Merchant Korloff had a smug grin on his skeletal face, which is actually quite difficult to accomplish. "The **** princess can't offer anything. She's just a pretty ****ing face at the front of the Mayor's army."

A hot wave of anger swept away all her fear and uncertainty. The undead merchant was another reminder that, like the Mayor, some authority figures were clueless windbags that didn't deserve her respect.

"Go **** yourself," said Maryan, squaring off with Korloff. "It's not the Mayor's ****ing army. He didn't do ****. He's ****ing useless. It's *my* ****ing army. And I'm going to wipe that ****-eating grin off your face and smash your entire army into a quivering pile of bones." She turned to King Bofor. "And as for you and your ****, pathetic attempts to barter for gain at the cost of our blood, I'll give you a ****ing choice. You can either cower behind the town walls like that piece of **** Mayor and watch some *real* **** fighters take out the Lich King, or you can ****ing fight with honor and join us in eliminating these ****s for good."

The undead merchant recoiled, his jaw working furiously, but no noise came out.

King Bofor rose from his chair, glaring at them with small, beady eyes, but likewise said nothing. His officers bored holes in her with their own fiery stares.

"Don't just stand there like a steaming pile of the Mayor's ****," she told them. "Get your ****s out of your mouth and line up next to the militia."

Somewhere far to the west on the walls of Bluntworth, a crow cawed, and in the silence they could hear it take flight.

The ogre king turned to Korloff. "**** you. I'm taking the princess' ****ing offer."

Merchant Korloff continued to sputter.

King Bofor turned and roared back to his officers and the ogre army beyond. "You heard Her ****ing Highness. Grab your ****." Then he smashed the ebony chair into splinters with a single strike of his massive club. "Negotiations are ****ing concluded."

"Sweet work, ma'am," said Onkar.

"Indeed, Your Highness, even I learned something about negotiating today," agreed Councilor Wilson.

Gunthar's eyes were wide. "I didn't know you spoke ogre so well!"

"I what?"

Cornelius fanned his face. "Oh my, that was horrible. Such language! I'm going to have to burn this pen when I'm done."

King Bofor approached and stared down at her. "Right. Let's get this **** over with."

Chapter 28
Battle

> *There is no greater joy than bumping into acquaintances whilst traveling.*
>
> — *Considered Revelations*, Book 67 *"How to Meet Sociopaths"*, Chapter 17, Verse 3

Maryan gathered the captains around her in the blue-and-white command tent. She pointed to the crude map on the table. "The Lich King has assembled most of his forces here at the center. He vastly outnumbers us, but his soldiers aren't very strong and they shatter easily."

"**** yeah," echoed King Bofor.

"The ogres, the Bluntworth militia, and Sir Humphrey will be our center, with the Haffleton archers behind them."

"Indeed, ma'am, methinks we can destroy the army of the undead in an hour."

"I think the Lich King is aware of that. So I'm worried what he'll try on our flanks." Maryan pointed further south. "He's got most of his magicians here. Our right flank will be held by Wizard Yang."

Yang bowed.

"That ****ing twig of a girl is going to stand against the Lich King's wizards? Those ****s are as strong as a ****ing ox with a **** up its ****."

"King Bofor, I assure you that Wizard Yang can handle whatever they try."

"And she won't stand alone, ma'am. We'll join her."

Everyone turned at the unknown voice, and found a tall wizard with thick, curly black hair in a headband and a flowery white robe, holding a crystal staff. Beside her stood another wizard with a long, gray beard with a staff of silvery metal.

Yang gasped. "Mage Niane! Warlock Tyrheus! What are you doing here?"

Niane bowed back to her. "Hello, Gardener. Er, Apprentice. Er, Wizard. We came to represent the North Hills School of Wizardry in this battle against the Lich King and his legions."

"Also, the barista at the Hall of Refreshment was eaten by an undead alligator." The warlock shrugged. "So there was no point in staying."

"Very well." Maryan nodded at them in greeting. "Mage Niane and Warlock Tyrheus will assist Wizard Yang on the right. And Gunthar will be there to protect them."

The barbarian raised his axe. "And, you know, to have some fun with the undead, too."

"That leaves the left flank." Maryan gestured at the northern part of the map. "The Lich King has almost no forces there at all. Almost as if he's tempting us to leave it undefended."

Sir Humphrey narrowed his eyes. "You think it's a trap, ma'am?"

"I won't take any chances. I'll need a contingent of ogres and a squad of Haffleton archers to hold our left."

King Bofor sneered at this.

Maryan sighed. "Come on, you sack of ****. Unless, of course, you don't think ogres can handle the ****ing danger."

"I'll ****ing go." Huknar, the captain with steel-capped tusks, stood behind Bofor. "It'll be nice to have more room to smash those undead ****s on the flank. And if I get hungry, I can eat the ****ing archers."

"No eating the archers," admonished Maryan. "If the **** gets heavy, just hunker down and hold them off. We don't have any reserves, so I'll have to break units away from the center to assist."

"What—****ing—ever," waved Huknar.

"Overall," said Cornelius, "the left flank seems the least dangerous. I might set up station there."

"Go wherever you'd like, Chronicler. But stay out of harm's way."

* * *

The sun's light filtered through layers of mist and clouds, wan and sickly. Everything had a gray tinge to it, like asparagus that had been left in a back drawer of the icebox too long.

Cornelius had just settled down on a slight rise with a good view of the battlefield when a shadow fell across his pages. A great barrel-chested man with a large turban stood over him.

CHAPTER TWENTY-EIGHT: BATTLE

The Chronicler clambered to his feet. "Librarian Banda! What are you doing here?"

"I'm here to help, of course." The librarian pulled out a quill of his own. "As they say, the pen is mightier than the sword."

Cornelius looked across the plain to a small group of skeletal warriors. "I hope the saying is true."

"Oh, it's not. Swords are much better." Banda stuffed the quill back into his robes. "So I brought the Archive's letter opener as well."

"Oh."

"I also brought this, just in case." Banda held up a miniscule glowing blue orb which dangled from a small chain around his neck. "An artifact from the beginning times. You can see verse here, in the lost tongue of the ancients. It says it's a tiny demon repellent."

"Hello there, scholars," called out the blue-haired customs officer. She led a contingent of Haffleton archers before them.

"Hello, Captain Emma," returned the Librarian. "So you're leading the forces on this flank?"

"It's a joint leadership role," she said with a grimace. "That ogre captain Huknar leads his forces."

"Does anyone have any extra arrows?" asked one of the archers. His mustache sported large handlebars, his beard very long and crisply squared off. "I could use a few more."

"Yes," said Banda, extending a small bundle. "We had these in the Archives."

The Haffleton archer eyed the arrows uncertainly. "Are they from a certified sustainable forest?"

"Can anyone loan me some blue arrows?" Another archer waved her hand. "Coral also works. Something to match a turquoise-colored bow."

"Where are the ogres?" asked Cornelius.

"Hold your ****ing horses," called Huknar, advancing with a force of his own. The ground shook with the steps of dozens of ogres, the weak light reflecting off armor and weapons and no small amount of drool. "Try to stay out of our ****ing way. And hope we don't get hungry." He leered at them.

Emma bowed. "Hello, Captain—"

"Whatever." Huknar turned away from her. "Get your **** set up!" he called to his ogres.

The customs officer frowned. "Captain, the princess said we had to work together—"

"**** that. I don't see her here, do you?" Huknar grinned, but not in a friendly way, his steel-capped tusks glinting. "Stay the **** back here and let us handle these ****s."

Emma rolled her eyes but said nothing more, and Huknar walked down and started exchanging dirty jokes with his troops.

"Indeed, Captain," said Cornelius, "there is a long history of ogres and humans not getting along very well."

She scratched her chin. "I usually stick to customs work. Like, what's the history?"

"There was the Battle of the Three Rivers. Lost to the invading vikings because the defending ogres ate their archers."

"Ah."

"Don't forget the Skirmish of Gray Hill," said Banda. "Lost because the ogres trampled their archers."

"And the Siege of Fort Calwell. Lost—"

"I think I get it," said Emma.

"Well, the archers were fine in that one," said Cornelius. "But the siege was lost because the defending ogres ate everyone else."

"Right."

"It may not matter." Banda pointed across the plains, where only a small force of skeletons faced them. "There could be very little action on this flank today."

"Good." Cornelius sat down again. "I was hoping to avoid any excitement."

"Wait." Banda narrowed his eyes, staring across the field. "Who is that? Someone in poncy black-and-white clothing, with five red armored guards."

"Oh, no." Cornelius squinted. "That must be Prince Mikhail. What the devil is he doing here?"

They sent a messenger to the princess, and soon she herself appeared, riding an unperturbed Daisy. "Oh, bother," said Maryan as she dismounted. "Why is he siding with the Lich King? That's insane."

"He's a sociopathic murderer, Your Highness," said Cornelius.

CHAPTER TWENTY-EIGHT: BATTLE

"Very well," said Maryan. "Let's go talk to him."

"What?"

"Sociopathic or not, the Lich King can only be a threat to him as well. Let's get him to switch sides, or at least leave the field."

"But—"

"Captain Emma, you hold the lines here."

The blue-haired customs officer nodded. "Yes, Your Highness."

The princess marched out, one of the Haffleton lieutenants behind her with a flag of parley. The lieutenant pointed up. "See?" he said. "It's a hemp flag. The latest thing in parley."

"Come along if you'd like, Captain Huknar," said Maryan as she walked by. "I'm going to talk to Prince Mikhail."

"Can I ****ing kill him yet, Your Highness?"

"No."

"**** it, I'll come anyway." Huknar walked next to her.

"Hello, Prince Mikhail," called Maryan as they neared.

He stood in front of the small company of skeletal warriors, his five red-armored Death Knights next to him. His filigreed jacket glittered in the weak light, although the Prince had a small, thick cloud some distance above that sheltered him from any direct sunlight.

"Hello, Princess." He smiled graciously, and the temperature dropped noticeably. "I presume you have come to reconsider my offer? Or perhaps to surrender?"

"Just a flag of parley, good prince." Maryan gestured further south. "We wanted to talk you out of your destructive alliance with the Lich King."

"I fear you are spending your time fruitlessly, princess. You may think you have my best interests in mind, but I wouldn't be here unless it suited my ambitions."

"Didn't you have six Death Knights before, Prince Mikhail?" Cornelius pointed at the five red-armored fiends. "What happened?"

"One was crushed by those undead bison you left us with on the Golden Plains." The Prince's smile dropped. "A most unfortunate event, for which you all will pay dearly, I assure you."

"Oh?" Cornelius' eyebrows went up. "How much does a Death Knight cost?"

"I wasn't talking literally. It was a metaphor. I meant I was going to kill you."

"Ah." Cornelius made a note.

"And to answer your question, yes, they're also very expensive. Even a used Death Knight will set you back almost seven hundred sovereigns these days, and that doesn't include the armor."

"Oh, wow."

"Look, are you ****s done talking? Can I start killing **** now?"

"Charmed, I'm sure, Captain Huknar." The Prince bowed again.

"Look, you ****ing—" The ogre took a step forward, but all five Death Knights turned their heads in synchrony, five hands moving to five hilts.

"Everyone, stay calm," barked Maryan. "We're still under a flag of parley."

"A *hemp* flag of parley," noted the Haffleton lieutenant. "It's even stronger than cotton, and holds color better."

"It's a white flag," said Mikhail. "It doesn't have any color."

"Well, whatever."

Prince Mikhail waved them away. "Thank you for coming. But you should get back to your lines before the battle starts."

"If the Lich King wins, you won't be safe. He'll kill you and take your lands." Maryan didn't move.

"Fair Maryan, the Lich King is going to let me have the northern lands and a fair amount of the west as well. He gets all the sunny bits and I get the shady bits. It's a great deal." The Prince's polished exterior started to hint at irritation. "Now if you don't mind, unless you are going to accept my marriage proposal, I need to get ready to cleanse this area of your unwelcome presence."

Maryan shrugged. "Fair enough, Prince Mikhail. If you reconsider, let us know." And she led the party back to the Bluntworth lines.

"I told you, ma'am," said Cornelius. "He's a sociopath."

"The Lich King has promised him a lot, much more than King Bofor was offered. And all the Prince has to do is hang out here on the flank? Keep your eyes on him." She swung atop Daisy's saddle again, and waved as she departed. "I'll head back to the center. Battle is imminent. Good luck."

Chapter 29
Assault

> *Most people don't realize this, but facing a large horde of undead skeletons isn't as perilous as it sounds. Unless they cheat. Then you're screwed.*
>
> — Considered Revelations, Book 18 "Ways In Which An Otherwise Non-Perilous Horde of Skeletons Can Be Made Perilous", Chapter 29, Verse 43

Captain Emma frowned across the field at Prince Mikhail, her blue hair tousled by the breeze. "I think he's up to something."

"Yeah, he's up to getting his **** kicked," said Huknar. "Once we get the signal, I'm going to **** his ****, and then I'll **** his five ****s."

"Our orders are to hold the flank and contain the Lich King's forces here. We need the joint protection of your pikes and our arrows—"

"Oh, **** that. As soon as they give the signal, I'm kicking their ****. You and your archers should stay here and hope I don't get ****ing hungry."

A long, evil tone rasped over the plains, echoing back from the walls.

"The Lich King has sounded his advance," noted Emma. "We should get ready."

"How can a tone sound evil?" asked Cornelius.

The bright trumpets of Bluntworth sounded in response, and a great cry went up from the troops further south.

Librarian Banda pointed. "They're marching out to meet the Lich King's troops. You can see that knight, Sir Humphrey. He's the big ball of blue lightning in the front. And that green blob next to him must be King Bofor."

"What a ****ing wanker." Huknar slammed his helmet on with a force that would have crushed a man. Then he roared to his troops. "All right, you useless ****ing kobolds. Stop sucking your ****s and grab your ****. Let's kill this ****ing prince."

Cornelius strained to see over the mass of marching ogres. "What's the Prince doing?"

"He's just sitting there." Banda frowned. "Like he's waiting for something."

The assembled ogres marched across the battlefield. Further south, the militia and the larger force of ogres engaged with the Lich King's main armies. They could see Sir Humphrey's electrified armor sparkling and vaporizing undead.

A great peal of thunder echoed across the plains, and the sunlight dimmed. A cold breeze blew in from the north.

"What was that?" The Chronicler shivered and covered his arms.

"Look," said Banda. "Sir Humphrey no longer glows."

Indeed, further south the Bluntworth troops continued to march to meet the larger undead forces, but the crackling blue aura around the knight had disappeared.

"That's not good," said Librarian Banda. "Someone unleashed an anti-magic blast."

The ogres in front of them had marched halfway to the Prince's lines.

"And that vampire Prince isn't waiting anymore. He's chanting now."

"Chanting?" Cornelius shivered again. "Why is it getting so cold?"

"Captain Huknar, come back!" The blue-haired customs officer waved to the departing ogres. "We need to stick together."

Huknar didn't look back, but made a rude hand gesture over his shoulder.

"Were those there before?"

Banda looked around. "What, Chronicler?"

Cornelius pointed north. "Those."

A large mass of demons marched towards them, making a strange hissing sound that grew louder by the second. Large demons moved ponderously upon great cloven hooves, whilst other demons ran, some slithered, and some flew on leathery wings.

"By the gods of long-overdue Archive materials! The Prince has opened a portal to the demon world." Banda stepped back.

"Release!" At the Captain's command, a flight of arrows shot forth, and the lead rank of flying demons fell screaming to the

CHAPTER TWENTY-NINE: ASSAULT

ground, most pierced with multiple arrows, but uncountably many swarmed behind.

Banda shoved Cornelius out of the path of an advancing demon. "Watch yourself!"

The demon clawed at him, but the Chronicler managed to stumble back out of the way. Another of the beasts slithered up, not like a slug, but more like a murderous speed skater, and the poor scholar was just saying his final prayers when Banda's sword cut both fiends in two.

Cornelius' eyes boggled at the greatsword, over five feet long, which the librarian swung with both hands. "Holy dragon snot! What is *that*?"

"I told you." Banda swung a return stroke, and a severed demon head went bouncing past the Chronicler. "It's the Archives letter opener."

Another flight of arrows mowed down the rest of the nearby demons, and for a moment the field cleared.

"I don't think your demon repellent works."

"Oh, it's useless." The Librarian ripped off the miniature blue orb and threw it far into the Badlands in disgust. "It turns out, it only repels tiny demons. Curse the lost tongue of the ancients and its vague, torturous syntax!"

"We're doomed!" Cornelius pointed at the legions of fiends advancing from the north, each of which was not tiny at all.

Ahead of them, the ogres advanced on Prince Mikhail, but they were bogged down by many demons assaulting them from both the side and the air. At least one ogre had fallen already.

Banda wiped demon blood off his sleeve. "And it's not just the demons. Who knows what else may come through the portal the vampire opened?"

"What's worse than demons?"

"I don't know. Maybe one of the elder gods made incarnate?"

Great fleshy tentacles burst from the ground in front of the ogres. Each was as thick and as tall as a tree, and covered in flabby suckers, although here and there a fleshy mouth appeared instead.

"Yes, like that." Banda sighed. "Anzu the Destroyer. He consumes all."

"Huknar, get back here!" Captain Emma screamed at the ogre,

but the green warrior was too busy fighting demons to notice.

Indeed, the ogres' charge had been stopped by a flurry of massive tentacles, and the pack of soldiers flailed madly in all directions now. Hissing, bubbling demon blood covered the ground, as well as dozens of bodies of fiends of all description. At least one tentacle had been chopped through, but another took its place.

Huknar screamed at his troops to advance, but the front line stalled, desperately hacking at great tentacles which lunged and struck back with immense power. A tentacle smashed an ogre in the lead and it went flying over his fellows, crashing to the earth in front of the archers in a great cloud of dust, where it lay unmoving.

"Eyes up!" called Captain Emma. "Another group in the air!" Her soldiers let fly a storm of arrows, the air thick with shafts and the twang of bowstrings. Many flying demons crashed to the ground, pierced with multiple arrows, but several others remained unscathed and dove into the ranks of archers, who had to defend themselves with knives and clubs in the tight quarters.

"How do we stop that Anzu thing?" asked Cornelius.

"We can't stop it." Banda sliced through another group of advancing demons, and stepped back to avoid the spray of corrosive blood. "It's a god."

The Chronicler waved. "Huknar, come back!"

Somehow, the ogre captain heard him, and looked back. Cornelius stared into the eyes of a furious berzerker ogre who was also slightly terrified.

And when ogres get into that state, they get *hungry*.

"Oh, no." Cornelius went pale.

Huknar raced towards him in great, thundering strides, his blazing red eyes locked on Cornelius, a bubbly drool at his tusks.

"Oh, no," repeated the scholar.

A flying demon dove at the ogre, but Captain Emma shot it before it could reach him, and it crashed to the ground. Huknar scooped the twitching beast off the ground and bit into it as he reached for Cornelius with his other hand.

The ogre recoiled, hacking and coughing. He spat the bit of demon flesh out of his mouth. "Oh, yuck." Huknar's jaw went slack and his massive green shoulders slumped. "Demon tastes like *vegemite*."

CHAPTER TWENTY-NINE: ASSAULT

The ogre's eyes no longer blazed red, and his pupils returned to something like normal size, though wide in shock. He looked around, then stared at Cornelius again. "A world inhabited by demons will taste horrible, won't it?"

"Yes." In truth, the scholar had no idea, but it seemed like the appropriate response to a hungry ogre. Huknar had to be out of his mind, since he'd stopped swearing.

A cloven-hoofed demon with bat wings and a cruel sword lunged at Huknar, but the ogre back-handed it, and the fiend's broken body went flying over the ground, directly into a fleshy mouth on one of the tentacles. Huknar turned back to Cornelius again, and now his eyes flashed a mixture of anger and contempt, which was refreshingly normal. "Well, you stupid ****? What do I ****ing do now?"

"Ah—"

"Get your warriors around my archers!" Captain Emma directed another flight of arrows, and a rank of advancing demons fell. "We can hold our ground longer that way."

Huknar spat, then grunted. "**** it. We'll ****ing do it your way." Then he marched out into the plains. "All right, you **** ****s. Get back to the ****ing archers."

A tentacle burst from the ground, right in front of Huknar, but dozens of arrows immediately pierced it and it fell to the ground, twitching. Huknar hurdled over it. "Get back to the ****ing archers!" he repeated.

Other ogres finally heard him, and began jogging back to take positions in front of the archers. Two of the green warriors furiously hacked at tentacles and demons in the front, so Huknar grabbed them by their collars and dragged them back.

Cornelius and Banda stayed with the back ranks of the archers, the librarian disemboweling any demons that tried to come at them from that direction with great sweeps of his two-handed sword.

"We're still doomed," fretted Cornelius. He pointed past the ogres. "The Destroyer is coming for us."

Indeed, tentacles further away zipped back into the ground again, and new tentacles burst out of the packed earth much closer to them. The constant roaring of angry demons washed over them, and the scholar lost count of how many fiends were killed by angry strikes of Huknar's sword. Again and again, waves of demons would press at the ranks of the ogres, but again and again, flights of arrows would decimate the attackers, and the green warriors would slice or smash the few remaining. The bodies of demons and the mangled remains of tentacles covered the ground, but more kept coming.

"Death Knights!" The Librarian pointed at the advancing red-armored undead.

"Make your arrows count!" Captain Emma shouted. "We're almost out."

Cornelius swallowed, watching the Death Knights swarm the ogre captain.

A tentacle wrapped around Huknar's arm, yanking away his sword. It would have lifted the ogre entirely, but many arrows pierced it, and it retreated. Huknar grabbed the club of a fallen ogre next to him, and brought it down on the red helmet of the closest Death Knight, crumpling the fiend all the way to the ground. Hundreds of tormented souls escaped, sighing in release, and a cool breeze blew by them.

"These things make the coolest ****ing sound when you kill them!" Huknar cried, and turned to the Death Knight nearest him.

Two tentacles grabbed the ogre, and lifted him high off the ground. A third tentacle whipped forward, a smacking mouth opening to receive him.

A few arrows slammed into the tentacles, but not enough to stop them this time.

"We're out!" Captain Emma dropped her longbow and drew her sword. "Last stand, everyone!"

A tentacle wrapped around Huknar, pinning his arms, and it lifted him and guided him to a gaping pink maw. "Farewell, you stupid ****s!" the ogre shouted to them. "Take a few of these **** with you!"

But then a great rippling *crack* echoed across the plains, as if thousands of stones struck in quickening succession. The demon in front of Captain Emma screamed with a harsh caw, but was sucked *sidewise* into some dimension between the usual three, and disappeared. All over the field, demons and tentacles vanished in a split second, leaving only a lingering scent of sulfur.

With the tentacles gone, Huknar found himself suspended in midair. He crashed down upon the Death Knight below him, crushing it like a pile of straw. Another grateful sigh of released souls washed over them.

The ogre stood and brushed dust and blood off himself. "I'll never get tired of that ****ing sound."

Chapter 30
Victory

Along with pretending to be left-handed, killing an invincible Lich King is a bad idea.

— Considered Revelations, Book 97 *"Lich 101"*, Chapter 6, Verse 2

The sun regained some of its strength, and a warm breeze blew over the battlefield from the south again. The demons and tentacles had disappeared, even the dead. But many fallen archers and ogres lay around them.

Princess Maryan and Wizard Yang dismounted from Daisy, who promptly grazed on the scrub near the town walls.

"It's great to see you, Your Highness, Wizard," said Cornelius. He hugged himself, surrounded by many dead and wounded.

"Sorry we were late." Wizard Yang wiped her brow. "Things got a little crazy on the south side."

Librarian Banda leaned against his letter opener and wiped his brow. "How did you kill Anzu?"

"I didn't. I only closed the portal. He was re-banished to his own dimension."

The remaining three Death Knights found themselves staring at a band of very angry ogres and archers. They marched in reverse, all the way back to Prince Mikhail, the ogres and archers following every step, with Maryan and Yang accompanying.

"Oh, hello everyone." Prince Mikhail had been sitting on the ground, chanting, but now staggered to his feet, swaying a bit. He blinked. "What happened to Anzu?"

Huknar swung his club, crushing the Death Knight on the right with another wail of escaping souls.

"Stop killing **** for a moment, Captain Huknar."

"Just for a ****ing moment, ma'am."

Prince Mikhail panted. "Can you keep that green monster away from me?"

Maryan glared at him. "Your Highness, we'll entertain discussion about your surrender, but that's about it."

CHAPTER THIRTY: VICTORY

"Surrender?" Mikhail took in the battlefield. "Oh, by the dark lords. You really did close the portal, didn't you? How did you do that?"

"It was easy, once I found the keystone. Most interdimensional portals are recursive layers built on top of a foundational connection, you know." Wizard Yang snapped her fingers. "Once I broke that, the rest of the portal collapsed like a bunch of fractal dominos."

Mikhail pulled his hair. "Do you have any idea how much preparation went into that? I powered it with one of the world's only Stones of Misery. Where will I get another one?"

"A Stone of Misery?" Maryan looked at Yang, who shrugged.

"Stones of Misery are from creation, Your Highness," said Librarian Banda. "They contain tears of the gods. Few remain."

"Yes, well, one less remains now. Thanks for that." Mikhail pursed his lips, staring at the empty plains.

"Can I ****ing kill him now?"

"This discussion is over, Prince Mikhail. If you'll come with us—"

"I'm not going anywhere with you."

"In that case—"

But Maryan never got to finish her sentence, as the vampire prince turned into a small bat. It fluttered away clumsily, as if exhausted.

Captain Emma grabbed her bow, and drew an arrow she'd scavenged from the field. She tracked the small bat, but lowered her bow without releasing.

"What? Why didn't you ****ing shoot that ****?"

"It didn't feel right," said Emma. "Shooting a helpless bat."

"**** that."

"I know what you mean, Captain Emma." Maryan also watched the departing animal.

"It's time to kill **** again." Huknar swung his club, shattering another Death Knight in a release of souls. The remaining Death Knight tried to chase its master, but fell under many swords and clubs.

Huknar licked his lips. "Where's the ****ing Lich King?"

"Battle is still joined at the center." Maryan pointed south. "But we've exposed the Lich King's right flank. I suggest we teach him a lesson."

"Right. You heard Her Highness, you ****s! Line your sorry ****s up."

The ogres lined up in ranks and marched upon the Lich King's flank, the archers in a group behind.

"Put your bows away, all," called Captain Emma. "We don't have enough arrows." The archers drew their blades and marched, and Maryan led them all to the center.

Despite his sword being drained of all magic, the knight still swept through ranks of skeletons, the rest of the Bluntworth militia with him. King Bofor and the main ogre army marched next to him, destroying the Lich King's heavy cavalry.

Maryan and her ogres and archers crashed into the side of the Lich King's reserves. Huknar clashed weapons with an undead troll, then the ogre flung the creature over his shoulder, where archers hacked it to pieces. Maryan impaled a skeleton chief on her spear, and it collapsed with a dry rattle.

More skeletons turned in confusion, and the lines of the undead armies disintegrated into chaos as they collapsed on multiple fronts. In only a few minutes they eliminated the Lich King's army, shards of white bone everywhere. The lich himself stood defiantly in front of his throne of skulls.

Captain Emma eyed him warily. "Why isn't he shooting spells at us?"

"He's not going to try that with me around," said Wizard Yang. "I'll just bring it back on him."

King Bofor approached them. His armor sported several new nicks and notches, dripping undead ooze. "Your Highness, Wizard Yang! I see you **** those skeletons on *both* ****ing flanks."

Yang bowed. "I was late to arrive on the left, Your Majesty. Somehow the ogres and the archers managed to withstand a god of destruction."

Huknar snorted. "Anzu was a piece of ****."

A shadow passed before the sun, and a distant moan rippled over the plains.

Librarian Banda coughed. "Ah, Captain Huknar, I recommend that you not taunt a murderous Elder God."

Huknar opened his mouth to reply then, quite

CHAPTER THIRTY: VICTORY

uncharacteristically for an ogre, thought better of it.

"What now, ma'am?" Captain Emma pointed at the Lich King, who stood glaring at them.

King Bofor grunted. "What now? Now I ram my ****ing club right up his ****."

"Well, King Bofor, ordinarily I'd be all for it, but I wonder if we should simply capture him."

"What?"

"If we kill him, he'll only come back stronger."

The Lich King leered at them. "Ha! We are at a standoff, Princess. You can't—"

"Surprise!" Gunthar popped out from behind the throne of skulls, and brought his axe down upon the Lich King. The skeletal form exploded with the impact, and a shower of bone splinters pelted the armies.

"That was great!" The barbarian picked up his axe, which he'd dropped, and pointed to the pile of robes in front of him. "You distracted him, and I was able to take him out!"

"See? That's what I'm ****ing talking about."

Maryan sighed. "I guess we'll try it your way, Your Majesty."

"'Tis the end of him, am I not right?" Sir Humphrey beamed. "We have *thrice* beaten him!"

"What?"

The knight ticked off the victories on his fingers. "First, in the cave, where Wizard Yang dispatched him. Second, this morning, when I defeated his champion. Third, just now, when Gunthar smashed him."

Yang frowned. "I'm not sure if defeating Grom counts."

"It totally counts, right?" Gunthar swaggered over to join them. "We beat him three times!"

Maryan scratched her head. "I don't know. Grom wasn't in the prophecy."

"*My* victory doesn't add to the tally, because I'm not in the prophecy?"

"Sir Humphrey, it's nothing personal, it's just how the prophecy works." Princess Maryan shrugged. "And didn't you say there was more to life than prophecies?"

"Well, yes... Wait! Where is Maiden Andi?" The knight looked about frantically until they heard the Ex-Bookkeeper's voice.

"What? Is someone looking for me?" Andi appeared, still holding the mace she'd taken from the bandit prince. "I was with the militia."

Sir Humphrey put a hand on his heart. "Indeed, good lady, 'twas a great fright when I couldn't find you."

"I'm fine, thank you for asking." She stretched up and kissed him on the cheek.

The knight blushed. "What were we talking about, again?"

"Oh, by the gods of the icy wastes." Gunthar brushed at his khakis. "I got Lich guts all over my new pants."

"What happened to your sword, Sir Humphrey?" Librarian Banda's eyes went wide with concern. "It no longer sparks. Is it broken?"

"Not permanently." The knight tapped the hilt. "That elder god sucked all the magic out of it, I guess. But our wizard said it will recharge."

"The ancient elves put a very clever pendulum mechanism in there," said Yang. "The sword slowly recharges just by being carried around. But it will take years to get back to full strength."

"In the meantime, Gwendoline serves me fine as a regular sword."

"What happened on the right flank?" Cornelius held his pen over a page in his notebook.

"The Lich King had all of his wizards attack at once. Warlock Tyrheus tried to charge them on his own, and, well..." Yang looked away.

The others could see Mage Niane, standing tall near the militia, but could see no sign of the warlock.

"Mage Niane and I got the situation under control, and demolished most of the undead wizards. When the Lich King saw we were winning, he flashed a signal to Prince Mikhail."

"Hmm, I knew he was waiting for something," said Banda.

"The Prince opened a portal to a forbidden dimension, and summoned the elder god Anzu, and a whole host of demons. Anzu dispelled all the magic on the battlefield right away." Yang shivered. "Princess Maryan and I galloped over as fast as we could."

King Bofor waved in irritation. "I don't know what the **** you all are talking about, but I'm as tired as a **** after a full day of ****."

CHAPTER THIRTY: VICTORY

"Me too, Your Majesty," agreed Gunthar.

"Anyone up for restorative yoga?" The Haffleton lieutenant looked around. "That helps me sleep better after a big battle."

"**** that," snorted Huknar. "Ogres aren't into that ****."

"And not at your ****ing prices," said another.

"Oh, my studio could do you a deal. Like, a free introductory session, and then a half-price series after that. Since you saved the city and all."

"**** that," repeated Huknar.

"Well," said the other ogre, "a free session is a pretty ****ing good deal. Even the ****ing gnomes don't do that ****."

"Fine," said Huknar. "One ****ing session, maybe."

"Let's get back to our lines." Princess Maryan looked back across the Badlands, where the perpetual stormclouds still loomed over the site of the Castle of Terror, lit by flashes of lightning. "And let's keep sentries posted."

Chapter 31
Night

> *There is no greater sense of fulfillment of purpose than when a government agency confronts the very situation for which it was established.*
>
> *— Considered Revelations, Book 126 "Things That Give a Great Sense of Fulfillment of Purpose to Government Agencies", Chapter 82, Verse 7*

Over the course of the evening, the wind picked up, and dark clouds obscured the moon and stars. The adventurers retreated to the princess' command tent. The tent flaps shuddered with the wind, and rain pelted the canvas in erratic bursts.

"Definitely a storm to accompany an angry, rebirthed Lich King," said Maryan.

"Nay, Your Highness." Sir Humphrey stood adamant. "We defeated him three times."

"I don't want the wind to take these." Maryan rolled up the maps from the table and placed them in the large wooden chest.

A peal of thunder rolled over them, the booming noise fading into the distance.

Wizard Yang stood. "I wonder if Her Highness might be correct. What if the Lich King attacks at night, with even larger forces?"

The knight shook his head. "A night attack? 'Tis a dangerous thing to attempt. His forces wouldst be blind."

"Maybe." Princess Maryan pursed her lips in worry.

Gunthar poked his head in the tent. "Has anyone seen my pants?"

"What?"

"I gave my khakis to the tailor for cleaning, but now I can't find him. Maybe he dropped them off?"

"Well, there are no pants here."

"Right, thanks. I'll look around more." The barbarian left.

"Let's take a look outside," said the princess. "I know we have sentries posted, but I'm not going to sleep in this storm anyway."

They woke the napping candidate Onkar and went outside,

CHAPTER THIRTY-ONE: NIGHT

where the dark plains lay deserted. A few tents and stakes marked the locations of the defending armies, but no soldiers remained.

Maryan jogged to the nearest sentry, and pointed back. "Where is everyone?"

"Hello, Your Highness." The sentry waved vaguely in the direction of the town walls. "The archers and the ogres went up to Haffleton for a free yoga session. And the Mayor called the Bluntworth militia back."

"He what?"

"He said there was little risk of a night attack, given the storm. And he said he didn't believe in the undead anyway."

"How do people still not believe in the undead? We just fought a huge battle with hordes of them!"

"I know, ma'am, but he's very persuasive. And most people don't want to believe in the undead, even though the evidence is right there."

Onkar frowned back at the gatehouse. "I was like, 'Hey Mayor, we kind of need the militia here.' And he was all, 'Well, having the militia lined up makes people nervous. Like there is something to be afraid of out here.' And I was like, 'Yeah, there is!'"

Maryan put her hands on her hips. "We'll have to find that Captain Vikal and get the militia out here again right away."

"Hey, you lot. Have you seen any khakis?" Gunthar walked up, wearing a towel. "Oh, it's you all. What are you doing outside?"

"No khakis here, sir," noted the sentry.

Sir Humphrey pointed out across the Badlands, where lightning flashed briefly. "Your Highness, the plains appear empty. If the Lich King intended to attack tonight, he'd have to summon the undead directly from the ground, and they'd all have to be magically endowed with night vision."

Lightning flashed again, and in its light they could make out the forms of thousands of skeletons clawing their way out of the ground. As the light faded, the Badlands dissolved into darkness again, but thousands of pairs of glowing eyes remained.

"Oh, great," complained Gunthar. "He's summoned the undead directly from the ground, they're all magically endowed with night vision, and I can't find my pants."

"Methinks the skeletons are bigger this time," noted Sir

Humphrey.

Wizard Yang sighed. "The Lich has come back stronger, and created stronger undead as well."

Gunthar ran back to the tent. "Where in the name of frozen kobolds are my khakis?"

"Are these good tactics?" The sentry waved behind them. "Being attacked by hordes of even larger undead, while our own forces have abandoned their positions? I'm still learning, but that's bad tactics, right?"

A large skeleton broke out of the ground in front of them.

"I've got him!" Sir Humphrey dashed up with Gwendoline, and smashed at the skeleton with the hard edge. But instead of shattering bone, the sword rang with the impact, as if it had struck a rock. The knight staggered back with a yelp. "These undead don't break! Oh, if only Gwendoline had any magic left in her!"

"Wizard Yang, can you disenchant them?"

"Oh, that Lich King was very clever." Yang motioned in the air, as if parting curtains that only she could see. "He used magic to harden their bones, some sort of calcified titanium, and added enhanced photonics in their eye sockets so they can see at night. But the skeletons aren't really magic now. They're like machines." She sighed. "I can't stop them, ma'am."

Sir Humphrey thwacked at the skeleton again, but it had no effect, and he had to dodge a brutal return punch from the angry undead. "I don't understand your magical terms, Wizard, but these are definitely harder to stop."

More skeletons had emerged nearby, and a larger host approached from the plains.

The sentry took a step back. "Um, what now, ma'am?"

"Run!" she ordered them.

"Or, like, hide!" Candidate Onkar dashed into the tent.

Gunthar ran out with his axe, wearing his old furs. "Are we running at the Lich King?"

"No!" Maryan pointed at the swarm of large, fast-moving skeletons just behind them. "Run back to the town!"

"Right. You lot go, and I'll hold them here." Gunthar swung his axe at the nearest skeleton. "Die, fiends!"

But the axe clanged off the skeleton harmlessly and flew out of his hands, and the barbarian chased after it. Then he vanished in a crowd of giant undead.

"Gunthar!"

Princess Maryan started to run back, but another group of skeletons rounded the other side of the tent. She dodged in time to avoid one's sweeping arms, but Yang wasn't so lucky. A large skeleton captured her and hauled her back towards the plains.

"Run, Your Highness!" cried Yang as she disappeared.

"Quick," said Maryan. "We need reinforcements. Sprint for the gates!"

She and Healer Nyala and the Chronicler charged headlong for the walls and the east gates of Bluntworth, the skeletons in pursuit.

The Mayor stood above the gates, waving them in. "You can make it!" he yelled. "And if you don't, that will be fun to watch too!"

"Where is Sir Humphrey?" Maryan cast about the dark Badlands as she ran.

"There, Your Highness!" Nyala ran next to her, pointing further along the wall. "But he is cut off from us by a large force of skeletons."

By some great fortune, and the excellent sprinting of at least one out-of-shape Chronicler, they beat the undead to the gates, which shut behind them with a crash.

"Whew, we're all safe," said the Mayor, joining them. "Except for all of your friends stuck outside, of course. Too bad about them."

A large boom echoed around the gatehouse as the skeletons outside smashed into the doors.

"I don't think the gates will hold very long," said Maryan.

"Oh, come now," said the Mayor. "Nothing can break these gates. Especially the undead, which I've decided not to believe in anyway." A large man in a black robe stood next to him. "Look, I have the Chief Advisor from the Centers for Undead Control and Prevention right here."

Another boom echoed around them, and one of the doors began to splinter, its hinges sagging.

"The Centers for Undead Control and Prevention?" Maryan turned to the Chief Advisor with relief. "Perfect, this is exactly the sort of situation the Centers were created for! Can't you explain to the Mayor that we should all be wearing sprigs of lemongrass, the undead are real, and the gates won't hold?"

The Chief Advisor cleared his throat. "Mayor, I think the Princess may be right. Those skeletons are especially strong—"

"Look, man, don't contradict me. Stick to the narrative, or I'll fire you."

"Um, yes, Mayor." The Chief Advisor turned back to Maryan. "Sorry, ma'am. We can't say whether lemongrass is helpful or not. There are a lot of opinions out there. And these gates will definitely hold up to the furious assault of the undead which we also don't believe in."

The town cooper stood nearby, waving his *Burn the Lemingras* sign. "That's right!"

"See?" said the Mayor. "The head of the CUC agrees with me. He's a great, smart man."

The gates shattered, and they all ducked to avoid a shower of wooden splinters. Large skeletons streamed in the opening.

"I blame my experts!" The Mayor pointed back at the Chief Advisor. "He kept changing his story. I never liked him anyway."

"Mayor, don't you believe in the undead now?" asked Maryan as they sprinted away from the charging skeletons.

"I think people are making too big a deal out of the rising tide of the undead," he retorted.

They had to stop when a large skeleton barred their way. The Mayor, the Chief Advisor, and the cooper huddled together as the fiend reached at them.

"Protect me!" screamed the Mayor. He tried to push the cooper in front of him, but the cooper pushed back.

The skeleton snatched the Chief Advisor and ran away.

The Mayor spread his arms triumphantly. "See! There's a sixty-seven percent survival rate. I don't know what all the fuss is about. People should go on about their normal lives."

More skeletons streamed from the gatehouse. The undead loped towards them, carrying not weapons but chains, their large hands outstretched, grabbing everyone they could reach.

"Run!" cried Maryan.

The Princess, the Healer, and the Chronicler dashed further into town, heading towards the main square. Calls of alarm spread all around them, and screams. Further back, a skeleton smashed the

CHAPTER THIRTY-ONE: NIGHT

wooden door of a house, then charged inside.

"The undead are taking people from their homes!" exclaimed Cornelius.

"What?" The cooper looked back behind them where the skeleton dragged a man away in chains.

"Ignore them!" said the Mayor, pushing past the cooper. "Remember what I told you? The Princess doesn't care about our economy. She's blowing the undead menace out of proportion."

"Oh, that's right," said the cooper. "I believe you, Mayor, and no one else!"

"To the main square!" called Maryan. Raindrops pelted them, the wet cobblestones reflecting the glowing eyes of pursuing undead.

The Mayor and cooper fell behind, the Mayor yelling at people as he ran that they shouldn't worry, they should ignore the Princess, and the whole situation was a false crisis created by his political opponents.

A large skeleton jumped out of an alley, grabbing the Mayor. The cooper screamed and cowered in the gutter, wrapping his *Burn the Lemingras* sign around himself.

The skeleton chained up the Mayor, then dragged him away. "Only my narrative is true! What you're seeing is not what's happening!" shouted the Mayor as he passed the trembling cooper.

Maryan and the others turned a corner and reached the square in front of the cathedral. Many townspeople thronged against the locked cathedral doors, standing behind lines of the remaining town militia.

The leader of the militia waved at her. "You're still alive, Your Highness!"

"Hello, Captain Vikal. Likewise, I'm happy to see you here."

"What do we do now, ma'am? The undead have overrun all of Bluntworth. We're the last line of defense."

The Princess turned to face the large skeletons who charged out of the side streets. "Hold your lines, Captain! We'll just have to do our best."

The militia crouched down, their wooden shields at the ready, pikes held forward in repeated rows, with the princess standing defiantly in front.

* * *

A group of skeletons wrapped Gunthar and Yang in chains, and dragged them across the dark, flat plains.

"Why didn't they kill us?"

"I'm sure the Lich King has something particularly disgusting in mind for us," said Yang. "Torture, or disfigurement, or a campaign rally of the Mayor's idiot followers."

"Oh, wow. What a sadistic monster." The barbarian's face went pale. "Can't you use your un-magic to get us out of here?"

"I don't have any power of my own. I can only repurpose what magic is already out there. And the Lich King cleverly built these skeletons to be non-magical."

"What an absolute wanker."

"Hold on a minute, I'm getting a faint reading. A magic item is lying ahead on the plains."

"Here? We're far from the walls. How would a magic item just be lying out here?"

"Whatever it is, we're getting closer."

Gunthar squinted. "Maybe a small blue thing ahead?"

"Yes. A tiny demon repellent. How did that get here? It's not very useful, but even so, it's got a fair amount of power."

"Can you use that?"

"Yes, get ready. I'll drain it and blast these skeletons."

Gunthar yelped as the skeletons dragged him over a rock. "I'm ready when you are!"

"Close your eyes!"

A second later, a great explosion echoed on the plains, and bits of sand and bone rained down on them, ringing against the chains.

"You blasted those undead into splinters!" The barbarian stood up in triumph.

Yang staggered to her feet next to him. She shook her bound hands, and a long length of heavy chain rattled in response. "Yes, but we're in chains, and more skeletons are coming."

Indeed, several of the large undead loped towards them from the throne of skulls. The Lich King had directed a small host to recapture them.

"I'll get the chains." Gunthar stooped, gathering their trailing

CHAPTER THIRTY-ONE: NIGHT

chains over his shoulders. "Run as fast as you can!"

They ran on the cold, hard ground back towards the town walls.

"The skeletons have breached the gates." Yang pointed at the shattered east gate of Bluntworth, some distance south of them.

"North it is, then," panted Gunthar. "To Haffleton."

"They're gaining on us!" cried Yang.

Behind them, the skeletons sent by the Lich King approached, the largest one bounding in long strides, its arms outstretched.

"Faster!" Gunthar gathered more of the chains on his shoulders.

They sprinted for several more minutes, their breath coming in ragged gasps. The high walls of Bluntworth faded behind them, and they neared the suburbs of Haffleton. Little homes with glowing windows glittered some distance ahead.

Their legs burned, and every breath hurt. Yang slowed.

"Keep going, Wizard!" shouted Gunthar.

She picked up the pace again, stumbling but still running as fast as she could. Behind them, the nearest skeleton continued to close the distance.

But then Gunthar collapsed, falling to the dirt with a thump. "I'm sorry, Wizard Yang. I don't have the strength to go on."

Yang turned back, her legs wobbling beneath her. "I feel terrible, Gunthar! You've carried the weight of the chains all this way."

"Look, go on without me. We're almost there."

"No." Yang grabbed him by the shoulders and dragged him along the ground. "We'll make it," she said through gritted teeth.

"Leave me!" he wailed. "I'm useless! I've lost my axe, which I can't use very well anyway, and I don't have a style move. I've failed as a barbarian."

"Oh, come on." Yang wheezed as she dragged him.

They could hear the nearest skeleton now, its feet pounding the earth as it ran.

"Just leave me! This is fine. I deserve to be here, lying on the lifeless ground of the Badlands. This is a fitting end for me, a useless, failed barbarian lying in the midst of a desolate wasteland."

"I've pulled you into someone's backyard now. We're not in the Badlands anymore." Yang peered around them in the dim light. "Actually, it's quite pleasant. We're on fresh grass, and there are flowers all along the side, and there's a cute little fountain over there with carved statues of fairies and gnomes."

"Well then, maybe it's kind of an ironic end for me. Like, the garden is a metaphor for refined civilization, and I'm this uncouth wannabe barbarian lying sweaty and useless in the middle—"

"Gunthar, you're not useless, and you're not a failure. You're a great ally."

"I'm not! I'm a horrible ally!" he wailed. "I always say the wrong thing. Remember when we met? I thought maybe you knew whack-fu, just because you were from East Kathandar. And I said Nyala was a great dancer, just because she was from Adnam. I lack the cultural context to be aware of what I'm saying sometimes, so I keep putting my foot in my mouth."

The lead skeleton reached the edge of the yard and spied them on the grass. It ran over and grabbed the Wizard.

Gunthar jumped up, but the skeleton swatted him away in annoyance, and he collapsed in a large rhododendron bush.

"It's fine, Gunthar!" cried Yang. "An ally isn't perfect. An ally is someone that always tries their best and learns from their mistakes. You've always done that for us." The skeleton carried her into the darkness, and she vanished from sight.

"Yang!" he called, but no one answered. "I'm such an idiot."

He staggered up and pounded on the door to the low house, then kicked it open. "Oh, it's a yoga studio!"

Ogres filled the studio, other Haffletonians standing around in concern.

Gunthar's jaw dropped. "What's going on?"

"It's the ogres." The Haffleton lieutenant ran up in his yoga pants. "It turns out they're super flexible. But then the battle cries rang out and they all tensed up and we can't get them untangled."

"Someone hand me my ****ing sword!" Huknar waved a big green arm nearby. "I can fight those ****s anyway."

Gunthar winced. "Huknar, how did you get both legs up over your neck like that? Can you breathe?"

"Look, you ****ing ****, don't just stand there. Roll me out on the ****ing plains or something."

"See?" The lieutenant wrung his hands. "They're all like that."

"Look, relax them somehow! Don't you have incense or something?"

CHAPTER THIRTY-ONE: NIGHT

"Not the ****ing incense again! It smells like **** farts."

"Maybe some down tempo world music?"

"We'll figure it out," said the lieutenant. "But you need to protect our families! They're in the side yard." He gestured at another door.

"Right, I'll do that." Gunthar dashed over, then paused and called back to the ogres. "Relax! Don't worry about the hordes of attacking undead, or the Lich King."

"Get outside, Gunthar!" pleaded the lieutenant.

The barbarian hopped out the door into the side yard. "Oh, wow," he said as he crossed the patio. "You've got terraces and flower beds and a trellis and everything. I've seen a lot of great gardens here! But I won't extrapolate to everyone in Haffleton. I'm sure not *all* Haffletonians are dedicated gardeners, just some."

The families of all the archers huddled nearby, a large crowd of all ages.

"Well," said a man in a green cloak, "thank you for not making a generalization about people from Haffleton. Not everyone here is a great gardener. And likewise, I'm sure there are many barbarians who aren't good with an axe."

The ground shook with the growing clamor of hard feet on the Badlands, and bones and chains rattled in the night air.

"The skeletons are coming for us!" screamed a small girl. "I can see them!"

"Hey, your hands are chained together." The green-cloaked man stepped forward with a small pouch of tools. "I'm useless in the garden, but I am a *very* good locksmith." In a flash, he had the padlock open and Gunthar's hands dropped free. The wrapped chains fell to the ground with a rattling clang.

"Save us!" cried the girl.

"I don't have my axe anymore. And I'm not really much of a barbarian."

"Oh." The girl dropped her eyes.

Gunthar took a deep breath. The skeletons approached, it was true, but he could also smell the scent of the garden, and several roses, and the grass. It reminded him of all his travels, and the smell of wildflowers on the tundra at his home.

He turned to the locksmith. "You know, you're right. I *reject* the idea that all barbarians have to be good with an axe. That's just a self-limiting stereotype. I can be the type of barbarian *I* want to be."

"I believe in you," said the little girl. "Even though I kind of wish you still had an axe or something."

Gunthar stepped in front of the huddled families and spread his arms. "This is who I am. I'm a barbarian that wears fake fur. I'm horrible with an axe, I don't have a style move, and I'm not really much of a fighter. I'm more of a hugger. And maybe I'm a clumsy ally who keeps making ignorant mistakes. But even so, I'll never stop trying to be the best ally I can, so that everyone has a fair chance to be great at whatever they are. Even if that means I keep making a fool of myself sometimes." He took another deep breath. "Wow, it felt good to say that."

"Thank you for taking us along on your journey of self-discovery," said the locksmith. "But we're about to be captured or pulverized by giant skeletons with night vision."

The barbarian turned. Several large skeletons had reached the edge of the side yard and advanced with leering grins, their arms outstretched, their eyes glowing a ghostly green.

"Right." Gunthar rolled his shoulders, and picked up the chains from the ground. "Who needs a hug?"

Chapter 32
Moonflow

A great leader's true character shines forth in moments of crisis.

— *Considered Revelations, Book 112 "Leaders Who Are Very Smart", Chapter 94, Verse 1*

Princess Maryan stood at the front of the militia, her sword at the ready. The troops assembled in front of the cathedral stairs under Captain Vikal's direction. The remaining residents of Bluntworth cowered behind the princess and the sparse lines of soldiers.

Nyala stood beside her. "Aren't we better off *behind* the lines of pikes?" asked the healer, eyeing the advancing skeletons.

"It doesn't matter." Maryan's mouth set in a firm line, her voice raspy. "These skeletons won't be stopped by pikes either."

The undead grew closer, giant fiends plodding forward with their mouths open, eye sockets burning. The lead skeleton headed straight for the princess, reaching for her with one hand, while the other held a large coil of chains.

"Get ready!" called Maryan.

Just before the hand reached the princess, chains wrapped around the skeleton from behind. It stopped, a frown on its skeletal face as it looked back and forth, trying to find its assailant. The chains tightened with a creak, and the rib cage collapsed inwards in an explosion of bone.

The skeleton crumbled into a heap of rubble, revealing Gunthar standing behind, holding the chains.

"Hello, everyone!" He waved. "It turns out these skeletons aren't really huggers. Who knew?"

Wizard Yang stood next to him. "Gunthar's found a way to stop the undead!"

A man in a green cloak waved from further back. "Hi! I'm a locksmith. Usually I'm not needed in battles, but with so many people being locked up in chains, I'm much more relevant tonight."

The barbarian turned and flung lengths of chain around another skeleton, then strained as he pulled and tightened the chains. That skeleton likewise frowned in confusion, then imploded like the first.

The militia cheered, and Captain Vikal raised his spear. "*Style move*, barbarian!"

Wizard Yang kicked at the skeleton rubble. "The calcified titanium bones are resistant to impacts, but suffer cascading failures when subject to extended compressive strain. I think the Lich King should have studied more materials science before dabbling in ossified alloys!"

"You see?" The librarian waved his letter opener in the air. "This is why people should spend less time on prophecies, and more on other parts of the Archives."

Maryan turned to the militia. "Captain Vikal! Have your units use the chains against the skeletons."

Gunthar destroyed a third giant skeleton while teams of militia picked up the discarded chains with cries of vengeance against the undead.

Yang kept staring at the piles of bones. "I'll never understand how the Lich King got titanium microcrystals embedded in an organic matrix like that. I thought titanium atoms were too big."

"And how are the skeletons frowning?" wondered Banda. "I don't see how that's possible with the facial musculature decayed away."

Gunthar stopped in his tracks. "For that matter, who makes fake fur? Isn't that beyond current textile manufacturing capabilities?"

"You're right, barbarian." Healer Nyala scratched her head. "I never thought about things before. For instance, why are we even using a Gregorian calendar? I mean, I know it's a modification of an earlier Julian calendar, but there has never been an Emperor Julius here, or a Pope Gregory. Nothing makes sense."

"You're over-thinking it," said Maryan. "Let's just advance on the Lich King."

The princess led the charge. Captain Vikal walked at her side, directing units of militia as they destroyed the great skeletons one at a time. With every skeleton destroyed, another length of chain was made available, and another unit was able to destroy more skeletons.

In only a few minutes they'd cleared out most of the streets near

CHAPTER THIRTY-TWO: MOONFLOW

the cathedral, and advanced on the east gate. They found the gates shattered with the gatehouse collapsed on top. Captain Vikal directed units of militia and nearby townspeople as they cleared the rubble, while Maryan and the other adventurers climbed to the top of the wall.

"Look!" Nyala pointed out across the Badlands. "It's Sir Humphrey. What's he doing?"

"Oh, my," said Ex-Bookkeeper Andi, her hand on her heart. "I can see him now, galloping on top of Daisy. He's charging the Lich King, isn't he?"

"It's hard to see." The healer wiped a wet dreadlock out of her face. "We only get the occasional flash of lightning."

"I thought he'd been captured!" Lightning flashed again, and Maryan spotted the distant armored form, running across the plains. "But it appears he'd escaped to the south. Now, with most of the skeletons moving up here, he's able to take the Lich King's position from the side."

"Maybe," said Nyala. "But see there? The Lich King has many ranks of undead defending him. Sir Humphrey can't defeat all those. Not now that his magic sword isn't working."

"Come back, you great fool!" Andi screamed into the storm. "Don't charge the Lich King on your own!"

"He can't hear us." Maryan waited for another flash of lightning, then pointed. "See, he and Daisy are closer to the Lich King now."

Librarian Banda climbed back down the stairs. "I'll help the militia clear the gates. We need to get out there to help the knight as fast as we can."

"We won't make it in time." Maryan shook her head. "He's almost to the Lich King's lines."

Another flash of lightning illuminated the plain, and Nyala squinted. "Wait, what is he doing? Now it looks like he's charging *past* the Lich King's forces."

"Perhaps he's attempting to turn the Lich King's flank?" Maryan shrugged.

Multiple lightning strikes on the plains flared in succession, and they could see the distant armored form far away.

"He's run past them now." Nyala squinted. "He's charging up the hill behind the Lich King."

"Of course!" Wizard Yang's eyes widened. "He's heading for high ground."

"Why?" Maryan looked back and forth between the distant knight and the wizard. "That's fine tactics for an army, but it won't matter for a single person. He's still badly outnumbered."

"It's not a tactical move," said Yang with a grin. "It's strategic."

"Strategic?"

Another flash of lightning lit the plains, but this time, the bolt struck at the distant hilltop, where an armored form sat bestride a remarkably calm horse, the rider's sword extended to the sky. Everything went dark again, and thunder rolled across them from the mighty bolt, as well as a triumphant eleven-note Chord of Recharge.

Then a bright blue form lit the plains, bolts of lightning now flying out from the armored knight. The horse grazed on the hilltop while Sir Humphrey advanced on the Lich King's position. Even from here, they could see electrical arcs sparking between his raised fists.

"Gwendoline is back!" cried Andi, clapping her hands.

"See?" said Yang. "He used a lightning strike to power the sword again."

"The gate is clear!" bellowed the librarian.

The group hurried down the stairs and out the gate, where Vikal led the militia on a sweep forward, clearing the way of mindlessly advancing skeletons.

"Look out, Your Highness!" Ex-Bookkeeper Andi pointed at a large skeleton charging Maryan from the north.

The princess raised her sword to block the undead's attack, but the skeleton was slammed to the ground with a powerful strike of a giant club.

"Have a seat, you ****ing ****!" cried Huknar.

Another ogre wrapped the fallen skeleton in chains and tightened, the bony form disappearing in a dusty explosion of titanium shards.

"The barbarian in the ****ing fake furs told us about the **** chain trick," explained Huknar with a toothy, tusked grin.

"You got out of your yoga poses!" Gunthar waved.

"Yes," said the Haffleton lieutenant, still in his yoga pants. "We

CHAPTER THIRTY-TWO: MOONFLOW

finally relaxed them with some Upper Estorian throat singers."

"Throat singing!" Gunthar nodded. "Works every time."

"That **** is tight," agreed Huknar.

"Forward!" commanded the princess. "We advance on the Lich King now."

The armies advanced on the skeletons, smashing the undead with chains. In only a few minutes, they met up with Sir Humphrey at the throne of skulls.

"Well met, Sir Humphrey!" Maryan waved at him. "We won't get any closer to you, since we don't want to get zapped."

"Also, you generate a lot of ozone," added Yang.

"Well met indeed, ma'am! 'Twas a close thing for a while there, I won't lie to you." Sir Humphrey waved to them from a safe distance away, arcs playing across his armor plates. "But once Gwendoline was recharged, I was able to smash through these undead without much trouble."

"The high current weakens the carbon-titanium bonds," explained Yang.

The knight bowed. "Again, wizard, I defer to you in the magical arts."

"We have defeated the Lich King's forces." Maryan waved her sword at the empty throne. "But where is the Lich King himself?"

"He ran away!" Sir Humphrey pointed further into the Badlands behind him. "He threw his ranks of skeletons at me as a diversion."

"Oh, that coward." The princess cursed, then shrugged. "Very well, then. We advance on the Castle of Terror."

The armies advanced across the plains. Councilor Wilson sensibly organized a supply train, and carts of food and water followed them as they walked east.

They overtook a group of skeletons carrying prisoners. Captain Vikal and his band smashed the undead and freed the townspeople, including the Mayor and his Chief Advisor for the Centers for Undead Control and Prevention. "Thank you," said the black-robed man as the locksmith opened his chains. "I thought I was a goner for sure. Not that anyone at the CUC believes in the undead, of course," he added with a sidelong look at the Mayor.

The Mayor himself sighed in relief as his chains fell to the ground. "I'll certainly consider mobilizing the citizens in our defense now."

Maryan blinked. "Really? You'll finally use your authority to marshal the town's resources and face the imminent threat?"

"What? No." The Mayor waved her off. "I was just making conversation. I'm too cowardly to face threats directly. That's why I refuse to believe in the undead." He considered the vast, dark plains that stood between them and Bluntworth. "But I might stick with you a while longer, rather than venture back to town on my own. You know, in case you need my very smart leadership or anything."

"You can come along, Mayor," said Maryan. "But try not to interfere and make things worse."

"I promise not to interfere. Not until the next election. Then I'll go back to suppressing the votes of the majority that dislike me." He looked at them with concern. "Cheating in elections won't help the not-real undead, will it?"

"Just stay out of my way," said Maryan.

No skeletons or other undead stopped them as they crossed the plains, although at one point a ghostly form materialized right in front of Gunthar, and he jumped back with a yelp.

"You frightened me, ghost fairy!" he cried.

"Get over it," she snapped back, her translucent butterfly wings flapping lazily in the darkness.

"Oh, hello Fairy Queen Inga!" Ex-Bookkeeper Andi waved at the flying ghost from beside Daisy. "We're on our way to destroy the Lich King once and for all."

"You mortals should listen to me," said Inga. "It doesn't matter. You'll die alone, abandoned by anyone that ever claimed to love you."

"I'm sure," said Maryan. "But you're welcome to accompany us in the meantime."

"Oh, very well." Inga threw up her hands in disgust. "It's not like I'll be able to get anything else done tonight, what with your armies stomping around." She fluttered after the princess, occasionally muttering about the dust and noise and futility of free will.

At last they reached the Moonflow, the calm waters burbling over rocks and pebbles as the stream cut across their path. "We've made it this far. It's nice to reach a familiar landmark, but I don't see how we'll cross it." The princess waded into the water and tested the

CHAPTER THIRTY-TWO: MOONFLOW

path forward, but once again, the invisible barrier stopped her from getting past the center of the stream. "The barrier is still there," she told the others as she returned, "We'll have to find another way across."

"See?" said Inga. "I told you it was pointless."

"Wait," said Gunthar. "Who is that?"

Someone or something stood across the stream, shrouded in darkness.

"Who's there?" called Maryan. "Show yourself!"

A constellation of pale green globes rose from the dirt, and by their unearthly glow the adventurers could make out the tall form of a robed skeleton. He stood with his arms folded inside his sleeves, regarding them with luminous eye sockets.

Maryan raised her chin. "We've come for you, Lich King."

Chapter 33
Dragon

> *Held as metaphor, the dragon is a potent symbol of the unlimited possibility of willpower and ambition.*
> *Held as beast, the dragon will rip the arms off whoever is holding it, roast everyone it sees, then devour whatever smells vaguely of meat. Approach only the metaphor.*
>
> *— Considered Revelations, Book 122 "Minimum Safe Distances from Common Literary Devices", Chapter 12, Verse 3*

The Lich King regarded the army from across the stream, his head at a tilt. "Oh, princess," he said in a mocking tone. "To have come so far, and then be thwarted by a shallow stream."

"We've beaten you, Lich. And it's just a matter of time before we find a way across the Moonflow."

"On the contrary, Your Highness," he sneered, "you've only beaten my weakest allies. Let's see how you fare against a *real* challenge." The Lich King gestured to the side, where green-lit figures stepped out of the shadows.

Nyala squinted across the stream. "Who are they?"

"It's the vampire prince," breathed Captain Emma. Prince Mikhail leered at them, the silver filigree on his jacket glinting in the dim green light.

"Gnomes," muttered Gunthar. Indeed, several blue-clad gnomes waved at them, with wide eyes and bright smiles. Their large cage loomed in the darkness behind them.

"Editors," cursed Cornelius. Editor Larsson stood beside the gnomes, her lips pursed, her arms crossed with her fingers thrumming.

"And researchers of markets!" added Yang.

"Oh, hello, adventurers." Kwento waved his clipboard. "I'm researching this market now. Most unusual, don't you think?"

"Prince Mikhail?" Maryan kept her focus on her supposed fiancé. "We don't fear you anymore. And don't even think of bringing up your marriage proposal again."

The Prince looked much restored from the previous day's battle,

CHAPTER THIRTY-THREE: DRAGON

eying them contemptuously from across the stream. "My dear Princess, I am through with you. Through with all of you." He held up his arm, where a fragment of bone glittered in his hand. "Meet my final artifact, the soul of an Ultimate Dragon!"

Mikhail tossed the glowing shard into the stream, and began chanting. As his voice grew louder, bones rose from the ground.

Wizard Yang stepped back with a look of concern. "Your Highness, this is a magic more powerful than anything I've seen before. The relic isn't something I can break."

More bones rose from the ground, everything from knuckles to spinal vertebrae to ribs. But these bones dwarfed the previous skeletons, and once out of the ground they spun in a large maelstrom over the Moonflow, kicking up dust and water.

"What is that?" Sir Humphrey shielded his eyes. "And why do the bones flock so?"

Gunthar hefted his chains. "Whatever it is, it's big!"

"I doubt you've encountered one of these before, barbarian," chortled the Lich King.

The bones stopped orbiting and condensed into a long, lizard-like skeleton with great wings. It landed on the ground with a thunk and a splash, easily spanning the stream.

Prince Mikhail sprinted to its spiky tail, then deftly ran up the bony spine. "Say hello to my latest pet," he shouted as he sat between two great, bony wings. "A reanimated Ultimate Dragon."

The beast lifted its head and roared, a fearsome call like a phalanx of trumpets, and followed that with a gout of fire that went sizzling over their heads.

Sir Humphrey's armor switched off, plunging them all into darkness.

"Gwendoline!" The knight's voice rang out. "Has she been drained again?"

Wizard Yang gripped her staff with white knuckles. "The dragon lays down some sort of suppression field, Sir Humphrey. Headmaster Morozov warned us about this."

"'Tis most inconvenient!"

A loud thump shook them, and Sir Humphrey went flying back with a shout.

"Look out!" cried Maryan. "The dragon is striking with its wings now."

"You are all doomed!" laughed Mikhail.

The adventurers scattered, dodging the mighty sweeps of bony wings, the long ridged claws whistling by overhead.

"Get them!" Mikhail spurred the dragon forward by digging his heels into massive ribs.

Mage Niane stood far from the suppression field, and she lifted her crystal staff. It sent out bright white beams, beacons in the night.

By her light the adventurers could see that most everyone had run away, except for Librarian Banda and the Chronicler, standing exposed before the bony horror.

"Look out!" cried Maryan.

Mikhail hissed at them, and directed his mount to strike. The dragon swung its long tail, and Banda raised the Archives letter opener to meet it. The hard bone of the tail smacked into the long sword and both shattered, sending the librarian tumbling back, where he lay unmoving on the ground.

"Librarian Banda!" Cornelius dashed over to the fallen man, then raised his bound pages to protect him as the skeletal beast charged.

The dragon ripped the tome out of his hands with the flick of a single talon. Papers scattered all over the area and fluttered in the air.

"No!" Cornelius turned this way and that, grabbing at errant pages.

Another talon slashed, and another blizzard of paper erupted.

"No!" repeated Cornelius. "Those are my notes!"

Mikhail howled with laughter from atop the dragon.

Cornelius leapt and caught a page before it fell into the stream. "You think this is funny? To destroy my work in front of me, as a joke, after all the time I spent on it?" He grabbed the thick binding and swatted away another claw.

"'Tis a calamity!" Sir Humphrey sat up in the shadows, his hand to his head. "The curse of chronicling prophecies!"

"You're dead, Chronicler!" gloated Mikhail as he urged the dragon forward again.

"You're no better than the Guild, you know that?" The Chronicler dodged another claw to save a third piece of paper. He swatted again with the binding, yelling at the dragon and its rider.

"You think I'm not used to this? Everyone trying to rip apart my manuscript? This happens every day." He smacked again, harder now, at a giant claw and grabbed a fluttering sheet. "I work and work and work and all that happens is that the Guild sends the pages back and I have to cut the best parts out and then send it all back and then an editor tells me the entire middle section isn't cohesive"—here the Chronicler stomped on a claw, using it as a springboard to jump to a rock further in the stream, where he picked up a soggy page—"and then I have to revise again and all the while I see really crappy Chronicles being published like that last one about the Cyclops in the southern wastes, and honestly, what was the point of *that* one, and—hey, do you *mind?*"—now the Chronicler began swatting claws and wings away with wild abandon, ignoring the bellows of the dragon and a protesting Mikhail—"but somehow it gets published while I have to cut an entire chapter and get two more publisher rejections while the only way to put bread on the table is to keep ghost writing for these spoiled celebrities who let's be honest can't even spell and how do people read that tripe but I'm stuck as a byline at the very end and the whole time all I can do is write but the universe keeps throwing the manuscripts back at me—"

"Whoa there, Chronicler, ease up!" Gunthar had him in a light bear hug. "You've won. Just calm down, now."

The Chronicler stopped ranting and smashing with his notebook binding and looked beyond his pages. Fragments of bone littered the field, all that remained of the reanimated Ultimate Dragon. Most of the shards lay still, but a few wobbled faintly in a lingering attempt to get away from him.

"Yes, well, fine then," he said. "Can you help me gather the rest of the pages?"

"Of course," said the barbarian.

Yang's jaw dropped. "How did Cornelius defeat an Ultimate Dragon?"

"Ultimate Dragons don't read anything except shallow posts like Prince Hugo's." Healer Nyala gestured at the field of broken bones. "That makes them quite vulnerable to books."

Sir Humphrey lit up, blue arcs of electricity illuminating the scene. "'Tis a relief! With the Ultimate Dragon dispatched, Gwendoline is working once more."

Prince Mikhail stood amidst the ruin of his Ultimate Dragon. He glared at the Chronicler. "You..."

Maryan walked forward, her sword at the ready. "Now you will pay for all of the evil you've committed, Prince."

Mikhail stumbled back into the stream, backing away from her until he smacked into the invisible barrier. He pressed his back against the unseen wall, his hands scrabbling for any sort of gap.

"You're finally trapped, good Prince," said Maryan.

"Ah, Lich King?" Mikhail called over his shoulder, keeping his eyes on the approaching Princess. "Can you invite me across the stream? I'd like to come back."

The Lich King rolled his eyes. "Fine." He lifted a skeletal hand, and flicked a finger over. With that, Mikhail floated into the air, then sailed over the gnomes and an astonished Kwento. The Prince landed in the gnomes' large cage, and the heavy door swung closed with a loud click.

"No!" wailed Mikhail, gripping the heavy iron bars. The gnomes gleefully rushed back and hauled the cage away, the Prince's pleading screams fading into the distance.

Gunthar and Cornelius finished gathering all the scattered pages, and the Chronicler stood with his arms crossed over his folio. "Editor Larsson, I think you'll agree Mikhail's book can't be published now."

"Not at all, Chronicler." The Editor waved a finger at him. "*My Values: Dangling Kidnapped People in Cages for the Good of the Country* is a guaranteed success. The Guild stands to make a considerable sum of money by selling his offensive and inciting book to the many people gullible enough to buy it."

Kwento raised his clipboard. "Editor Larsson, we're no longer polling quite as well in Bluntworth, or with the ogres. Apparently Mikhail's multiple displays of evil *and* cowardice have made many people change their minds about him." The researcher's face shone pale and sweaty in the green light. "Not only are Mikhail's book sales at risk, the notoriety could impact other titles offered by the Guild. We're talking about a potential revenue hit."

Editor Larsson harrumphed. "It's like I've been saying,

CHAPTER THIRTY-THREE: DRAGON

Chronicler. Prince Mikhail's book does not meet our high editorial standards. We'll never publish it." She turned away. "Let's go, researcher."

Kwento waved as he followed Editor Larsson into the darkness. "Good luck, adventurers!"

Maryan approached the stream, and the Lich King beyond. "We've defeated your latest attempt, Lich, and your last allies."

"No, princess, you've lost. I am safe, on this side of the Moonflow, free to strike again at my leisure. And earlier in the evening I was able to regain the Teacup." He smiled, a wide grin of gray teeth lit by his green orbs, and hoisted Yang's satchel.

"Oh, crap," said Yang.

Chapter 34
Bishop

> *Throughout the ages, the Bishops of Bluntworth have been most notable for their greed, corruption, and venality. Indeed, there are but few exceptions.*
>
> *— Considered Revelations, Book 49 "Reasons Bluntworth Bishops Are So Fun at Parties", Chapter 12, Verse 3*

A wave of exhaustion washed over Maryan. She gritted her teeth and steadied her legs beneath her. They'd fought two battles the previous day, then marched across the Badlands all night, and her feet were killing her. Stars appeared through rents in the clouds above, and she could see by the constellations that dawn approached.

"I am in your debt, princess!" The Lich King laughed triumphantly. "You freed the Teacup for me, and now I can transport it anywhere I want. After centuries of being stuck under the rubble of the Castle of Terror, I am finally free to conquer the world."

"Go ahead, take the Teacup," taunted Wizard Yang.

"Oh, I am not so foolish as you think, *Wizard*. The Teacup cannot be handled directly, except by those immune to magic." He smiled. "But as the current owner of the ruins of the Castle of Terror, I have inherited all of its denizens, including two elementals."

A small party joined the Lich from further south. A troop of skeletons carried a chest and a table, led by two elementals.

One elemental was a shifting humanoid form made of fire, crackling and popping. The other was of the purest ice, a deep glacier blue, and it moved with the creaking of frost and snow.

"And as you know, princess, elementals are immune to magic."

"Is that true?" Maryan looked back at her fellow travelers.

"Aye, Your Highness," grumbled Librarian Banda. "Elementals are beings immune to all magicks."

"Place those here, servants," commanded the Lich. The skeletons put the table in front of him, and the chest beside.

CHAPTER THIRTY-FOUR: BISHOP

"Hey!" Princess Maryan put her hands on her hips. "That's *my* table, and *my* chest."

"You fled the field of battle, princess," sneered the Lich. "And so I ransacked your command tent and carried everything back here."

"Why, you..."

The skeletons placed a heavy leather bag on top of the table, as well as Yang's canvas satchel. They used long wooden tongs to open the bags, and remove an item from each.

The Lich King spread his arms. "Behold the Teapot, and the Teacup, together again after centuries apart!"

On the table stood a teapot, made of deep black stone, covered at the top and bottom with faintly glowing runic inscriptions. Next to it sat a teacup-sized hole in spacetime, revealing another universe within. The air buzzed with power, and ripples spread in the Moonflow as the ground trembled.

"Oh, no," breathed Wizard Yang. "He's got both artifacts now. Who knows what he's capable of?"

"I believe there are maps in your chest, are there not? I'm sure they will be invaluable when planning my siege on the civilized kingdoms." The Lich King leaned towards Maryan. "Where did you say you were from, Your Highness? Offerdell, was it?"

"You demon." Maryan glared at him.

"Let's prepare our assault, shall we? Elementals, take the artifacts!"

The ice elemental picked up the teacup, while the fire elemental held the teapot. Instead of exploding or disintegrating or turning into a flock of birds, the elementals just held the magical treasures as if they were regular tableware.

"Open the chest! Let us examine the maps."

Two skeletons heaved open the top of the chest. But rather than pull out maps, they backed up as the bishop candidate Onkar climbed out.

"Oh, wow. Hello, everyone." He blinked in the light of the elementals, and the Lich King's floating green orbs.

"Onkar!" Maryan gasped. "What are you doing there?"

"Well, Your Highness, when the skeletons first attacked at night, I hid in the chest in your command tent. But then they carried me here." He looked at the Lich, standing a few paces away. "In retrospect, maybe it wasn't the best hiding spot."

The Lich opened and closed his mouth, staring at Onkar.

A long whistle pierced the silence, and everyone looked at the fire elemental. "Sorry," it said. "I've been holding the teapot, so it got hot." It raised the whistling black teapot. "Tea's ready."

"Put those down," ordered the Lich.

The fire elemental put the teapot on the table and backed away, and the ice elemental did the same with the teacup. The teapot's whistle faded as it cooled.

"He's no bishop. I know that." The Lich glowered at the adventurers across the stream. "And you have wasted enough of my time. Elementals, attack!"

The elementals strode into the Moonflow, one creating loud hissing footprints of steam, the other creating chunks of ice which floated downstream.

"Oh, my," said Wizard Yang. "I'm not sure how we can defeat those."

The Mayor waved his hands. "Look, I know I said I didn't believe in the rising tide of the undead, and I told people not to wear sprigs of lemongrass even though it would have protected us, but that's only because *my* life wasn't in immediate danger. But now that *I'm* facing a direct threat, can't you do something?"

The elementals advanced across the stream, very tall and moving with merciless precision. Even the skeletons had sometimes betrayed hints of emotion, of anger or surprise or malice. But the elementals were older, from a forgotten age before mortals first walked the earth, and they betrayed no feelings at all, just a ruthless and brutal efficiency in carrying out their orders.

Sir Humphrey raised his fists, electricity crackling. "'Tis most unclear whether I can stop them at all, but I will die trying!"

"We can't face them directly," said Maryan. "Mayor, you have to approve Onkar as bishop!"

"What?" The Mayor shook his head. "That's ridiculous. He'd be a horrible bishop. I need someone more malleable, someone that can back up my inane political posturing with shallow appeals to false faith."

The elementals reached the near side of the stream and loomed over them, their powerful arms raised.

"Now, Mayor! Or we're all doomed!" cried Maryan. "And by that I mean, you'll die too!"

"Oh, by the gods of fraudulent recounts. Fine!" The Mayor raised his hands in disgust as the elementals advanced. "Onkar, I pronounce you Bishop of Bluntworth!"

But nothing changed. The elementals kept marching, and Maryan and the Mayor and the others had to scatter, fire and ice close on their heels.

"I'm still standing, mortals, though you have summoned your bishop." The Lich King raged beside Onkar. "I will destroy you!"

"We'll find a way to cross the stream, and crush you to a pulp," responded Maryan as she ran, furious.

"Everyone, please, just chill! Perhaps we need less fighting, and more listening. Why don't we have some tea?" And Bishop Onkar used the wooden tongs to pour the hot tea from the teapot into the teacup.

A crack of lightning and peal of thunder reverberated across the Badlands. The stormclouds over the ruins of the Castle melted away in a single heartbeat, like a guilty thief slinking sideways into an alley. With the eastern clouds gone, the bright sky illuminated the plains with tints of rose and coral, dawn imminent.

The elementals stood still.

On the table, the teacup-shaped hole in spacetime closed with a snap, while the teapot crumbled into a fine gray dust that dissipated in the breeze. Bishop Onkar stepped back. "That was, like, totally weird. What happened to my tea?"

Most surprising of all, however, was the appearance of people. Amongst the militia, many more members appeared. Captain Emma's squad of archers doubled in size. All around them, people cried in astonishment and joy.

And many ogres appeared next to King Bofor's forces.

"Kogon, you ****! What the **** are you doing here?" exclaimed Huknar to a recently-appeared ogre.

Kogon himself blinked in confusion in the predawn light.

"What just happened?" Gunthar kept turning around.

"Everyone who fell in battle was brought back." Maryan staggered back, taking in the celebration. "The Lich King has finally been defeated."

Cornelius whooped and waved his pen, then attempted an

awkward high-five with Librarian Banda. Gunthar said nothing, but kept staring back and forth between Onkar and the cheering militia.

"Congratulations, Your Highness," said Wizard Yang.

"Thank you," replied Maryan. "It doesn't seem real."

"Queen Inga, you're not a ghost anymore!" Ex-Bookkeeper Andi stared up at the flying queen, no longer a ghost, but a living fairy again. Her large butterfly wings were no longer translucent, but now a brilliant iridescent blue and yellow.

Inga kept trying to say something caustic, but appeared too shocked to come up with anything, so she just opened and closed her mouth repeatedly as she hovered over the barren ground.

"Who is that?" Gunthar gestured across the stream.

A tall, dark man with short curly black hair stood between Onkar and the Lich. He wore robes of green and yellow, with a simple mahogany staff in his hand.

"Oh, my," gasped Wizard Yang. "That's the legendary Archmage Omondi. He was killed by his apprentice in the Castle of Terror long ago."

"Hello, everyone." Omondi beckoned to them. "Please, approach. I've dispelled the barrier."

The adventurers waded across the stream, relieved to find that the invisible wall no longer barred their way. They stood on the eastern side of the Moonflow, gathered in front of Omondi.

"You lot have fulfilled the prophecy," he explained. "You thrice-defeated the Lich King, and got him to invite the bishop across the Moonflow for tea."

"I don't remember him inviting anyone," said Gunthar.

"The lich book of manners is fairly terse, but if a lich carries you in a chest somewhere, that's about the same as an invitation."

"Oh."

"The teapot and the teacup are no more. And once they were destroyed, everyone that was ever killed by their foul influence was returned." The Archmage nodded at the restored ranks of humans and ogres. "No one really knows how titans think, but I suspect that bringing people back is a kind of apology, or a final closure of the joke."

"And why did the elementals freeze?" Gunthar waved at the

beings of ice and fire, standing on the other side of the Moonflow.

"Property ownership laws, and wills in general, are very complicated when people can die and return to life later," said Omondi. "In this case, once I was restored, ownership of the Castle of Terror reverted back to me. So the elementals freeze until given instructions by their new master."

"And why is the Lich still here?" Maryan pointed at the figure of the Lich, standing in his robes, though he seemed to have shrunk somewhat, and the hood obscured his face.

Archmage Omondi addressed him. "Well, Apprentice, what do you have to say for yourself?"

The figure pulled back his hood, revealing not a Lich King, but just a regular person with nervous black eyes and a thin mustache. "You losers ruined everything. I *liked* being a Lich King," he hissed. "And when I finally got the Teapot and the Teacup, you destroyed them. I'm going to get even, do you hear?"

"Look, man. I think you need to be nice, okay?" Bishop Onkar patted him on the shoulder, and the Apprentice promptly disappeared in a puff of black smoke.

"Whoa!" Onkar's eyes went wide.

"You gave him a direct order to be nice, but not a single atom in his body could obey," said Omondi, sadly shaking his head. "So he was banished to the underworld."

"Serves him right," muttered Banda.

"I know one shouldn't speak ill of the dead, but he was a **** apprentice," said Omondi. "Now, let me look at the people who fulfilled the prophecy, and saved me!" And he regarded each in turn.

He stopped first at Onkar, and nodded. "Greetings, Bishop. It has been a long time since the people of Bluntworth have had a Bishop worthy of their faith."

"I'll, like, totally do my best, Archmage."

The Archmage stopped next in front of Gunthar. "Ah, the Wise One. A pleasure."

Gunthar blinked. "What?"

Then Omondi came to Wizard Yang. "And the Protector. And not just a Protector, but a Void Mage!" The Archmage bowed deeply. "It has been millenia since a Void Mage last walked the firmament.

Truly, the honor is mine."

"Um, thank you, I guess?" said Wizard Yang. "And it's great to meet you too."

Omondi looked at the rest of them. "I'm sorry, but I don't recognize you."

"We're not really in the prophecy," said Maryan, bowing. "But we wanted to help."

Sir Humphrey waved from some distance away, blazing in his electrified armor. "Sorry about the ozone!" he cried. "That's why I'm standing downwind!"

"And now, where is Fairy Queen Inga?" asked Omondi. "She is the one I most wanted to see."

"Really, Omondi?" Inga fluttered next to Maryan. "I noticed you spent all of your time talking to everyone else, and *then* you asked about me."

Omondi stared at her. "You are as beautiful as the day we met."

"Oh, knock it off." She waved a finger at him. "You abandoned me, you know. I waited at the altar all day. You'd better have an amazing excuse."

"I'm sorry, Inga. I was murdered by my apprentice on the morning of our wedding, and then my soul was trapped in a teapot for over six hundred years." He sighed. "I thought of you every day."

"I don't know if that's good enough."

"Please, walk with me." The Archmage extended an elbow to her.

The fairy queen pursed her lips, her butterfly wings flapping slightly faster. "Fine," she said. "Just for a minute." She landed and took his arm, walking stiffly beside him as they headed towards the dawn.

"Remember, I promised to make the Badlands your own personal garden," said Omondi.

"If I recall, you said I could do what I wanted, and *I* told *you* that I'd turn it into a garden."

"Yes."

The couple walked away, grass and flowers sprouting wherever Queen Inga stepped. Omondi and the fairy spoke in hushed tones now, and the adventurers could no longer hear what they were saying.

CHAPTER THIRTY-FOUR: BISHOP

"Oh, of course. It's what the soothsayer said. A romance that spans the ages." Maryan brought her hands to her cheeks. "We found it, but it doesn't belong to any of us. It belongs to them."

Further out, Omondi and Inga still walked together. But the fairy queen no longer held his arm so stiffly, and after another few steps, she rested her head against his shoulder.

"I think the Badlands are going to be all right now," said Maryan. "Let's go back and see what we can do for Bluntworth."

Chapter 35
Farewells

Parting is such sweet— Wait, ignore the sorrow bit. Sometimes you are happy to leave.

— *Considered Revelations, Book 44 "How to Ghost a Party", Chapter 13, Verse 12*

The armies spent the rest of the morning marching back to Bluntworth, and finally arrived at the town walls in the early afternoon. Word of their victory had already reached the town, and people had set up banners and tents outside the walls.

"I'm going to stay here and enjoy the victory party," said the Mayor. "Since I'm the person that saved the day. You know, by appointing the Bishop and all." He turned to Councilor Wilson. "Can I fire the Bishop now?"

"Sorry, Mayor," said the councilor. "Onkar is now Bishop for life."

"Shoot," said the Mayor. "Still, I can make him a political foil and blame him for all my mistakes from here on out. Voters eat that up."

"We'll head up to Haffleton first," said Maryan. "We want to accompany the archers back to their homes."

"We'll go with you," said Vikal, at the head of the Bluntworth militia.

So they all marched north to the eastern outskirts of Haffleton.

"It's great to be back at my studio," said the lieutenant. "These yoga pants were pretty comfortable during the battle, but I'm over them now. This is why I normally just wear shorts."

"We and the archers will stop here so we can rejoin our families. But you should go on ahead." Captain Emma waved to the center of Haffleton. "Bluntworth's eastern gate is still constricted with rubble. But the northern gate is open. You can get in that way."

"Thank you," said Maryan.

The lieutenant pointed to Librarian Banda's broken greatsword. "Do you want us to re-forge that for you?"

"No, thank you." Banda patted the hilt. "It works better as a letter

CHAPTER THIRTY-FIVE: FAREWELLS

opener this way."

The adventurers said goodbye to the archers, then turned to the company of ogres.

"We'll ****ing wait here," said King Bofor. "I can't stand that ****ing Mayor. What with having misled his own citizens, ****ing over his scientific advisors, and generally **** with ****, I think he's a complete ****. And I don't mean that in a good way."

"I hear you, Your Majesty," said Maryan. "Cool your **** here, and we'll come and rejoin you once we've returned the militia to their homes."

The princess and her fellow travelers walked further into Haffleton, the militia streaming behind. People waved to them from windows, and tossed flowers down.

A group of stylish Haffletonians sauntered past them.

Yang stared after them. "What were they wearing?"

"I haven't seen that fashion before," said Princess Maryan. "Was it... Was it fake fur?"

"Aye." Gunthar scratched his head. "Most odd. Maybe they also couldn't find their khakis?"

"Oh, look," said Librarian Banda. "There's another group."

Several Haffletonians sat at a table outside a kombucha bar. They wore fake furs, either kilts or dresses, with matching jackets, and they waved at the adventurers as they passed.

"Perhaps Saturday is wash day?" wondered Gunthar.

They rounded a corner and entered Haffleton's main square. Many brightly-colored stores crowded around the square, with hanging signs advertising hemp clothing, hot chai, and shields made from fast-growing sustainable hardwood.

At the head of the square, a large shop sported a sign that read "Fake Furs," with a smaller sign that said "It's back! Stylish and Ethical!" In the display window hung a poster of fur-garbed barbarians hugging each other and flashing a thumbs-up sign.

Yang pointed at the shop. "Gunthar! You've ended up being the most stylish person in the kingdom!"

He snorted. "All in all, wizard, I liked the Forest of Madness better."

In the center of the square stood four people that the adventurers recognized right away.

"Oh, wow," said Wizard Yang. "Your Highness, all of your suitors are back!"

"Wait! Don't move!" Prince Hugo dashed up and wrapped an arm around the barbarian's shoulders. "Smile! Bigger! Yes, more big!" The prince held up a small mirror and sketched their reflection on an easel which an aide had supplied.

Gunthar raised an eyebrow. "What is this?"

"You're the hot thing right now," said Prince Hugo. "Big and vulnerable and also setting the fashion trend." The influencer turned to his assistant. "Quick, get copies of that sketch posted in all the nearby towns!"

"You seem to be fine now, Prince Hugo," said Maryan.

"Never better, princess! Can you believe I got a selfie with the Fake Fur Barbarian? This is great! Now, if you'll excuse me, I need to get my summer collection updated. Furs in summer, who would have thought?" And the influencer dashed off again.

"Whoa, like, who was that dude?"

"Oh, hello Sir Chad, Squire Brock." Maryan nodded to the two of them. "I hope your brief death wasn't a major imposition."

"We spent the time in purgatory, and guess what? We *rocked* it!"

Sir Chad and Squire Brock did their fistbump-handshake-elbow bump again, and the adventurers backed up a step to make room.

"Purgatory was totally boring. It was a good thing we brought drums and this!" Squire Brock waved his flask.

Sir Chad scratched his head. "I've heard that the overseers of purgatory don't like to have people go back to the land of the living, but they seemed delighted when we left!"

"They were probably happy for you," said the princess.

Squire Brock bobbed his head. "Oh, yeah! For sure!"

"We need to get going, Your Highness." Sir Chad pointed up at the Mayor's palace, beyond the Bluntworth walls. "There's a big party later, and we need to get to the prefunc now."

"Of course, gentlemen. Have fun!"

"Will do, ma'am! Later!"

The two men in fringed leather swaggered through the northern gate of Bluntworth.

"Is that Princess Maryan's voice I hear?" Prince Juan waved from nearby. "I'd greet you, but I don't want to tear my eyes away from my love."

"Oh, wow," said Maryan. "How wonderful that you should already be in a relationship, so soon after returning from the land of the dead!"

"Oh, yes, princess. As I told you, I find life too frightening to face on my own. So I jumped into a relationship right away, once I was alive again."

"Hello, Your Highness," said the object of Prince Juan's affections. "I'm Sarah, the daughter of Merchant Klaus."

Maryan nodded. "Hello, Sarah. I trust you are happy in your relationship with Prince Juan?"

"Oh, yes," said the merchant's daughter. "I've always had these vague feelings that I should be doing more with my life of privilege, and I thought there was no better way to bury those feelings than by diving into a relationship with a total stranger."

"I'm happy for the two of you," said Maryan. "You were meant for each other."

"Thank you, princess," said Prince Juan. "And congratulations to the rest of your party, since although I never got a very good look at them, I know them just by their sound. I heard you all saved the city."

"Thank you, Your Highness." Sir Humphrey bowed. "'Twas our pleasure."

"Now, if you'll excuse us," said Sarah. "We need a little privacy, where our repressed anxieties and lack of purpose outside our relationship can fuel our first fight."

"Of course," said Maryan. "Good luck."

The swaggering barbarian Rangvald jumped out to hassle Gunthar again, but Gunthar hugged him back, and it took two teams of Haffletonians several hours to untangle the bully from all the chains.

"Thanks for the help," Rangvald told the Haffletonians who worked to free him. "And take your time. This is a good opportunity for me to reconsider many of my life choices."

The adventurers walked through the large gates into Bluntworth, the militia following them. The Princess and her entourage stopped in front of the Mayor while the city's returning troops streamed past.

The Mayor greeted her with open arms. "How wonderful to have you back, Your Highness!"

"How is the city, Mayor?"

"Just fine! I told you that the rising tide of the undead was no big deal. And like my advisors said, not doing anything except distorting facts was a great way to head off the crisis."

Nearby stood the Chief Advisor of the Centers for Undead Control and Prevention. "Oh, I know what you're thinking," said the black-robed man. "You're thinking that I should be ashamed, and that the CUC will be forever remembered as a bunch of sheepish bureaucrats who, when their city really needed them for the first time, buckled under political pressure and produced distorted lies rather than stand by the truth, and that the CUC will be a new synonym for intellectual cowardice."

"There's a bit more I'm thinking," said Librarian Banda, "but let's start with that."

"Well, I'd tell you not to worry." The Chief Advisor spread his arms with a smile. "The tax dollars will keep flowing anyway!"

"Maybe the CUC should be put under the control of the Council or another legislative body, so that it won't be as crippled by political pressure next time?" suggested Maryan.

The Chief Advisor of the Centers for Undead Control and Prevention gasped, and placed his hand over his heart. "What? And miss future opportunities for the CUC's critical mission to be subverted by a pathological demagogue? Why would we do that, ma'am?"

"Of course," said Maryan. "I don't want to rock the boat."

"Good advice." The Mayor nodded to the Chief Advisor. "Stick to my inane narrative, or you're fired."

"Aren't you worried that your citizens won't trust you now, Mayor? Since you were obviously wrong about the undead the whole time, and often flat-out lied?"

"Not a problem," he replied. "I'll just tie my authoritarian misbehavior to jingoistic patriotism. You'll see, my followers will love me even more. Works every time."

"Can we go now?" asked Gunthar.

Maryan nodded. "Definitely. Bishop Onkar, you're welcome to come with us."

CHAPTER THIRTY-FIVE: FAREWELLS

"Thank you, Your Highness, but I will stay here. My duty is to the citizens of Bluntworth." Onkar gestured back to the town cobbler, still waving his *Burn the Lemingras* sign. "I know a lot of Haffletonians were like, 'Those Bluntworth citizens have lost their sense of community, thanks to poor political and spiritual leadership.' But I was all, 'Don't worry, they'll bounce back.' People are naturally good, you know? Especially if their leaders aren't focusing all their attention on artificial divisions."

Princess Maryan bowed. "You are a braver person than me, Bishop Onkar. Good luck."

"Thank you, ma'am. Good luck to you too."

Maryan turned to the remaining worthies. "Councilor Wilson, Librarian Banda, we'd love to have you in Offerdell, or wherever our travels take us next."

"Thank you, ma'am, but I'll stay here." Councilor Wilson sighed. "I'll need to clean up after the Mayor, as usual."

"And I need to stay here to provide some intellectual backbone, for when the CUC caves again," added Banda.

"I don't envy you, but I'm glad that the citizens of Bluntworth have you two and Bishop Onkar looking out for them, despite their horrible Mayor."

"Good luck, ma'am."

"Goodbye Councilor Wilson, Librarian Banda."

Healer Nyala bowed. "And I'll also head back now, Your Highness."

"Oh, Healer Nyala! I was hoping you'd stay with us for a while in Offerdell."

"I'd love to, ma'am, but I've already left Rob, Bob and Bartholomew alone for too long. And like I said, I'm a *retired* Ranger. I've got plenty to do in the mystic forest, and the Badlands will be changing a lot soon. I'd like to be there for that." She nodded to all of them. "You're welcome to stop by whenever you're in the area."

"Indeed, Healer!" Sir Humphrey saluted her. "And likewise, the doors of the Happenhouse estates are always open to you."

Maryan led them up back to the northern gate. On the way, they passed the Halls of the Merchant Houses.

"What happened, Sir Humphrey?" Maryan gestured at the ornate doors. "Did you shut them down?"

"No, ma'am. In truth, I don't have it in myself to put anyone through bankruptcy. And now that I have the deed to my estates again, and more wealth besides, I don't feel the need to be vindictive. The Ex-Bookkeeper came up with a different solution."

"Microloans, Your Highness," said Andi. "We've told the Merchant Houses that they have to run a microloans program to discharge their debt."

"And what do the Merchant Houses think of that?"

"They don't like it much, ma'am, but they prefer it to insolvency. And with the Badlands turning into a garden, Bluntworth will need some sort of economy besides taxing traffic. This way, the Merchant Houses will help grow the next generation of entrepreneurs."

"I would say, Ex-Bookkeeper Andi, Sir Humphrey, that I like your solution."

Maryan and the others returned to the northern gates of Bluntworth where King Bofor and his ogres waited for them. "Let me guess," said the king. "That ****ing Mayor didn't learn **** from the whole experience."

"No," said Maryan. "He's still a complete ****."

"Some ****ing things won't change." Then Bofor roared back to his army. "Grab your ****, you ****s! We're following Her Highness!"

Chapter 36
Home

> *The last chapter of a Chronicle is often an afterthought inflicted upon the reader by distracted Chroniclers who are already battling with editors over their next manuscript.*
> *Unless, of course, a trickster titan is involved. In that case, all bets are off.*
>
> — Considered Revelations, Book 2 *"On the Last Chapters of Chronicles"*, Chapter 88, Verse 2

Maryan and the ogres marched up through Haffleton, the residents cheering and waving and throwing locally-sourced bouquets of flowers. They discovered blue-haired Captain Emma standing by the docks, staring out at the river.

"Captain?" asked Maryan.

"I don't know what to do," she replied. "You see, with trade routes moving away from Haffleton and across the Badlands, there will be less work for customs officers now."

"Well," said Maryan, "I could use a squad of archers."

"Very well, Your Highness." And Captain Emma and several of her archers joined them.

They marched for a day and a half up the Goldswell, then paid the river traffic to ferry them across at a calm stretch of the river.

"Oh, it's you again!" The captain waved at the Princess and her entourage when they boarded his boat. "I'll have you on the west side of the Goldswell in fifteen minutes, or my name's not Captain Marco!"

An hour later, they disembarked. "Sorry we're so far downstream," said Captain Marco sheepishly. "I wasn't expecting the currents to be so strong there."

"Don't worry about it, Captain. Thank you again."

They marched up and rejoined the ogre army and the archers, then camped on the Golden Plains. The ogres sang and danced by the campfires, which is just as frightening as it sounds. Then they all marched again at dawn after far too little sleep.

A few minutes before noon, they reached the walls of the North

Hills School of Wizardry.

A red-robed figure waved down at them from the top of the wall. "Hello!" cried Headmaster Morozov. "I'd let you in the gates, Your Majesty, but I'm too scared of ogre armies."

"Go **** yourself," replied King Bofor. "And don't worry, we won't take it ****ing personally."

"Hi there!" Thristletoramallicus, Keeper of the Gates, also waved from atop the walls in his brilliant blue robes. "Warlock Tyrheus suddenly appeared here three days ago. He sends his greetings!"

Mage Niane called back, her hands cupped around her mouth. "Good to hear he returned to the land of the living! Why didn't he rejoin us?"

"The barista also re-appeared in the Hall of Refreshment. So Tyrheus decided to stay."

"Well, Your Highness, this is where we ****ing head our own way." King Bofor pointed to the hills further north. "We'll march home, so **** you."

"**** you too," said Maryan warmly. "Fighting alongside your ogre army was ****ing ****."

Huknar rubbed his jaw. "I don't know about you ****s, but I'd prefer to keep wandering and kill some more ****."

"Huknar," said Maryan, "if King Bofor says **** ****, you'd be the most ****ing useless companion I could imagine."

"Oh, **** it," said the king. "Huknar, go **** yourself. And anyone **** enough to go **** with a **** like you."

"Thank you, Your ****ing Majesty." Huknar bowed deeply.

Gunthar whispered to the princess. "Is it wise to have a company of ogres accompany us? I'm a little worried about Huknar especially, since he seems to have a better grasp of battlefield tactics now. Who knows what he could do to Offerdell, or other kingdoms?"

"I know. But that's all the more reason to keep a close eye on him. And who knows? Maybe he'll be useful." Then she spoke loudly to Huknar and his assembled group. "All right, you ****s, try not to get in our ****ing way."

The main force of ogres headed north, following King Bofor, while the smaller group under Huknar stayed with Maryan.

"I'll stop here, Your Highness." Mage Niane stood before the

CHAPTER THIRTY-SIX: HOME

gates, her white robe flowing, her crystal staff gleaming in the sunlight.

"Thank you for all of your help, Mage Niane."

"Of course, ma'am." Niane tilted her head. "Wizard Yang, won't you join us? You're the most powerful wizard at the school now. At some point, Archmage Morozov will retire, and we'll need a new headmaster."

"I'm not really the type," said Yang. "I think you'd be a much better headmaster than me, Mage Niane."

"I'll certainly think about it." Niane's eyes twinkled. "I'll see you all someday soon, I hope." Then she disappeared.

The party continued on, much smaller now although still the most formidable force in the area given that it consisted of a Void Mage, a huggy barbarian, a knight in electric armor, a warrior princess, a unit of ogres, a squad of archers, a dependable horse, an accountant, and a Chronicler. They traveled across the plains and passed through the Forest of Madness without incident since, as you've probably realized, that Forest is only dangerous to those who bring malice with them.

In fact, the only notable event to occur in the Forest of Madness was when Sir Humphrey presented Ex-Bookkeeper Andi with a wreath of wildflowers. She promptly put it on and kissed him again and he blushed a deep red.

They entered Offerdell on Saturday, the twenty-third of May. The palace had all its flags flying and the road to the entrance lined with troops in their finest livery, standing in salute. The king and queen stood at the steps to the entrance.

"Are those ogres?" The King squinted at Huknar's unit, which had stopped at the main gates. "Are they housetrained?"

"Oh, Maryan, didn't anyone feed you?"

"Hi, Mom. Hi, Dad."

"Well, you've got your own army now, or at least, a start." King Albert waved at the ogres and archers. "Although, you should get more horses. Cavalry's the thing, you know."

"Where's my brother?" asked Maryan.

"Oh, he's at tennis camp," said Queen Sally. "Have you met Ambassador Shimsusa?"

Next to the queen stood a tall young woman, regal in silk robes of white and silver, a graceful platinum necklace glittering in the sun, with long matching bracelets on her arms. And around her shoulders lay a bright red shawl.

"Ambassador Shimsusa." Maryan bowed. "Or should I say, Titan Ereshkigal?"

The titan smiled, perfect white teeth behind ruby lips. "I am flattered that you recognize me, Your Highness."

"You appeared last time as a peasant woman, but somehow you feel the same. I'm surprised no one else recognizes you, Ereshkigal. The red shawl is a big hint."

"You are the only one that can see my shawl, ma'am. Just as you are the only one that is paying attention to this conversation."

Indeed, the rest of the princess' party greeted the King and Queen of Offerdell, somehow ignoring both the princess and the titan, though they stood but two paces away.

Maryan's eyes narrowed. "What are you up to with your magicks this time, trickster?"

Ereshkigal laughed, a warm and friendly laugh that reminded Maryan of an embrace and a mountain stream at the same time. "Some call me a trickster, Your Highness, but that's not a label I give myself."

"Librarian Banda said you were known as a trickster, and you mislead people with false promises. Like you misled us with your false prophecy."

"Was it a false prophecy? I think I steered you more true than the official prophecy, and with less tortuous verse to boot."

"I suppose so." Maryan scratched her head. "You could say the Mage, the Axe, the Ranger, and even the romance were all a part of the prophecy in the end. But none of them were what we were expecting."

"They never are, Your Highness. And telling the future is a difficult thing."

"So if you aren't a trickster, what are you?"

The titan smiled, and the palace courtyard brightened. "I'm not sure what I am, exactly. But suppose for a moment that I had dedicated my existence to cleaning up the traps and snares laid by other titans at the dawn of creation. Those other titans would call me a trickster, and other names besides, wouldn't they?"

CHAPTER THIRTY-SIX: HOME

"Perhaps. So why are you here now?"

"I wanted to congratulate you, of course. And say thank you. That Teapot was never supposed to leave the forbidden dimensions. I know it was a lot of trouble to return, but I always knew you could do it."

"Well, thank you too, I guess."

"Also, I wanted to give you some advice, Your Highness." The titan gestured back at the palace. "Your older brother is in line for the throne. But let's be honest. You would be a much better ruler. Offerdell is beset on all sides by danger. You are the only one in the kingdom that can prevail."

"I can serve just fine as princess, Ereshkigal."

But there was no answer, for the titan had disappeared.

"What are you doing, Maryan? Staring into space again?"

"Sorry, Mom. What were you saying?"

"We were inviting you all into the palace, of course." The queen gestured back into the open doorway, where a red carpet led into hallways lined with rich furniture and fine art.

This was an invitation to return to the comforts of the castle, and others' expectations of what a princess should be. Maryan's body tensed, as if ready to fight or flee, and she swallowed. Wasn't this what the titan had mentioned? Returning and jockeying for position behind the throne?

But the sun warmed her back, and a breeze tugged at the strands of her hair that had escaped her bun. She belonged outside the palace now, and knew better than anyone else how she could help her kingdom and its people.

And the guidance of titans wasn't always what you thought it was.

"Thank you, Mom, but I won't be coming in."

"What?" King Albert sputtered. "You've only just arrived. We've got a banquet planned, then a ball, and then this amazing brunch—"

"Sorry, Dad. I need to see Prince Mikhail."

Queen Sally clapped her hands together. "Oh, I just *knew* that you and that dashing prince would make up someday."

"No, Mom. I'm going to march into his mountain stronghold and drive a stake through his heart."

King Albert frowned. "Young people today and their new-fangled ideas of romance. That's not how we did it."

"And then I'll take my forces across the River Halstrop, and conquer the Wild Lands. I'll make it a kingdom of my own. Offerdell will be stronger and safer with a friendly kingdom standing next to it." Maryan jerked her head back at the ogres. "And I think Huknar and Emma will conquer the unknown lands beyond that. They'll need help."

Her parents looked at each other, then shrugged.

"At least take a sweater with you, dear. Mountain strongholds can get chilly at night, even in June."

"I'll consider it, Mom." Princess Maryan hugged them, then turned around and marched out of the palace grounds.

I'm sure you've already heard tales of Maryan's epic battles with Prince Mikhail, and her adventures in the Wild Lands, accompanied by her friends, a band of very limber ogres, and some hip archers.

But that, dear reader, is a Chronicle for a different Chronicler.

Lyrics

Here follow the uncensored lyrics of *Plucky the Dragon from Huck*.

Disclaimer from the Senior Editors of the Chroniclers Guild:

We are allowing this appendix only in service of the historical record.

This material is intended for mature readers only.

Plucky the Dragon from Huck

There was a young troll from Halden
He had a big cart but his wheels were stuck
He pushed them and pushed them but they just wouldn't budge
What did he need? He needed a duck!

I'm Plucky the Dragon from Huck!
I'm plucky and I'm lucky and I just love a good duck!
In Huck we're all happy and raise ducks galore
And lucky for you, I have come to your shore
I know what you want and I have what you need
You need love and to give is my creed
And most of all you need a good duck
Nothing says love like a fair winged duck

So the troll left with a smile on his face
His cart was rolling and his wheels were placed
Plucky the Dragon gave him a crazy good duck!
He got himself a crazy good duck

There was a young goblin from Howe
With a house and a yard with a buck
But her deer kept begging for an animal friend
What did she need? She needed a duck!

(chorus repeats)

So the goblin left with a smile on her face
Her buck was happy and the yard a shared space
Plucky the Dragon gave her a crazy good duck!
She got herself a crazy good duck

About the Author

Alexander Thomas has worked at various times as a physicist and mathematician, and now makes a living as an engineer. He reads a lot of history, writes some fantasy and science fiction, and tries not to take anything too seriously.

He lives in the United States, in the Pacific Northwest, with his family.

You can follow him at www.AlexanderThomasAuthor.com.

Acknowledgments

Any book requires the assistance of a small army to get it to publication, and that's doubly true of an author's first book.

Over twenty people—fellow writers, beta readers, and editors—generously gave their time and energy to review and critique all aspects of the manuscript as it evolved. Here are the brave souls that agreed to have their names associated with this work! Fellow Writers: Chetan D, A. y. Johlin, Adam Kispert. Beta Readers: Amanda Adkins, Kristopher Ballard, Margo Brialis, Gabby D'Aloia, Shalini G, Mikayla Gray, Lauren Lanier, Andrea Nortje, Rachel Welsh. Editors: Lisa Wong.

I deeply appreciate their help! Anything fun or interesting in this book is almost certainly due to their kind influence, and any errors are mine alone.

This is a self-published book. Please leave a review if you have a minute! That makes a big difference to indie authors.

Most of all, thank you for reading.

Made in the USA
Coppell, TX
22 May 2024